THE
WIDOW *of*
HARTFORDE

Before there was Salem, there was Hartforde

J. F. Baker

FOXBURG & STERN Books, LLC

Designer
MAD Studio

Editor
Maithy Vu

Copyright © Foxburg & Stern Books, LLC
ISBN: 979-8-9989913-1-8

Visit www.FoxburgAndStern.com for more info.

Illustration
Baker, Lucas John, *The Sigil*. 2025 Charcoal. Foxburg & Stern Books.

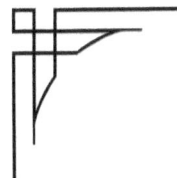 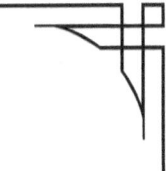

Prologue

Her dream was always the same.

Rebecca walked toward the rear deck of *God's Hope*, gripping Caleb's arm as the creaky ship rolled through the freezing ocean beneath them. Dark waves pounded its sides, sending up spray. As they climbed the stairs to the stern deck overlook, she could hear the ship's weather-beaten sails pulling their tethers, straining against a harsh wind.

Rebecca sat on a crate, praying the rocking wouldn't be as severe up above as it was down in the ship's belly. She sucked in fresh air, almost tasting the salt spray, glad of the clean winds.

Below them, the belly held the smell. The stench of the dead seemed trapped down there, even though the bodies and their bedding had long been tossed overboard. She closed her eyes and inhaled in the cold salt air again, desperate to rid herself of the pungent stink of death.

Yards away, the captain stood at his midship post, nudging the ship's wheel back and forth. She pulled her cloak up over her chin and gazed out over the lower deck, where a handful of passengers, swathed in black, huddled together near the railing, shielding their faces from the wind. Caleb rubbed her back, then leaned down and murmured something in her ear, but a gust swallowed his words.

Suddenly, her white bonnet whipped away, taking to the air like a sea bird flying over the stern. She chased it to the rear of the ship, gathering her loose hair up in one hand. Below her, the churning water carried it away, never to be touched by human hands again.

When she turned back toward Caleb, the place where he'd stood on the overlook was empty.

"Caleb?"

She took a step.

No answer. No sign of him.

She looked down from the overlook to the midship deck. The captain was missing from his post. Her stomach clamped tight at the sight of the ship's wheel, unmanned, spinning out of control as the sea pulled it from below.

Ahead, the lower deck was empty too; the passengers who'd occupied it just minutes earlier were gone. A wind howled across the deck, slapping her dress against her legs. The ship let out a monstrous groan.

She felt a pull to the sea and headed to the nearest railing. An object floated directly below: a shadow, bulky and blunt, hovered just beneath the surface. Slowly, other similar shadows emerged around it.

Rebecca squinted as the sea mist kicked up. She gripped the ship's railing, the wood cold against her palms, and peered at the sea. Holding her breath, she was unable to look away as dozens of shapes rose to the surface.

Then the shadow closest to the ship breached, revealing a man's leg in dark pants and boot. Rebecca's breath caught in her chest as a wave tumbled it about like a log—just a single limb, torn pink and jagged at the hip. Then a dark-haired head broke the surface nearby. Closer to the hull, another shadow broke the waves: a bearded man's torso, severed below the chest, its pink entrails dangling. Rebecca stepped back.

Another wave came, and all around her, other bodies— no, *fragments* of bodies—rose to the water's surface. All torn.

Severed. Dead. Another wave slapped them against the ship. The dull thudding sound sickened her.

Rebecca staggered. She heard a crack somewhere deep in the ship's belly. She glanced down at her feet just as the deck shuddered, once, twice, and then with a *snap* as the planks began to splinter. Rebecca lost her footing and lunged for the nearest railing, just as the balusters shook apart and plunged into the water. The deck planks spread like fingers beneath her, and she fell onto her hands and knees. The ship's mast fractured. Its top half soared toward the deck, ripping the ship's white sails down with it. Rebecca covered her head as sail and rope and flinders of wood rained down. The crow's nest fell, splashing into the water behind her.

She raised her head, furiously searching for any sign of Caleb—or anyone—on deck, but instead saw water begin to rise through the splintering deck. On the midship, crates bobbed around the broken mast; water began to lap over the ship's sides toward her. Rebecca's feet slipped through the deck, and she grabbed onto a plank to keep herself from falling through entirely. She winced as the sea's icy bite tore straight through her boots and stockings. All at once, water flooded the deck from all sides and *God's Hope* disintegrated around her.

Rebecca clung to the plank as the deck ripped apart below her. She sank into the sea, clutching the board and watching as pieces of the dead floated closer.

She screamed.

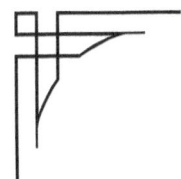 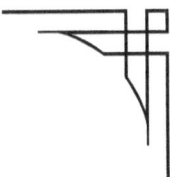

DECEMBER 1662

CHAPTER 1
Rebecca

Rebecca batted back a swarm of blankets as visions of the body-filled sea fell away, replaced by the outline of quilts stretched across the end of her bed. She lay back, panting, and stared at the ceiling as light from the fireplace flickered across the beams above. The dream's visions of bodies so torn, broken and lost, stayed with her.

She and Caleb had arrived in Connecticut Colony, safely, three months ago. No bodies in the water. No smashing of ships. And yet, it secretly drove her mad to wonder what it could possibly mean for her, a reverend's wife, to have such a gruesome dream.

Rebecca exhaled and slipped out of bed, plucking her sweat-soaked nightdress away from her body. The December chill found her skin, and she winced, then padded to the window and cracked the shutter. Outside, the last rays of a burnt-orange sun were sinking behind the forest that surrounded their house. At this time of night, the forest looked vast and endless, like a dark ocean of another kind. She wondered—not for the first time—about the things that might swirl beneath its tree line and if her dream had been some kind of warning.

The forest was the reason she had Bow.

She'd been walking back from South Puritan one afternoon a month ago and had seen some kind of animal watching her from the edge of the woods. At first, she thought it was some kind of wild bull—with most of its body blocked by trees—but as she passed, it appeared to rear up on its back legs. It looked at her with shiny black eyes. What she'd thought were low-hanging branches above it weren't branches at all; they were the top part of its head. Its forehead split at the top and extended up into horns, twisted and impossibly thick.

When she realized it was taller than she was, with its gaze unbreaking, Rebecca ran the rest of the way home. They'd argued that night, she and Caleb, over what she saw—and they never argued. She'd almost told him how much she hated it in the colony. The words had been in her mouth.

The forest. The isolation.

Caleb purchased a brown-and-white hound from a local farmer the next morning to give Rebecca a sense of security for when he was away. It was the best he could do for now, he'd said. Rebecca named him Bow.

She snapped the shutter closed again and clasped her arms over her chest, shivering. On nights she had the dream, it took hours to fall back to sleep. She'd go downstairs to sew or read or pen letters home for news on her baby nephew. She'd write by the fire until she barely had enough energy to walk upstairs.

But tonight was different. Tonight, night had come early.

She and Caleb had just sat down to dinner when Constable Hindstall pounded on their door—ruddy-faced and dusted with snow, with a four-horse wagon waiting outside. She'd overheard him asking for Caleb's help with an urgent matter in town.

Rebecca had only met the frizzly bearded Constable once before, the day she and Caleb had arrived in Connecticut Colony. Their first stop had been to the constable's house, where Rebecca found herself staring up at six severed wolves' heads nailed above his front door.

Insects buzzed at their nostrils and the blood saturated the door's frame. Seeing the horrified look on her face, the Constable simply explained the heads were there to encourage the men in town to hunt down the wolf population. "Otherwise, we'll have to seal up in our houses again in winter or risk getting picked off on the way to church," he'd said, as if exposing the risk of a wolf attack could make anything better.

Rebecca hadn't seen the Constable since.

So, when he unexpectedly showed up at their door, she'd busied herself with dinner while he talked with Caleb outside.

Caleb dashed back in a few moments later with a serious look on his face. He'd given her a kiss on the cheek, grabbed a hunk of bread and promised he'd return as soon as he could. When they'd gone, Rebecca took two pieces of bread for herself and her bowl of stew upstairs to bed. She threw extra logs on the fire in her room and then buried herself under blankets, devouring the stew before it, too, dared to get cold.

She hadn't counted on falling asleep so early.

Now, she sighed. Thanks to the dream—no, *the nightmare*—her mind was already wide awake, and night had barely begun. The visit from the Constable certainly hadn't helped, either. She shivered again and ran her hands over her arms.

Rebecca stepped through the dark and plucked Caleb's tan breeches from the chair in the corner. They were a knee-length pair that Caleb had asked her to mend weeks ago, before the snow began. She'd survived twenty-three English winters in her lifetime, but she'd never experienced cold like this. The Connecticut cold whipped straight through her clothes, seeped into her skin and nested in her bones, refusing to depart no matter how close she stood to the fire or how thick a gown she wore (or how much she complained).

A week ago, she'd finally given up fighting the cold and had begun secretly wearing his breeches underneath her wool dress during the day.

She'd be horrified if Caleb found out—but equally horrified if she had to give them up.

Rebecca pulled them on, thankful that their height difference made Caleb's knee-length pants nearly reach her ankles. She waited and listened for Caleb, wondering why he hadn't come up yet. After a few minutes, she realized there was no noise downstairs. No clatter of the dishes she'd left out. No scratch of a quill. No squeak of a chair.

Night had fallen and he hadn't returned.

Dream or no dream, she'd never be able to get back to sleep now, so she grabbed the lantern she always kept on her night table.

She walked to the fireplace, dipped the candle from inside the lantern into the fire to light it, replaced it back inside, then padded over to the door.

She inched the bedroom door open and raised the light, illuminating the windowless upstairs hallway. The house's other three bedrooms were closed, their doors undisturbed. She paused. Rebecca hated being alone in the house. It was an older two-story log structure—one of the first built in the colony, created for the colony's first, and recently retired, reverend. The old man had had a huge family, but now it was just her and Caleb. The sight of so many empty rooms often left her feeling a pang of sadness. She adored children, but she and Caleb hadn't been blessed yet, despite trying for months. When they'd moved in, she'd mentally reserved the first room to the right of the stairs for their baby, but still, no luck. No babies left a lot of empty rooms to creak, shutters to slam, and windows for the wind to whip. Everything about the house made her jump.

"Caleb?" she called.

She took a step out into the hallway and—*oof!*—tripped over something ankle-height just outside the threshold. She scrambled to find her footing while steadying the lantern, knowing she'd find Bow standing at her feet, thumping his tail and looking at her through sleepy brown eyes. He'd taken to sleeping outside her door.

"I'm sorry, boy! What are you doing up here?" Rebecca whispered, leaning down to scratch his head.

Rebecca took a step toward the stairs and sniffed the air, hoping for a scent of Caleb's pipe. Nothing. Ever since that thing had frightened her in the woods, Caleb promised to return home before nightfall. If there was ever a delay, he was to send word so she wouldn't worry. Perhaps she had slept through a knock. Maybe a messenger had been sent and with dusk approaching, slipped a message under the door to reassure her that everything was fine.

"Come on, Bow. Let's go look," she said. Feeling braver with the dog beside her, she descended the stairs. The temperature seemed to drop with each step.

It wasn't just the house that unnerved her—a fact she tried to hide as much as possible from Caleb— but Connecticut Colony was more desolate and dangerous than any place she'd ever imagined. All she'd ever known was England, its green hills, stone buildings, and her father's farm where she'd grown up riding horses and raising foals. When Caleb received the letter calling him to be the youngest leader of a Puritan congregation in Connecticut Colony, Rebecca had heard the colonies were primal and undeveloped, but never really knew what that meant. The town's mud-and-log structures looked jagged and hazardous. Snow piled higher than houses themselves. Illness had popped up in different parts of town twice since they'd arrived and had killed entire families. And there were the Pequots—savages native to the land she'd heard terrifying rumors about—living in tents made of animal skins, decorating their naked bodies with painted symbols. To Rebecca, it was as if the colony was land forsaken by God, plucked from *The Bible* and made real.

But the worst was the isolation. In the colonies, meeting houses were intentionally built outside of town. South Puritan was a full mile away and atop a hill so it could double as a stronghold in case of an attack by the savages. Rebecca and Caleb's house was the only building built beyond South Puritan, deeper into the forest.

Rebecca shivered as her feet hit the landing at the bottom of the stairs. She held up her lantern, its light sweeping across the first floor. The fireplace had run cold. The room's empty pair of rocking chairs were still. Their rungs twisted odd shadows across the fireplace as she moved the lantern. Rebecca shone the light into the kitchen on the other side of the stairs. Caleb's stew still lay on the tabletop, untouched, just where she'd left it. Rebecca turned back toward the front door. His coat was missing from the peg next to it. So was his gun.

Her teeth started to chatter. She pulled her own black cloak down, swept it over her shoulders, and yanked it closed.

"Did you hear anyone come by?" she asked Bow, ducking down and scratching his head. He let out soft, sleepy yips and began to dance around her feet at the prospect of going outside. She nudged him back from the door with her foot in case a note had been slipped underneath, but the floor was bare. She set the lantern on the small table next to the door. Perhaps someone had left a scroll outside, seeing that it was getting dark and didn't want to disturb her. Rebecca pressed a hand against the door and felt the cold wind press back. She took a step away from it, grabbed Bow by the scruff of his neck, and pulled his lanky body against the side of her leg, his front paws tapping at the floor, more excited now that the chance to go outside was confirmed.

"Shh! Shh!" she hushed.

She gripped the door handle, took a deep breath, and cracked it open, shivering as a draft snaked in around her legs. She raised the lantern against the dark to find that the front stoop and footpath out to the road had been covered in a perfect blanket of snow. No footprints, no note.

Just then, Bow started to growl, a low warning rumbling from deep inside his ribcage. His round eyes narrowed, his gaze locked on something deep in the woods on the other side of the road.

"What do you see, boy?"

Rebecca stared into the darkness of her front yard and listened for any sounds of an animal. Bow growled again. She glanced down to see him crouch and bare his teeth, transforming from pet to wild animal in seconds.

"What is it?"

Rebecca gripped his scruff tighter with one hand and raised the lantern slowly with the other, but the light died off past the bushes that lined the front of their house, long before the end of their yard. She squinted at the wall of trees that grew fifty yards ahead. With the sun fully set now, the outline of the forest's bare red maples and bushy evergreens blurred together into what looked like a big dark nest scattered with snow. Other than that, she saw nothing.

She swallowed hard and took a step back.

Bow continued growling, eyes locked at something in the woods. Rebecca hesitated, taking a step back toward the house, pulling him back with her.

"Come, boy! Back inside!" She crouched down to pet him, but Bow's growl exploded into a vicious snarl. He darted forward out of her grip and ran out into the blind night, his back legs kicking up fresh snow. He barked wildly, chasing after something she couldn't see.

Rebeca lunged after him. "Wait! Bow, stop!"

As she did, the lantern swung back in her hand, shattering against the doorframe and sending tiny glass shards everywhere. The candle toppled out and landed in the snow, blotting out all light. Rebecca tossed what was left of it and sprinted out into the yard, ignoring the icy bite of wet snow on her feet. She ran up to the rock wall that divided their property and the road, but she had already lost sight of the dog. Rebecca squinted into the dark in the direction of Bow's fierce bark as it sank deeper and deeper into the forest that loomed ahead of her.

She put her hands up to her mouth and called his name. "Bow!" Her breath evaporated into icy mist.

The barking continued to move away from her.

"Bow!"

Rebecca pivoted to run back into the house to get another lantern, but as she turned, something else caught her attention far down the road through the edge of the forest. A blur of bright light moved about in the darkness among the trees that ran up the hill and bordered the property line of South Puritan Meeting House. *Their* meeting house.

Was it fire? Rebecca gaped at the orange-yellow glow, trying to make sense of it. No. The light was moving, separating, reconstituting. Torch light? She squinted. Dozens of torches moved in the distance, up the hill and around the base of the church. Not just that, but she could see boxy shadows shifting in the snowy field next to it. Horses and carts were pulling in. She tugged her cloak up around her chin as a breeze passed. South Puritan only held one church service per day, just after lunch. There was no reason for a crowd to be there at dusk. Something was wrong. She had to get to South Puritan now.

Rebecca spun back toward the woods again, hopeful she'd see Bow trotting back to her, but there was still no sign of him.

"Bow, come back!" she called. The damn woods.

The barking had stopped.

"Bow!" Rebecca shrieked so loudly her own scream echoed against the winter-bare forest, causing her to recoil a few steps. She stood at the end of the rock wall, out of breath, exhaling white puffs into the night air. Shivering, she pulled her cloak tighter around her shoulders, suddenly feeling very aware that she was completely alone and unprotected.

Her eyes flitted back toward the church just as a loud crack of branches startled her, coming from the woods. She turned in the direction of the noise to see a thickly hoofed foot and dark leg in the forest's edge. She froze. It was the same thick hoof. The same slow movement. The angled leg. The muscles protruding beneath fur. Rebecca backed up just as the creature moved, stepping back into the trees. Her breath caught in her throat. She blinked once and it was gone—receded into the darkness.

Heart pounding, Rebecca backed away, then turned and sprinted back into the house.

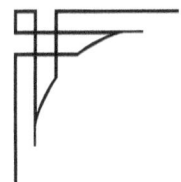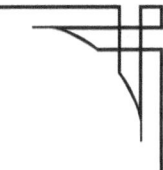

CHAPTER 2
Rebecca

Rebecca ran back up to her bedroom and flung open her clothing trunk. As Caleb had said, there were a million explanations as to what the creature in the woods could've been. Her mind ran through a list of anything hoofed. Cattle. Donkey. A wild horse. Did they have those here? No, that hoof was much too thick to belong to any of those.

With Caleb still gone, their horse, Charlie, would also be with him, which meant her only way to South Puritan was to walk. She shed her cloak and white nightgown as fast as she could, then picked through the trunk. As the Reverend's wife, she'd be expected to role model for all the other colonists, even in a time of crisis. She debated removing Caleb's breeches for a second, but decided against it—if anything, she could justify wearing extra layers walking through the snow at this time of night. She grabbed the thickest wool gown she could find and slipped it over her head. She traded her wet stockings for two pairs of dry ones, then shoved her feet into her brown leather boots. Then she turned and ran back downstairs, pulling her cloak on as she moved.

Rebecca paused at the bottom to pluck her white bonnet from the hook on the wall and twisted her dark hair up underneath it. As she did, her eyes swept through the first floor of the silent house. With her lantern smashed to pieces outside, she'd need some kind of light, something, anything.

Caleb's lantern was nowhere to be seen. Rebecca eyed the door. She'd have to go in the dark.

Her hands shook as she inched the door open and peered out. Without any light, the yard appeared full of still and silent shadows. Rebecca studied the outline of the forest beyond for any sign of the creature. Nothing. After a few seconds she stepped out of the house and tugged the door closed quietly behind her. She leaned down and grabbed the shovel that sat propped next to the front door. She held it across her body and walked slowly to the edge of her yard.

Rebecca stepped up to the rock wall and paused again as her eyes adjusted to the dark. She gripped the shovel tighter and stared into the woods without daring to blink, looking for any sign of movement. Her chest hurt when she thought of Bow being injured—or worse—but there was no way to search for him safely until sunrise. She stilled herself and sneaked a glance toward South Puritan. A sea of light flowed up the hill to the meeting house now, illuminating the base of the building, even from this distance. Why hadn't Caleb come for her? Rebecca stepped one foot out onto the road, ice crackling beneath her foot. The sound made her jump and her heart race. She waited, staring into the woods and listening for any movement. She gripped her shovel tighter in both hands and pivoted her body left, slowly, and moved softly out onto the road. She took one careful step and then another, gradually picking up her pace.

Her ears absorbed any sound coming from the woods, but at this time of year, there were no birds left to chirp, no small critters skittering in the night. She heard only the puff of her own breath in the frigid air and the light crunch of ice beneath her feet. Both seemed to echo against the bare trees that surrounded her on both sides of the street. She slowed her pace, willing her body to be quiet. Rebecca blinked as snowflakes landed on her eyelashes. She pulled the hood of her cloak up over her head and continued moving forward, keeping her eyes on South Puritan.

Minutes passed and finally the marker tree—a felled evergreen on the side of the road that marked the halfway point between their home and South Puritan—came into view. She relaxed a bit at the sight of it, dropping the shovel to one side.

Just then, a loud hissing noise, low and deep in tone, issued from far behind her. The sound seemed to pass straight through her ears and fill up the inside of her head. She winced as it grew louder. The noise swept the entire length of the road, shaking the ground beneath her. She jumped back. The hiss grew louder, echoing off the trees around her. Rebecca threw the shovel to the ground, covered her ears, and spun back in the direction of the sound. There, in black shadow against the dark purple trees of the forest, she saw the outline of a tall figure—easily several feet taller than Caleb—emerging from the edge of woods across from her house. But it was no man. It had twisted horns, just as she'd seen before. Its body was muscular as a steer, but this creature walked upright on its back legs. It took another step. Even from this distance she could hear the echo of a heavy hoof clacking on the ground.

Rebecca leaped behind the downed evergreen and covered her ears as the hiss swelled louder. She felt it vibrate deep in the core of her brain. As she squeezed her eyes shut, she was certain that her head would split in half from the pain.

Then, as suddenly as the noise started, it stopped. The stabbing pain vanished with it.

Rebecca held perfectly still for a second and waited. She pushed herself up and peered around the end of the evergreen. The creature, this...beast...was still there, pacing about the road in front of her house. She stared at its horns. Each one was as long as a man's arm. It turned back toward the place in the woods from which it had come, the shift in its body revealing that something small and limp swung from one of its claws. Whatever it was, it wasn't moving.

Rebecca felt the contents of her stomach rise toward her throat.

Run.

Feeling her legs take over, Rebecca threw herself forward and darted in the direction of South Puritan as fast as if she were running from fire. She pursed her lips, holding in a scream, and didn't dare to look back. If she could just get close enough to the townsfolk driving in from town, she could scream for help. Far up ahead on her right, the forest line ended and ten acres of field that lie between the forest and South Puritan began. She debated running up through the field as a sort of shortcut, but there was no way to tell how deep the snow in the field would be.

Before she could decide, Rebecca's boots hit an icy patch on the road. Her feet scrambled underneath her, and she slipped, smashing down onto the road and landing on her hands and knees. She scrambled to push herself up, but her right knee throbbed. Suddenly, she heard the sound of hooves racing toward her from behind in the road. She squeezed her eyes shut.

The pounding of hooves grew closer.

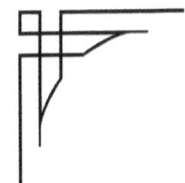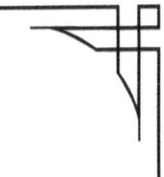

CHAPTER 3
Rebecca

Rebecca hunched her shoulders up to her ears and braced herself for an attack, terrified at the damage this Beast could do to her after seeing Bow's body dangling from its claw. The hooves thundered closer along with other noises now, too. The creak of wood in the cold. The clatter of wheels. And then the dull shouts of a voice.

"Whoa!"

A *human* voice. Rebecca popped her head up just as a shadowy outline of a trotter horse and wagon skidded around her, showering her with slush, and coming to a stop not ten feet away from her. A single lantern dangled from the driver's bench.

Rebecca flipped herself onto her bottom and squinted back down the road in the direction from which she'd just run from. Her eyes darted around, looking for any movement from the trees on either side of the road. There was no sight of it. Rebecca froze for a few seconds and waited. The only movement was the gentle flutter of snow, falling silently through the dark. She stared back down the road toward her house, trying to process whatever she'd seen. It *hadn't* chased her. Whatever it was had gone.

"Ma'am? Are you alright?" he called.

Rebecca flipped around facing the driver, who was making his way back to her.

"That looked like a nasty fall!"

Rebecca looked up to see a dark-eyed boy not much older than thirteen peering down at her, his eyebrows pressed together with concern. He wore an oversized workman's coat, and a maroon scarf he'd yanked down under his chin to speak to her. A shiny musket was slung over one shoulder.

Rebecca pointed a shaky finger back down the road. "Tell me, did you see..." Her question fell short as she heard the tremble in her own voice. She swallowed hard, pressing her lips together.

With the boy's light casting over her now, Rebecca could see the damage the fall had caused. Her wool cloak had torn in two or three places, and where it hadn't torn, it was covered with slush and ice. She ran a hand carefully over one tear, feeling her knee throb underneath. Both of her feet felt numb and useless, but the boot on her right foot felt heavy— the toe had completely been soaked through with icy water during her fall. She yanked the boot's lace and slipped the knot apart, freeing her foot and cringing at the bite of cold air on her bare skin. She tried to warm it up by rubbing it between her hands, but the simple movement sent a dull pain shooting up the outside of her ankle.

"You'll be needing to wrap that," the boy said. Leaving the lantern with her, he raced back to the cart and returned with a wool blanket. He pulled a hunting knife from his pocket, cut one long strip of cloth from the end of it, and handed it to her.

As Rebecca struggled with stiff fingers to work the strip into a tight makeshift stocking, she glanced up at him, bewildered.

"Tell me, how is it that you're traveling east on this road?" she asked. "My...my house is the last in town. The road ends there. I've just come that way. There's nothing beyond my home except for the forest."

"I took a shortcut through the woods, over there." He pointed to the edge of the forest line behind them, where the woods ended and South Puritan's field began. "I know we're supposed to stick to the main road, but there's a great shortcut from town to where the trees end along South Puritan's property just over there."

"You traveled through the forest at night? Alone?" Rebecca tucked the end of the blanket strip snug into the stocking. She then accepted the boy's forearm for leverage, pulling herself up fully on her left leg. She gingerly set her right foot down to test her strength.

"Oh!" she flinched, digging her nails into the boy's sleeve as the pain shot up her ankle to her knee. She shifted her weight back to her left leg, touching only the tip of her right toe to the ground for balance.

The boy nodded his chin toward her leg. "Let me give you a ride."

"Yes, thank you." She looped her elbow through his, noticing he stood only about as tall as she. "Weren't you afraid to travel through the woods in the dark?"

He yanked his scarf down again and guided her toward the wagon—a four-wheeled cart that stretched only a foot or two longer than the horse that pulled it. As they moved closer, Rebecca could make out the words "Poole Blacksmiths" inked in white on the side.

"No reason to be," he shrugged. "We've hunted there for as long as I can remember."

"We?"

"Chancer and I." The boy nodded toward his horse, who stamped back and forth, grunting and snorting in the cold. "And my brothers, of course. I have three. I'm Levi Poole. Our father's the blacksmith in town. We all hunt when we can. I have for as long as I can remember."

"Nice to meet you, Levi." Rebecca hobbled next to him.

He glanced back toward the forest. "There are a lot of wolves there in the springtime. There are times when the Constable will pay a half-pence a head for a wolf! But hunting's pretty sparse now, especially when it's this cold."

"Nothing at all worth hunting?"

"Mmm, maybe an occasional bear, but that's really rare," Levi said. "When the season's right, it's great for turkey, pheasant, opossum and like. We aren't afraid of the woods—ever, are we Chancer?"

The horse turned her head back toward him, swinging her spotted mane as if acknowledging her name.

"She's a lovely one." Rebecca paused at the foot of the cart, holding onto one wheel for balance. "I grew up on a horse farm. My father bred them. We had one that looked just like her."

The horse's faint spots, even in the dim light of Levi's lantern, made her think of Belle, her favorite mare that she'd had as a child. Even this horse's mane looked almost identical.

"Thanks," Levi said, hanging the lantern from the driver's hook, then shedding his musket and placing it in the back of the cart. "Besides, Chancer and I didn't have much choice but to take the shortcut if we wanted to get here in time. The road from town is completely boggled."

"Boggled?" Rebecca rotated her ankle beneath her. The pain was still there but seemed to be slowly waning.

Levi boosted himself up and slid onto the driver's bench. "We live right above father's shop in town. After the Constable and his men rode through town raising the hellfire they did, the entire town was awake. By the time I could get Chancer saddled up, it was nearly impossible to get out onto the road. The shortcut was the only way."

"The Constable, you said?" Rebecca puzzled, stepping her good foot up onto the driver's step and grabbing onto the bench for balance. "He asked everyone to head to South Puritan? You're certain?"

Chancer whinnied as Rebecca sat down, scanning her surroundings from the elevated height. Woods that lined the left side of the road ran all the way from here to town, one mile away. The deep field Levi had cut through stretched out on their right. Her home—and Bow and the Beast—were lost somewhere in the darkness behind them.

"What's the hurry to get to South Puritan?"

"Well, it is the Particular Court, ma'am." Levi said matter-of-factly, snapping the reins. Chancer picked up into a steady trot.

Rebecca looked at him blankly. "The what?"

"Did the Constable not send word to your house?" He paused. "Probably because you live all the way out here. They went door-to-door hours ago to say the court is nearly here. They've traveled all the way from Massachusetts Bay to hold an emergency trial tonight. Everyone is to meet at South Puritan immediately."

Rebecca felt her cheeks flush despite the weather. Constable Hindstall had indeed come to their home but hadn't given any such warning. She struggled to recall anything odd in the conversation she'd overheard between he and Caleb. The Constable had sounded urgent, but there was certainly no mention of a court or a trial.

"What's the Particular Court? What are they doing at the meeting house?"

"You're new to the Colony, aren't you?" Levi glanced over at her. "I mean no offense, ma'am. I can only tell by your accent. You sound, well, more *English* than most of us."

"Yes. We came from Dover in the fall," she said. The dark woods slid by on her left as Chancer pulled them toward South Puritan. "I'm Rebecca Easton. My husband is the new Reverend at South Puritan." She turned toward Levi. "What's this Particular Court?"

"Well, the colony doesn't have a full-time court, or money for a courthouse, so the Particular Court is a sort of traveling court," he said, pulling a wool blanket up onto his lap and tossing Rebecca a wolf skin. "Most of them technically live in Hartforde Towne, but they travel to different parts of the colony every three or four months to hear trials all at once and deliver sentences. Then they move on to the next town.

They always meet in the biggest building they can find. Here, that's your meeting house." He paused to rub his chin underneath his scarf. "They've never come in the middle of winter, in the middle of the night like this, though."

"Any idea what's happened?" she asked.

He shook his head. "None, ma'am. I told you I have three brothers and one soon-to-be sister-in-law. If there was gossip about a major scandal, I'd know. That's why I'm so interested. The entire town is abuzz, but no one seems to know anything."

Rebecca suddenly turned to him, the wagon rumbling beneath them.

"Levi, could the trial be about an attack?" She gripped the edge of her seat with one hand and, with the other, drew the wolf skin fur all the way up to her nose, She huddled underneath it to block the frost from whipping her face as they sped toward the church.

"An attack? What do you mean?"

"Have there been any attacks in town, any severe enough for this court to come in the middle of the night?"

Levi held Chancer's reins in one hand and made a fist with the other, blowing warmth into it. He squinted ahead. "No, I don't remember there being an attack or brawl or anything. A fight is usually minor, something the Constable would handle himself. Besides, a man would face a few hours in the pillory for something like that, he wouldn't face the Particular Court. They handle serious crimes, like..."

Rebecca waited as Levi pursed his lips for a moment, as if deciding to say more.

"Forgive me, ma'am, but they hear cases of divorce. Not that we've ever had one of those. Treason—there have been a few of those, considering the state of everything. And murder," he whispered. "Only the really serious stuff."

"Oh," Rebecca said. Her sense of unease at not knowing where Caleb was rushed back.

"But if there was an attack," Levi reasoned aloud, "—and the court's already on the way, that would mean they had the man in custody ready for the trial, right? So, there's nothing to worry about. Why, have you heard of something?"

Rebecca gripped the wolf skin tighter, debating again if she should tell Levi about the Beast. The young man had just plucked her out of an icy mess, wet and injured. He'd think she was hysterical if she tried to describe what she'd seen, wouldn't he? Then again, if he did believe her, he may want to go back and investigate. Levi was just a boy. She'd be responsible if anything happened to him.

"It's nothing," she said." Please, let's hurry."

Within minutes, Levi slowed his horse to face a crowd waiting at the bottom of South Puritan's hill that stretched four, even five wagons wide and back toward town as far as Rebecca could see. She gawked at the mess of wagons and carts in front of them. Many drivers, dressed in Puritan black, were struggling to steer their donkey- or horse-pulled carts, up out of the road and toward South Puritan at once. They hollered at one another, inching forward and angling their carts so they'd be the next to move into the already bottlenecked turn-in. Anger erupted at any man riding on horseback or those traveling on foot, who dared try to snake their way through any space between vehicles. Others shouted at anyone whose flaming torch got too close to their horse. A tiny white dog riding in the flatbed of a hay wagon in front of Levi and Rebecca ran from side to side, yipping at everything.

Levi let out a soft, slow whistle. "Looks like I was wrong. The whole town is here and then some."

"But why have so many come, Levi?" Rebecca estimated that the crowd was easily triple the size of the normal congregation. "At this hour?"

"The Particular Court, Mrs. Easton," he swallowed. "You have to understand. Their trials, well, the most awful ones... they almost always end with a trip to the gallows."

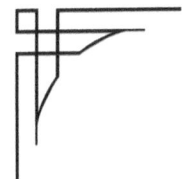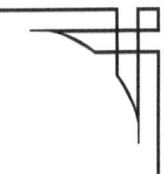

CHAPTER 4
Rebecca

"The Gallows?" Rebecca's eyes widened. But Levi had already straightened his back and was driving Chancer toward the line of people waiting to turn in, nudging her in line behind the hay wagon with the yipping dog.

"Levi, there's no way all these people will fit inside the church," Rebecca shouted over the commotion. She glanced left, toward the stone churchyard wall that blocked everyone from circumventing the line to turn in and up the hill. A man holding a torch hopped over it, then reached his arm back over to help two small boys make the climb. Others followed them.

The line of carts in front of them suddenly shifted, and the yipping dog lurched ahead. Levi butted Chancer ahead in line. An ancient wagon—with its front wheel missing two spokes and led by two straw-colored ponies—pulled up right behind them from the opposite side of the street.

"Hey, you there!" The wagon's white-bearded driver called to them, the ponies' reins gripped tightly in his gloved hands. "Either of you hear what the trial's about?"

"No idea! Have you, sir?" Rebecca called.

The bearded man punched a gloved fist toward them. "I heard it's a murder!"

"Who told you that?" Levi called in a skeptical tone.

"You folks talking about the trial?"

The three looked down to see a chubby woman hiking on foot, cutting in between the two of them, a sack slung over her shoulder. The woman paused momentarily, panting—her face so red and the puffing breaths she exhaled so white that Rebecca felt certain she'd walked the whole way from town.

"I heard it was those Pequots," the woman said,. She put a hand to her chest. "Bet they got caught stealing wheat again. Third time this year, too! They'll be tarred for it, mark me!"

"That can't be true," the white-whiskered driver bellowed. He peered at her out of the corner of his eye as he inched his ponies forward in line. "The Particular Court doesn't waste time on savages! They're burned alive if they're caught committing a crime." He poked his thumb toward Levi. "Isn't that right, boy?"

"Burned alive?" Rebecca repeated to Levi, but before he could answer—

Boom!

Boom!

—two thundering snaps exploded from the direction of the church. The noise echoed off the trees behind them.

Rebecca ducked in her seat, her hands shooting up to her ears. Levi did the same next to her.

"Musket shots!" Levi yelled.

Several horses waiting in line whinnied out of surprise and tugged at their reins. The white-whiskered driver across from them struggled to control his ponies.

Boom!

A third shot echoed from the church.

Carts knocked into one another as the horses rumbled again. Drivers rushed to untangle their animals from one another. Other men hurried to pull out their own arms, then looked around with guns in hand, unsure of where to point.

Levi held Chancer's reins with one hand and twisted around, reaching behind him and feeling for his gun—but Rebecca grabbed his forearm and held it frozen in mid-air.

"Wait! It's all right!" She nodded. "Three gunshots. Three. It's a signal!"

They stared at each other for a second, both of them listening. Levi's horse gnawed her bit and pulled in mild concern against her reins.

A few seconds of silence passed.

"See, just three." Rebecca released his arm. She sat up straighter, feeling for the first time in months, proud to be in possession of useful knowledge.

"It's the emergency signal for all the church members to report to church immediately. I've never heard it used before, but—" Rebecca turned toward the bell tower and pointed at the thin snake of white smoke that billowed out against the night sky. "Look, just there! They fired from the bell tower. See?"

"Gunshots?" Levi looked at her, wide-eyed. "Don't you Puritans have a big expensive bell to ring?"

She turned back toward him. "Don't you understand? The signal has to be a good sign, right? It means someone of authority is at the church! Someone's in charge."

Hopefully Caleb, she wanted to add. Rebecca glanced back at the road. Everyone was pushing forward at once now, trying to force the line forward.

"Levi!" Rebecca warned, gripping her seat as horses approved from every angle.

"Go! Quick!" the white-bearded driver yelled, waving them ahead. Levi didn't waste a minute snapping the reins. Chancer turned, taking the next place in the line that was moving uphill.

As they passed through the church gates, Rebecca looked back over her shoulder to thank the man, only to see him and his ponies being swallowed into the crowd. Just before he was out of sight, she caught him yelling at a younger man in a small carriage attempting to cut the line, its wheels coming dangerously close to his ponies. Behind them, a cluster of fiery torches loomed as the voices of angry men grew louder.

"Levi, it's madness!"

"And it's only going to get worse," Levi said, handing Chancer's reins to her. "I'm going to go down and lead her by hand. You just keep her steady."

"Be careful!" Rebecca called as he climbed down from the wagon.

She took the reins, a horse's leather straps feeling like a happy memory to her hands. It felt like ages since she'd driven a horse, let alone ridden one. The terrain here was mostly thick forest—not the best riding conditions for horses.

Levi stepped down and vanished from view just as a blue delivery wagon pulled by a solid brown trotter horse passed them on the right. Jeers from the crowd chased it up into the yard. The driver, a black-bearded man flanked by two daughters, kept his chin down, pretending not to hear.

Levi reappeared at the side of Chancer's head seconds later, where he gripped the horse's bridle and pulled her head down close to his own. He led her to the right, tugging them all carefully out of line, around the flatbed in front of them and uphill, while Rebecca kept a steady grip on the reins.

"Look here, boy! How dare you!" The driver with the yipping dog shot to his feet. "I've been waiting for more than an hour to—" The man stopped short, fumbling with his horse's reins for a split second, yanking them backwards when he realized Levi wasn't going to stop.

"Good evening, sir!" Rebecca interrupted, giving the man a hard smile and a cordial wave as Levi tugged them past. The man's jaw dropped in confusion, his mouth forming a perfect "o" as he pointed at Levi. Before he could protest again, Rebecca interjected. "And thank you for the kind gesture of letting a good woman of the Lord pass! Surely, He will remember your kindness!"

With that, Rebecca faced forward, following Levi as he weaved her and Chancer through the chaos. The whole way,

Rebecca quickly apologized for every bump or knock of their wagon on another's, kept Chancer's reins pulled so taut she couldn't get injured or tangled, all the while keeping an eye on Levi as he led them up toward the building.

Just as they crested the top of the hill the church was built on, the front of South Puritan finally came fully into sight.

"Lord, help us."

The words dropped from her mouth as Rebecca's eyes swept across the church yard, which was cast in eerie yellow torch light. The building's doors hadn't opened yet and at least one hundred men, women, and even some young children waited in a cluster outside the doors. The cluster of people were close to being pinned against the base of South Puritan by the townsfolk who continued to flood in with them. Some people in the crowd banged on the front doors. Some were attempting to form a line, while others bickered with one another about where the line should start. Those on the edge of the crowd shouted frantic directions to drivers who were still trying to find a place to stop their horses. One wide-eyed mother, on the ground two carts distance away from Rebecca, stood gripping her chest, calling out again and again for a misplaced child. To the far left of the churchyard, where the cemetery lay, a group of men had assembled, lending their lanterns to a driver who'd apparently driven his cart atop a tombstone concealed in the snow. The cart's rear wheel stuck up awkwardly in the air. Two men struggled to lift the back of it while a third pointed and shouted directions.

Rebecca felt the wagon stop underneath her. She looked up at Levi, who was waving in front of Chancer.

"Look! There!" He pointed past the building to the right, toward the church barn. Just alongside the barn sat two of the longest and most elaborate black coaches Rebecca had ever seen. Pairs of perfect white horses sat at the lead, outfitted in black-and-silver harnesses that glinted in the torchlit yard. Stiff red plumes adorned the heads of the two lead horses, who stamped patiently in the snow. Behind them, a man sat atop the wide driver's bench, nearly invisible under a pile of black blankets. Every edge of its black exterior was perfectly curved, with gold trim framing the door and each of the coach's glass windows. Rebecca hadn't seen anything so fanciful since she'd left England.

She looked back at Levi with raised his eyebrows. He nodded, but she already knew. It was the Particular Court. They were here.

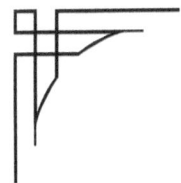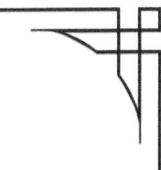

CHAPTER 5
Caleb

Reverend Caleb Easton sat sunken into his chair in South Puritan's tiny vestry room. His knee bounced as he absently rolled a quill pen back and forth between his fingers, its feather dancing in an odd shadow across the bare wooden floor in the light of the room's candle.

Caleb sighed and shifted in his seat, tossing the quill onto the desk. He reached over, slid his Bible off the desk and leaned forward, placing his elbows on his knees and gripping the book with both hands. He traced a thumb over the ornate golden embossment on the spine that read Geneva, then lifted the cover and began to flip through the book's thin pages. He stopped at Psalms Chapter Ninety-One, Verse Eight, and read the line almost silently: *You will only observe with your eyes and see the punishment of the wicked.*

He closed his eyes a second, snapped the book shut, and dropped it back on the desk with a soft thump.

Caleb could tell by the noise of muffled shouts swelling on the other side of the door that the crowd swarming into the nave of South Puritan was immense. A woman's laugh reverberated through the wall. Caleb rubbed the spot in between his eyes where a stabbing headache was forming. Never in all his months of planning and preparing to take on his post of reverend in South Puritan could he have predicted he'd testify in a trial against one of his very own parishioners. Now, he'd not only have to testify, but his words would likely send her to her death. Caleb looked back at the Bible on the desk.

Unless—

Just as he moved to reach for the book again, the vestry door opened. A tall man with dark hair and a ruddy red complexion stepped through, musket in hand.

Caleb nodded to him. "It's done then, Constable Hindstall?"

"Yes," Hindstall said, tugging the door closed behind him. He leaned over and propped his gun against the shelves. "You should see the crowd outside. One family has come as far as Boston. Boston! You'd think they'd followed the court straight away. This will be one for the records, for sure." Hindstall dusted his hands off and looked around the tiny space. Failing to find a place to sit, he crossed his arms and leaned back against the door.

His ears burning with embarrassment over his tiny space, Caleb got to his feet to prepare for the trial.

The vestry was an afterthought of the church's construction—a tiny room tucked away in the front right corner of the church that builders originally intended to be a firewood closet. From his first day at South Puritan, Caleb considered it peculiar that its builders had focused so much time and money on creating an interior that would delight the wealthy members of the congregation. Somehow, a room designated for clergy had slipped their minds. Compared to the body of the meeting house, the vestry was pathetically small—only about three paces deep and four paces wide. Aside from Caleb's chair, a tiny wooden writing desk had been wedged inside and took up at least a third of the space.

He headed to the opposite wall, which offered two shelves, both stacked with the church's service valuables: offering plates, candles, a white-sanded hourglass, and a stack of Caleb's carefully folded service vestments. A tiny looking glass hung on the wall next to them, which Caleb used to dress for services or occasionally practice a sermon he was especially eager to share with the congregation. It was one full of hope that would encourage each man and woman in attendance to seek out a closer connection with God. His words would make a real difference in their lives.

But tonight felt nothing like a service.

Caleb stepped past Constable Hindstall to the mirror, his eye catching for a moment on the shiny brass badge on Hindstall's dark blue coat. Caleb plucked his black cassock from the shelves.

"My men have broken up three fights so far out in the yard," Hindstall said. "We also caught two other men trying to bring ale inside."

"Ale in a church?" Caleb shook his head free through the neck hole of the cassock and shimmied the black garment into place over his arms and body. "Isn't that a five-shilling fine?" He leaned over and grabbed his white collar from the shelves.

"Aye. Not much you don't see at something like this, Reverend. People have come from all over town. I swear, I even saw a few babies being brought in despite the hour." Hindstall kicked one black boot over the other, crossing his legs at the ankles. "Speaking of families, are you certain you don't want me to go and fetch your wife? We have horses waiting out back. I could take the shortcut through the field over to your house and—"

"No!" Caleb locked eyes with Hindstall in the mirror and froze, his fingers mid-tie with the collar. He paused and picked his next words carefully. "I appreciate it, Constable. It's just that . . . Rebecca's having a bit of a rough go lately. Trouble adjusting, you know? I'd prefer to leave her at peace tonight."

"Ah. Still finding her place, eh?"

"She's happy here, just...it's the woods, the isolation. It gets to her." Caleb finished with the collar and turned back toward Hindstall, eager to change the subject. "Please, tell me, what's the status of the court?"

"They're setting up now up front. Should be just a few minutes more."

Caleb walked back to the desk and ducked down, reaching underneath it and retrieving a tattered brown box. He lifted the lid and pulled out his services wig. He shook it out, its white goat hair unnaturally rough on his fingers. Caleb detested it. It itched the back of his neck endlessly, but such a valuable item was a status symbol in the Colony, not that his was of terrible note. It was short in length, falling only two curls past his ears, a sign of his limited years in service. But still, it was more than most people had, and Caleb had a feeling that everything about his station in the community would matter tonight.

He headed back to the mirror and pulled it on, tucking any loose piece of his own dark brown hair underneath.

"And the Widow?"

"Out back, secured in my coach. Two of my men are guarding her." Hindstall cleared his throat, then lowered his voice. "Just so you're aware, Reverend, I've already sent two of my men back to town to prepare the gallows."

Caleb caught Hindstall's eye in the mirror as he fiddled with the wig. "Is that really necessary? The trial hasn't even started yet."

"I've been Constable here for ten years, Reverend," Hindstall said, balling one hand into a fist and squeezing it with the other, popping his knuckles. "Crowds like these, well, they can turn into a mob very quickly. I passed at least two of the wagons out there in the yard that are stacked with rope. At least three quarters of the men present are armed, probably more. I personally don't want to risk anyone taking punishments into their own hands. Do you?"

Caleb paused, eyes averted, fiddling with a button on his cassock.

Hindstall stood up straight. "What's wrong, Reverend? You don't believe her?"

The biblical passage ran through his mind again.

You will only observe with your eyes and see the punishment of the wicked.

Caleb turned toward Hindstall. "I'm the leader of a church, Constable. I'm not in the business of sentencing people to—" His voice broke off as he paced back to the desk, putting his hands on the back of the chair. He hung his head, brow furrowed. "How could I not believe her? Exodus Chapter Twenty, Verse Three: 'Thou shalt have no other gods before me.' She's confessed!" He shoved the chair underneath the desk. "But that doesn't mean I have to like a minute of this. What will this do to the congregation? The town? You're right to think there will be a panic!"

"You leave the panic to me," Hindstall told him. "And you can't blame yourself. You've only just arrived in Hartforde."

"I don't. Well, maybe I do, I don't know." Caleb rubbed the back of his neck and gazed off. "I presided over her husband's funeral the first week I was here, but other than that, I knew little of the family. Still, that's not right. I should've made them a priority considering the odd circumstances of the man's death, but that doesn't make what I have to do any easier. Have your men found any evidence?"

"Out searching now, but it's dark and the weather's no help." Hindstall crossed his arms and cocked his head to one side. "She could be mad."

"And wouldn't she have to be to—"

Just then, the doorknob on the vestry door rattled and the door burst open, thumping into Hindstall's back. Hindstall sidestepped out of the way as a gray-bearded gentleman wrapped in flowing judge's robes pushed inside.

"Good evening, sirs. I'm Judge Madden of the Particular Court." The Judge towered over Caleb by at least six inches, his head coiffed in a pure white wig that flowed down from the crown of his head and ended past his shoulders. A thick maroon cloak was draped over one arm, and he carried a thick brown travel case in the other. He extended his right hand—manicured fingernails adorned with gold and ruby rings— toward Caleb.

"Reverend," he said, studying Caleb with narrow icy blue eyes framed from underneath wiry gray-black eyebrows. Deep frown lines notched in between them.

"Reverend Easton, Judge," Caleb said, stepping out from behind the chair to grip his hand in return. "And I believe you already know—"

Judge Madden nodded toward Hindstall. "Constable Hindstall. A pleasure, sir. Thank you for your detailed letter. It should come in very handy tonight."

"We are thankful the court could attend so quickly, Judge," Hindstall said. "We've never had an issue of this matter in Harteforde before."

"Of course." Judge Madden stepped in front of Caleb, tossing his cloak over Caleb's chair and plunking his case down on the desk. "It is my personal mission to investigate every possible moral and spiritual violation in the colony. Understand, there must be no mercy in situations like this."

"We have the most earnest of intentions, Judge," Caleb said.

Judge Madden gazed back over his shoulder and cocked an eyebrow. Caleb knew what was coming.

"An Englishman? Tell me, Reverend, how recently have you crossed?"

"Three months' time, Judge."

Caleb saw a flicker of a small smile form on the Judge's lips, just for a moment. "Three months is not a long time, Reverend."

"Well, I served the Lord for three years prior in my hometown."

"Three years. I see." Judge Madden turned back to his case and opened it. Reaching in, he retrieved a roll of parchment which crinkled as he unrolled it across the desk. "And are you, Reverend, familiar with the law?"

"I am."

"How so?"

"Constable Hindstall educated me earlier tonight." Caleb glanced at Hindstall over the Judge's back, who shrugged in return. "We were blessed back in England not to have such troubles of late, not in Dover anyway. There's been no record of such incidents in Connecticut."

"You're new here. You don't know the Colonies well," Judge Madden grumbled, running his finger across the parchment. Caleb watched as the Judge reached into his jacket pocket and retrieved a small eye glass, which he held up to his left eye and dove down close to the parchment.

Caleb clenched his jaw and forcing a smile. "I know the Bible well, Judge."

The Judge turned back to him and slipped the eye glass back in his pocket. "Fair enough. I expect you're schooled in double predestination? You will be providing testimony as such."

"Double predestination? Of course." Caleb nodded. "God has a plan for us all."

Hindstall raised his hand. "Double predestination?"

Caleb turned. "Double predestination is the theory that God has predestined the fate of every person. Part of a person's fate is that they are destined to spend eternity in one of two places: in eternal salvation or eternal—"

"Damnation," Judge Madden interrupted.

"Wait. God willingly damns people?" Hindstall looked from man to man. "But what about forgiveness? Repentance? The Bible talks about them, too. I know. I've read it."

"But neither outweighs predestination," Judge Madden responded.

"Double predestination is God's will," Caleb said. "If He wills your soul to Hell for eternity, no amount of repentance—"

"—or begging, or pleading, or lying, or promising to repent can save you," Judge Madden interrupted again, his voice growing louder with each word. "Every violator of these charges protests the same: it was a mistake, a lie, a rumor, they'll change, repent, devote their every breath to serving God. But we mustn't be fooled. If God predestines that you are to be damned to Hell, so you will be. Such is the case for the vial creature on trial tonight. She's nothing more than someone God himself has willed to burn in damnation for eternity."

The Constable opened his mouth to ask another question, but quickly closed it, fixing his eyes before his feet.

The Judge crossed his arms and turned to face Caleb again. "Reverend, you are a soft speaker for one who presides over such an exquisite meeting house. A soft voice for one who's about to condemn a woman to her death."

Caleb could feel Judge Madden's eyes rake over him, assessing every black button, every stitch of thread that held together his garment. For the millionth time that night, he wished he hadn't answered the door when Hindstall fetched him to hear the Widow's confession.

"You may know The Bible back and forth," the Judge pressed, his voice rising, "—may have studied it your whole life. May think you know the people of this church, but you're new here in this world, Reverend. I can tell you from my own experience that you don't know this world."

Caleb was ready to protest, but the Judge leaned in, placing his hand on Caleb's shoulder. "This type of problem, well, it's something we need to...contain before it spreads. We are the men who can put an end to this vile creature and the sin she's brought upon herself—to cast the miserable being into her eternal damnation—as God has obviously willed her."

The Judge leaned back and pulled a black Bible out of his case, thumping it on top of Caleb's on the desk. Then he reached into the bag again, this time, retrieving a crude necklace—a black cord with a vial of something white at the very bottom. The vial was inscribed with wording too small for Caleb to read. The Judge offered no explanation as he lowered it around his neck.

"But to stamp this problem out for good, your town must witness and remember what she's done so it's not repeated. She must be sentenced. Every detail must be drawn out during the trial. And her death must be celebrated. That, Reverend, is our unescapable, God-chosen destiny. I hope you agree."

Judge Madden backed away. Turning toward the desk, he gathered up his parchment under his arm, left his Bible behind, and yanked the vestry door open. He looked back over his shoulder, his beady eyes locking with Caleb's. "I trust I can count on you, Reverend Easton."

With that, Judge Madden swept out of the room, his black robes fluttering in waves. Caleb heard the Judge's boots squeak out onto the church floor and realized the buzz of the crowd must've been dwindling since the moment the Judge had walked into the vestry.

Caleb slipped his own Bible off the desk and under his arm, making a move to follow him before stopping short at the door. He ducked back inside, tugging the door closed a mite behind him for privacy, and turned to Hindstall, who was shouldering his musket.

"On second thought, Constable, I would very much appreciate it if you could send someone to my house to see my wife is secure," he whispered.

"Of course," Hindstall replied, nodding. He tipped his gun toward the door. "I'd best stay and tend to Judge Madden, but I'll surely send one of my best men to fetch Mrs. Easton right away."

"No! You misunderstand me, Constable." Caleb gripped Hindstall's forearm and stepped closer, dipping his head, his voice lowering. "Whoever you send must be sure that under no circumstances can my wife leave the house."

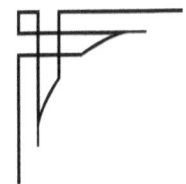
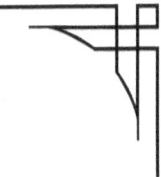

CHAPTER 6
Rebecca

"Ouch!" Rebecca exclaimed, knocking her chin and elbow into the doorframe of South Puritan's women's entrance as the crowd surged forward from behind.

She and Levi had separated out in the yard when the doors to South Puritan opened and everyone rushed for the entrance. Levi told Rebecca to hurry ahead as he stayed behind to search for an appropriate tie-up for Chancer.

Now, all around Rebecca, a crowd with many family members in tow, had tossed the meeting house's rule of men and women entering through separate entrances and were pushing in wherever they could.

Rebecca, still squashed against the doorframe, glanced over her shoulder to see the offender who'd pushed her—a pudgy woman wrapped in a filthy shawl. She was knocking into everyone, shuffling in sideways, her elbow raised ahead of her like a sail on a ship.

"Sorry, miss. We're in a hurry!" The woman continued past her, dragging her small daughter of about ten years old behind her by the wrist. She stopped a few steps ahead of Rebecca, stuck behind a blockade of tall men, and hissed back at the girl, "Keep up, now! Before they're full!"

Rebecca cursed the fact that she was shorter than just about everybody. She gritted her teeth as she stood on tiptoes to look over the crowd that pressed inside the church, having no doubt the pushy woman was right. Everyone was edging forward to get a seat inside. Judging by the dress of the people around her (farmers in stained work clothes and shopkeepers in fine grays and blacks), there were more townsfolk here than South Puritan members.

"I heard it was a stabbing!" a grumbly male voice said behind her. "Two men killed!"

Rebecca looked back to see a balding man with a bulbous nose and a patchy brown beard in debate with a younger man next to him.

"No, no! It's a robbery for sure!" the younger man said, dusting snow from the sleeves of his cloak. "I'd guess something big, from the shipyard."

"You're both wrong! I bet it's treason again," said a deep voice. Rebecca and a few others turned to look at a tall skeleton of a fellow, with a gruff black beard and a worn gray cap. He ran his tongue over his teeth and nodded. "That's the only way they'd come at this hour and demand we all be here! Some fool didn't learn his lesson last time."

Rebecca turned back around as the crowd pushed forward, enabling her to fully slip inside the building. Then she came to a cramped stop again. Someone had lit the series of lanterns that ran along both walls, illuminating the interior of South Puritan with dim orange light. The noise of nervous conversation filled the air, echoing off the eaves high above. Rebecca scanned the crowd, hoping to spot Caleb or anyone else who worked there. But all she saw were backs of heads. Both the right and left banks of pews were nearing capacity, and those who hadn't found seats yet stood in the aisles, shouting at others to move in, make room. The crowd at the very back of the church, where she stood, seemed to be moving in a slow stagger toward the clogged center aisle.

Rebecca peered over at the men's entrance at the far left of the church. Standing in the exact place of the entrance where Caleb normally stood to greet parishioners was Solomon "Sol" Willis, the church's tithes man, whose red hair, pale white skin, and tall stature made him stand out in just about any crowd.

"Sol!" she yelled. Rebecca held her hand up, waiting for him to turn so she could wave, but something was wrong. Normally good-natured, well-liked and capable in his position of keeping order at the church, the profile of Sol's face was as red as his hair. The words coming out of his mouth to someone at the door were falling fast and hot. Rebecca waited for the family next to her to move forward before she made her move.

"Excuse me," she apologized to two terrified looking gray-haired women who clung to one another by the arm, eyes darting from person to person as if anyone around them could be the accused. Rebecca then sprung sideways across the women's entrance and shimmied along the back wall toward Sol. She squeezed in front of the Dollens, a family of fair-haired pig farmers who attended church daily and had at least five freckled boys. They appeared to have resigned to standing in the back of the church for the trial, leaning against the wall. As she passed them, she nodded at round-faced Mrs. Dollen. She stepped up behind Sol, who was standing with his back to her, his full attention on a man stopped at the door, still in heated conversation. Rebecca's gaze dropped to the wall behind Sol, where she saw the biggest pile of weapons she'd ever seen—muskets of all sizes, some black with filth and age, others new with shiny barrels, and every condition in between. There were also a few knives, and even one bow. But why were they all here?

Sol stood guard in front of the pile, glaring at a stout man in a midnight blue coat, poised two steps inside the men's doorway, his eyes bulging and teeth gritted as he held his gun across his chest in two white-knuckled fists.

"I said your arms now, sir!" Sol jabbed a finger at him.

"No!" The man only gripped the gun tighter, lifting it toward his chin. "Like I said, it cost a fortune! Not only is it brand new, but—"

"Constable's orders!" Sol thrust one thick hand forward. "It's for the safety of everyone."

"But—"

"Your gun, sir, or a ten-shilling fine for defying the Constable's rules and I throw you out anyway!" Sol's neck flushed red up to his ears.

The man's eyes grew wider, his nostrils flaring. "Ten shillings? Fine, then!" He thrust the gun into Sol's chest. Sol snatched it with one hand, returned the man's glare, then turned, adding the gun to the pile behind the door.

"Sol, are we starting our own militia?" Rebecca asked once the man had stepped past.

"Mrs. Easton?" Sol twisted back and looked down at her, the redness in his face slowly melting away. His red hair stood up awkwardly, proof that Constable Hindstall's men likely pulled him out of bed for this. "It's nice to see a friendly face, if I may say. This crowd is a nightmare." He pointed at her cloak. "Wait, are you all right?"

She glanced down, seeing in the light for the first time that her fall on the road had left her splattered with muddy slush from chest to foot; a jagged rip stretched across one knee of her cloak. Her cheeks reddened and a stray piece of hair fluttered across her forehead, making her wonder how bad the rest of her looked.

"It's a long story," Rebecca said, slipping her arms out of the cloak, hoping her black wool dress underneath would be more presentable. She tilted her chin toward the gun pile. "Really, what is all this?"

He leaned down and waved her closer. Sol was the kind of tall who had to practically bend in half to talk to most women. Most people, really.

"The Constable is afraid there'll be a riot," he said. "He asked me to collect all weapons at the door. Blades. Bows. Guns. No one is to bring anything inside."

Rebecca furrowed her brow as she slung her cloak over one arm. She glanced back in the direction from which she came. "But no one monitoring the women's entrance."

"I know. I have no help," Sol shrugged, then turned and tugged two guns from a pair of farmers walking in, who surrendered them without issue. He turned back to her. "People are bringing in much more than guns, too. Axes. All manner of things!"

"Here, let me help you, then," Rebecca said, reaching for the guns in his hands.

"No, I'll be fine. And honestly, you should get a seat." He turned and nodded toward the front of the church. "My wife and son are up in the front pew—came along early with me. They'll be happy to make room for you."

"Are you sure?"

He glanced back at the men's entrance, where the crowd continued to push in.

"Listen, we're nearly full," he whispered to her. "I'll be forced to close the doors soon and not everyone is going to make it inside. The crowd's not going to be pleased. Go! Now!"

Rebecca took a step, then hesitated. "Sol, you said you spoke to the Constable. Was my husband with him? Did they tell you what this trial is about?"

Sol blinked a moment, then frowned. "The Reverend's in his office, I think. At least, he was walking that way when I got here. The Constable went in a bit later." Sol turned and held his hand up, stopping an older boy with the faint beginnings of a beard and a musket over his shoulder.

Rebecca shifted her cloak in her arms, glanced up toward Caleb's office.

"And about the trial?"

He placed the boy's musket onto the pile, then ducked his head, putting his hands on his hips.

"Sol? What did he say?"

"Aye, he told me." He stopped, looked over her head, off toward the front of the church. "I know what the charge is. Forgive me, ma'am. The court may be fine holding the trial here, but...there are just some words I can't say in God's house. It would be...immoral of me, I'm sure."

Rebecca stepped back, nodding blankly.

"Okay, then," she said. What offense could be so bad that he was afraid to say it out loud? "We'll find out soon enough, right? Stay safe back here, Sol."

"You as well, ma'am." Sol gave her a final nod, then turned toward the door again.

Rebecca pivoted and stepped into the crowd heading down the aisle. With Sol's odd response still stuck in her mind, she squeezed into place in line behind two gentlemen with similar dark beards and muddy boots, brothers maybe. She looked toward Caleb's office up on her far right, its tiny door closed with no sign of movement. Her cheeks began to burn a little. Why hadn't he come for her, sent for her, or at the very least, sent word to the house? Anything other than allow her to show up here, clueless to their staff. As the Reverend's wife, it was her job to help out during dark times, a duty she wanted to fulfill.

As she made her way down the aisle, she scanned the newly filled pews for familiar faces. Parishioners dotted the crowd dressed all in black. She also picked out Mr. Jacobsen, the town chimney inspector. Behind him sat a fair-haired seamstress who worked in town and her husband. Up ahead, she could see the side profile of Sol's wife, Grace, chunks of her curly blonde hair peeking out from under her black hat as she leaned over to whisper something to her tiny son, whose mop of brown curly hair barely peeked above the pew. Still, more than half of those in the crowd were strangers to her.

Just as she neared the front of the pews, Rebecca came to a dead stop as the brothers in front of her argued with those seated to their right to make room. While she waited, she glanced down at an old man in a brown waistcoat sitting at the very end of the pew her hand rested on. The man leaned forward, reaching with one arm for something at his feet, mumbling.

"Have you dropped something, sir?" Rebecca asked when he didn't immediately pop back up.

The old man looked up at her and smiled, the skin around his eyes crinkling with age, then leaned back, revealing a shaggy brown mutt laying over his feet.

"Fond of dogs?" he asked, leaning forward to stroke the dog's head. The pup tilted its nose up at the man's touch, its warm brown eyes similar to Bow's, but with the fur around its eyes white. Rebecca suddenly felt dizzy.

"Do you have one yourself?" he asked.

She looked at the old man. "Um..."

Rebecca swallowed, feeling hollow inside. She bit her lip and looked away from the man and his dog. Shame washed over her.

When had she stopped being brave? She'd been as excited as Caleb was at the chance to start a new life in a whole new world, to cross the ocean, to not just see a new land, but experience it, help build it.

She looked back at the old man and shook her head.

She should have Bow with her. She should've been brave, chased him into the woods and brought him here with her. She should've burned whatever she had to in order to light up the forest and find him.

"Ma'am?" An impatient female voice called to her from behind. Rebecca looked up to see the men in front of her had won their argument and were shuffling into the aisle, clearing the way for her.

"Sorry." Rebecca rushed forward and began to round the front pew toward Grace when she froze at the sight of the sanctuary in front of her. It looked nothing like she'd left it just hours before. Their beautiful hand-carved wooden altar had been pushed back from the center of the room up against the left wall, its cloth cover and greenery crumpled in a ball on top of it. In the altar's place sat a large table piled at one end with what looked like a month's supply of flaming beeswax candles. A stack of parchment lay at one end and Caleb's hourglass was at the other. An empty chair had been placed at the end of the table, turned out to face the congregation.

Rebecca swallowed. The accused's chair.

Caleb's lectern had been pulled forward and placed next to it. Behind all the shifted furniture, a cluster of older gentlemen dressed in expensively thick great coats, frilly cravats, and all manners of white barrister wigs swarmed about. They hurriedly unpacked rolls of parchment from leather cases, unfurled them, then ran them up to the table.

The men of the Particular Court.

As Rebecca took it all in, she heard the familiar creek of Caleb's office door on her right. She looked over to see the door swing open midway. A hand held it ajar, as whomever it belonged to paused to speak to someone back inside the vestry. The wigged heads of the men from Court swiveled toward it, the view of whoever it was sent them hurrying back to their seats on a bench that had been dragged behind the table. This was it. Behind Rebecca, those left standing scrambled for seats. The crowd began to hush.

"Mrs. Easton! Here!"

Rebecca pivoted to see Grace signaling to her from her seat in the front pew, just opposite the accused's chair. Rebecca rushed to join her, speeding down the pew so fast, she knocked her leg against the knee of the man occupying the first space in the row.

"My apologies," Rebecca whispered as she passed. The man silently tucked his feet in under his legs, giving her room to pass. Rebecca continued, then did a double take over her shoulder. There was something peculiar about him. He was dressed in Puritan blacks, as was the tiny, brittle looking woman who sat by his side, perched on the very edge of the pew, her silver hair pulled tightly back into a bun. Their faces were twisted into grim expressions and their eyes swam in dark circles on their faces, but they sat staring straight ahead, as if oblivious to the commotion around them. They were Puritans, but she was sure she'd never seen either of them before.

"We're happy to make room for you, Rebecca," Grace said and scooped little Jonathan up onto her lap. He chewed on his pointer finger and studied Rebecca with sleepy blue eyes.

"God bless you," Rebecca whispered, taking a seat. The pew was hard, but it felt wonderful to sit down again. She glanced to her left at the strange Puritan couple.

"Grace, do you know them?" she tilted her head slightly toward them.

Grace leaned forward, looking past Rebecca, and shook her head, the ends of her blonde curls bouncing from underneath her hat. "No, I don't think so."

As soon as Grace had gotten the words out, the door to Caleb's office swung all the way open and a wall of a man, a Judge, dressed in black trial robes and a sprawling white wig, emerged from the room. He stalked across the front of the church and into the sanctuary, carrying a brown travel case in one hand. The Judge scanned the crowd with fierce blue eyes framed with thick eyebrows and a heavy forehead. He walked in front of Rebecca, dropped the case with a heavy thud onto the table—the candle flames trembling at the motion—and stepped behind it. With his back to the crowd, he quietly addressed the gentlemen of the court. Each of them snapped to attention at his presence, pausing mid-step or dropping various papers onto their laps.

Rebecca sat up straight, suddenly feeling like cold water had been poured down her spine. This was real. Someone they knew had done something terrible and could die for it. Her mind ran over all the possibilities she'd heard on her way here. Savages. Murder. Treason. The Gallows. She could tell the people around her felt it too, as all conversations behind her fizzled into silence. The only sounds she could hear now were a creak of a pew, a rustle of a coat, or a muffled clearing of the throat from far back in the room.

As the Judge conferred with the court, Rebecca again heard the creak of the vestry door and turned to see Caleb and Constable Hindstall emerge from the office.

Her annoyance at him for leaving her in the dark about the trial dissipated the moment she saw her husband. She breathed a huge sigh of relief at the sight of him, that he was here and safe and in charge, walking to the head of the church, Bible in hand. The sight of him up front felt like a touch of normalcy, a sudden pause in the town's storm of insanity.

But as he moved closer to the center of the room, everything wasn't all right. Caleb looked terrible, as if he'd aged a thousand lifetimes in the few hours he'd been gone. His eyes were bloodshot, with heavy shadows underneath. His wig made everything worse. She'd always hated the thing, but now, paired with the pained look on his face, it made him look like an old man and not at all like a distinguished member of society.

As Caleb took a few more steps into the sanctuary, his gaze fell on Rebecca in the front row. He took a sudden step back, bumping into the Constable walking behind him. Caleb's eyes shot from Rebecca to the Judge, who was still speaking to the Court, then back to her. Caleb motioned the Constable to sit, while he walked over toward her, lips parted as if something urgent to tell her.

"Rebecca," he hushed, motioning for her to meet him halfway. She began to stand when the Judge turned around.

"Gentlemen," the Judge snapped, peering at Caleb over his shoulder.

Caleb and the Constable both stopped dead and looked over at him. The Judge waved one hand toward two unoccupied chairs at the end of the Court.

"To your seats. We're about to start."

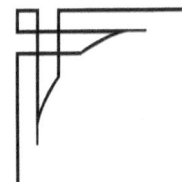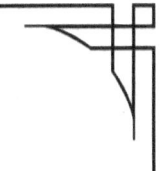

CHAPTER 7
Rebecca

Rebecca watched as Caleb rushed to take his seat. The Judge put his fingertips together, turning and nodding to Constable Hindstall.

"Bring her in."

"Yes, Judge." Hindstall crossed the front of the church and disappeared out of the side entrance to the left of the choir box. As the door closed behind him, the two strangers sitting at the end of Rebecca's row caught her eye again. Like most in the room, they were staring at the Judge, but their expressions were different. Ferocious. The man sat leaning forward in his seat, his face flushed red and nostrils flaring. His wife, too, looked furious despite her tiny stature. She was on the edge of the pew, her eyes narrowed at him and her lips pursed as if physically struggling to keep words from spilling out.

Rebecca nudged Grace with her elbow and whispered, "Are they relatives, do you think? Of the accused?"

Grace shushed her and nodded toward the Judge as he walked around the table and stepped up into Caleb's lectern. Rebecca loved that lectern. The congregation had presented it to Caleb upon their arrival in the Colony as a welcome present. Two sparrows depicted in a joyous flight—their faces turned upward as if flying to heaven—had been hand-carved on the front. Now, as the Judge took his place, the extra two feet of elevation—combined with the thickness of his dark robes and thick white trial wig—made him look like a massive raven hovering over the tiny birds. They were trapped with nowhere to go.

Rebecca snuck a glance over her shoulder at the congregation behind her. Everyone was silent and still, waiting on his words.

The Judge spread out a roll of parchment across the lectern's tabletop, cleared his throat, then looked out over them to study their faces. Rebecca glanced again at Caleb in his seat with the Courte, facing them. Caleb looked from her to the Judge's back, his brow furrowed. She felt uneasy. What had he tried to tell her in that moment before the Judge interrupted?

"Residents of Hartforde Towne," the Judge said, his voice grave and deep. "I am Judge Mordecai Madden, of Particular Court of the Colony of Connecticut. You may have heard rumors that we've come all this way from proceedings in Wethersfield Village, despite the snowfall, to be here tonight. That is true."

He leaned forward and gripped the tabletop with his aged hands, jeweled rings glittering in the candlelight. "We've come here tonight to conduct an immediate trial, the details of which I am afraid, are so blasphemous in my professional opinion, that any delay would surely put every member of this colony at great risk for the purity of their very souls."

"Ahhh!"

Rebecca jumped in her seat at the sound of a muffled shriek issuing from outside the church's side door, where the Constable had disappeared moments ago. Rebecca glanced at Grace, then back at Judge Madden, who continued speaking as if he hadn't noticed. The crowd rumbled uncomfortably behind her.

The Judge drew his fingers back together, forming a tent in front of his chest. "I'm afraid a member of your commu-

nity has committed one of the most unnatural and dangerous violations a soul can commit here on earth."

The church's side door creaked open, and a blast of win-
tery air swept in as Constable Hindstall emerged in the
shadow of its frame. He grimaced as he dragged in a figure
shrouded in an oversized black cloak backwards. The figure underneath appeared to be small and should've easily
been managed by the Constable, except that it fought him
the entire way, its two white hands—the only parts visible—
scratching at his arms and tearing at his beard. Constable
Hindstall struggled to hold the creature at arm's length
while pulling it inside. Then, one of the Constable's men appeared in the doorway behind them and pushed it forward.
The figure stumbled, shuffling and tripping over the cloak
that dragged on the ground. Bare feet protruded out from
underneath the cloak.

Hindstall continued to wrestle the accused into the room
as a murmur rolled through the crowd.

"It's all right, son," Rebecca heard Grace whisper next to
her. She turned to see Grace wrapping her arm around little
Jonathan, pulling him tighter to her chest, using one hand
to partially block the child's view.

Rebecca turned toward Grace and mouthed, "Who is it?"

Grace shook her head, her green eyes wide. "No idea."

"Sirs, if you please." The Judge motioned Hindstall to
bring the accused to the chair that sat at the end of the table,
facing Rebecca.

She put her hand to her mouth and exchanged horrified
looks with Grace as Constable Hindstall yanked the cloaked
figure across the floor and dropped it into the chair. He then
stepped behind it, hovering close enough to lunge if the figure dared to move.

The accused sat perfectly still, except for its hands, which
gripped the end of each armrest tight enough for its knuckles to whiten. Rebecca could see the hands were old, twisted
by age, with thick veins wrapping around the tiny bones like

vines. The fingernails grew jagged and filthy and were lined with dirt as if the person had been digging. Its feet were similar. Pure white skin, reddened by the snow outside, but the toenails caked with dirt.

The figure lifted its trembling hands toward its face and slowly pushed back the hood. Rebecca sat transfixed at what was before her. It was as if time slowed when those white, shriveled hands grabbed for the hood, and—for an instant—all sound stopped as the hood dropped behind the person's head.

Feet away from Rebecca sat a woman greatly advanced in age. Her face looked gaunt, her skin thin and wrinkled as wet parchment. Her eyes were pale and beady, made worse by the fact that they were also lash-less. Her eyebrows, too, appeared to have long faded away into the paleness of her forehead. Her face was framed by damp tangles of white hair, matted on the sides from utter lack of care and flecked with what looked like bits of dirt.

The woman's name slipped, almost silently, from Rebecca's lips.

"Widow Goodness."

The Widow was one of the oldest members—if not the oldest—in South Puritan's congregation. Rebecca knew her only by name and face, but certainly not this state of face. Caleb had presided over the funeral of her husband just three weeks after they'd arrived in the Colony as one of his first official duties. Rebecca searched her memory for anything Caleb may have mentioned about her or the family. The Widow attended services almost regularly despite her age but had always departed before Rebecca had time to speak with her afterward.

Rebecca studied the old woman's face, feeling a pit forming deep in her stomach. The creature who sat before her now looked nothing like the Widow who'd mourned her husband months ago, dressed in the black finery prescribed for dutiful Christians. No. The Widow who Rebecca saw now, facing the hundreds who'd packed the church, had her mouth twisted into a bitter scowl, her eyes narrow and glaring.

The expression on her face almost looked like one of ...defiance.

Judge Madden stepped down from behind the lectern to stand next to Widow Goodness, who sat motionless in the chair, her gaze piercing the air above Rebecca's head.

"One week ago, I received word from your Constable that multiple merchants in this town reported odd inquiries made by Widow Goodness, requests for specific herbs, mugwart and pennyroyal. And, most disturbingly, illicit books with the darkest of origins, including 'De Praestigiis Daemonum' and 'The Lessor Book of Abe,' both of which are banned in most of Europe due to their dangerous nature."

The Judge paused, looking over the crowd. Everyone was still, except for one man sitting among the Court who scribbled notes as the Judge spoke.

"Upon the Constable's further investigation, which was conducted over the course of a week, as well as the search of her home and a questioning of Widow Goodness earlier this evening, there's sufficient evidence to suggest that deplorable, soul-shattering crimes have taken place at her hands." Judge Madden stopped to unroll a piece of parchment, which he read aloud, his voice booming. "Let it be known to all present and let it be recorded that Widow Evanora Goodness, nee Evanora Brown, born in the year sixteen eleven, is hereby formally charged with engaging in witchcraft."

All around Rebecca, the room erupted with gasps of disbelief and confusion.

Rebecca's hand covered her mouth again as her eyes shot to Caleb, who was leaning forward in his seat and wiping his brow on his sleeve. He only stared silently at the floor in front of him.

The Widow, on the other hand, had no reaction that Rebecca could see. She remained sitting completely still, the look of defiance still frozen on her face. No movement other than the slow blinking of lidless eyes every few seconds.

"Witchcraft? Can this be possible?" Grace whispered over Jonathan's head to her.

"Silence!" Judge Madden shouted at the crowd. He plucked a document from the table and stepped closer to Widow Goodness, holding it up above his shoulder for all to see and pointing at the heading with one finger. "I have here a copy of the Statue of 1641, established by the General Court of the Massachusetts Bay Colony, which states..." He lowered the document and flipped it over to read. "'Any man or woman be a Witch, that is, one who hath consult-eth with the Devil or a familiar spirit, they shall be put to death.' Knowing this, Widow Goodness, how do you plead to this charge?"

The Widow tilted her white face, examining the Judge out of the corner of her eye.

"Guilty," she hissed through her teeth.

The crowd erupted again.

"Guilty!"

"She's really pleading guilty?"

Rebecca's mind spun. Witchcraft? What had she done?

"Blasphemy!" Someone shouted from the back of the room.

"Sinner!" a man at the far end of Rebecca's pew yelled.

"Witch!"

"Hang the witch! No, burn her!" thundered a man's voice from close behind. The gruffness of it caused Rebecca to twist around in her seat, turning to see a wealthy shopkeeper from town up on his feet three rows behind her. And he wasn't the only one. A handful of red-faced colonists were now standing with looks of confusion, anger. Within seconds, the Constable rushed into the crowd, squeezing down the aisle toward the man who'd yelled "hang her" at a pace fast enough that all others on their feet quickly dropped back into their seats.

"Silence! Listen, everyone!" Judge Madden stepped to the center of the room and held his arms up. "Although the Widow has chosen to plead guilty to these charges, the trial must continue. We must understand the extent of the darkness here, and how far it is spread so we are sure to stamp it out. Each of you must serve as witnesses."

The Judge rushed back to the front of the church. "First, we will establish the moral severity of engaging in witchcraft, an act that has been clearly condemned by God himself. To do so, I summon Reverend Caleb Easton forward."

Judge Madden raised a hand, motioning for Caleb to rise. Rebecca held her breath as she watched him stand. He pushed himself out of his chair, holding his Bible in his left hand and smoothing down his black robe with the other. His eyes found Rebecca in the front pew, his brows pressed together with worry. She looked back at the Widow and felt a knot form in her stomach.

"Please, take a seat." The Judge motioned Caleb to a chair that one of the Particular Court's men was carrying forward. He positioned it in front of the lectern, just feet away from the Widow. Caleb lowered himself reluctantly into it.

"Reverend Easton," the Judge began, pacing in front of both of Caleb and Widow Goodness. "What does the Bible say about witchcraft? Does it condemn it?"

"Yes, the Bible condemns the act in multiple places," Caleb said.

"Elaborate."

Rebecca watched as Caleb flipped the Bible open to one of the early books.

"Well, here in Exodus, it's clear." He glanced at the crowd and cleared his throat. "In Chapter Twenty, Verse Three, it says, 'thou shalt have no other gods before me.' The word 'me' obviously means the Lord, our father. To worship any other god, nature, spirit, would be an act of blasphemy, an absolute lack of reverence for the Lord."

Rebecca studied Widow Goodness for any reaction, but she remained bizarrely motionless in her chair, unmoved by the words. Rebecca examined the awful mats in her hair again and wondered if the Judge was absolutely certain the Widow was of sound mind and knew what she'd agreed to.

Judge Madden put a finger to his lips as he continued to pace. "What else does the Bible say, Reverend?"

Caleb paged further into the book, stopping in the middle. "In Second Chronicles, we learn the story of Manasseh. He was a King of Judah, who the Bible recorded as practicing witchcraft during his life. The book describes this particular act as one of 'evil in the eyes of the Lord.'"

"Evil in the eyes of the Lord!" Judge Madden echoed. He walked back toward the Widow, his black boots mashing the floor with each step. "And Reverend, does the Bible prescribe a punishment for those who engage in witchcraft?"

Caleb hesitated, glancing from the Judge to the book and back again. "It does."

"Show us."

Rebecca clenched her jaw and glared at the Judge. Her husband was a good man, faithful to the Lord and his subjects. Why couldn't Judge Madden move on and question someone else? The Constable, or the merchants the Widow had made those requests too?

"Reverend?" the Judge pressed.

"Here it is," Caleb said softly, pointing with his index finger. "Exodus Twenty-Two, One Hundred and Eighty-One."

"And what does it say?" the Judge demanded after a moment of silence.

"'Thou shalt not suffer a witch to live.'"

"Thou shalt not suffer a witch to live!" Judge Madden annunciated each word, pausing in front of the Widow, looking again for any reaction. She only stared straight ahead.

Rebecca jumped as someone touched her elbow. She turned to see Grace, stroking the head of her teary-eyed child.

"I'm sorry, but we must go," Grace whispered. "I know it's our duty to serve as witnesses, but he's terrified. He's too young for this."

Rebecca nodded numbly, feeling as if she was in a stupor. "Of course. Go!"

Grace bundled her son against her chest, slipped out of the pew and down the side aisle, turning toward the back of the church.

"Does the Bible describe how a witch should die?" the Judge snapped.

Rebecca looked back at Caleb. His hand hovered over the Bible, fingers shaking. She stared at the Judge. Was he really going to make her husband—a reverend—prescribe a woman's death?

"Do I need to remind you that you are under oath, Reverend?"

Caleb exhaled, then raised his eyes to meet the Judge's.

"Leviticus Twenty, Twenty-Seven. 'A man or woman who is a medium or spiritist among you must be put to death.'"

"And? Read the rest, sir."

Caleb took a breath.

The Judge turned. "Reverend!"

Caleb dipped his head, not needing to look at the book. "'You are to stone them; their blood will be on their own heads.'"

Rebecca's stomach turned.

"Their blood will be on their own heads!" The Judge pivoted to face the Widow. "Widow Goodness, do you understand the gravity of pleading guilty to this charge of engaging in witchcraft, a crime that the Bible records as a crime against the Lord God himself? Are you prepared to admit all that you've done before your town?"

She said nothing. Only watched him with her feral eyes.

"Constable, the basket."

Constable Hindstall backed up from his place behind the Widow's chair and retrieved a basket from underneath the table. He lifted it and turned it upside down, scattering what looked like tightly wound bundles of dirty sticks across the tabletop.

Judge Madden grabbed one of the tiny bundles and held it up high.

"Poppits were found during a search of your home!" he said, dangling one in front of her. Rebecca could see it closer now, a cluster of twigs divided into the shape of a human with cloth twisted between the limbs. "Fifteen or so in all, made from sticks, mud and cloth, stuffed with herbs. A child's toy, yes, but not quite an innocent frivolity for an aged woman. Common artifacts of a witch who wishes to inflict torture on their real-life counterparts."

He turned to the Constable.

"Where were they found?"

"Hidden in the fireplace, sir," the Constable said.

"No doubt they were stowed above a burning fire in order to inflict burns and fevers on others," Judge Madden said.

"My husband and children have been down with fevers for three weeks!" a woman's voice shrieked from the back of the room.

Holding one hand up to silence the woman, Judge Madden turned toward the Widow and slammed his other fist on the table, making Rebecca and those who remained in the front row flinch.

"Well, Widow Goodness? You've pled guilty and we have physical evidence. It's time to admit the extent of your crimes. Understand that no mercy can be given here on earth for what you've done. You will die for what you've done. But if your last act on earth is done to correct some of your wrongs, if you're lucky, the Lord may show a hint of mercy on you in the afterlife!"

The Judge's spit had flown everywhere with the exclamation, but the Widow just sat there, gritting her jaw and staring over Rebecca's head.

"Miserable bastard!" someone whispered.

Rebecca's head spun in the direction of the whispered curse. The strange Puritan couple at the end of her row! The husband was glaring more viciously at Judge Madden than he had before. His wife was gripping his arm, holding him back. Rebecca turned to the Judge to see if he'd heard, but he only continued hovering over the Widow.

"What did you use the poppits for? To curse others in town? To curse some of those present? To curse some of the women and children present?"

This elicited cries from the crowd.

"Our baby!" another woman whimpered from the back. "He was born stillborn two months ago! Ask the midwife!"

"It was her!" another voice shouted.

But the Widow remained silent, staring straight ahead.

The Judge took another step, now directly in front of her. "The herbs, the books you ordered in town, what were they for? What spells have you tried?"

The Widow offered no response.

The Judge backed up and crossed his arms over his chest, peering down at her. "Your husband, Elias," he took a step forward. "He died in a somewhat unusual manor, didn't he?"

The Widow glared at him, her lips parting, but no words came out.

"Dismembered, am I right?"

Her white hands gripped the chair tighter.

No one breathed.

Judge Madden suddenly backed away, throwing his hands up. "Reverend Easton, maybe you can be of assistance."

Caleb twisted in his seat. "I'm sorry, Judge?"

"She spoke with you earlier this evening. Get her to speak again," the Judge commanded.

"Sir?"

"Get the information out of her! You and the Constable took her confession. She's your parishioner. Do it."

"Oh, I think the Constable or someone else from the Court would be more appro—" Caleb raised his hand in protest and looked over his shoulder at Constable Hindstall, still standing guard behind the Widow's chair.

"I order you to do so!" The Judge lunged in two furious steps past the Widow and towered over Caleb in his seat. "Or are you not an authority figure in your own place of worship?"

Rebecca saw the look of shock on Caleb's face melt into one of contained fury as he pursed his lips. His neck flushed red up into his ears, and he stood, looking unsteady on his feet as he turned to drop his Bible on the chair behind him.

As Rebecca watched him move, she felt her pulse race and her cheeks burn, baffled that anyone would speak to a man of the church like this. She looked up at the Constable, who ordinarily had the most power in town. He offered no interference, standing stock still with his arms crossed. Behind him, the secretary and the rest of the Particular Court, too, sat perfectly still on their bench, all eyes on Caleb. Rebecca shook her head. Would no one stand up to this man?

Caleb moved slowly around the Widow, the Judge taking a few steps back, his eyes glaring as Caleb paused to take a seat on the tabletop next to her.

Caleb looked down at his hands, squeezing them into fists in his lap, then released them.

"Evanora," Caleb began, speaking in a gentler tone, one Rebecca often heard him use with those ill or grieving. "You've been a member of this church for many years. It's obvious that you've been led astray. Can you tell us how this all started?"

A few seconds of silence passed, then the Widow's face slowly eased into a smile, her cracked lips spreading to reveal rotting yellow teeth with deep brown gaps in between them. Rebecca recoiled, averting her eyes for just a moment.

"He came to me. To me," the Widow said in a frail, raspy voice, tapping her chest with a bony white thumb. "He did. I was chosen."

"Who did?"

She ducked her chin to her chest, still smiling, then threw her head back and laughed. Too loud. Absurdly loud. The sound of her laughter lit a fire under the Judge again, who jumped in between her and Caleb.

"The dark spirit came to you? Lured you himself?" Judge Madden pressed. He leaned in toward her. "How? Was it in a vision? A dream?"

"No," the Widow laughed straight through the Judge's questioning, then shifted her gaze back to Caleb. "He's real."

"Who?" the Judge asked.

"The Devil," she said, her eyes still on Caleb. "He's as real as you or I."

Rebecca froze. The Devil? She studied the old woman's face. Her eyes sparkled. Her lips curled up into a smirk. She was serious. She really believed what she was saying. Rebecca glanced quickly over her shoulder. About a fourth of the congregation appeared to have fled out the rear doors, while those who remained sat perfectly still, in all forms of spellbound shock: leaning forward, elbows on knees, hands over mouths, jaws agape.

"Where?" the Judge asked.

Rebecca turned back to see the Widow closing her eyes, as if envisioning the meeting. "He came to me, and at first, I was afraid. Terrified at the way he looked. His eyes, they were round and black, but somehow burned like fire."

"Then what?"

"He came closer and bowed to me." She swept a gnarled hand through the air. The Widow's mouth closed and twisted up into a smirk. She turned back forward, this time—for the first time—meeting Rebecca's eyes. They looked to Rebecca like watery puddles, fading slightly into the whiteness of her face. Rebecca shifted in her seat, terrified to think of what this woman had seen, what she'd done, what she was saying.

"What next?" the Judge repeated. "Did you sign your name in the Devil's book of names? Did you seal a carnal pact?"

Rebecca stared at her hands as she twisted them in her lap, feeling the Widow's pale eyes lingering on her, feeling exposed, wishing she'd left along with Grace and Jonathan. It shocked her how easily a Judge, a man unknown to any of them, would dare to speak of an old woman's carnal behavior in a meeting house. In front of such a crowd. In front of children!

A moment of silence passed before the Widow responded. "He let me pet him."

Rebecca's head jerked up. The Widow was staring straight at her.

The Judge paused, his brow furrowed. "What?"

"The Devil isn't a man, fool." Widow Goodness smiled. "The Devil is an animal. A Beast."

An animal.

Rebecca's jaw dropped and her eyes shot to Caleb, who was already looking at her, his jaw clenched. Just for a split second, Rebecca swore she saw him flick his head to one side: no.

She returned her gaze to the Widow, feeling dizzy as her thoughts whirled. Animal. She'd said an animal had approached her from the woods.

"Repeat that!" the Judge ordered. Behind the desk, a few of the Court's men rose and began digging through the pile of parchment at the other end of the table. Their expressions were bewildered.

"The Devil is an animal. He lives here, right here, in the dark woods of Hartforde. He roams the forests and fields at night."

"Can you describe this Beast?"

"He's tall like a man, but much bigger, with a humped back and silky black fur," the old woman said, dipping her head so that a few clumps of her white hair swung in front of her face. "His eyes are wide, and he has a snout from which he roars. His jaws can tear flesh clean from bone. He's crowned with two gray horns."

Rebecca felt her breath catch in her throat. The Beast she'd seen in the woods was exactly as the Widow had just described. Rebecca looked back at Caleb and suddenly understood his no. Caleb must've heard about the Beast from the Widow earlier tonight. That's why he hadn't sent for her. He'd done it intentionally; he'd known how dangerous admitting to seeing this Beast would be and wanted her to stay away.

She looked back at Judge Madden as he carried on demanding that Constable Hindstall strip the Widow and search her for something called a witch's mark. Their voices blurred as Rebecca's thoughts raced. If she admitted to seeing the same Beast, she'd put herself at risk for being accused of the same vile acts as Widow Goodness. If she said anything, Caleb, maybe even their whole church, would be placed under suspicion.

She turned back toward the Widow, who Constable Hindstall was now yanking out of the chair by her arm as the woman shrieked.

But Rebecca hadn't run toward the Beast. She'd run from it. Twice. It certainly hadn't bowed to her; it had chased her, killed her dog. The Widow may be a witch, but Rebecca wasn't, and they'd both seen the same horned creature in the woods. What if the whole town was in danger? Not just the other members of the church, but the entire town?

She swallowed and glanced back at the church doors. She couldn't imagine going back outside, knowing such a creature was roaming the woods. How could she let anyone else?

Rebecca looked up to see Constable Hindstall struggling to pull the old woman out of her chair as Caleb leapt to his feet, rushing back out of their way. The Constable had run to her husband in his time of need. He'd protect them, vouch for them if he had to, wouldn't he? Better yet, he'd go after this Beast, wouldn't he, whatever it was? Her eyes followed the Constable as he dragged the Widow toward the side door, followed by all the men from the Court who abandoned their seats. The Judge stayed behind, raising his arms up to calm the crowd left inside the church. She glanced at the people sitting in the pews. Those in the church, they'd vouch for her, wouldn't they? This was still their town, their church. She looked back at Judge Madden. It was the Judge who was the outsider.

"Lord, give me strength," Rebecca whispered, closing her eyes for a second. Opening them again, she stood up, twisting her gray cloak in her hands, the Puritan strangers seated next to her looking over.

"Judge Madden," she called into the scuffle. "May I have a word?"

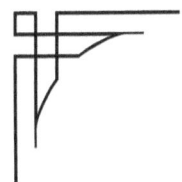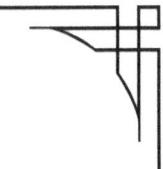

CHAPTER 8
Rebecca

Judge Madden recoiled from the Widow, turning his head toward Rebecca and squinting at her, clearly laying eyes on her for the very first time.

"What did you say? How dare you interrupt these proceedings!" he said, his voice rising.

Rebecca cleared her throat and glanced over the Judge's shoulder to Caleb, who had risen from his bench the instant she'd spoken up. The Judge took a step past the Widow's chair toward Rebecca. The narrowness of his pale blue eyes aimed right at her made her feel exposed, vulnerable. She shivered.

"Well?" he barked.

Rebecca swallowed, then started again. "I said excuse me, but—"

He thrust a hand toward Widow Goodness, who was still struggling to pull back from Constable Hindstall's grasp. "Ma'am, are you a witness to this woman's evil deeds? Her dark worship? If not, I suggest that you remain quiet and let us carry out justice swiftly and uninterrupted. A trial of the Particular Court has no room for emotion."

"I wanted to tell you—tell the court, I mean—that I saw it too," Rebecca stammered, her voice sounding much weaker than she'd meant it to. She twisted her cloak in her hands, her nails digging into its rough wool, suddenly feeling all the attention in the church turn to her. The men from the Particular Court gaped at her from the front of the church over their parchment and legal books, and the eyes of the congregation behind her bore into her back. She stared straight ahead at the Judge and swallowed, feeling her cheeks flush.

"Repeat that," the Judge commanded, walking closer. He placed his fists on his hips, the sleeves of his black robe tenting out around him like a black raven's wings.

Rebecca cleared her throat again, determined to speak louder. "I said, I've seen it. The animal, the Beast, in the woods. A creature just like the one the Widow described."

The Judge blinked at her for a second. "What?" He turned back toward Constable Hindstall, who was leading the Widow back toward her chair in the center of the floor. She dug her feet into the ground, trying in vain to yank herself away from him.

"Constable, who is this woman?"

"Rebecca Easton. I'm the wife of Reverend Easton," Rebecca said before the Constable could open his mouth.

"Wait—" Constable Hindstall, motioning to have the Widow deposited back into her seat, put a hand up, looking at Rebecca. "You say you've seen a creature like the one the Widow described?" His tone sounded skeptical.

"Yes." Rebecca looked from the Constable to the Judge and back again. She'd spent so much time debating if she should come forward that she never considered whether or not they'd believe her. "I saw exactly what Widow Goodness described. A huge creature with silky black fur. It walks upright like a man, but so much bigger."

Constable Hindstall furrowed his brow. "Like a bear?"

Rebecca shook her head. "No, not a bear. It's taller, and its legs are lean, muscular. It also has hooves and moves fast. It doesn't lumber like a bear. And it has wide horns."

"Like antlers on a stag?" Judge Madden asked.

"No, they were too thick. As broad as a stag, maybe, but horns thick like a bull's, except they were twisted." Rebecca pursed her lips together at the thought of Bow's final squeal as he'd disappeared into the woods. "It also hunts."

She waited a moment, then looked back at the Judge, standing now opposite her, and staring silently as if waiting for her to continue.

"I'm a good Christian, sir, and a member of this church, a leader here with my husband, Caleb," she said, sneaking a look over the Judge's shoulder again at Caleb, who was wiping his brow with one hand. "I didn't have any...interaction with the beast like Widow Goodness described. But yes. I've seen the creature in the woods between our house and here. In fact, I've seen it twice now."

The Judge put an index finger up to his lips and began pacing in between Rebecca and the Widow, who had slunk back down into her chair and was glaring at Rebecca, perfectly still—her beady eyes peering through her lash-less eyelids.

"Twice, did you say?" the Judge asked.

"I saw it earlier tonight on my way here, actually." Rebecca moved the cloak she held in her hands to the side, revealing the tear and wet slush stains at the bottom of her dress. "It came out of the forest across the way from my home. It chased me part of the way here. A boy from town picked me up and gave me a ride in his carriage." She snuck a look over her shoulder, back at the pews, wondering if Levi was still among those seated. If he was present, he made no note of himself.

"Maybe the noise of his horse scared it away, I'm not sure. I arrived here just as the trial started. I hadn't had time to tell anyone."

"And the first time you saw it?" the Constable asked.

Rebecca paused. "A few weeks ago. I was walking home from women's choir practice when I heard a noise, a loud hissing noise. I turned and saw it come out of the woods behind me. I was so terrified, I ran all the way home."

"And did you report that sighting before now?" the Judge pressed.

Rebecca's eyes shot to Caleb. His face looked white.

"Um—" she stammered.

Caleb rushed forward and paused next to the Judge, who stood now, just a pace or two away from Rebecca. "Judge Madden, I assure you, my wife is a devout Christian and a woman of excellent moral character."

"Mmm. And is she a sympathizer to this witch?" Judge Madden continued staring at Rebecca. She glanced at the floor, suddenly unnerved at seeing the judge up close. She shrunk under the immensity of his white trial wig, his ruddy complexion, his thick black eyebrows that framed his pale blue eyes—eyes that raked over her, suspiciously, as if evaluating her face, her windblown hair, her torn garments.

"Of course not, Judge," Caleb said. "I'm sure she's come forward now out of her concern for the safety of those in town, especially if someone else has seen it."

"Yes, he's correct," Rebecca nodded. "It's not safe." Just feet away from Rebecca, the Widow began to rock silently back and forth in her chair. Her eyes squeezed shut, and she began mumbling something through her peeling lips.

"Mmm." Judge Madden turned back and pointed to the man seated on the end of the court's bench, quill in hand, taking notes. "Let Mrs. Easton be listed as a witness and her testimony recorded as evidence in support of the charges of witchcraft."

The man ducked his head, moving his quill in a flourish across his page.

"Wait, no! I'm not—" Rebecca started.

"Silence, woman!"

"But the safety of the town!"

"The court thanks you for your contribution." He nodded, then turned away.

Rebecca froze, her cheeks burning. This Judge was impossible! She wasn't a witness. She hadn't seen anything the Widow had admitted to doing. She looked back at Caleb, who stared down at the ground, jaw clenched, yet he made no effort to interrupt.

Rebecca sat down on the pew beneath her and looked at the Widow, who continued to rock, lips moving. There was no other reaction from her, as if she hadn't even heard.

"Judge Madden." Constable Hindstall stepped forward, pulling his musket off his shoulder and holding it in one hand like a walking stick. "If Mrs. Easton did see something out in the woods tonight, devilish Beast or otherwise, I must insist that my men and I be dismissed to go hunt it down. If there's an animal of any kind chasing after our townsfolk, we simply must take a look. Now. Whatever it was may still be nearby."

"I agree with the Constable," Caleb said, folding his arms over his chest and looking down at his boots. "I'd also suggest, Judge, that we delay these proceedings until the Constable finds the animal."

"There will be no delay," the Judge said through gritted teeth. "Finding the Beast is secondary, a separate matter than Widow Goodness's admission to wicked and immoral deeds, and we will deal with one matter at a time. The Widow has confessed to consorting with the Devil. You read the passages aloud here tonight yourself, Reverend. Joshua Six, Ten: 'You are to stone them; their blood will be on their own heads!' There is no other resolution to this case other than the ultimate punishment."

Rebecca blinked, something striking her as odd in his quotation. Before she could think on it, the Judge pivoted and headed back up to Caleb's lectern, stepping up and grabbing his gavel from its tabletop. Caleb backed up and took a seat on the bench with the court's men. Constable Hindstall remained standing guard over the Widow in her chair, his arms crossed over his chest.

Was this it? Rebecca's eyes darted from one man to another, but Caleb and the Constable were locked on Judge Madden.

The Judge looked out over the crowd, his eyes looking fierce and narrow underneath his wiry black eyebrows.

Rebecca peeked over at the Widow, who began rocking faster now, strands of her stringy white hair falling over her forehead. Her mumbling had stopped, her mouth had stretched again into a queer little smile. Rebecca glanced back over her shoulder as the Judge leafed through papers. At least half of the congregation had made a run for it during the Widow's questioning. Those who remained in their seats now sat stock still, staring at the Judge. Some wore expressions of fury, as if they held back their own accusations and blame against the Widow for their problems, illnesses. Others leaned forward, their elbows on their knees, captivated.

As Rebecca turned her attention toward the front of the room, her eyes caught again on the odd Puritan couple seated at the end of her row. Tears streamed down the old woman's face, silently but heavily. The man attempted to quietly console her, one hand rubbing her upper back while he glared up at the Judge.

Rebecca shifted in her seat and looked back at Judge Madden, who ran a finger over a piece of parchment on the lectern in front of him.

"According to Statute of 1611 of the General Court of Massachusetts Bay, upon which we base decisions in these trials, two things are required to find a person guilty of witchcraft—" The Judge's voice boomed low and heavy across the room. He lifted two fingers in the air, the ruby ring on his forefinger glinting in the candlelight. "—an accusation and a single piece of evidence. I hereby declare the need for an accusation in this case to be nullified, due to the fact that the Widow herself came forward with an admission, first to the town's Constable and Reverend, and then repeated that confession before all of you here tonight."

He shifted behind the podium, then continued. "As for the second point, the evidence in this case exists in the form of poppits which you see here." He gestured to the table in the middle of the floor behind the Widow's chair where the crude stick and thread dolls lay in their pile. "As you heard from Constable Hindstall, they were uncovered earlier this evening during a search of the woman's home. In addition, you also heard supplemental witness testimony from Mrs. Easton."

Rebecca lowered her eyes and slunk down in her seat a few inches.

"Therefore—" The Judge lifted a brown gavel from the lectern top and raised it high in the air. "The Particular Court of Connecticut does find that the accused, Widow Evanora Goodness, guilty of the charge of practicing witchcraft."

Rebecca raised her head as whispers immediately rippled through the crowd behind her.

"Silence! I am not done!" Judge Madden held both hands up, and the crowd's noise immediately ceased. "The only remedy that exists to cure a soul infected by evil of this magnitude is to send it into the afterlife for true punishment. Understand that the Widow will go to Hell and burn for what she's done, according to God's own law of double predestination." He lifted the gavel high. "Widow Goodness, I hereby sentence you to death by hanging!"

With that, the Judge smacked the gavel down hard on the lectern. Rebecca turned as members of the crowd rushed to their feet, shouting.

"Hang her! Hang the witch!"

"Kill her!"

"She's bound for hell, she is!"

Just then, the Widow sprung to life before Rebecca, leaping out of her chair and standing up with the vigor of someone decades younger. It appeared as if life had flooded back into her face, and her eyes lit with excitement.

"Praise him!" the Widow yelled through her cracked and ancient voice. The crowd fell silent. The Widow balled up one bony hand into a fist and punched the air, then spun backwards to face the Judge. "You fools with your Bible verses and holy talk. You send me exactly where I want to go, to be with my beloved. He waits for me!"

"You foolish woman!" the Judge yelled. "If you still think you have a chance at reuniting with your deceased husband in the afterlife, then you are sorely mistaken. You will burn in Hell for the choices you've made!"

Ignoring his remarks, the Widow turned to face the crowd again, smiling and taking a few slow steps down the aisle. "I can hear him now. My beloved approaches from the forest," she said, staring toward the church's front door. Rebecca peered in the same direction, her jaw dropping as she understood who the Widow really meant as her *beloved*. Around her, the townsfolk had also fallen silent, everyone listening.

The Widow's eyes watched the church door. "He comes for me, now! We are to be married in Hell, where we will live forever!"

She broke into a run, tearing down the aisle, her black cloak dragging on the floor behind her and her arms out as if trying to grab someone invisible. People in the pews shot to their feet. Some yanked their loved ones back away from her. A handful of men stepped out into the aisle, red-faced and shouting threats, but making no move to touch her. Rebecca put her hand to her chest, suddenly unable to breathe.

"Stop her!" the Constable yelled as he and one of his men took off down the aisle after her. They caught her just a few feet away from the women's entrance doors. Constable Hindstall got to her first, grabbing her around the waist and dragging her back as she laughed—high and shrill with delight, still staring back at the church doors.

The Constable dragged her to the front of the church where his men took her from him. One man gripped her underneath each arm and rushed her across a cluster of horrified townspeople seated in the choir box, and out the church's side door, where Rebecca could see a portion of a horse and carriage waiting in the dark.

"Don't you understand?" The Widow yelled at Judge Madden before they pulled her through the doorframe. "I need you to murder me. That's why I came forward! That's the only way I can be his queen! He desires only a murdered bride!"

"Constable, wait!" the Judge called from the lectern, ignoring the Widow.

Constable Hindstall urged his men to continue on, then slammed the side door shut behind them— the sounds of the Widow's shrill laugh silenced at last.

He hurried back to the center of the floor.

"As I said, we're dealing with one matter at a time." The Judge pointed to him. "Now that the Widow has been sentenced, I approve of your request to conduct an immediate search of the forest for this Beast, if you truly believe there is a safety threat to the town."

"Yessir."

The Judge turned and looked directly at Rebecca. "Second, Mrs. Easton will be transported to the jailhouse immediately for questioning."

Rebecca sat up straight, feeling like buckets of freezing water had been poured over her. "Questioning, Judge?"

"Naturally. You and a condemned woman have seen the same thing."

"But Judge, I must protest—" Caleb stood up, calling from his seat.

The Judge ducked his head, signing a piece of parchment one of the men from court had slipped onto the lectern. "She's had contact twice with this beast creature," he said. "As I told you earlier in your office, this problem of immoral behavior must be contained before it spreads."

"Immoral behavior?" Rebecca repeated, the words ringing in her ears. She slowly rose to her feet, glancing at Constable Hindstall, wondering if he was about to grab her, too.

Caleb rushed up to the side of the lectern, his face beet red, nostrils flaring. "But my wife is not a witch, sir! Look at her! She hurt herself this very night trying to escape it!"

Judge Madden glared down at him. "Restrain yourself, Reverend, or you'll find yourself in jail for the rest of the night! I will indeed question your wife, in private."

He nudged the signed paper back to the man from court, who was now staring at Rebecca through a tiny single eyeglass.

The Constable stepped forward, holding his musket in both hands. "If you please, Judge. I'd like to take Mrs. Easton with me into the woods to hunt down this Beast. She's seen this creature with her own eyes. She can lead us to the exact spots she's seen it."

The Judge paused.

"Think about it, Judge," the Constable continued. "Only Mrs. Easton and Widow Goodness have seen this animal. The Widow has been convicted. She's in no shape to be trusted or taken anywhere at present. We could find any manor of beasts out in the Hartforde woods at this time of year, especially if food sources are scarce. We can track it, but we need Mrs. Easton's eyes to confirm we've captured the right creature."

Rebecca swallowed hard as the Constable turned to look at her. She could tell the Judge was considering it.

"Fine then," Judge Madden spat. "Take the Reverend's wife. But I must warn you both that if any woman under the suspicion of witchcraft attempts to abscond, she is, by law, automatically declared guilty."

He turned, addressing the Constable only. "I'll give the two of you until dawn to find and surrender this animal, dead or alive. Be assured, Beast or no Beast, the Widow hangs at first light."

He looked back at Rebecca as she sunk into her seat. "And I will question Mrs. Easton immediately after."

"Judge," Caleb said, stepping around the lectern and trying to work his way into Judge Madden's gaze. "Judge, I must request that I, too, accompany them into the woods to—"

"No," the Judge dismissed, looking down again at the documents in front of him. "But, Reverend, you bring me to my third matter. You will accompany me into town immediately to help prepare the Widow for the carrying out of her sentence. End of story."

The Judge raised his head and looked out over the crowd, then banged his gavel again. "This court is dismissed, though I desire anyone within earshot who worries about his or her soul to report at dawn to the gallows in order to see the justice of the Lord carried out in our world!"

Rebecca stared ahead blankly as the men of the Particular Court rose, stuffing their legal books and papers into their bags, and yanking on travel cloaks. The Judge stepped down, picking up his black travel bag from behind the table and stomping toward the side door. The noise of conversation immediately swelled again behind Rebecca—shrills of hatred toward the Widow, excitement for the hanging, shouted offers to help bring the Beast in—but Rebecca only heard the echo of them through numb ears as the crowd behind her began to depart.

She stared at the floor in disbelief. She felt frozen in her seat. It couldn't be real. Her, a witch? How could anyone think that?

Rebecca slowly rose to her feet, her cloak sliding off her lap and dropping onto the floor in front of her. Her hands shook as she wiped them across her face, pushing stray strands of her hair back out of her eyes. She quickly tried to make herself look neat and tidy, the complete opposite of the Widow. Caleb rushed over and pulled her into an embrace—her cheek pressing against his shoulder—regardless of whoever in the remaining congregation saw. How could she defend herself without Caleb present? Without the Constable or the ladies of the congregation to testify in her favor? She'd only spoken up to try to warn them. She squinted her eyes, suddenly feeling dizzy.

"Rebecca, my darling, I'm sorry I didn't send for you. This is why I didn't tell you," Caleb whispered down into her ear, still holding her against him. "Trials like these..."

She nodded, her forehead crinkling and her chest heaving. She fought the urge to cry. "I was only trying to help," she said into his chest. She leaned back, Caleb's hands sliding down to her forearms. "I know what I saw. I just didn't want it to hurt anyone. What do I do?"

Caleb released her and took a step back, looking across the room at the church's side door. He thought for a moment. "If the Judge forces me to go with him, I'll try to delay the Widow's execution as long as I can. She can't possibly mean the things she's said. It's obvious her mind has gone feeble since the death of her husband, tragic as it was. In the meantime, if anyone asks you anything, stick to the truth. You've just seen this thing in the woods, nothing more. You've done nothing wrong, I know that, but I don't want them charging you with anything."

"They can't possibly!" Rebecca covered her mouth with her fingertips.

"We're new here and the Particular Court doesn't know you yet," Caleb told her. "This Judge Madden is—"

"Pardon me, sir," a deep voice interrupted them. Rebecca looked to her side to see the odd Puritan couple from the end of her pew standing next to them. The man removed his hat, revealing a nearly bald head with just a few strands of gray hair swept across. His wife stood a step behind him, no longer crying, but sniffling and looking down at the ground.

"Yes?" Caleb said.

"I'm Josiah Martin of Wethersfield Village." He stuck out his hand. "This is my wife, Mary. May we have a word in private? I'm afraid it's urgent."

Caleb shook his head. "Now is not a good time, sir."

"Reverend, I'm afraid now is the only time." Mr. Martin looked over his shoulder at the handful of stragglers still left in the room. He turned back toward them, his brow deeply lined and the corners of his eyes watering. "It's about the Judge. If he wants to question your wife, then you must hear why we've come all this way."

Rebecca bristled. Caleb looked back at her with raised eyebrows.

"Okay," she said, nodding.

Suddenly, the church's side door swung open, and Constable Hindstall stepped in, dusting snow off his sleeves. He waved them both outside. "The Judge's carriage is waiting for you, Reverend. Mrs. Easton, you're to ride with me. Come quickly now!"

Rebecca looked back at Caleb.

"Constable—" Caleb stepped in front of Rebecca. "Remind the Judge that it's South Puritan's standard to offer every dying congregant the option to receive a final Holy Supper. I need to run to my office to retrieve the bread and wine. I'll be out as soon as I have it."

The answer seemed to satisfy the Constable, who nodded and stepped back outside. Rebecca and Caleb watched until the side door snapped shut.

"We don't have much time," Caleb said, turning to Mr. Martin. "Please, whatever you have to say, be quick."

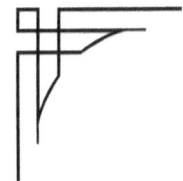

CHAPTER 9
Rebecca

Mr. Martin furrowed his brow and began.

"Our daughter, Catherine," he paused, his voice cracking. Then he wiped his brow and continued. "Sorry. Our daughter was tried of witchcraft three weeks back. She was hanged immediately at the order of this Judge." He'd spat out the last word, "Judge", with ultimate detest.

Behind him, his wife fell into a soft sob.

"He didn't have any evidence, except an accusation and a handful of dolls! Poppits, just like those—identical to them— that he said were found in our home." Mr. Martin stabbed one finger toward the table of dolls that lay lifeless on the table, forgotten by the court.

Rebecca and Caleb exchanged a look.

"Those dolls were never in our home!" Mr. Martin shook his head.

"You're sure?" Rebecca asked.

"Weaving is my husband's trade. Mine, too." Mrs. Martin raised her head, tears still lining her face. "My daughter wanted to start taking in work as a seamstress. She was so skilled with needlework. She never would've made dolls that crude looking." She looked from Rebecca to Caleb and back. "Don't you understand? He had them! That Judge and those men from the Particular Court! He blamed them on our Catherine! Our daughter no longer draws breath because of what that evil man did with a pile of dolls made of sticks and thread!"

Mr. Martin dipped his head, his fingers dancing nervously along the brim of the hat he held. "We followed him here," he said. "Catherine was our only child. We have no reason to be home now. Home just reminds us of what happened. We hoped we were wrong, but he's using the same evidence again to—"

"But the Widow confessed," Caleb said slowly. "You heard her."

"And he had the evidence he needed to convict, just in case she didn't, didn't he?" Mr. Martin and Caleb stared at one another for a few seconds. Rebecca's mind whirled. Judge Madden was awful, but lying in order to convict someone of such evil would be...immoral.

"Joshua." The name fell out of Rebecca's mouth before she realized what she was saying.

"What?" Caleb said.

"The Bible verse. The one he yelled at you just now when you asked him to delay the trial until the Beast was found. It was wrong. The Judge quoted Joshua, but that passage is—"

"Leviticus," Caleb finished. The two stood in silence.

"Judge Madden made quite a name for himself in our town. A fortune, too," Mrs. Martin said, her eyes narrowed in anger. "You'll notice he doesn't dress in Puritan standards with the glorious robes and those rings he wears."

"He's led at least twelve witch trials in our Wethersfield, all of them ended in hangings," Mr. Martin said. "We heard of more in other towns we stopped in on our journey here. It's as if he convicts to seek fame. Fame from these trials."

Rebecca looked straight ahead at Caleb, who frowned at the floor, deep in thought.

"Caleb, what do we do?" she said.

Before he could answer, the church's side door popped open again. The Constable poked his head inside.

"Reverend, I can't hold him off much longer," he said, peering back over his shoulder into the inky blue darkness of the churchyard. "Mrs. Easton, we must go. Now."

Rebecca turned back to the Martins. "Thank you for the information. We'll keep it in mind."

"Please do," Mrs. Martin said in a tone that neared begging. She reached over and grasped both of Rebecca's hands in hers.

"God be with you both in what follows."

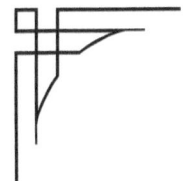
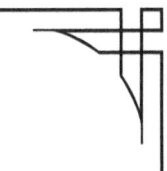

CHAPTER 10
Rebecca

"Caleb, what do we do?" Rebecca asked again as Caleb snapped the vestry door closed behind them. She put her hands up to her cheeks. "Can we trust him? Constable Hindstall, I mean? Will he arrest me?" She choked out the words.

"I certainly hope not." Caleb pulled off his white wig and tossed it down on his desk next to his Bible, itching his scalp with both hands. "I don't know the Constable well, but the Judge hasn't made the best impression on him either." He turned to Rebecca.

"The problem is witchcraft isn't just morally wrong in the eyes of the Lord, it is illegal here, like the Judge said. That would put pressure on Hindstall to follow the law, and from what I know, he's a law-abiding man."

"I certainly haven't done anything illegal," Rebecca said. "I can vow to it."

"You don't need to vow, not to me." Caleb rose and stepped toward her, pulling her hands down and taking them in his. "Sweetheart, I promise I'll do everything I possibly can to make sure you stay safe. All right?"

"Okay." She squeezed his hands back.

"But listen to me." He laid her hands against his chest. "You and the Constable must find this Beast, Rebecca. That will be the best way to steer clear of Judge Madden."

"But Caleb, I'm not on trial."

"You're right, you're only coming in for questioning, but if the Martins are right about him, we'll..." His voice trailed off. Rebecca raised her eyebrows. "Let's just keep it that way."

"Twelve women." Rebecca pulled away and stepped past Caleb, walking into the center of his tiny office and staring down at the room's small rug beneath her boots. Caleb quickly shed his black robe and threw it and his wig into a satchel hanging next to the vestry door.

"What kind of conscience would a man have...to have twelve innocent women hanged?" She looked back at him, studying his face. His expression was stern, yet vacant as he fiddled with the straps on the bag. He clearly hadn't heard a word she'd said.

"You wish I hadn't come forward, don't you?" Rebecca turned.

Caleb stood silent for a moment. "It would be easier if you hadn't, yes." He ducked his head. "Witch hunter or not, that Judge is a monster of another kind. I'm your husband. I don't want him anywhere near you, under any circumstance."

"But you understand why I spoke up, right?" She backed up and sat down on his desk chair, facing him.

He dropped his head, turned away, his hands on his hips.

"Caleb." Rebecca sat up straighter in the chair and stared at him, willing him to look at her. "I hate it here." She felt her face flush as her words hung in the air between them. His head twisted back to look at her. She froze, waiting for his reaction.

"Do you?" he said.

"I'm scared all the time," Rebecca continued. "All the time. I feel like I'm living in a nightmare. Do you know what that's like? I'm scared of the woods, of the fact that you're gone all day and our house is miles away from any neighbor. I'm scared of the fact that every man in town carries a gun with him everywhere he goes."

"Rebecca—"

"No." She slipped off the chair and stood up, taking a step toward him. "We came to the colony because we thought it was God's will. A way that we could finally worship free from the monarchy, but it's worse here!"

She crossed her arms over her chest. "I haven't slept a full night through since we arrived, and in the small chance I do sleep, I have nightmares which I can't even begin to explain to you—" Her chest heaved, and tears filled her eyes. "And now, there's this thing that lives in the woods near our house, and I'm apparently the only one who sees it aside from a woman who has been sentenced to death!"

"Rebecca—" Caleb interrupted.

"A woman who claims to be a witch, that is. You don't think that terrifies me? Don't you understand? I came forward because I'm tired of being a coward. I stood up at home and defied the Church of England, even the King himself for what I believe."

She took a few steps back from Caleb.

"Do you understand what that's like for me? I'm not some fraidy-cat wife! I crossed that ocean, the same as you did! Do you know I can still feel the rocking when I lay down at night? I can still smell the odors of fish and vomit and sweat and God knows what else that we had to live in below deck for a month. I'm not a skittish person."

Caleb sighed and opened his mouth to speak. Tears came to her eyes, and she squeezed them shut. "It's nothing like I expected."

"I understand." Caleb put his hands on her shoulders. He sighed. "Listen, life here is certainly not what I expected, and it hasn't been easy for me either."

"Really?" She looked up at him, seeing tiredness in his blue eyes. He'd barely said a word of negativity since they arrived.

"All the Puritan leaders here fight with one another over how literal our interpretation of the Bible should be, not to mention the general uneasiness among the people." He stepped over to the shelves and picked up the box of bread and a bottle of wine, Last Supper supplies. "The Puritans hate the Quakers; everyone hates the Dutch. Everyone is jockeying for what's right and who should be in control, not to mention the King has been reinstated in England. Lord knows what that means for the future of the colonies." His eyes found hers in the mirror. "But I do know that God has led us here for a reason. You still believe that, right?"

"Of course I do. God has a will for us all," she recited. Her eyes found Caleb's Bible on the desk. She ran a thumb over its smooth embossed leather cover. "I was on that road. I saw the Beast. Maybe I was chosen to see it because He knew I would be the only one to come forward."

"Maybe. God works in mysterious ways," Caleb said, stashing the bread and wine into his satchel.

"Caleb, what do you believe?"

Caleb blinked, confused. "What do you mean? About God having a will for us?"

"No," she said. "Do you believe that Widow Goodness is really a witch? Really?" Rebecca turned.

"I think the Widow is very ill," Caleb said, returning to the shelves. He sorted through their clutter until he found a candle and dropped it into the bag. "I think the death of her husband has upset her so much that she's living in an imaginary world, a world inside her head."

"It killed Bow," Rebecca said, finally.

Caleb added South Puritan's chalice to his bag and stopped. He turned back toward her. "This Beast? When?"

"Earlier tonight."

"And you saw this happen?"

"In the forest across from our house." She met his gaze. "Caleb, it happened right across from our house! And then I ran like a coward. Don't you see that's why I had to say something? I had to stand up."

Caleb stepped over, dropping the satchel onto the desk and taking both of her hands. He grasped them in his and raised them to his lips, kissing her thumbs then resting them on his chin.

"Don't mistake me, Mrs. Easton," he said. "Witchcraft? A Beast no one can explain? This is a situation I never thought I'd be in either." He squeezed her fists tighter. "I'll try to stall the Judge as long as I can. I'll dig into his background to see if I can learn more about those previous trials, try to figure out if there's anything to the story the Martins told us. That concerns me most of all. In the meantime, you and the Constable must find this thing. Have Hindstall take you back to the last place you saw it. He may be able to track it depending on how much snow has fallen since the trial began."

Rebecca picked up her gray travel cloak from Caleb's desk and pulled it on.

Caleb plucked his from a peg near the door. "Here, take mine, too. You'll need it going out in this weather."

"But what will you wear?"

"I'll be fine. Take it." He wrapped it over her shoulders.

"I'll do everything I can, I promise," Rebecca said as she slipped her arms through his cloak and rolled the sleeves up two folds on each side. "Caleb, I'm so sorry about all this."

"What you did was brave," Caleb said, picking up his satchel from his desk and strapping it shut. "If there is something in the woods, Beast or otherwise—if it's as dangerous as you say—you're right in that it could hurt a lot of people in town." He looped his arm around her and pulled her close, putting his forehead against hers.

Almost immediately, there was a knock on the vestry door.

Rebecca held on tighter.

"Yes?" Caleb called, releasing his grip on Rebecca. She quickly wiped the tears from her cheeks and wiped her hands off on the wrists of her double cloak. Constable Hindstall pushed the door open. He had fully dressed for the hunt, wearing a wool cape lined with thick gray wolf-fur around the neck, gun draped over his shoulder.

"Mrs. Easton, I'm sorry, but we must go," he said. "It's snowing harder. Every minute we wait will make the creature harder to track."

Rebecca looked back at Caleb. "We'll find it," she said, then leaned into Caleb's arms again, burying her face in his chest. "I have no choice."

"God be with you, my love." He kissed the top of her head. "Now, go. Quickly. Constable, keep her safe."

"Aye." Constable Hindstall nodded at Caleb. "Reverend, I'll have her back in town before dawn."

Rebecca fastened the last button on Caleb's travel cloak and left Caleb behind as she followed the Constable out to the church's main hall.

Although she moved on her own accord, she felt the eerie sensation as if she were floating. As she followed the Constable across the front of the church to the side door, everything in her surroundings stood out to her with a strange new clarity and vividness. A mess had been left by so many who'd departed abruptly: papers were scattered on the pulpit, the altar had been pushed back against the wall, wet footprints made the floor gleam, a left-behind glove lay on a seat in the choir box.

When they reached the side door, Rebecca turned back and gave the interior of the church a final glance, an odd thought popping into her head. Would she ever see the inside of South Puritan again?

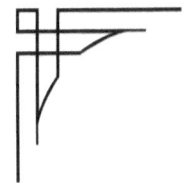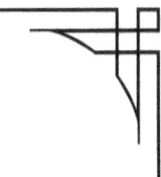

CHAPTER 11
Rebecca

"Damn it to hell, the entire town's gone off!" Constable Hindstall muttered as he closed the church's side door behind them. He pulled a brown wolf-skin cap out of his cloak pocket and yanked it on. "An old witch. A Beast in the forest. A hanging in town, a mob that's been growing by the second. And a Judge who's been on a bloody nightmare, ordering my men around since the moment he got here!"

He picked up a lantern that sat just outside the door, then stepped around Rebecca, leading her into the church's side yard. The crowd had gone, but the wheels from so many wagons and coaches had rutted the yard's snow down into slushy mud—and judging by the bitter, earthy smell, they'd left plenty of horse droppings behind as well. The lantern swung back and forth in the Constable's hand as they moved. Rebecca kept her eye on its little circle of light, dodging a pile here and there while doing her best to keep up with his giant stride. He led her toward the far end of the church property, where she could see the blackened outline of a cluster of steeds waiting. Beyond the horses—and the rock wall that outlined the church on all three sides—lay miles of forest, still deep in shadow in the moonless night.

"I should've kept my mouth shut about the Widow and just let your husband deal with it as a church matter," Constable Hindstall huffed. His boots crunched through the snow toward the horses.

Rebecca's ears perked up at this. She studied the back of the Constable, his musket swinging with each step, and wondered how much she could trust him. He'd called on Caleb a handful of times in the few months they'd been there, but Rebecca had never had a single conversation alone with him before.

She clutched Caleb's cloak tighter around her as they walked through the dark, pulling it up to her ears to block the wind from whipping her cheeks. She tried to rub the feeling back into the tip of her nose with the side of her forefinger.

"If you aren't fond of this Judge, why did you write for him to come?" she called to him. "Surely a court has many judges."

She heard him huff again.

"I'd never met him before tonight," Hindstall said, the handle of his lantern making a squeaking noise as it swung from his hand. "Judge Madden is from Massachusetts Colony, and apparently, specializes in witch trials."

"But I thought—"

"When the Widow came and confessed to me, I had to turn her in. It's my job." Hindstall glanced over his shoulder at her, his face barely visible between the bottom of his thick fur hat and the top of his scarf. "She confessed to witchcraft. That's a crime, so I did what I do in any arrest matter that I alone can't resolve. I wrote to the Particular Court. They were due to return in spring to hold trials. I thought they'd try her then." He glanced back at the church behind them. "In truth, between her state of mind and her age, I thought she'd most likely die in jail before then and would never have to face a trial. Then this morning I got a letter from the court announcing they were arriving today to hold a special trial."

"Constable, what if we can't find the Beast?" Rebecca's heart pounded as his steps quickened. "By dawn, I mean."

The Constable stopped and turned toward her, rubbing the space in between his eyes with one thumb. He glanced back at the church over Rebecca's shoulder and shook his head, gritting his jaw.

Seconds passed.

"Then we'll hunt the largest thing we can find and take it in," he said, avoiding looking at her. "The faster this bastard Judge is gone, the better for us all."

Relief flooded out of her like water.

The constable turned, his pace quickening toward the hunting party that waited for them. At this distance, Rebecca could make out the shadows of two figures sitting on the church's side rock wall, waiting with the horses. She'd never met any of the Constable's hired men, although she'd seen them plenty—weather-beaten men in wolf-fur hunting cloaks. Constable Hindstall always seemed to be accompanied by at least one or two, following him around to do his orders.

"Surely the Widow is mad, don't you think?" she asked, her pace picking up to match his.

"As long as they're here, it doesn't matter what I think." The Constable tilted his head ahead toward the front corner of the church, fifty yards or so ahead of them. Rebecca looked back to see the dark outline of the Particular Court's black coach repositioned at the corner of the church, with Judge Madden, no doubt, waiting comfortably inside.

Just as Rebecca went to turn back toward Hindstall, her eyes noted something odd about the Judge's grand coach, her view from the side yard offering a new perspective of it. She stared at its shape for just a few seconds, when suddenly, one of the horses moved forward a step, stretching the coach forward a few feet while the back wheels remained still. It took her a second to realize what she was seeing.

"There are two coaches," she blurted out, studying the shadows. She squinted to be sure, her eyes adjusting more to the dark as Hindstall continued on with his lantern, its light moving away from her. There were definitely two—identical in size, both paired with two horses each. To the left of that, the dark outline of not one but two drivers meandered among their horses. When she'd seen the coach walking in from the main road earlier that night, the two must've overlapped, creating the appearance of one giant coach.

With the Judge's arrogance so evident, Rebecca wondered who he'd possibly allow to have lush travel accommodations equal to himself.

"Constable, you said that's the Judge's coach," Rebecca said, jogging to catch up to him. "Who is in the second one? The one parked next to it?"

Hindstall paused, standing twenty feet or so just out of earshot away from his own men waiting at the rock wal., He turned back to her, lowering his voice. "Aye. That's another oddity, isn't it?"

"What is?"

He looked past her toward the coaches. "The child."

"A child?" Rebecca repeated, not understanding. She couldn't imagine a terror of a man like Judge Madden having a child.

"Aye, a girl. A wee thing, too, maybe seven or eight years old," Hindstall said, shaking his head at Rebecca. "What's even more bizarre if you ask me is that the Judge arrived in one carriage, the girl in the other. I saw her only for a short time, maybe a minute."

Constable Hindstall waved his men over. They'd taken note of Rebecca and Hindstall a minute earlier and were already leading the horses over, meeting them midway.

"She didn't come inside for the trial, which is even stranger," Hindstall said quickly. "He must've brought her all this way for a reason, but it's a dangerous journey in this weather. The stretch between here and Wethersfield is mostly wilderness—hostile wilderness at that. If they'd been attacked—"

"Constable?" one of his men called as they approached.

"Forget what I said," Constable Hindstall hushed, glancing down the hill toward the road and out into the woods behind it. "We've got work to do, and fast."

Rebecca followed the Constable over to the men. As their features came into view, Rebecca tugged her scarf up to her nose, wishing she could hide her face completely. Had they been inside for the trial? Did they suspect she was a witch like Judge Madden did? She glanced at their faces for any sign of recognition. She nodded silently to the man closest to her, who was young and stout around the belly, with a narrow face and a thick beard the color of wheat that stretched across his square jaw. The other man appeared to be tall and slim underneath his coat, with the ends of black shaggy hair visible from underneath his hat. Behind them towered three of the biggest and most intimidating horses Rebecca had ever seen. Each horse stood at least two, maybe three feet taller than Hindstall himself. Impossibly thick muscles seemed to wind around their forelegs from shoulder to heel, and their coal-black coats glinted in the light of the men's lanterns.

"Saddle up, both of you," the Constable barked, pointing at the horses. "We're off on a hunt."

"A hunt, Constable?" the man closest to Rebecca asked. Both men glanced at one another. Clearly, they were expecting to head off into town to assist in the Widow's hanging, not dash off on a midnight hunt.

"Aye, you heard correct." The Constable turned to Rebecca. "This is Mrs. Easton, the Reverend's wife. Mrs. Easton, this is Cooke and Banks."

Rebecca nodded as the Constable pointed to each man in turn, Cooke being the fairer of the two.

"Mrs. Easton saw something in the woods, a creature of sorts, that may be a danger to the people in this town and is critical evidence in tonight's trial." Hindstall glanced at her, then back to his men. They were rapt with attention. Rebecca felt her shoulders relax a bit. Obviously, they hadn't been at the trial. She let her scarf drop a bit.

"We're to hunt it down now? In the dark?" Banks asked in disbelief. "It can't wait until morning?"

"Aye, it can't. And there's no room for failure," Hindstall said. He stepped over to one of the horses and adjusted its saddle. Cooke and Banks followed and did the same to their horses. "Mrs. Easton is one of the only people to have seen the creature and is to accompany us to identify we've captured the correct beast."

"What type of Beast?" Banks asked over his shoulder at Rebecca as his fingers worked out a knot in the horse's reins. His horse stamped in the cold air behind him, steam snorting from its nostrils.

The Constable interjected before Rebecca could respond. "We're not quite sure of its nature. The sightings were at dusk, so we'll have to be on alert for just about anything."

"What type of animal should we expect?" Cooke asked, gathering up the reins on the middle horse and pulling him forward from the group. "Is it fast? Violent?"

"I'd guess it was ill, or starving and desperate for food, most likely."

"Makes sense at this time of year," Cooke returned.

"Where are we to look for it, sir?" Banks asked.

The Constable disappeared behind his horse for a second, then reappeared pulling himself atop it. He lowered himself onto the saddle. "Mrs. Easton lives west of here in the old Reverend's house."

"That place is still standing?" Banks gawked. His gaze flew to Rebecca and his mouth shut quickly.

"Yes, Banks. And we'll start in that direction if it's okay with you," Hindstall said.

"There's a tree, an old oak that's fallen partially onto the road midway between here and there," Rebecca interjected. "That's the last place I saw it. It may have gone into the woods somewhere around there."

"Then that's where we'll head," Hindstall said, readying himself on the saddle. He looked down at the three of them. "I'll take the lead. Banks, you follow me. Cooke, I'd like you to take Mrs. Easton with you on your horse and bring up the rear." He looked Cooke directly in the eye. "You're to stay at the back of the pack and keep her safe."

Cooke nodded.

The Constable then glanced at Rebecca. "If we come upon something, you'll be safest in the back, ma'am."

"I'm afraid I don't carry a side-saddle with me, ma'am," Cooke apologized, removing the horse's saddle entirely, leaving only its reins and bit in place. "You'll have to ride astride."

"It's fine," she said. "I used to ride like this plenty when I was a child."

Banks gave Cooke a boost up onto the horse first.

"You'll ride behind him, ma'am," Banks said. He knelt down and let her step up onto his knee. Cooke reached down and grabbed her arm, pulling her up. She swung one leg over the horse, as Banks pushed the other foot up for leverage.

"Thank you," she said, settling into place behind Cooke, wondering if it was predestination that made her start wearing Caleb's breeches under her dress last week.

"Hold on, ma'am, round my waist if you can manage it," Cooke said. Rebecca wrapped her arms around his belly, the two of them so padded with winter gear it felt more like hugging a giant bundle of quilts, except he smelled a little like sweat and dirt and the outdoors.

"For decency, ma'am," he said, sliding something that she assumed was a small pack between his back and her front. "And don't worry, no one is safer than those who ride with us."

Rebecca nodded weakly, then peered into the woods that started just a few feet past the rock wall, safe being the last thing she felt.

The group, now on horseback with loaded muskets, one ax or knife per man and two large coils of rope, had made their way around the front of the church. - The Judge's mysterious pair of carriages were now vacant of their drivers. They headed down the hill, out onto the main road, and turned left in the direction of Rebecca's house. Each of the three horses, Constable Hindstall in the lead, Banks behind him, and Cooke and Rebecca in the rear, had been outfitted with a lantern, which cast eerie shadows as they moved. Once they turned onto the road, the horses kicked up into a trot and moved into a one-by-one formation behind the Constable.

Rebecca glanced behind them for a second, taking one last look back up at South Puritan and the Judge's coaches. The lights of the church grew smaller, eventually disappearing into darkness. She wondered about the child the Constable had mentioned. Could it be possible that such a terror could have a shred of softer side *and* be a parent? And what of the mother? The Constable hadn't mentioned seeing a woman traveling with them. What kind of woman would dare lay hand on such a man? The thought of it made her recoil.

She shook her head and leaned a little to the left, trying to look past Cooke and the horse's bobbing head into the shadowed road ahead. Trees had already formed a thick wall of darkness on their right, and within seconds, they passed the end of the shorn churchyard on their left before the forest surrounded them on both sides. The only sound was rhythmic pounding of the horses' hooves as they moved. Her eyes wandered about the trees as they trotted on, blinking as she tried and failed to discern the mess of dark branches and shadows. Everything was perfectly still.

From the bottom of South Puritan's hill, it was a one-mile ride to Rebecca's house.

"Lights down!" the Constable called back from his place in front.

"That means us," Cooke whispered over his shoulder. He passed her the lantern. "Mind dousing this?"

"Why?" Rebecca pulled it back around him. "Why no light?"

Ahead of them, Hindstall's light went out completely.

"So we'll have the benefit of surprise. It won't have time to get spooked," Cooke said. "We have a better chance of grabbing it with as little light as possible."

Rebecca did as she was asked, opening the lantern's little glass door. The wind coming from the movement of the horse was enough for it to douse on its own. The clacking sound of horse hooves began to slow.

"When exactly did you see this animal?" Cooke said out of the corner of his mouth, his eyes forward.

"Earlier this evening. I was walking to South Puritan." Rebecca blinked into the trees next to them as their horse continued on, unfazed. Her eyes slowly adjusted to the shadowed darkness. She glanced at the sky, which was an inky shade of black-purple, and searched for the moon.

"Just one creature? It was alone? Not a pack animal, then?"

Rebecca hadn't considered the possibility of there being more than one. The thought made her stomach twist. "Yes, just one," she said. "At least, I think so."

She turned and glanced at him out of the corner of her eye. "Have you heard of such an animal in Hartforde before? A creature that's unlike anything anyone has seen before?"

"Can't say I have, but that doesn't mean much." Cooke paused, pulling back on the reins a touch with his thick fingers, adjusting their horse's place in line. "God knows there are all kinds of things out there in those woods. Wolf packs. Bears bigger than men, though bears tend to travel alone. The savages to the north are just about as wild as beasts if you ask me."

"But if we get into trouble, there's no one around to—"

"We've got enough weapons on us to go after just about anything, especially if there's only one," Cooke said, his tone sounding overly certain, as if he thought his list of beasts had scared her into silence. "Guns, knives." He dropped the reins with his left hand and reached back to pat his right hip. "And I have my lucky ax here. Have faith, ma'am. When it comes to hunting, there are no better men."

Rebecca nodded silently and exhaled. Her shoulders and forearms were beginning to ache, and she realized how tightly she was gripping Cooke. She loosened her grip, trying to force herself to relax.

"Wait! Shh!" Cooke pulled their horse to a stop. Rebecca felt her heart jump as the reins tugged around her waist, pulling the horse to a stop. The other horses in front of them paused, the Constable turning to look back at them.

"Hear that?" Cooke said.

Rebecca sat up, ducked her head, and listened, hearing the tiny sound of an echoing clack coming from the dark road behind them.

It was the sound of hooves.

"Aye! Who goes there? Identify yourself!" Cooke boomed back over his shoulder into the darkness.

Rebecca turned and looked back down the road in the way they'd just come. She saw nothing, but could hear the clacking approach closer and closer.

"Aye!" Banks yelled, pushing himself up into a standing position in the saddle and holding their last remaining lantern up. "Who's there?"

Constable Hindstall wasted no time and rode his horse back up parallel to Rebecca and Cooke, his horse stamping its feet and yanking forward against Hindstall's grip on its reins. Rebecca squeezed her eyes shut for a second.

"In the name of the Constable, who approaches?" Hindstall snatched his musket from around his shoulder and raised it, aiming straight into the darkness. Rebecca saw Cooke unloop his musket that he'd strung across his chest, holding it up in one hand.

"Head down," Cooke whispered through his clenched jaw to Rebecca, who was still peering straight behind them. Rebecca turned, her arms gripping Cooke's belly tighter, she buried her face in his back.

"Constable?" a voice called from the darkness. The sound echoed off the trees around them.

... ...
... ...
... ...

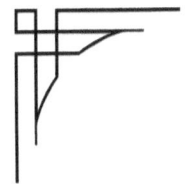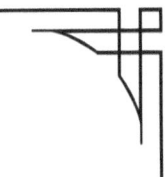

CHAPTER 12
Caleb

Caleb nudged his office door closed behind him. He'd stalled long enough and estimated he had minutes at the most before Judge Madden sent someone looking for him. Was the Judge's misquote of the Bible a simple flub, or really something more as the Martins had claimed? Caleb stood behind his chair, grasping the back of it with both hands. He stared at his copy of the book on his desk as if the words inside would condemn Rebecca directly. There was no doubt that the Judge was vicious and arrogant and self-righteous—just the thought of the way he'd spoken to Rebecca made Caleb furious. Of course, the Martins had been so sure about his role in condemning their daughter to her death, but that was a serious accusation to make.

Caleb took a breath and slid the Bible over. There was one thing he'd kept to himself from the Martins—and even Rebecca—that had bothered him even more about the Judge's credibility. If Judge Madden had really wanted to condemn his wife, then and there, in front of everyone, the Judge had failed to pull out what would've been the most logical and damning biblical connection: The Book of Revelation.

Caleb was grateful that no one in the congregation had made the connection, although he wasn't surprised. Very few families in Connecticut Colony owned a Bible and even fewer had the ability to read it if they had one. Instead, most of the townsfolk got their religious enlightenment during services at South Puritan, and anyway, Caleb rarely if ever preached from Revelation. People were always more interested in parts of the Bible that related directly to their biggest and most immediate concerns, like sin, death, and God's promises of forgiveness and eternal life. The Book of Revelation was the final chapter in the Bible, and if someone read that far, the chapter's horrific predictions of the end of the days were too terrifying for most to wrap their minds around.

Caleb lifted the Bible up into the light of the candle on the corner of the desk. He flipped to the very back, scanning the pages until he found Revelation, Chapter Thirteen, Verse Five.

Suddenly, a scuffling noise issued from outside his office. Caleb froze, clutching his Bible back against his chest for a second, concealing the pages. A light footstep, perhaps. He stepped over to the vestry door, cracking it open and silently and peeking out, searching the main hall for any signs of life. It appeared empty, just as it had been when Rebecca had departed with the Constable minutes ago. The only movement now came from the flickering lanterns that lined the church walls. Caleb ducked back into his office and secured the door again. He ran his fingers over the lines, silently reading the words in Revelation:

"The Beast was given power to wage war against God's holy people and to conquer them. And it was given authority over every tribe, people, language and nation. All inhabitants of the earth will worship the beast—all whose names have not been written in the Lamb's book of life, the Lamb who was slain from the creation of the world. Whoever has ears, let them hear."

Caleb's eyes refused to move any further—but he remembered the gist of what came next. The warning predicted that the Devil would someday walk among men on earth in the form of a vicious Beast, his appearance signifying the beginning of the end.

He shut the book and ran a hand over his beard. If the Judge really knew the Bible as well as he'd claimed, wouldn't he have made this connection to condemn the Widow further, as evidence that the Beast truly could be Satan in his predicted physical form? Not just the Widow, but Rebecca, too? Caleb closed his eyes and gripped the tiny wooden cross he wore around his neck with one hand, unwilling to let himself consider the possibility.

He glanced over at his closed office door. Hopefully, Rebecca could lead the Constable to this creature, and they'd discover it was nothing out of the ordinary—a gargantuan bear of record size or a rabid wolf, perhaps. Hindstall's hunters would capture it, or better yet, kill it and bring its carcass into town, serving the Judge a purely logical answer.

In the meantime, Caleb needed to stack the odds in their favor. He looked around the room for an idea. In the corner opposite his desk, he spotted a pile of Judge Madden's belongings he'd stored: a travel case, a stack of parchment and court documents, and on top, the Judge's copy of the Geneva Bible. It was a large folio edition, the biggest and most expensive Geneva made, with an evergreen cover and brown raised-band spine. The word *Bible* was written in gold between the spine's divots. Caleb paused. The Judge couldn't reference Revelation if he didn't have a Bible. Stealing was wrong, so says the Lord, but surely such a sin could be forgiven if it saved his innocent wife from a tyrant.

Caleb snatched the heavy book from the Judge's stack of belongings. Immediately, something struck him as odd. He tilted the book back and forth in his hand. The weight of it felt unbalanced, the bottom heavier than the top. Caleb stared at it as he took a step back and felt something inside the book shift, hearing a little clinking sound coming from within. He flipped the cover open and gasped.

An entire interior square of Judge Madden's Bible had been crudely carved out with a knife, making the interior of the book into a sort of hollowed out box. Lying within that empty space was a small dagger, the same length as a man's hand. It looked ancient, its handle was long discolored, and its blade rusted and stained with something black. A small red bottle, likely the source of the clinking noise he'd heard, occupied the space next to it, and its dark coloring concealed its contents. His heart pounding, Caleb dropped the Judge's book onto his desk and snatched up the bottle, pulling a tiny cork out of the top of it. He glanced one more time back at the vestry door and emptied the contents into the palm of his other hand.

A wave of nausea gripped his stomach as a dozen human teeth tumbled out and scattered onto his palm. All sizes and shapes, roots still attached to some. A few appeared to have been pulled out whole, while some smaller ones were partially cracked, as if a blow to the tooth or jaw had caused them to break. One massive molar still had the jagged root attached. Almost all of them were stained with dried blood.

Mr. Martin's words rushed back to him: twelve women had been hanged in Wethersfield for witchcraft under the Judge's direction. Twelve. Caleb stared at the contents in his hands. Were these some kind of sick souvenirs of the Judge's success? He took a step back, staring at his palm. Forget stalling the Judge. Or waiting for Rebecca and Hindstall to track down the creature. He had to get to Rebecca now.

Caleb quickly funneled the teeth back into the bottle with the palm of his hand. He shoved the plug back in, stashed the bottle back inside the Bible, and returned the book to its place on the stool. Then he rushed to the wall near the door, slipped on the thin maroon cloak he kept at the office, and snatched his musket from the shelf, slinging it over one shoulder. He stepped over to the vestry door, then stopped cold. The Judge's Bible could be used as leverage if Caleb took it with him—unless the Judge caught him with it first. Caleb debated both outcomes for a second, then turned back and plucked the book up again. The folio edition was huge, twice the size of a normal bible, and would be difficult to hide. Caleb yanked an old cassock from the peg on the wall and wrapped the Bible inside it until it was completely concealed, then tucked the black bundle underneath his arm. He stepped over to the door and inched it open, staring out into the body of the church. From what he could see, it was still empty. Again, there was no sign of what caused the sound he'd heard earlier.

Caleb bolted out of the vestry, speeding back into the main hall of the church then rushing down the aisle toward the front door. If he departed immediately, through the church's front door, he'd bypass the Judge's entourage parked on the other side. He could grab Charlie, his horse, from the barn and race to catch up to Rebecca and the Constable. He estimated that they couldn't have gone more than a half-a-mile or so in the time since she'd left. Then he and Rebecca could leave town, damn the Judge's warning that doing so would confirm her guilt. They'd take only what they had on them. They'd ride straight, night and day, and not stop until they got to the nearest port. If they didn't have enough money, he'd beg his way onto the next ship to get them out of here. Work his way over if he had to.

Caleb pushed the front door of the church open, a blast of cold winter air flooding in against him when he heard the church's side door slam shut from far behind him. He jumped forward, trying to make himself completely clear and free out of the front door before he was seen.

"Reverend Easton!"

Caleb stopped cold in the doorframe and looked back over his shoulder. Judge Madden was walking toward him, his fists on his hips and his mouth twisted into a scowl. He was now dressed in a hooded wool travel cloak and dark gloves.

"We've been waiting a frivolous amount of time for you to join us on our route to town," he snarled, narrowing his eyes at Caleb. "The Widow, and the rest of the court, have likely already arrived at the jailhouse. Have you failed to understand the importance of serving justice swiftly? Or is witchcraft now an acceptable practice in this part of Connecticut?"

"My apologies, Judge." Caleb took a step back inside the church, the door slamming shut again as he kept his body angled away from the Judge to conceal the bundle under his arm. He nodded at the door. "I was just heading to get my horse now. I'll be right with you."

Caleb turned away from him to push the door open again.

"Enough with the delays, Reverend." The calmness in Judge Madden's deep voice made Caleb freeze, one foot inside the church, the toe of his boot across the door's threshold. Caleb quickly glanced out into the church yard, searching for any sign of Rebecca, Hindstall, or any of his men or their horses, but the lawn sat in darkness. There was no one he could run to or yell for help.

He clutched the bundle under his arm tighter and stared back at the Judge.

"I understand your hesitation," Judge Madden said, making his way down the aisle slowly. "Your wife has seen something terrible." He took another step toward Caleb, studying him. "May have done something...terrible. That's a lot for a young Reverend to absorb."

Caleb stared into his cold eyes, determined not to back down. "My wife has done nothing wrong," he said through gritted teeth.

"Do you want to know the truth, Reverend?" The Judge took another step.

"Sir?" he looked back at the Judge, who continued to move toward him.

"When women fall," Judge Madden said, shaking his head and stepping forward until he was an arm's length from Caleb, "once they are snared by the darkness, they are beyond saving. They are not worth the breath they steal from the living."

Caleb turned to him fully, shaking from fury. "My wife has already been saved and is saved again every time she proclaims herself a daughter of the Lord and Savior, Jesus—"

Before Caleb could realize what was happening, Judge Madden slapped him across the face.

"Wake up, man!" the Judge shouted, flecks of spit flying on Caleb. "Must I remind you that ours is a battle against the vilest individuals and blackest of hearts? Nothing must come in the way of justice in the name of the Lord, nothing. Not even marital vows. And—" Judge Madden stepped closer and jabbed his index finger sharply into Caleb's chest. "If you insist on standing by a woman who's accused of witchcraft, well, let me tell you now—that's as good as loving a corpse."

He snatched Caleb's jaw in his hand, turning his face to one side and leaning in to whisper. "If you intend to pull more foolery with me, I will finish you, do you understand?"

"The Judge released his grip. "We'll leave now." He spun back, marching down the aisle and motioning toward the side door. "Now! Or when your wife reports for questioning at dawn, you'll be there alongside her!"

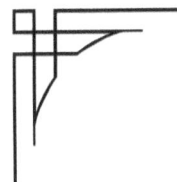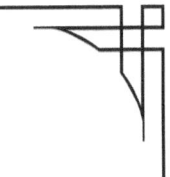

CHAPTER 13
Rebecca

"Constable Hindstall, sir!" the voice called.

Each man sat frozen atop his horse, gun aimed back down the road. Rebecca, her face still buried in Cooke's back, waited a few more seconds, then turned her face to glance at the Constable. He was still on his horse next to them, his gun steady.

"Identify yourself!" Constable Hindstall boomed. The warning tone of his voice made her shiver. The Constable leaned over from his steed, taking Banks's lantern and raising it high, shining its light back onto the road. The clacking sound of hooves slowed.

"It's Levi, sir! Levi Poole!"

Levi? She hadn't seen him since he disappeared on the stairs of the church before the trial. Rebecca leaned to one side, looking over her shoulder, back down the road. Behind them, the shadowy outline of a lone figure atop a horse approached.

"Poole?" Cooke repeated, his gun still aimed.

"What do you want, boy?" Hindstall called to the figure.

"I wanted to offer my help, sir, to hunt this Beast," Levi called back, slowing Chancer—whom Rebecca could see in the light of Banks's lantern —now unhooked from the Poole Blacksmith cart.

"Go home, son!" Cooke shouted over Rebecca's head. "Leave the hunting to the men."

"Actually, I was a wolver for you last winter, Constable." Levi pulled the horse to a stop and glanced over the group. His eyes locked temporarily with Rebecca's, then moved to the Constable, making no acknowledgement of her. "I brought in at least eighteen heads myself. My horse still has the scars to prove it."

A wolf hunter? Rebecca looked to see faint pink ribbon-like scars twisting up and down Chancer's forelegs.

"I do remember." The Constable nodded, then dropped his gun, shouldering it again. "We can use all the help we can get. Besides, the sooner we bring this thing in the better." Constable Hindstall nudged his horse with his heels, turning the steed in the road and heading back to the front of the group. "Everyone, let's ride. Up with me, Levi."

Rebecca watched as Levi drove his horse past them and up to the front of the group, his own musket draped across his back. She wished more than anything that she could have a word with him, but he kept moving forward, keeping Chancer at the Constable's horse's heels.

Ahead of her, Cooke blew out.

"You dislike the boy?" Rebecca whispered, as their horse picked up, its hooves clopping down the path behind Banks. The forest stood as a dark wall of trees, branches barely perceptible, in a wall on both sides of them.

"You know Levi Poole?" Cooke's protective tone turned cold.

Rebecca paused for a moment. Levi had made no acknowledgement of her. She felt the need to follow suit for now.

"No...His family don't attend."

"Bah! I wouldn't expect it," Cooke replied. "The Poole family is not too fond of South Puritan."

Rebecca furrowed her brow. "Why do you say that?"

"They have their reasons."

She peeked over Cooke's shoulder, watching Levi teeter back and forth on his horse, yards in front of them in the limited shadow of Bank's lantern.

"His family. They're blacksmiths, aren't they?" she asked.

"Aye, they are," Cooke said. "Father's a bloody good one. I'm surprised they still live here though."

"Why do you say that? Apparently, he's quite the hunter, otherwise the Constable would never have let him join."

"It's not me who has the problem with the Pooles, it's South Puritan."

"Why?" Rebecca's mind ran.

"The reverend your husband replaced, the one who led the church before the new South Puritan was built—"

"What about him?"

"He ordered the church to burn down their house."

"What?" Rebecca sat up on the horse, wishing she could see his face to see if he was serious. "South Puritan burned down their house? Why? Are you sure?"

He turned his profile toward her and nodded. "I was there when they lit it."

"But why on earth—"

Before Rebecca could finish, a thrashing noise came from the forest up ahead on their right, then the sound of branches cracking, snapping as fast and as easily as twigs.

"Whoa!" Rebecca heard the Constable call as the horses at the front of the line skittered to the left side of the road. Rebecca dug her nails into Cooke's cloak and peeked over his right arm as their horse shuffled to the side behind the others. Up ahead, Rebecca could see the source of the sound—a cluster of treetops ten feet or so into the woods were moving. Their dark black tops trembled violently against the purple-black sky, shaking several feet back and forth.

"Hush, everyone!" the Constable whispered.

Rebecca heard the metallic sounds of guns being pulled from the men's shoulders again, as they positioned them to aim, the horses quieting.

"Hold on tight, ma'am," Cooke breathed over his shoulder, his eyes locked on the woods up.

Rebecca placed the side of her head against Cooke's back, wrapping her arms tighter around his stomach until her fingertips faintly touched in the front, and stared into the woods on her right.

The thrashing sound moved closer, just as deep in the woods, but moving in their direction, treetops swaying in the night.

"Is that it?" Cooke asked out of the side of his mouth. Beneath them, their horse let out a soft whinny and shuffled a few steps back in the road.

"Mm-hmm." Rebecca pursed her lips, digging her forehead into Cooke's back. She squeezed her eyes shut for a moment. She'd be safe—the Constable had promised.

Suddenly, the movement stopped as quickly as it had started.

"Can anyone get eyes on it?" the Constable whispered.

"No," Cooke answered.

"I think—no, never mind!" Levi said.

"Shh!" the Constable hushed. "Banks, the light!"

Banks shifted his lantern to brighten the forest that grew just six feet or so off to Rebecca's right. As the beam of light moved, it illuminated snow-dusted evergreens, the bases of which were as thick in body as their horses were in length. Bare oak and magnolia trees, looking skeletal without a trace of green, grew tangled in between. Snow piled atop the wild brush of the forest floor at knee-height—even higher in some places. As Banks moved the lantern, every dark shadow in the forest seemed to bend into the form of the Beast's arm or leg, and every bare branch seemed to twist into a claw. Rebecca's heart pounded as she gripped Cooke tighter.

A few seconds of silence passed. The horses shuffled their hooves on the icy street, exhaling hot breaths through their nostrils.

Banks moved the lantern again, its light moving in the other direction, back up the road toward Rebecca's house. She could see the front of the group had stopped near the edge of the felled oak tree—Rebecca's midway point from her house to the church.

She raised her head up to warn them that this had been the last place she'd seen the Beast, but was interrupted by an ear-piercing snap of wood—as sharp as a crack of gunfire—that issued from the forest directly next to them.

Cooke's horse spun toward the noise, backing up.

"Watch there!" Banks yelled, his light falling from the forest to the ground as he fumbled with handling both the lantern and his gun. But Rebecca, and apparently Cooke too, didn't need full light to see the two tall pine trees plummeting toward them, falling straight through the forest as if severed at the base of their trunks. Snow slid off the branches as they bumped and smashed against other trees, making a whooshing noise.

"Ho! Back up! Back up!" the Constable yelled.

Rebecca buried her head into Cooke's back as he and the other men drove their horses up off the road until their tails nearly touched the forest on the other side. She peered around Cooke's side just in time to see the tall ends of the two massive pine trees smash down onto the road where they'd stood seconds ago, showering them with pine needles.

Rebecca and the men stared at the destruction.

"Describe this animal again for me?" Cooke muttered to Rebecca.

"Aye! I see it there!" Constable Hindstall shouted as he whipped his horse's reins, the steed whinnying in surprise. "Follow me, men!"

Rebecca leaned around Cooke to see the rear end of Constable Hindstall's horse thunder forward and disappear into the forest up next to the downed pines. His voice became muffled as he sped ahead, deeper into the woods, calling back, "Ready your weapons!"

Levi's horse followed, disappearing into the brush, Banks speeding close behind them. Rebecca's eyes shot to the woods again, her visual clarity of the forest dying off into darkness as the lantern disappeared into the woods with Banks.

"Hang on!" Cooke said to her, as he charged their horse forward.

"What? I thought we were to wait here!" Rebecca shouted, clinging on tight as Cooke drove the reins down hard on the horse's shoulders. His leg knocked against hers as he kicked the horse's side, jolting it forward.

"We'll stay in the back of the pack! We won't get too close!" he called over his shoulder. "Whatever this is, it's huge. They may need our help!"

Rebecca and Cooke bolted into the woods after the others, slipping in between two oak trees. Rebecca gritted her teeth as the tree's frigid branches tore against her hood and coat sleeves. There was no path here, only the jagged and frozen-over wild. Branches snapped all around her as Cooke's horse fought to keep up with the men who'd entered before them. She gripped her legs tighter as the dark of the forest, and the smell of evergreen and sap, enveloped her. Clumps of snow fell on them from above as Cooke's horse knocked into trees, dashing blindly through the brush.

"Whoa!" Cooke yelled suddenly as Rebecca felt his arms yank the reins back. The horse slowed so fast that it threw her forward a little. She looked around Cooke's shoulder to see that Banks, still with his lantern lit, had come to a dead stop a few yards ahead of them. His horse was pulling against its restraints, whinnying and thrashing its head back and forth, its large teeth chomping at its bit. In Banks's light, Rebecca could see that his horse's tail and back legs were tangled in a deep thicket of thorns up to its knees.

"We can't get through!" Banks called to them over his shoulder. "She's tangled in the brush! Go 'round me!"

Off to the right, Rebecca heard the far-off shouts of Constable Hindstall, his words unintelligible, but the force in his tone urgent and terrifying.

Boom!

A gunshot fired from the direction of the voices.

Cooke launched his horse forward toward the sound, sliding off to the right behind Banks as they fought their way into the woods. The light of Banks's lantern dimmed behind them, and the silhouettes of dark trees began rising all around them. Their horse slowed in the shadows, but Cooke snapped its reins in response, driving it faster despite the darkness. Without light, they were moving nearly blind with only the sound of shaking trees up ahead to guide them. Rebecca ducked as a shower of pine needles rained down on them. Cooke yanked the horse to one side and bolted forward again, the horse's forward flank bumping against a tree trunk.

Boom!

Another gunshot blasted a few yards ahead. Rebecca's heart jumped in her chest.

The shouting of men's voices followed, their words indistinguishable among their push through the brush and their horse's panicked breath.

"Can you see them?" Cooke, out of breath, asked Rebecca.

"No!"

Cooke kicked the horse again, pushing it toward the noise.

"Constable, did you get it?" Cooke shouted in the direction of the gunshots. Rebecca felt the horse pull right, then left, underneath her as Cooke drove it blindly through the thick forest floor.

"Constable?" Cooke yelled again. Then he called back over his shoulder. "Banks? Did you get through?"

Rebecca turned around, looking behind her, unable to see Banks's light. "How did they get back this far?"

"Damned if I know!" Cooke said, forcing the horse forward. "Constable? Waterhouse?"

Boom!

Another musket blasted up ahead, closer this time, then a third blast before all sound stopped. No voices. No shouting. No thrashing in the trees.

Cooke pulled the horse to a stop. Rebecca sat up, tilting her ear toward the last blast she'd heard, listening for any sound.

Nothing.

"Constable?" Cooke yelled again, his voice echoing eerily off the trees and back at them.

Cooke turned and bellowed over his shoulder. "Banks?"

They waited for a call back, but none came.

An awful silence crept around Rebecca, wrapping around her, squeezing her ribs. What had happened? Why wasn't anyone answering? A hint of moonlight was coming through breaks in the trees where they stood, illuminating Cooke's profile as he turned his head in different directions.

"Are we lost?" Rebecca whispered.

"No. Just separated," he said, matter-of-factly. "Our horse was able to get through. Banks should be along in a minute."

She nodded. Cooke sounded certain, but the rapidness in his breath when not speaking made her wonder if he was really that confident.

"Could you make anything out of what they said?" Rebecca asked, their horse shifting on its feet underneath them. "They fired at it. If they got it, why haven't we heard anything?"

"It could be wounded," he hushed, holding one finger up and listening.

A few seconds of silence passed as they sat still upon the horse.

A low hissing noise slid about the trees, the sound originating from their far right.

Rebecca's senses heightened. Her pulse began to race.

"It must be them," Cooke said, shifting himself atop the horse. He swung one meaty leg high over the horse's head, and dropped to the ground, branches crunching under his boots—leaving Rebecca alone on the steed.

"No! Wait! You don't understand. That sound—"

But Cooke handed the reins to Rebecca. "Take these. I'm going to investigate."

"No! Don't leave me alone!" Rebecca frantically scooted forward on the horse, gripping the reins as he let go and took a step back. Trees surrounded them. A few more steps and the darkness or the forest would swallow Cooke from her limited sight completely.

"Cooke, you don't understand." Rebecca dug her thumbs into the reins. "That's the noise it makes! We don't know what's happened, and I can't see anything!"

"If they aren't answering by now, they could be in trouble!"

She heard the metallic sounds of a musket lock clicking.

"Cooke!" Rebecca sat up and pulled the reins taut.

"Shh!" he hushed, his voice coming from beside her ankle. "I promise I won't go far. Here, take this for safety." She saw him raise the shadow of his arm and felt something heavy and solid tap against her thigh.

She reached down to the thump and grabbed a cold, heavy square the size of her palm. She ran her thumb along it. His ax. She grabbed it and slipped it into the pocket of her cloak.

Then she looked at his silhouette in the night, blotted out and featureless.

"Can you count to one hundred?" he asked.

"Of course!"

"Then wait here. Count to one hundred, slowly," he whispered. "I'll be back by then."

"Please don't go too far! Please be careful!"

"Just to the count of one hundred," he said.

"All right," she conceded, but Cooke was already creeping up toward the front of the horse, gun clutched in one fist, the other hand on the horse to guide his steps. The only noise now was the light crunching of Cooke's footsteps as he walked across the frozen forest floor. The outline of him passed the horse's head, disappearing into the trees ahead of them and off into the sightless forest. Cooke's horse waited with her, its chin angled toward the ground. Every now and then, its ears perked straight up and twitched, listening.

Rebecca turned back the way they came—at least, the way she thought they'd come—hoping to see even the dimmest glimmer of Banks's light off in the woods. But there was no sign light.

"One, two, three, four..." she began to count, slow enough that one number leaked out with every one of her exhales.

Above her, the sliver of moon shifted, slowly plunging the woods into total darkness, the little sight she had leaking away.

Rebecca blinked her eyes, willing them to adjust. The black silhouettes of trees smeared together, disappearing into one another. The darkness around her seemed to grow closer, feeling so close and present that it felt overpowering. It was as if she could breathe it, and if she did so, it would smother her. She continued to count. Rebecca gripped the horse's reins so tight, her fingernails dug into her palms. The horse underneath her, too, seemed to be listening intently in his own mysterious way, frozen in his stance except for his head nudging from side to side, tugging the reins a touch.

Her heart pounded so fast, it felt as if it would give away their location to the Beast somehow. She sat up and puffed out her chest, filling her lungs and holding the air in, willing herself to get some control over her runaway heart, which remained fluttering in her chest like a wild bird caught in a cage.

She sat in the silence, counting.

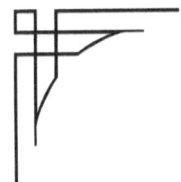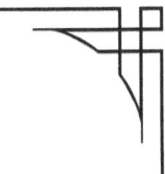

CHAPTER 14
Caleb

Caleb wiped away beads of sweat from the side of his face as he secured the church door, then followed Judge Madden out into the side yard. He glared at the back of the Judge's hooded head as they walked, his pulse racing and cheek still stinging over their violent exchange back in the church. Caleb shifted his spare black cassock—in which he'd bundled the Judge's Bible—under his arm, trying to silence the tiny *chink! chink!* the teeth made inside.

There was no doubt now that the Judge was no normal man of justice. There had been truth to the Martins' claims, and then the ugly discovery in his office. But what to do about it?

Caleb's eyes darted across the silent churchyard. Not a soul remained. As he moved, he spotted a faint outline of the moon glowing dimly behind heavy clouds, its perfect white curve skimming the top of the tree line that began an acre or so away from where the church's land ended and the forest began. Caleb stared at it, willing it to slow its descent in the sky and leave his wife as much time as possible until dawn to capture this creature.

"This way! Faster!" the Judge barked without turning back to look at him. The ugly demand in his voice made Caleb bristle.

The Judge led Caleb through the wheel-rutted snow—littered with animal waste, burnt out torches and the like—around to the front of the church where Caleb stopped cold.

Just feet from the church's front steps stretched two of the most ornate horse-drawn carriages Caleb had seen since he left England. It was clear that no expense had been spared in their making—both were black, except for the wheels and the bottom third of the cabin, which had been painted a deep and alarming red. The carriage door sported a brass handle that glinted in the light of the driver's lantern. The driver's bench up top was outfitted in gray cushioning. Hitched to the front of both carriages stood pairs of solid gray horses, speckled all over, up into their smoke-colored manes, their harnesses jingling lightly as they moved. Among them stooped a white-whiskered driver in a black cloak and hat, hunched over and polishing one of the horse's leather breeching straps.

Caleb stared. How was it possible that a Judge in the colonies could acquire not one, but two such vehicles?

"You'll accompany me in my carriage," Judge Madden ordered, stepping toward the one positioned closest to them. The Judge looked up toward the driver and banged a balled fist against the carriage door. "Fineas!"

The ancient driver jumped to attention and rushed toward them, his limbs moving loosely under his cloak like a scarecrow. He stuck his chin in the air, the polishing cloth disappearing behind his back.

"Ready then, Judge?" the old man asked, addressing only Madden. Caleb detected the slightest hint of an English accent in his voice.

"Into town. As fast as possible," the Judge ordered as the old man lowered the folding step for them and opened the carriage door.

The Judge pushed back his hood and ducked inside, the cabin tipping just a touch as it took on his weight. The driver glanced at Caleb out of the side of his eye, as if waiting for him to follow. Caleb squeezed his bundled cassock against his chest and climbed inside. The door slammed behind him before he had a chance to sit.

The interior of the carriage, dimly lit from the exterior lanterns, was even more luxurious as its exterior. Its benches, upholstered in light-brown hide, stretched wide enough to seat three men comfortably on each side, with a heap of furs strewn over each one. The walls above the seatbacks were painted the color of a red mulled wine.

As Caleb dropped down on the bench opposite the Judge, his knuckles grazed a cream-colored fur closest to him, its softness surpassing the finest rabbit he'd ever felt.

"Lynx," the Judge nodded to the blanket. He removed his thick white trial wig and placed it on the seat next to him, revealing a head of wiry gray hair that matched his wild, unkept eyebrows. The Judge passed a hand over his head in a careless attempt to smooth it down. "The seats are reindeer hide, also. Gifts from a fur trader I know from the far north."

Caleb nodded, but didn't say anything and left the lynx fur where it lay. He'd freeze to death before he gave Judge Madden the satisfaction of watching him indulge in his extravagance. Instead, Caleb placed his bag on the floor, locked his forearms over the cassock-wrapped Bible on his lap, and leaned forward. He peered out the Judge's window at what he could see of their coach's twin. He hadn't seen anyone board it, nor could he see anyone sitting inside through the bit of window from his perspective.

"That second coach," Caleb nodded. "It's quite similar to this one, is it not?"

"Identical," Judge Madden grumbled, as he undid his travel case and pulled out several pieces of parchment, thumbing through them.

"Do the members of the court travel in that one?" Caleb asked, keeping his eyes on the coach, although that suggestion didn't feel right. At least twelve men from the Particular Court had shown up for the trial—not that Caleb could image the Judge being even the slightest bit comfortable allowing anyone else the same level of luxury as he.

"The court is likely already waiting for us in town," was all Judge Madden offered as he picked up one document and held it up in the light, squinting at it.

The roof shook as Fineas stepped up into his bench above them and snapped the reins. The carriage lurched forward, Caleb's back bumping against his seatback. He felt his chest tighten as the familiarity of South Puritan slid past his window. Within seconds, their carriage moved down the hill and swung to the right, out of the churchyard, making the turn onto the main road toward Hartforde Towne. As they turned, Caleb looked out of the Judge's window again, squinting out into the black night that existed beyond its pane, desperate for any sign of Rebecca and the hunting party returning on the main road. Perhaps they'd gotten lucky, and this business could be over with. Perhaps the Constable would be making his way back and Caleb could flag him down and slip him the Judge's hollowed out Bible. Or, if all else failed, maybe he'd jump from the carriage and make a run for the group, warning them all of the truth about the Judge.

But he saw no sign of anyone, only the shadow of their own carriage moving too quickly over the empty dirt road as they turned and headed off toward town.

Just then, Caleb heard a not-so-distant crack of a whip and turned to his own window, looking back up the hill toward the church in time to see the second carriage begin to move, following them.

Caleb tightened his grip on the hidden Bible and studied the Judge, who continued to leaf through the stack of documents before him, wondering how in the world he could delay the Widow's hanging—and his wife's questioning—until Constable Hindstall returned. Hindstall would listen to him. He'd find the Judge's Bible as disturbing as he had. The good Constable seemed to be spooked by religion in general. Caleb held in a deep inhale as he watched the dark forest move outside his window, his mind running through a directory of men he knew who lived in town who could come close to matching the Judge in power, stature—or even just wealth. Caleb held a decent status as Reverend, but he and Rebecca were still new in the colony. As a Puritan reverend, he was an unknown compared to other, more senior religious leaders in the colonies who'd published pamphlets on their own Puritan biblical interpretations—a massive expense! Especially that father and son duo in Massachusetts. The Mathers. Caleb sighed silently as he gazed back at the Judge seated across from him, his lips now pursed as his eyes ran over lines on the paper before him.

Then one name came to Caleb's mind.

"Has there been any word of the return of Governor Winthrop?" Caleb asked.

"Winthrop?" The Judge looked up from his papers through narrowed eyes. "Ha! He's hardly deserving of the title!"

"He lives in Harteforde Towne, does he not?"

"Aye, he has a home there," the Judge said. "But he's been fooling around England for more than a year trying to convince the King to give Connecticut a charter and he's done nothing but fail." He made a huffing noise and glanced for a second back down at the parchment in front of him. "Perhaps he's better off over there, leaving this work to serious men."

Caleb scrunched his brow, taking in the Judge's response. "What do you mean?

"With Winthrop gone, all witchcraft trials in the colonies have fallen to me," the Judge said. "I've been fortunate enough to bring several witches to justice. Lord knows Winthrop is far too soft on the topic."

Caleb took this information in. Fineas's whip cracked again and the trees outside Caleb's window began to speed into a blur. At this rate, they'd be in town in no time.

"All witchcraft cases? How many exactly?" Caleb pressed.

"How many?" The Judge tilted his head to one side.

"Witches. How many have you tried with the Governor gone?"

The Judge's eyes searched Caleb's face for a moment. "I'm not sure at this point." He leaned back in his seat. "The weaker sex has been feeble in mind since the Garden of Eden. To this day, women have little-to-no power to resist dark temptations."

Caleb pursed his lips as he looked away. He thought of Rebecca just then, who at that moment was hunting a violent creature through a dark forest, while the Judge rode in luxury.

"Do you know what your problem is, Reverend?" Judge Madden asked. Caleb looked back to see that the Judge was again staring at him. The light from Fineas's lantern swung back and forth outside, casting a shadow over the Judge's weathered face like a dark pendulum.

Caleb cleared his throat. "My problem, Judge?"

The Judge crouched forward, elbow on one knee, leaning toward him as if speaking in confidence.

"Your problem is that you don't believe."

The anger that flashed through Caleb made the soreness on his cheek from the Judge's smack back in the church sting again.

"Judge, my expressing the need for caution over executing the Widow—or anyone—should not cause anyone to question my faith!"

The Judge waved a hand at Caleb, his head shaking.

"No. Your problem, Reverend, is that you don't believe in the Devil."

Everything inside the cab went still for a second as Caleb locked eyes with Judge Madden. The carriage wheels shook underneath them. Farther away, the horses' hooves pounded in the sludge of the road.

"Sorry?"

Judge Madden narrowed his eyes and tapped a finger in the air at Caleb. "You believe in your God, that he'll protect you, forgive you, guide you through life and whatever else you feed your congregation during your six-hour sermons as dictated by your Bible. You love Him. You fear Him."

Blood rushed to Caleb's face. "My faith in the Lord is strong, sir!"

"I'm not talking about God!" the Judge shouted. "I'm talking about the Devil! The Dark One. The one who walks about us and tempts women—and occasionally men—to do his evil deeds. Tell me, how can a Reverend whole-heartedly believe in one biblical figure and not another? The Devil is just as present in the Bible and yet you choose not to believe in his existence!"

The Judge leaned back in his seat, his face back in swinging shadow again, and tilted his head to one side. "You probably don't even believe your wife, believe what she's seen, or what your condemned Widow has done."

Caleb opened his mouth to speak, but the Judge held a hand up and continued.

"You can't pick and choose! No!" he said. "We're in a battle between good and evil, perpetuated by the weakness of the fairer sex. Men like you and I have the chance to stop the Devil himself by ridding the world of as many witches as possible. They must be snuffed out like a candle before their flame spreads into an uncontrollable fire—and yet you hesitate. You're weak."

"And that's your destiny then?" Caleb said, his voice rising. "To be the one who stops them? To hang women for items you find in their homes? To sentence the aged and ill to their deaths?"

"Your Widow wasn't so innocent now, was she?"

"Widow Goodness is a sick woman!" Caleb shouted. "Her mind is ill, if she has any mind left at all, isn't that obvious? I doubt she even understands what she's saying!"

The Judge leaned forward in his seat. "How can you explain her husband's death?"

"How can *you* explain her husband's death?" Caleb returned. "The Widow is frail! Elias Goodness, what was left of him, was found torn limb from limb. She had no physical strength to do such a thing! To suggest she murdered her own husband is preposterous!"

The Judge only closed his eyes and shook his head in response, as if Caleb's words were preposterous.

"You have no concept of mercy do you, Judge?" Caleb asked. "Not even for the ill?"

"Boy, you have no idea the evil I've seen."

"What have you seen then?" Caleb challenged. He glanced out his window, just in time to see the woods they were passing were beginning to thin out. Plowed farmland would soon appear, a sure sign that they'd arrive in town soon. "What's the worst you've seen? With your own eyes?"

Judge Madden answered without hesitation. "The Cross family in Massachusetts."

"A family?"

"The mother, Bethany Cross, made a pact with the Devil in an attempt to raise the dead. Her husband had died earlier that winter. She claimed their family was near starvation and she was desperate." The Judge crossed his legs, one ankle over his knee. "She was seen by three neighbors making a fire circle in the forest late at night. She was dancing around the flames, naked and chanting for the return of her husband."

"Her *dead* husband?"

Just then, the coach hit a bump that jolted Caleb in his seat. His hand instinctively shot out to steady himself, but in doing so, he let go of the Judge's bundled Bible, scrambling to pull it back into place on his lap. His eyes shot to the Judge, searching for any suspicion, but Judge Madden only continued.

"Yes, her dead husband. After I pressed her, she admitted she'd made a pact with the Devil, as had her two sisters."

"What do you mean by 'pressed her'?" Caleb held one hand up. "Don't forget I am from England, sir, and am well aware of methods I'd hoped would've been left behind when the colonies were started—"

"We used the drowning test on those members who refused to cooperate."

"The drowning test? But it's barbaric!"

"The Bible condemns witchcraft," the Judge stated.

"But the Bible doesn't endorse torture!" Caleb pushed.

"I'll do whatever I need to in order to rid the world of evil," the Judge spat. "Bethany Cross and her siblings all floated. They failed the test. Proof they'd made deals with the Devil."

Caleb sat up straight, his fingers gripping the edges of the hidden Bible. "Or proof that they were swimming for their lives!"

"All three were hanged within the hour."

Caleb stared at him. "You put an entire family to death?"

"No," the Judge said, sitting up suddenly and leaning toward his window. "Not the entire family."

Caleb followed his glance. Outside the window, the yellow lights of Harteforde Towne had come into view and their carriage's pace began to slow accordingly. Caleb turned toward his own window. He could see the edge of the great wall that wrapped around Harteforde Towne—a vertically constructed log barrier that stood twenty or so yards up ahead and protected the town from invaders, animals, and savages. Yet now, Caleb could see dozens of carts and horses abandoned outside just as they had been back in the church yard. A few drivers rushed about them with lit torches, tying up their horses, filling buckets with rotten food—and God knows what else—to throw. Other drivers argued with the few other late-arriving coaches who were trying to push in ahead of them.

"We're nearly here. You said, not the entire family," Caleb rushed. "Was anyone in the family cleared of the charge?"

"Yes and no." The Judge yanked his wig back on and buttoned his cloak as he glared out the window at the traffic outside. Their carriage shuttered to a stop. "There was a girl," he said absently.

Caleb recoiled in his seat, disgusted at the thought that one of the tiny teeth inside the vial could belong to a child.

Just then, Fineas knocked on the Judge's window.

"What is it?" Madden barked through the glass.

Fineas popped his door open slightly. "Excuse me, gentlemen. It seems the town's interior is full. Everyone's driven in for the...execution. I can't get us in any closer."

"Then make them move!" boomed the Judge. Caleb felt bad for Fineas as he watched the old man pull his hat off and twist it in his hands.

"You may have more luck on foot, Judge," Fineas said. "It's only about fifteen meters from here to the wall. If I push us forward any further, those waiting may get injured—"

"Oh, damn them all!" The Judge lurched from his seat so fast that Fineas had to jump out of the way. Caleb scrambled out after him, the bundled book tucked underneath his arm. By the time Caleb's feet hit the mud, the Judge was already several feet away—striding fast in the opposite direction Caleb expected, back toward where the strange identical carriage was slowing to a stop.

"Bring her to me," Caleb heard Judge Madden direct over his shoulder at Fineas, who struggled to keep up with the Judge's bags. Judge Madden paused near the horses that were pulling the second carriage to a standstill. "I'll need her."

"Her, Judge?" Caleb called after him, rushing to catch up. Caleb fastened his travel cloak and pulled up his hood as the cold wind whipped by them. "The Widow is already in town, yes?"

The Judge's nostrils flared. "My carriages do not transport the afflicted."

Judge Madden paused next to the horses leading the second carriage.

"You asked who survived from the Cross family, Reverend," the Judge said, pulling gloves from his cloak pocket and sliding them on. "There was a child. She swore—her hand on my Bible—that she did nothing to participate in her mother's evil ways. When we presented her with witchcraft dolls found in her home, hidden of course, she admitted she'd made them as instructed by her mother and aunts. As I told you, witchcraft tends to run in families, especially among women."

"That's horrible," Caleb said. He stared at the judge, unable to look away from his profile, seeing a small smile push up his cheek.

"The child came in rather useful. She netted us six other witches in town."

Caleb's heart pounded. "Six? How?"

"She was an Innocent." The Judge's narrow eyes glinted as he turned and looked at Caleb. "Some children have a special ability. They're able to see things that adults cannot. Some, like this young girl, had the unique ability to detect a witch by sight."

"What happened to her?"

The Judge turned back, watching the second carriage, where Fineas was opening its door. Out stepped a tiny, booted foot, followed by the ends of a blue cloak. Fineas stepped in front of the figure, bending and nodding at it. Caleb stepped to the side and craned his neck to see who it was.

The tan boots padded around Fineas, as the old driver pointed a thumb back over his shoulder in the direction of Judge Madden. Caleb shook his head no, clutching the Judge's concealed Bible to his chest, wishing to stop everything he was afraid was about to be confirmed true. Around Fineas stepped a girl, no older than eight, with her hood pulled up around her oval face, the ends of two fair braids draped both sides of her face. Even in the dim light of the torches being carried around her, she looked in every way the opposite of the Judge. Her face showed the innocence of any child: flawless skin, round eyes that reflected the light of the lanterns being carried high around her. Her mouth offered no expression of fear—she appeared oddly unfazed by the commotion of the horses, the men, the shouting and noise outside the town gates. Her arms were wrapped around an immense book she held against her chest as she walked toward them, Fineas and the driver of the second carriage rushing behind her, now carrying her luggage as well as the Judge's.

Caleb stepped forward. "Judge, who—"

The Judge crossed his arms over his chest.

"I told you, the child in the Cross case was a huge asset to us. She was an Innocent. I couldn't afford to put her to death." He turned to Caleb as the girl approached. "So, I put her into my employment instead."

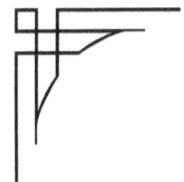
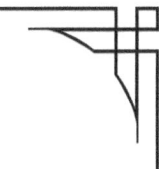

CHAPTER 15
Rebecca

"Ninety-six, ninety-seven, ninety-eight, ninety-nine ... one hundred."

Rebecca stiffened. She'd counted to one hundred three times—twice more than what Cooke had asked her to do—with no sign of him. She held perfectly still, listening for any noise and gripping the horse's reins so tightly that her freezing knuckles ached from the strain. Her fingertips were nearly numb against the leather. She'd seen no movement among the blue-black trees that surrounded her.

Her mind scoured the possibilities: what if he'd gotten lost? What if he'd been killed while she continued to sit here waiting? What had become of Banks? And what about the Constable and Levi? There had been no sign of them since they'd torn off into the woods.

Rebecca turned her head ever so slightly, hoping to catch any sound, but heard only the faint shuffling of her horse's hooves in the brush below.

She could try to steer the horse back through the dark maze of the forest to find the main road, and if she found it, ride for help. But what if Cooke returned and found her gone? And if she could find her way out, could she ever find her way back?

Above, the clouds shifted, allowing a touch of moonlight to shine through. Its light revealed the inky blue outlines of the evergreens she'd been smelling. They surrounded her, just inches from brushing against both sides of the horse. Snow hung heavily on their branches.

Then, a branch snapped from somewhere far ahead of her. She froze, but nothing followed.

"Missus!" a man's out-of-breath whisper called.

Cooke! She could hear him now, judging by the sound of branches crunching several yards north of her, moving sight-blind in the thicket.

"Cooke!" she hushed back, mimicking his tone. She listened for him again, but it was quiet.

The horse's ears perked.

"This way!" she said, the volume of her voice faltering. The horse whinnied softly as it tried to take a step. She leaned forward and stroked the side of its head, holding the reins steady.

She heard his steps resume, slowly crunching across the frozen forest floor.

Rebecca remembered the ax he'd given her and pulled it from her pocket. She held onto the saddle and leaned over, tapping the ax on the nearest evergreen branch.

Tap, tap, tap.

The motion shook clumps of snow free from the branches above, a frosty shower fluttering down onto Rebecca's sleeve.

She stared ahead, looking for any sign of movement. Nothing. She waited another few seconds.

Tap, tap, tap.

Up ahead several yards, her eyes caught on something moving between the trees, slow and faint. She squinted and waited, her heart pounding, ears on alert. It was the shadow of a man moving in the brush several yards ahead. His features were indistinguishable in the faint light except for the broadness of his belly and shoulders.

Cooke.

The horse's ears perked and twitched.

Tap, tap, tap.

Almost immediately, she saw the shape of him pivot toward her and heard the crunch of his steps pick up. Rebecca waited a few more seconds, then tapped the ax, gentler this time. Cooke moved in response, disappearing behind some pines, then with lightly crunching footsteps, partially reappeared into view, ten yards or so away, his gun gripped in his fist.

She tapped the ax again. He turned his head toward her, his face still in shadow.

"I found the Constable!" Cooke's words traveled in a hushed whisper. His tone sounded restrained, as if he was struggling to stay calm and not frighten her. His footsteps crackled as Cooke fought his way through a tangle of low-hanging branches, then high-stepped through a thick patch of bushes, arms out to steady himself as he moved toward her. "He's been mauled. I'm not sure he's alive! Stay there. The brush is thick. Let me come to you. We'll need to back out! We need to get help!"

As Cooke rounded a bare oak tree, his horse whinnied underneath Rebecca, flipping its head to one side, then the other, agitated.

"Shh!" she hushed.

"There's a bit of a clearing, to the north and—" Cooke's steps stopped suddenly. Rebecca listened, trying to hear whatever it was that had given him pause, and wound the slack of the horse's reins tighter around her palms. Just as she steadied herself on the horse, eyes locked on Cooke, the cold sensation she'd experienced just before she encountered the Beast on the road that evening crept over her once again. It moved over the back of her neck and swept around her ears. She tilted her head, wiping the sensation off on her shoulder. She took her eyes off Cooke for a second and peeked behind her. It made no sense. No breeze could blow through a forest this dense.

She faced forward to see Cooke moving toward her again.

"Perhaps its Levi?" she whispered.

Cooke shook his head. "I only saw the Constable. His horse is down as well." He paused behind a felled log, the trunk thick enough that it measured up to his waist. He swung a leg up and over it. "Banks?"

Just as Rebecca opened her mouth to respond, a tremendous hissing noise stirred from the trees to the right of Cooke, who froze, one leg stuck on either side of the felled tree. As he turned to look back at the noise, Rebecca saw the tall trees behind him tremble. A few branches shuttered. Then stilled.

"Cooke, move!" she yelled. Before he could react, the tree behind him shattered into a shower of splinters. A horned figure sprang through the forest and launched itself on top of Cooke, knocking him off the log and onto the forest floor behind it.

"Ahh!" Cooke screamed. The Beast slammed Cooke into the earth, pinning him to the ground.

"Your gun! Cooke, your gun!" Rebecca yelled, the horse jolting at the sound of her cry. The steed sped backwards, smashed into a tree, then turned and tried to move forward.

"Whoa! Whoa!" She yanked back on the reins, trying to get control of the horse, its head thrashing, terrified at the commotion.

Ahead, Cooke's scream was smothered as the Beast moved over him. For an instant, the Beast moved through a stream of moonlight that illuminated its profile: a dark snout and a steep jaw protruded from the lower part of its face. Its coal black eyes marked the start of where its face flattened out. Above its eyes, its forehead seemed to rise and separate into horns that corkscrewed up into three twists, ending in sharp points.

Ahead of her, Cooke screamed as the Beast hissed again, moving its immense shoulders behind the log and tearing at him with its claws.

"Help!" Rebecca yelled, but her scream only frightened the already terrified horse, who bucked beneath her, nearly throwing her off. She gripped the horse tighter with her legs and considered trying to ride close enough to throw the ax at the Beast—but who knew if they could get there or if a simple ax would even slow it down? The sounds coming from Cooke changed from a yell of surprise to a shriek of intense pain. She tugged twice on the reins, aiming the horse toward Cooke and the Beast, but before she could make a move, the thrashing noises disintegrated into a wet tearing, followed by a sharp crunch.

Rebecca's stomach lurched.

The Beast lifted its head and hissed again—this time so loud it seemed to echo through the trees all the way to Rebecca. The sound moved like an arrow straight through her ears and into her brain. The horse must've felt the noise too, as it began wrenching itself out of the grasp of the bridle, yanking its head back and forth, desperate to get away.

All at once, the noise intensified as the Beast raised its head and looked in their direction, the shadow of horns growing taller as it stood.

The horse reared up on its back legs, and Rebecca felt herself slipping backward through the air.

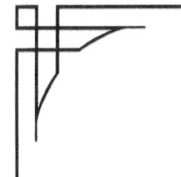
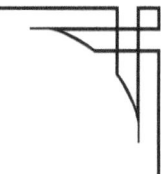

CHAPTER 16
Rebecca

Rebecca landed on her side, branches cracking underneath her. She rolled over and began pushing herself up as she looked back toward the noise—the hiss of the Beast made her cover her ears again. She sat back.

Just ten feet away, Cooke's horse lay flat on its side. The Beast now sat crouched on top of it. It pinned the horse to the ground with two immense clawed hands as the horse's hips bucked, its legs flailing sideways in the air in a hopeless attempt to rise and run away.

Rebecca kicked her feet, pushing herself back into the trees as the Beast dove down on the horse. Its jaws clamped down on its neck, the hissing sound smothering into its flesh. Before her, the poor horse struggled to scream, but the noise came out as a weak whine that drowned into a wet bubbling noise. The Beast leaned back, tugging back a mouthful of what Rebecca could imagine was flesh from the horse's neck. It widened its black jaws again and dove deeper into the animal. The horse's guttural groans dissolved, then its body stilled.

Rebecca shuttered. The horse had gone from standing strong to dead in seconds.

She had only one choice now.

Run.

Stashing the ax back in her cloak pocket, Rebecca spun around and pushed her way through the dark pines behind her. She stumbled blindly through the forest, moving as fast as she could, her senses on fire with the basic instinct to survive. There was no way to move quietly, not in the darkness or over the wild terrain of the woods. She stumbled over rocks, scrambled over felled trees. Her feet slipped now and then on fallen pine branches slick with snow. Shrubs snagged and clawed at the bottom of her cloak, tearing it again and again. She reached down and grabbed a fistful of it, lifting it so her feet could move faster. She ducked her chin into her cloak as branches tugged her sleeves and snagged her hood at every step. Her shoulders jerked up toward her ears at every noise, every branch snap that could be the Beast behind her. She was certain that the hissing noise would follow next and that it would devour her with its jaws, mash her with its strength, tear her to pieces with its claws—thoughts that only drove her to move faster.

She scrambled right, squeezing through a cluster of thick pines with branches that offered better coverage and appeared to lead up a gradual incline. Rebecca stayed close to the trees, grabbing onto branches for balance and pulling herself through as pine needles clawed at her bare palms. She ran uphill through the pines, fighting for every step, until her legs started burning, her face flushed with heat, and the pounding of her heart echoed throughout her entire body. Her steps slowed as she pushed through one last tree at the top of the incline, feeling herself near exhaustion.

Rebecca pushed free of the pines, her lungs heaving from the climb and her breath forming white clouds as she exhaled. She found herself in a tiny clearing no bigger than a backyard garden. It was a little patch of land, in which a twenty-foot oak tree with a massive trunk lay uprooted, its stringy roots dangling out. Past it, another thick sea of pines loomed. Rebecca dashed across the frozen field and hid behind the uprooted oak, pausing to catch her breath and listening for any sounds of the Beast, but all she could hear was her own gasping breath.

She leaned over, putting her hands on her knees and inhaling deeply, and threw back her hood. The weight of two cloaks atop her dress and Caleb's breeches underneath suddenly felt like she was wearing a heavy suit of armor—if she could only be so lucky. Her shoulder hurt from the fall. Her ankles ached from running on uneven ground. Her toes inside her boots had gone numb from the cold, except in a few places where they burnt with wicked blisters. She took a few deep breaths. Exhaustion from a night of no sleep shook over her in a wave, making her feel dizzy and nauseous all at once. She carefully stepped toward the roots of the oak and peered through them, squinting toward the pines she'd just run from for any sign of movement. She was surprised to inhale the stink of fresh soil. Rebecca looked at the roots and down into the small pit the tree's roots had been torn from. She reached out and wiped her fingers across one of the twisted roots, feeling the soil crumble easily in her fingers. It was fresh, not frozen. The tree had recently been torn from the ground. She took a step back. Could the Beast of done it? Pulled something this big from the earth?

She thought back to her fight with Caleb the first day she'd seen the Beast in the woods, how he'd thought it was a bear or a pack of wolves or wild boar—or an animal they didn't have back in England. She put her hands on the tree, its bark frozen and hard under her bleeding hands. He'd had no idea.

Just then, Rebecca heard a thick snap in the woods in the direction from which she'd just come. The noise was loud enough to have come from someone or something who didn't care if their presence was known. Rebecca turned and took off into the pines behind the fallen oak.

She was no more than three strides in, under the cover of the trees, when the forest floor disappeared from underneath her feet. She fell, feet first, skidding awkwardly on her heels, then falling on backside down the slope of a hill. She tried to dig the heels of her boots into the ground to stop herself, but it was no use. Her arms flailed, her hands feeling for a tree trunk or a root, something, anything to stop herself, but the hillside's downslope was too steep. As she slid, her hip hit a rock big enough to bump her onto her side, and she began to roll down the steep incline. She threw her arms up to protect her face and head, and after three or four painful rotations, she landed crouched on her elbows and knees at the very bottom of the hill. She froze for a few seconds, breathing and assessing the damage the fall had caused, which really was of no use because everything ached.

Rebecca sat back on her heels and lifted her head, suddenly mystified at her surroundings.

She appeared to be lying in the middle of an overgrown path in the woods—although it was no path she knew. Wide enough for only about one horse to travel on, the path was lined with the strangest trees she'd ever seen. They were completely bare of leaves. Their thin, stringy branches erupted from the top of their trunks, then—white with snow—dripped straight toward the ground, glimmering as if the trees themselves were made of icicles. She stumbled to her feet and crossed the path, reaching out and pinching one of the frozen branches between her fingers. It took her a minute to decipher what they were: winter-bare weeping willows. Trees like those, she knew, lived near water, but there were so many, it was as if they'd been planted here. She turned in a circle. The trees lined both sides of the path, evenly spaced out, before and behind her. She had to be someplace—a place she hadn't yet heard of.

Rebecca took a step back. Her lungs were on fire. Each icy inhale burned inside her chest. The scraped palms of her hands throbbed with heat and felt sticky from sap and blood. The cold of the forest floor bore directly through the soles of her boots. She lifted each foot, one at a time, shaking her ankles out. She was certain she was hurt, bleeding from somewhere, but her heart pounded too fast to care about that now. All that mattered was this path and that it led to somewhere. Perhaps it was a hunter's path that led back to the main road. Perhaps town.

She glanced over her shoulder at the hillside she'd tumbled down. It appeared quiet, for now. She looked down both directions of the path, knowing she had no time to decide. To her right, the path appeared to curve off into darkness. She looked left, which seemed to be a bit more well-lit, moonlight casting through the ice trees making their branches glimmer. Left it was. Rebecca pulled her hood back up and started moving, keeping her eyes on the woods on both sides of her, watching the bizarre icy trees for any signs of life.

Rebecca had no idea how long she'd been walking, only that every ounce of the heat she'd felt running through her body at the top of the hill had dissipated, replaced now by the freezing cold. She felt as if every slight breeze, every drop in temperature, blew straight through the wool of her garments and into her skin. She shivered and pulled Caleb's cloak tighter around her. She wiped her nose again and again, until the tip of her nose felt raw. Her feet felt like icy blocks beneath her, but her hands were the worst. She blew into them to try to warm them, but felt no sensation in her numb fingers. She tried to bend them, but her joints ached. Around her, she'd passed nothing but frozen willows. What if the path led to nothing?

She had no choice but to continue forward. If the Beast caught up to her now, she had little faith she could outrun it, or that she'd be able to hide among trees as thin as these. She scolded herself for leaving the shelter of the evergreens on the hill. As she glanced at the trees she was passing, her vision caught on something. At first, she thought it was exhaustion overtaking her vision, that she should doubt what she was seeing. She blinked a few times and wiped her eyes, then stepped toward one of the willows that lined the right side of the path. A patch of bark on one side of this tree had been hacked off. Carved right into its trunk at chest-height was some kind of marking. She stepped closer to see a double circle, one circle fitting inside the other, with an X scrawled through the smaller of the two. In between each limb of the X, the carver had notched a backwards letter C. The carving was jagged and thin, as if etched hastily with a tiny blade. She ran her finger over it, finding the tree bark sharp and jagged under her thumb. The carving was fresh.

She took a stumbling step back. Had she run so far into the woods that she was in savage territory? What if this was one of their marks? Rebecca backed away, looking the way she'd come, scouring the woods for any sign of movement. Nothing but still and silent weeping willows surrounded her with their frozen hair glinting in the night. She looked back at the circle with the dotted X. Or could it be a mark a daring hunter had left here, leading to the road?

Rebecca took a deep breath and continued forward, leaving the marking behind. It had to indicate something. As she walked, she glanced over her shoulder now and then, well aware that she was walking out in the open, visible and unprotected. No sounds followed her. In fact, there were no sounds coming from any direction, save for the soft crunch of her feet on the frozen path. She passed an endless number of trees when her eye caught on one next to her. Another willow with an identical double-circle symbol to the one she'd passed minutes ago. She squinted ahead down a path with an end she could not see.

The symbols were definitely leading her somewhere, but where?

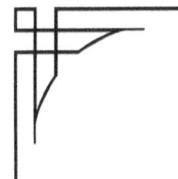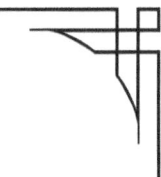

CHAPTER 17
Caleb

"May I introduce you to Miss Marguerite Cross?" Judge Madden nodded toward the little girl, his snarl widening into what Caleb could only guess was the closest thing the Judge had to a smile.

The little girl stepped up to Caleb, studying him with wide blue eyes framed by long, fair lashes.

"Good evening, sir," she said, adjusting a thick book under her arm to hold out one tiny, gloved hand toward his.

"Good evening, Miss," Caleb returned. She smiled faintly at his handshake, the corners of her mouth revealing light dimples on each cheek. Caleb studied the girl intently. She'd sentenced her own family to death—her entire family—and here she was, living and breathing and standing mere inches from him. Up close, her small round face was milky white, framed with clean blonde hair that would look like cornsilk if shaken loose from her perfectly identical braids, which were tethered at the ends with small blue bows. As he released her hand, Caleb tried hard not to recoil at the thought of this little innocent girl being groomed into becoming some kind of witch hunter. He wondered if she knew what was hidden in the Judge's Bible, if some of those teeth belonged to her own family, or worse, if she'd helped him place them there.

"We must go," the Judge ordered, pivoting and leading the group toward the Hartforde Towne entrance. "We have justice to serve."

Judge Madden and Fineas—loaded with baggage—led the way into town while Caleb accompanied Marguerite behind them. She kept up with the men well despite her small stature but struggled now and then to balance her thick book under her arm.

"What's that you're reading, Miss, if I may ask?" Caleb said, as he stepped carefully through the over-trodden muddy path that led into town. "Would you like me to carry it for you? It looks rather large for a young girl."

She glanced down at the text. The book had a rigid spine and was twice as thick as any Caleb had ever seen.

"It's *The Malleus Maleficarum*." Marguerite raised one eyebrow at him, as if it was obvious. "And I prefer to carry it, thank you."

"A Latin book?" Caleb tried to place the title. The Latin prefix "mal" meant "evil," but other than that, he couldn't decipher it.

"It means 'The Hammer of Witches'," she said matter-of-factly, pulling it out and holding it up to him like a shield. The copy was ancient, the page ends rough and yellow, the title hand-painted in black ink across the maroon cover. "It has everything inside, everything you need to know about finding and identifying witches. Torture methods, issuing death sentences—"

"Torture methods?"

With this, Judge Madden's steps paused, waiting for Caleb and Marguerite to catch up to him.

"Yes, torture methods," the Judge said. "I find it a failure of your education, Reverend, that you are not schooled in such texts. The *Maleficarum* is the most insightful text on trying and convicting a witch in the entire world."

Caleb felt his face redden. "I am schooled in many texts, but I prefer the Bible, Judge."

"Well, you should know of this one," the Judge continued as they walked. "It was published by the Catholic Church, but it turns out that exterminating witches from God's creation just may be the one thing we have in common with them. The Protestant Church has also agreed to endorse it as their leading guideline for those convicting witches. It's the standard book that lies in courtrooms all over Europe. The Colonies will follow suit soon, no doubt."

"It's very comprehensive," Marguerite added. Caleb looked down at her, doubting he knew what the word "comprehensive" meant when he was her age.

"You'll find that Miss Cross is a most insightful child," Judge Madden said. He reached behind Marguerite, placing his hand in between her small shoulders, guiding her forward. "Whereas Widow Goodness may fail to admit to others in your town are involved with witchcraft, Miss Cross can step in and prove her wrong."

"Is that so?" Caleb said blankly, eyeing the girl who walked unfazed as they moved toward the noise coming from inside the perimeter wall of Hartforde Towne. The wall itself, made from raw lumber from the woods, looked like a row of jagged teeth standing upright, and protected about a hundred structures within it from animals, savages and other intruders. It had contained the first homes and businesses in Harteforde Towne, before farmers began building outside the town walls to get more acres of land. Now, only about half of the town's population lived within its walls, above businesses like the butchery, the ship builder, the tailor, the magistrate's office, the old meeting house (a quarter of the size of South Puritan) and so on.

But now, it was obvious that the full population of Harteforde Town—and then some—had poured themselves within the walls to witness Judge Madden's extinguishment of evil. As the foursome scaled the tiny incline up to the Harteforde Towne gates, passing abandoned donkeys, horses, carts, wagons, and carriages of all kinds, Caleb could see that the light inside the town walls burned nearly as bright as day. The walls weren't just filled with light, but sound, too. It was the sound of a pent-up crowd, yelling, shouting, occasionally chanting, their individual words dulled by the thick walls.

But the tone of the crowd bled through.

The Judge dropped back and spoke to the girl as they walked.

"The accused in this case is being held in the town jail. The guards should be prepping her for execution as we speak."

"Tell me about her," the girl said, stepping twice as fast to keep up with Judge Madden's lengthy stride.

"You weren't present at the trial?" Caleb asked, thinking it strange and not wanting to relive the admission all over again.

"No, I never go in," Marguerite said. "I rely on my natural ability of seeing a witch's mark." She turned and scrunched her tiny brow at just him, readjusting the *Malificarum* in her arms. "I'm not the best at knowing when someone is telling a lie or not. So, I prefer to see them outside the trial."

"To answer your question, Miss Cross, the condemned is a Widow who's confessed in great detail to having a relationship with the Devil. Although, I'd still like you to get a look at her," the Judge said. "Especially if she is...uncooperative in the end."

"She confessed without eye witnesses? Without being reported?" Marguerite's eyes widened. "I'm sure that's never happened before! Is she remorseful?"

"On the contrary, she reconfirmed her adoration for the Fallen One," the Judge said, steering the child around a stilled cart in the road. "She wishes to die so that she can enjoy eternity in Hell. And so, she will."

"Guilt with no remorse." The girl shook her head, her blonde braids brushing against her cloak. "What deeds did she perform for him?"

"We suspect the death of her husband. Others in town, present at the trial, have suggested she caused illness, possibly one stillbirth."

Caleb craned his neck to look at the Judge, appalled. Those weren't filed accusations presented during the trial, those were remarks shouted by hysterical townsfolk—with no basis.

"And her covenant to him?" Marguerite continued. "Was it sealed?"

"Sealed?" Caleb interrupted. His eyes flashed to Marguerite, then up to Judge Madden as he dodged a wide cart pulled by two donkeys to keep up with them. "Judge! Don't you feel that's a bit of a mature topic to speak of in front of a child?"

Judge Madden ignored him and addressed Marguerite only. "In this case, the Wicked believes she's to marry the Devil in Hell, after her death. She wishes to die."

"Were there dolls?" Marguerite asked.

Caleb looked down at the girl, his breath catching in his throat.

"There were," Judge Madden said.

Marguerite shook her tiny head from side to side, making a *tsk! tsk!* noise. "Like so many others."

Caleb watched the girl out of the corner of his eye and wondered just how many cases she'd seen since her family's case where dolls were the damning evidence. He thought again of the Martins, and what they'd said about the Judge finding dolls in their own house.

The group continued on until they reached the back of the crowd that butted out of the Harteforde Town gates. Two enormous torches hung on either side of the entrance, flames lapping in the air. A sign posted on the wall closest to Caleb immediately caught his attention. Both parchment and ink were difficult to come by in the colonies, which is why he found himself staring slack-jawed at a public notice posted before him.

Convict Widow Evanora Goodness!
Convicted Witch!
Set to Hang Immediately!
Upon Order of the Particular Court
8 December 1662

Caleb whirled around to look at the Judge, who had backed away a few steps, admiring one with a half-smile on his face.

"Judge? You had these drawn up?"

"Just a handful," he said, leaning in to wipe at a smudge of ink with his thumb. "A legal technicality of the Particular Court."

Caleb's head spun. The speed with which he'd done this, not to mention the cost of ink and parchment alone, was baffling.

One of Hindstall's men, identifiable by their trademark wolf-lined cloaks, squeezed out of crowd and walked toward them. He was accompanied by a jailhouse guard, guns slung over the shoulder of each man.

"Judge!" the man called. He was bony faced, with a scar across his upper lip. "The gallows are ready and in place if you'd like to take a look."

"Gallows?" Caleb asked. Hartforde Towne had no gallows.

"Aye, set up in the center of town next to where the old meeting house was," the man replied. "We got them up in record time, too. There are men in town quite eager to help."

"Yes." The Judge stepped ahead. "I'd like to take a look to ensure they're up to standard."

Caleb saw his chance.

"I'll accompany Miss Marguerite to the jailhouse," he said. "We'll wait for you there. The crowd sounds a bit rowdy, and she is a child after all—"

The Judge scowled at him.

"That it is, sir. I've never seen anything like it," Hindstall's man broke in. He leaned in closer. "Honestly, if things get out of hand, I'm not confident we have enough manpower to control the crowd. Especially with the Constable and two of our team still absent."

"There's been no sign of the hunting party?" Caleb asked.

"Not here," he replied. "You've come from that direction. Have you seen any sign of them on the road?"

Caleb shook his head.

"We'll deal with the matter of the missing Constable after the Widow is disposed of," Judge Madden said, directing everyone back into town. "Reverend Easton, take Marguerite to the jailhouse. I'll excuse myself and see that the gallows are properly up to scale."

"Shall I speak with her if she's inside?" Marguerite asked.

"You shall," the Judge said, then looked over at Caleb. "But Reverend, you aren't to speak to her without me present." He took a step, joining the guards and Hindstall's man who waited for him. "There's no such thing as true repentance from a witch."

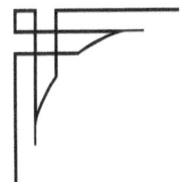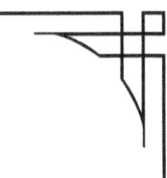

CHAPTER 18
Rebecca

Rebecca continued shuffling down the path between the strange frozen willow trees, uncertainty biting at her like the cold.

She'd followed the path for a while, but no cut-through to the road ever emerged. It seemed to be an endless trail of willow trees. Now and again, along the right side of the path, there would be shorn-off bark— revealing that mysterious symbol.

As she shuffled forward, her feet blistering in her boots, she wondered if she'd ever find her way back, and if the path really led to anything. She looked up at the sky, alarmed at the streak of purple and the sliver of gold that sneaked through the thin branches of the trees. Dawn wasn't far off. The Widow would be dead soon. And if she didn't return, she'd be presumed guilty of witchcraft. Would the Judge make good on his threat to her? Would he send a party out to hunt her down? Her heart sped up at the thought.

Her only hope was that someone from their hunting party had survived—Banks or Levi—and had run back to town for help.

That, and this path.

Suddenly, the high-pitched snap of splintering wood cracking echoed through the forest behind her. She turned where she stood, looking back toward the source of the noise. It had come from miles back in the direction of the hilltop she'd fallen from. Rebecca watched as the tops of two evergreens dropped from the tree line as if they were sinking straight down in the forest—as if a plug had been pulled beneath them.

The Beast.

Rebecca felt her legs take over like a bullet from a gun, shooting her forward, moving faster underneath her than she'd ever run before, speeding blindly forward, all pain in her feet forgotten. She felt like screaming, but who would hear her out here?

Another tree smashed down behind her, halfway down the hill, half the distance that the other trees had fallen. How could anything move this quickly through the forest? The vision of the Beast's jaws tearing Cooke's horse apart passed through her mind in an instant, causing her legs to find more power to push even faster. She sped past the willows as she darted down the path. Behind her, branches snapped wildly as the Beast closed in.

Far behind her, the hissing noise began again. The noise filled the inside of her head, seeping into her ears and filling her head with a cloud of pain that swelled larger by the second. Could it kill someone with just this sound? Rebecca pressed her hands over her ears, blocking out the noise as her feet pounded down the trail.

Up ahead, something came into view in the night: the outline of a dark square shadow. Something large. Something with straight edges. Equal dimensions. Something man-made.

A roof! Rebecca continued running. As she moved toward it, a small cottage appeared in the murky light twenty yards or so in front of her. A structure meant people! People meant shelter! Safety! Rebecca ducked her head and pumped her arms faster.

A tree crashed down on the path behind her, its branches brushing against her back as it landed.

She peeked over her shoulder, getting a glimpse of the wreckage happening on the hillside as the Beast made its way down the hill. A jagged path of trees had been torn from the hillside.

She turned and ran for the cottage ahead.

"Help!" she yelled. "Someone help me!"

But as she neared, the cottage's features became more discernible in the moonlight. It was decrepit. Its front windows were boarded up. The front wall of the cottage was overgrown with rotting weeds. Where the thatched roof wasn't covered in snow, it was blackened with mold. The chimney that jutted out of the right side of the roof had partially crumbled away.

Rebecca ran toward it anyway, the pounding of her heart blurring with the rapid inhalation of her lungs, her entire torso powering her legs to move. If she could only get inside, put any barrier between her and the Beast. Perhaps those who'd lived there had left something behind, a weapon or some kind of tool she could use as a weapon. Something larger than the pathetic ax she had in her pocket.

Behind her, another tree smashed again directly on the path behind her, this time, sending splinters of wood showering on Rebecca from behind. She didn't dare turn around to look, just propelled herself forward down the path, nearing the cottage by ten yards.

"Help!" she yelled, just in case.

A groan issued from the bushes a few feet ahead of her on the left side of the path. She glanced over to see black boots sticking out from snow-covered shrubs.

Her feet stopped so quickly underneath her that she nearly tumbled forward.

"Help me!" a male voice moaned.

"Constable?"

He lay on his back in the brush, one eye fully purple and swollen closed, the opposite side of his head covered in red-black blood. His torso was saturated with blood, but his legs were moving slowly, his heels scratching at the snowy dirt path.

"Hurry, it's coming!"

"It's back?" Constable Hindstall winced as he rolled over and pushed himself up onto his knees. "My gun—" He pulled his musket across the ground toward him.

"You must hurry! It's coming down the hillside!" She grabbed the Constable by the forearm and pulled him to his feet, his body weight nearly pulling her to the ground as he struggled to stand. As she steadied him, she noticed the tree he'd been lying under boasted another of the marked symbols. Constable Hindstall turned in the direction of the noise of the Beast.

"Go! Go!" he said weakly. He teetered on jelly legs and slapped Rebecca's shoulder, pushing her toward the cottage. She spun and ran for the door, the Constable followed behind her, gun in hand, his one good eye aimed back down the path.

The Beast's hissing unfurled toward them, this time close and loud.

"Cover your ears!" she yelled.

"Ugh!" The Constable slapped his hands over his ears as Rebecca reached the door of the cottage. She thrust one hand into the frozen green overgrowth that covered it, feeling for a latch or handle. Behind her, she heard the metallic click of Hindstall's musket snap into position.

She ran her hands along the dry rotted wood of the door. The Constable backed up against her.

"I can't find a—"

Boom!

His gun blasted high and loud, the noise exploding inches from her ear. She crouched, but she didn't stop running her hands along the door.

"Damn it!" Hindstall yelled. "I can't see it! It's in the trees!"

Just then, a giant branch smacked against the outside of the cottage, just feet from Rebecca's head.

"Rebecca!" Hindstall warned. Suddenly, the tips of her fingers slipped into a fist-sized hole where a doorknob should've been. She felt around for a second, her fingers tracing the rotted wood. The knob must've fallen out due to years of rot. Rebecca thumped her shoulder against the door, but it didn't budge.

"The door. It's swollen shut with cold!"

She pounded on it with both hands. Some of the fresh snow dusted off the door. She stepped back, then wiped one hand over the door, uncovering the bizarre symbol that had been carved in the willow trees on her way here.

"It's here!" the Constable yelled.

Boom!

Rebecca turned as the Constable's gun blasted again. She could see the Beast thundering toward them, a horned black figure moving in the dark, down on all fours. It twisted its head to one side as it neared them, opening its jaws wide. If it hissed again, Rebecca couldn't hear it thanks to the ringing in her ears from the gun blasts. Rebecca pounded on the door with both fists.

"Jesus," the Constable swore as he struggled to reload his gun. Rebecca grabbed his forearm.

"Help me!" Rebecca yelled to him, then took a step back.

The Constable turned, nodding at the door. "Together! Now!"

Rebecca stepped back to stand parallel with him, then they rushed forward in tandem, slamming their shoulders into the door as hard as they could and throwing all their weight against it. It burst open on its hinges. Flakes of rotting doorframe fluttered down on them as they pushed inside. The Constable slammed the creaky door shut behind them both, leaving them in total darkness. The Beast hissed in response on the other side. Constable Hindstall threw his back against the door as Rebecca ducked down on the floor, bracing herself for the door to be beaten down and the Beast to come tearing through at any second.

Then, the noise stopped completely.

Rebecca blinked into the black, suddenly feeling unable to breathe, unsure of what was—or could be—just within inches of her.

"Did you shoot it?" she whispered.

"No," Hindstall said from above her before erupting into a series of wet coughs. "Bullets seem to go right through it. Bollocks! Pardon me."

The Constable thumped down onto the ground near her feet, his bodyweight still holding the door closed. His breath deepened.

Rebecca crawled next to him and pressed her ear to the door, which stunk of mildew and rotten wood. The only sound she could hear outside was a gentle gust of wind.

"I don't understand. Why would it just go?" Rebecca hushed. "What is it?"

"I've never seen anything like it," the Constable said, breathing hard.

"Where are you hurt?" Rebecca whispered through the darkness. The window she'd seen from the outside had some covering over them, boards or shutters. She waited a few more seconds, listening for any sound outside, then stood up slowly. She guided herself to the window by running one hand against the door, then the stone wall next to it, until she felt the wood of a windowsill.

"What happened out there?" she whispered.

"We were attacked," he said, in between milky breaths. "It took my horse straight out from underneath me. Poor thing was dead before I could even get on my feet. It lunged after me, got me in the chest." He groaned again. "Levi and his horse charged the thing. Made it madder than hell. It drew the creature away."

"What happened to them?" Rebecca said, her hand finding a wooden plank wedged into the windowsill. She slipped her fingers in and tugged at it.

"Last I saw...the Beast was after them." The Constable's speech broke into phrases, with him gasping for air in between. "You? Banks? Cooke?"

"Cooke's dead." She tugged the board again, making a little scraping noise as she pulled it toward her. A beam of light streamed in on the packed dirt floor, illuminating the Constable's blood-stained coat and boots.

"The Beast?"

She nodded, kneeling down and peeking through the opening. "Yes. Cooke had no chance."

"Damn it to hell."

She peered outside in the pre-dawn light. The black sky was slowly lightening into violent shades of purple. There was no sign of the Beast outside, only snow fluttering silently down on the path they'd just run down.

The trees were still.

She turned back toward him. "We got separated from Banks on the chase. As far as I know, he could be alive."

"Mm." The Constable suddenly sounded sleepy. His gun clattered to the floor between them. "I'm sorry, Mrs—"

"Don't be." Rebecca rushed over and knelt at his feet.

"No, for not believing you." He leaned his head back against the door with a light thud. He struggled to unbutton his cloak, his right hand covered with blood, slipping over the buttons. "I've seen it."

"It's all right," she said, helping him unbutton his wolf-fur coat, realizing that her fingers were shaking. "Seeing is believing, right?"

"No," he swallowed again, his tongue lapping in his mouth. "You're right. It's—"He paused, his breathing labored. "—not of this world."

She pursed her lips and pushed his cloak back to reveal an impossibly thick wool pad strapped atop his shirt. The middle of it was shredded and stained with blood. The stains darkened within seconds.

"Wool armor." The Constable dipped his head, looking down at the damage. "Protects against savage's arrows." He tilted his head back against the door an instant later, closing his eyes. "Apparently not against claws."

"Here, hold still." Rebecca put pressure on the wounds with one hand as the fingers on her other hand tugged at the armor's ties to get the wounds underneath. "Constable, do you know where we are?"

The wool armor fell away to reveal two deep cuts across the Constable's belly, blood running through his vest and the shirt beneath it. The blood gushed out in spurts. She tossed the armor aside and thrust both hands on his belly.

"I'm not sure," he said, closing his eyes. "We're deep in. East of town perhaps, according to the moon. No idea how far. It happened so fast." He reached around his back and pushed something toward her in the darkness, a brown saddle bag that he nudged up against her knee. "My...pack. A lantern."

"I'll get it in a minute," Rebecca said, pushing a bit harder as warm blood flowed through her fingers.

Hindstall let out a deep sigh. A gentle tap followed as the back of his head dipped back into shadow and rested against the door, his chin sinking into his neck.

"Constable?" Rebecca hushed. "Sir!"

But there was only silence.

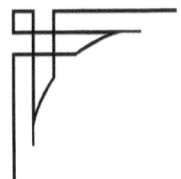
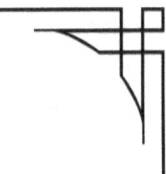

CHAPTER 19
Rebecca

Rebecca pressed her hands on the Constable's wounds. She held perfectly still, listening for any sound of life from his body, a breath, a sigh, a swallow, anything.

"Constable! Constable Hindstall!" she repeated, louder. "Constable, I need you! Wake up!"

He slumped to one side, sliding sideways toward the floor. Rebecca released the wounds and grabbed his strong frame by the shoulders, slowing his fall. She put one hand behind his head and laid him gently on the cottage floor, positioning him flat on his back, then resumed pressure on his belly with her hands.

Rebecca pressed harder into the warm stickiness of his abdomen—feeling the blood gush out in small spurts—as if the pressure could prevent him from dying and leaving her alone in this rotting cottage with the Beast stalking the woods outside. She knelt there in that position, hands on the Constable for not even two minutes when, from somewhere in the dim cottage behind her, Rebecca heard a whimper. She hunched her shoulders up to her ears and froze, listening, the Constable's blood still pulsing against her fingers. She squeezed her eyes shut, bracing herself for anything.

Another muffled whimper issued, followed by a stifled inhale from behind her. A person! Dear God, they hadn't been alone in the cottage!

Rebecca removed one hand from the Constable, sliding the other to press down on the center of his wounds, and slowly reached down to pick up his gun from the floor, having no idea if it was still loaded. She took a breath, holding the side of its cold barrel against her cheek. Her heart beat wildly, as if something could jump out of nowhere to grab at her. Rebecca stood and turned, cocking the gun and aiming it at the dark side of the cottage.

"Who's there?" Rebecca yelled. The anger in her own voice scared her even more.

There was no answer, only a wet, shaky inhale coming from across the room.

"Listen!" Rebecca peered into the darkness, seeing nothing but shapes in the shadows of the cottage. "I'm here with the Constable of Hartforde Towne. He's injured. We're both stranded here and are in need of help! Who's there? I can hear you! Answer!"

Rebecca listened as a moment passed in silence.

She took a step to the left, past the Constable's head. "Fine then, I'll uncover the window the whole way and give you no choice but to—"

"No! Don't!" a small, breathy voice rushed. "I'm sorry! You frightened me!"

Before Rebecca could move, she heard the sound of a soft scratch. On the floor in the corner opposite her, not ten feet away, a spark sprang to life and spread into a flame. Thin white fingers shook as a person placed the small light into a lantern, then pulled back into shadow.

Rebecca tightened her grip on Hindstall's gun, aiming inches above the lantern. As the light bloomed brighter, it revealed the scuffed toes of brown boots and the tattered ends of a brown cloak, then crept up to reveal the wearer of them—the chin, eyes, and forehead of a girl about fifteen. She sat huddled in a corner of the cottage, her arms hugging her knees tightly to her chest. A shawl of wavy dark hair draped her shoulders. Every part of her was shaking.

The girl sniffed again, openly this time, and wiped at her face with the back of one hand. Her dark eyes darted in a feral, fearful way, from Rebecca's gun to Constable Hindstall and back again.

"Please, Miss," the girl said, voice cracking. "When you burst through the door...I thought it was..." Her eyes flashed back to the door. "I thought I was dead."

"The Beast?"

The girl nodded.

"It seems to have gone. For now," Rebecca said, lowering the gun but keeping a grip on it. She glanced around at the interior of the cottage in the lantern's dim light. It was an old one-room log-and-mud cabin, the type of house they no longer built in the colony, and it appeared to have been abandoned for some time. All windows had been boarded up from the inside. Its thatched roof dipped down in patches, a sign of rat nests. To Rebecca's left sat a small, cobwebbed table, and next to it, a rocking chair with a broken back. A bed with a single quilt was pushed against the far wall. Rebecca looked to the right, back toward the girl. A cold stone fireplace anchored the wall in between them. A filthy black cauldron filled the space where a fire would've been, the hearth before it sat cluttered with a few cooking tools. Atop the mantel, Rebecca could see a collection of smudged vials and jars of different sizes. Fistfuls of herbs hung to dry from the ceiling above the fireplace.

Rebecca looked back at the girl, certain she'd never seen her before. "What's your name?"

"Hannah," the girl whispered.

"I'm Rebecca Easton," she said. Rebecca propped the gun against the wall and nodded toward the Constable. "My friend here, he's the Constable. Do you know him?"

Hannah sniffed and shook her head no.

"That Beast hurt him. We think it killed others we were with." Rebecca squatted down, resuming pressure on the wounds and reached one arm out toward her. "May I borrow your light so that I can try to help him?"

Hannah nodded silently. She uncurled herself from her tight place in the corner and stood up, grabbing the lamp and carrying it over. As she did, Rebecca could see that the cloak the girl wore was obviously not her own. The wool material draped over her shoulders, the sleeves hung past her knuckles. The bottom was jagged, as if extra length had been torn off to make the cloak wearable for a girl her size instead of a full-grown man. This close, Rebecca could see the girl's lips were badly chapped and peeling, and the cheeks of her heart-shaped face appeared red with windburn.

Rebecca knelt down beside the Constable, surprised that Hannah took a seat on the floor next to her, holding the lantern high so Rebecca could see. With his cloak and soft armor discarded, Rebecca could see the Constable's torn vest and shirt was saturated with blood. She peeled them up, revealing his belly and the source of the blood: two deep cuts across his abdomen, dozens of smaller scratches in between, and a puncture wound on his left side.

"It did that to him, ma'am?" Hannah recoiled.

The Constable exhaled softly, sending a gush of blood leaking out of the wounds. Rebecca grabbed the soft armor from the floor, turned it inside out, and pressed it hard over his entire abdomen.

"I'm sorry!" she said.

He groaned lightly, stirred for a second, then was still again.

"Here, we should start a fire to keep him warm," Hannah said, placing the lantern on the floor near his head. She walked to the fireplace, kneeling down and removing the cauldron. She quickly swept the fireplace's black ashes aside with her hands.

Rebecca looked at the girl over her shoulder. "Who are you, Hannah? Of what family are you? Where are your parents?"

Behind her, the girl continued sweeping out the ashes, finally answering, "Back home, ma'am."

"Oh."

Judging from the girl's age and her response, and the fact that she was wearing clothes that weren't her own, meant she was likely a servant. "Back home" meant somewhere across the sea.

"Who is your master?"

Rebecca turned and watched as Hannah got to her feet and reached up. She pulled down a few bundles of dried-out herbs that hung from the rafters. "My master is dead," Hannah said. "Has been for months."

"What was his name? My husband is the Reverend in town. Perhaps we knew him."

Hannah kneeled before the fire, packing the herbs under the logs as kindling. "Elias Goodness."

Rebecca spun around, trying to get a full look at her face as she continued.

"I serve...only his wife now," Hannah said. The girl hung her head, her voice faltering.

"You're the servant of Widow Goodness? This cottage belongs to her?" Rebecca twisted to the side, facing Hannah.

"You know her then." Hannah ducked her chin, her brow furrowing as if about to cry.

"I do. But this isn't their house. The Goodnesses lived in town."

"This is their old house. Their *first* house," Hannah said. "Master Goodness once told me that the first houses built in the colony were built out here. Then they realized how close they were to the savages, so everyone moved east."

"Are there others built out this far? Someone who could help us? Help my friend?"

"I haven't seen anyone else," she said, staring down at a cluster of dried dandelions pinched between her fingers as she added them to the mound. "But I haven't gone out too far. Master kept this place all these years as a hunting cabin, but that's it. After he died, she started bringing me here..." Her voice faltered. She tossed the dried flowers in and leaned over toward Rebecca, reaching into the lantern and pulling a candle out of it. She cradled it with one hand and tilted it into the fireplace, waiting as the herbs caught fire.

Hannah stood and leaned around the far side of the fireplace, pulling out two thin logs. She arranged them carefully over the burning bundle in the firebox.

"Widow left two days ago and hasn't returned. Our firewood is nearly out." Her eyes turned into little mirrors as she watched the flame spark into a blaze. "I can hear what's happening in the woods. I'm too scared to go outside to get more."

"Listen, Hannah, you're all right now. They've arrested Widow Goodness," Rebecca said, still holding the cloak in place over Constable Hindstall's wounds. "You've nothing to fear from her now."

Hannah looked down at Rebecca. The fear she'd seen in the girl's eyes before was gone, replaced with...something else. Alarm.

"Arrested? When?" Hannah's brow sharpened.

"Earlier this very night. She's confessed to witchcraft charges."

Hannah looked at the floor, her expression unchanged.

"You aren't surprised," Rebecca said.

"Did she have the book with her? Please, tell me she did!"

Rebecca blinked. "A book?"

The girl put her fingers to her lips, got to her feet, and began pacing back and forth. "I've looked everywhere, in all her hiding places. I can't find it anywhere."

"Hannah, what book?"

Hannah paused her steps and turned back to Rebecca, her face looking pale and ghost-like in the lantern's light. *The Grimoire.* Her spell book. It's how she summoned the Blood Demon." She nodded her chin toward the door behind Rebecca. "It's how she controls it."

"The Widow controls the Beast?" Rebecca repeated. "How do you know this?"

Hannah paused at the fireplace, eyes wandering over the collection of tiny vials that packed the mantel.

"I know because I helped her," she whispered. "She forced me." Hannah looked back at Rebecca and pushed up the sleeves of her cloak. She held out her wrists, showing red blistered burn marks on the insides of each wrist. "Please, forgive me!"

Rebecca swallowed, restraining herself from wincing at the pain the girl must be in. "Tell me about this book."

"It's very old. She told me once that it had been passed down in her family for generations. It gives the person who uses it...dark powers."

"What did she use it for?"

"All kinds of things." Hannah pulled her sleeve back down and resumed pacing. Behind Rebecca, the Constable moaned lightly. Rebecca grabbed a piece of wool armor and pressed it down on his wounds. He gave no reaction. She looked back at Hannah, raising her eyebrows for her to continue.

"She said she could use it to influence nature. Change the weather. Control an animal's behavior," Hannah said, locking her arms over her chest. Her eyes narrowed to the floor. "She said she could even pick and choose which women in town could or couldn't conceive a child—"

Rebecca swallowed.

"—she said she could transport herself from one place to another, traveling through the sky, unseen."

"And you've seen her do these things?"

Hannah paused, looking off into the corner of the cottage. "I wasn't sure at first, about any of it. You know how when people get very old, their minds can...change? I thought maybe that's what it was, when she started talking about doing these things. I thought that Master Goodness's death had caused her to have such thoughts. Until she brought me here."

"What happened when she started bringing you out here?" Rebecca shifted her position on the floor, her legs stiffening beneath her from running so long through the woods.

"She began performing spells from the *Grimoire*," Hannah said. "I can't read too much, but it's not written in English anyway. I couldn't understand what she was saying but watching her...She'd kneel in front of the fireplace for hours, screaming into the fire." Hannah glanced over at the fire snapping and popping, then looked up at Rebecca, her voice dropping to a whisper. "The terrifying part was she believed every word."

"And did you believe her?" Rebecca asked. She stood, grabbing the Constable by the boots, readying to move him in front of the fire.

"I didn't believe her until...it appeared," Hannah said, stepping up to the Constable's shoulders and lifting him a few inches off the ground. Together, they slid him over to the fireplace, laying him out in front of the hearth.

"Right away, it was too powerful," Hannah said, reaching up to the mantel and selecting two vials. "Here." She held them down to Rebecca. "Empty these onto his wounds."

Hannah took a seat by the Constable's feet and watched as Rebecca unplugged the two vials and did as the girl suggested, emptying one powder and one liquid into the cuts. Hannah reached over and mixed the two together in her palm, then used the mixture to plug the puncture wound on his side.

"It killed the horses that brought us here," Hannah said. "They were dead, in seconds." She looked over her shoulder at the cottage door. "When you burst through the door, I was sure that it had found a way inside. Even though she'd—"

"What is it? This creature?"

Hannah looked away for a minute, dusting the herbs off her hands onto her cloak, her cheeks flushed in the heat of the fireplace. "It's a Blood Demon."

"A demon? Where did it come from?"

"Hell," Hannah exhaled the word, her voice shaking. "It came from Hell. She summoned it here. She tethered it to the woods."

"But why?"

"It was part of her plan. After Master passed, Widow Goodness became obsessed with dying so she could marry the Devil." She looked back at Rebecca. "She wants to die! It was this vision she had in her mind, to become the Queen of Hell. She wouldn't talk of anything else. She'd sit in that broken chair and rock and rock mumble to herself!"

Rebecca held up one hand. "Tell me more about this Beast, this Blood Demon?"

Hannah looked back at her. "She summoned it here. She ordered it to kill anything and everything that exists in the woods, and it has. It tracks by blood."

"By blood? How?"

Hannah stood and walked toward the boarded-up window that Rebecca had pried loose and ducked down, peering one eye through its crack, but not getting too close.

"I'm not sure. I think it can hear it, smell it. It seems to have the ability to track down or draw out animals that should be hibernating. Deer. Wolves. A few bears a day." Hannah straightened back up and looked back at Rebecca. "I can't be sure, but I think it's also taken some of the savages who live nearby. I heard screams. They sounded human. I saw blood up by the frozen river, but that was the last time I left the cottage."

"If it kills anything with blood, how is it that you're still alive?"

"The symbol on the door."

"The double circle with the X? The symbols I saw on the trees in the woods on the way here?"

Hannah nodded. "She realized it was too powerful. She cast some sort of circle of protection, a boundary that it cannot pass. It protects the cottage. A bit of land that leads from here to the road, but that's it."

"But why? Why did she summon this monster?"

Hannah turned fully toward Rebecca. "As a reminder. She summoned the Demon here and tethered it to the forest to remind people that the wife of the Devil himself once resided here."

Rebecca's mind reeled. Before her, the Constable coughed weakly, his eyes still closed. She lifted up the armor to check his wounds. Whatever herbs Hannah had given her seemed to be slowing the blood, as the wounds hadn't gushed nearly as severely with this cough.

"Is there a way to stop it? Do you remember the spell?" Rebecca pleaded.

"No." Hannah shook her head. "That's why I've been looking for the *Grimoire*. I've searched the cottage, and I can't find it anywhere. I thought if I found it, I could try to make my way back to town and find someone who could force her to undo the spell. You're certain she didn't have it on her when she was arrested?"

"No, I don't think so," Rebecca said. "They presented evidence at the trial, but there was no mention of a book."

Hannah glanced at the Constable's gun, still propped against the wall where Rebecca had left it. "Your friend has a gun. Maybe if he wakes, we have a chance of getting out of here and into town for help. Where are they holding the trial?"

"Hannah, the trial is over." Rebecca shook her head. "The Widow hangs at dawn."

"No!" Hannah rushed toward Rebecca, her hand raised. "You don't understand! She cannot be killed!" Hannah stepped closer. "Widow Goodness cast the spell. She is the one who must undo it. The Blood Demon answers only to the one who summoned it. If Widow Goodness dies, there will be no stopping it."

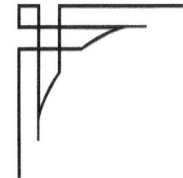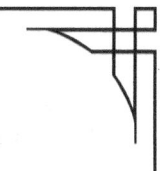

CHAPTER 20
Caleb

As the Judge hurried off to inspect the gallows, Caleb put a hand on Marguerite's back, steering her into the crowd in the opposite direction toward the jailhouse. The two were quickly swallowed into the filthy, angry, overtired mass that filled the walls of Hartforde Towne. Around them loomed the ragtag two-story, wooden shop buildings mixed with older thatched-roof homes. The second-story shutters of homes they passed stood cracked open—fearful women's faces pressed against the glass. Some young men had climbed up on the snowy roofs of the buildings for a better view and were shouting down from above, their words swallowed by the noise of the crowd below. Chimneys all around them piped black smoke into the marble purple-gray sky.

Dawn was not far.

As they were jostled through the sloppy streets, they passed women holding baskets of rotten food and at least three men holding coils of rope. All around them, people bickered about how awful the Widow had been to them, how terrifying she'd always been, and who the court should try next.

"My brother lost three steers this year! Bet it was all her doing!"

"My husband said she purchased a cauldron from his shop last month!"

"I'll bet you two shillings that fat midwife is next to hang!"

"Forget the midwife! Best question every woman in town, if you ask me!"

"Have they seen a hanging before, Reverend?" Marguerite inquired over her shoulder, squeezing in between two men—brothers from the looks of their matching red beards—and moved ahead.

"I'm not sure."

"A lot of people find them entertaining," she said. Her words made him glance down at her.

"I find nothing to celebrate in extinguishing a life," Caleb said, looking around for a break in the crowd as two young men shoved past.

Caleb had seen several hangings in his life, growing up back in England. He recalled the first one that happened. He guessed he was about Marguerite's age. He'd been excited. A thief who'd stolen from the Crown was caught in the town next to his, one he'd seen on wanted posters all over town for more than a year. He and his brothers used to run off and play "sheriff and scoundrel" in the woods, and Caleb had many times played the robber whose face was etched on the posters. Then, one day, word came that the thief had been caught and was sentenced to hang. Caught up in excitement of a capture, Caleb and his brothers had risen early and waited at the gallows in the center of town for hours until it was time for the execution.

But it was nothing like the younger version of himself had thought. Caleb could still remember standing at the base of the gallows, his chin barely reaching the wood of the base of the platform. When it was time, the thief was dragged out onto the platform. Caleb was confused. He didn't look dangerous or even much like the fearsome sketch of a villain on the wanted poster. He was a shivering bald man with a hooked nose. He was shorter than Caleb expected, shorter than his own father even, and his bound hands shook the moment he saw the noose. People had thrown rotten fruit and mud balls at him that splattered at his bare feet. Caleb could remember feeling his own breath catch in his throat and a deep pit form at the bottom of his stomach. The man's jaw quivered as they placed the rope around his neck, the robber shaking his head back in forth, whimpering a soft "no, no, no" that only those in the very front could hear.

Caleb remembered the sickening crunching noise of the man's neck breaking once the lever was pulled. He realized how fast life could be taken away. A two-foot drop. One snap. Just seconds. The crowd around Caleb had cheered, but all he felt was a deep wave of pity. Not long after seeing his first hanging did Caleb decide to one day become a minister, wishing to lead those who'd gone astray back to the light.

"Ouch!" Marguerite cried, looking down at her foot as a man carrying a barrel of ale collided with them.

"Sorry, miss!" the man yelled as he backed up, knocking into Caleb's shoulder as well.

"Careful!" Caleb stood on his tiptoes and craned his neck, trying to see if the crowd let up ahead, but it only thickened. The man pushed past.

"Here, this way!" Caleb steered Marguerite off to the right. The alleyways would be the easier route to the jailhouse. He led her down a dirt alley that ran next to the apothecary. At its corner sat a loaded barrel that someone had filled with hay and set ablaze. The barrel's flames burnt dangerously close to the bottom of the shop's yellow hanging sign.

The interior layout of Hartforde Towne was a mess that never made sense to Caleb. The town's original settlement buildings and homes had been built in necessary haste in the old style of wood and thatched roofs. Sturdier two-story stone structures were added as the town expanded out, leaving there to be a scramble of curved alleyways and side streets in between shops and homes.

"Here, up this way." Caleb nodded when they reached the back of the apothecary, turning left into the dark alley behind it. The putrid smell of human and animal waste filled his nostrils. Caleb knew this particular passageway ran in between the outermost line of shops and businesses, and the Hartforde Towne wall. From here, they could enter the jailhouse from behind, just a handful of buildings up.

Caleb glanced at Marguerite as they walked, her face still showing no fear or even sign of unpleasantness at the commotion. If he was going to get any information on the Judge or on his trial of the Cross family—her family—it had to be now.

"What is the job of an Innocent, exactly?" Caleb asked, keeping his voice low as he and Marguerite passed the back of the magistrate's office.

"I can identify witches—women, men, older children, even bewitched animals—by sight," she said, stepping carefully among the wheel-rutted slush that led through the alley.

"By sight how?" Caleb shook his head ever so slightly, disgusted that the Judge could've convinced a child of such a thing.

"It's hard to explain," she said. "I see a presence around them, a glow, but not a happy one, not like sunshine rising from behind a cloud. It's more like a black shadow that no one else can see but me. I can feel it too."

"A shadow you can feel? What does it feel like?" Caleb asked. Marguerite held tight to his sleeve for balance as they moved on past the town notary and onto the rear entrance to the pig butcher, where a cramped pen of piglets made soft grunting noises in the dark. It stunk of manure and wet hay and blood.

"It feels...cold, but in a strange way. Like going outside first thing in the morning during winter," she said. "The cold just sort of washes over you and makes you grab your coat tighter, only this cold doesn't stop. It goes all the way through you."

"And when you see this shadow, you identify the person as a witch?" Caleb asked, leaving behind the pigpen and moving on past two dim homes with thatched roofs.

"Uh-huh. What else could they be but evil?" She shrugged. "Judge Madden usually does the questioning. He gives them the chance to confess to witchcraft or evil acts, then asks if they know of anyone else in town who has done the same."

Caleb swallowed. "What do they usually say?"

"They all deny it at first. My own mother denied it when they arrested her," she said matter-of-factly.

Caleb's eyes shot to her, but he found her expression unchanged.

"The Judge often finds evidence, and evidence is proof of sinning against the Lord." She adjusted the book under her arm a bit.

"Was it difficult when your family was taken?"

"It was scary, because I didn't know what was happening and Father had just died," she spoke slowly. "But not after."

"After what?"

"After the Judge found these horrible dolls hidden in our house. They'd been stuffed up our chimney in a hiding place. One had long black hair like our neighbor. She'd been ill for weeks. When he explained it to me, how witches use dolls to cause others harm, I knew they were guilty. It's like he said, God put my mother on earth to serve as an example for the rest of us. I met the Judge after the trial. He thought it best for me to be his ward, considering so many from my family had been found guilty. That was two years ago."

They rounded two more residences that lay just before the jailhouse. Thatched-roof twin buildings, all lights burning inside. A dog barked from inside one of them.

"Was Judge Madden also the one who told you that you were an Innocent?" Caleb felt almost foolish asking. So much of what the Judge had constructed had been a lie—a false reality so he could chase down witches for fame and glory.

"No. I realized it myself."

"When?"

"At their funerals."

"I thought witches weren't allowed funerals." Caleb paused behind the jailhouse, an old stone one-story building that looked as if it were on the verge of tumbling with the pull of one river rock. Its black-barred windows were covered over with shutters at this time of year, but Caleb could hear that the coverings hadn't deterred townsfolk from gathering at the front of the jailhouse. They were banging their fists on the window covers, shouting threats that echoed off the building's surface.

"You're right," she said. "Witches don't have funerals. They can't be buried in cemeteries, of course. It wouldn't be right. They were hanged and their bodies were burned. To ash. Then dumped in a river along with the logs they were burned on."

Caleb turned and studied her face. How could a child use such a cavalier tone when speaking of the death of their own kin? He cleared his throat and looked at the jailhouse, hoping against all odds that the Constable had returned and could hear this madness.

"I was there when their ashes were dumped in the river," she continued. "Judge Madden told me I needed to see what happened to women who engaged in witchcraft, so I wouldn't follow in their path. A few other people showed up. There was a woman in a red cloak I'd never seen before. She was surrounded with the shadow."

"And you told Judge Madden?"

She nodded. "I was terrified. She was taken and tried under suspicion."

"What happened to her?" Caleb walked to the wooden door on the far end of the jailhouse building and pounded on it as loud as he could with the side of his fist, hoping a guard inside could hear despite the crowd's noise.

"She was declared a witch. I was confirmed as an Innocent. Judge Madden took me as his ward. Witches also tend to travel in packs called covens. Their friends or relatives or neighbors have been taken in by the Devil as well. He has me look over those who are in attendance when their sentence is carried out—for the shadow—just in case."

"And do you miss your family?" Caleb asked, quietly, as the two waited for a response from within the jailhouse.

He thought he saw the girl's face flinch for a second. She looked down at the toe of her boot, as she slid away a lump of slush in the road.

"The work I do for Judge Madden is important," she whispered. "It was God's plan for my family to die."

"Well, Marguerite. I know a lot about God, and I don't believe that," Caleb said, knocking again, louder this time. "I don't believe that God creates people just so they can die in agony."

The girl looked away, staring at something farther up the alley, and pulled her big book against her chest.

"They call that a murder. Did you know?"

Caleb turned fully toward her. "What?"

"A murder," she said, still looking away. Caleb followed her gaze to find a bundle of crows perched on a pile of trash behind the butcher, two buildings up.

"Like how a bunch of cows is called a herd," Marguerite said. "A bunch of crows is called a murder. I've read about it."

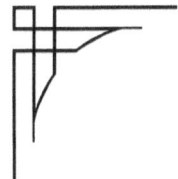
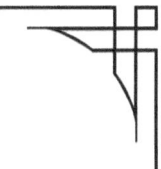

CHAPTER 21
Rebecca

Within minutes, the small fire Hannah had started had grown into a blaze next to Constable Hindstall. They'd dressed his wounds and covered him with his own heavy cloak and the quilt from the bed. Satisfied it was the best they could do for him, Rebecca had convinced Hannah to dig through the cottage one last time to look for the Widow's *Grimoire*. But Hannah had been right. The cottage, having been barely used for so many years and what little thread-bare furniture it had, left few places to hide anything.

"Where has she kept it in the past?" Rebecca asked, as she helped Hannah flip over a rug that ran along the edge of the fireplace for a second time. Only a line of dust marked underneath it. They'd already pawed through the bed and bedding, checked every empty container in the place. They'd even inspected the room's dirt floor for any sign of recent dig or scratch marks, but there were none.

"All sorts of places," Hannah said, getting to her feet. "Under the bed. Inside flower pots. There was no rhyme or reason why. She had the crazy notion that I'd steal it from her if I had the chance."

"I wish you had," Rebecca said as she lowered the rug back into place. As she did, a hard thump landed on the backdoor of the cottage, making both of them jump. They locked eyes through the light of the fireplace.

"What was that?" Hannah whispered. "Are there more of you?"

"I'm not sure," Rebecca said, keeping her eye on the back wall of the cottage. She studied the backdoor and boarded up windows. "Shh! Listen!"

A few seconds passed. Then, another thump, followed by a scratch against the door.

Rebecca stepped past Hindstall and grabbed his gun.

"The circle of protection the Widow placed in the woods—" Rebecca looked down at Hindstall, who was still unconscious. "Does it cover your backdoor?"

"I'm certain it did," Hannah replied. "She set a boundary around the entire house, so there's no way the Demon could—"

Boom!

Before Hannah could finish her sentence, a gunshot cracked, and the back doorknob exploded in a shower of wood splinters and smoke. Both women ducked to the floor, Rebecca still gripping Hindstall's gun in her fist.

The backdoor swung open.

"Hello?" a male voice called. The stink of gunpowder wafted in.

"Who's there?" Rebecca called back, one hand over her heart, which was smattering itself against her ribs. She looked up in time to see Levi stepping through the door, gun still aimed.

"You're alive!" Rebecca said, jumping to her feet. "Praise the Lord!"

"Barely!" Levi removed his hat and brushed pine needles and drips of slush out of his hair. He glanced at Hannah. "Sorry, Miss, for the entrance. The way this place looks, I thought it was deserted. I was having no luck with the door and that creature chased me all the way here. There was no other way for us to go. And from what I've seen out there, I'm afraid horses may be on short supply."

"You still have yours?" Rebecca asked, not wanting to picture Chancer at the mercy of the Beast.

"She's tied up outside," he nodded. Levi turned, noticing the Constable lying on the floor for the first time. "Holy! Is he...?"

"Alive," Rebecca said. "So far."

Hannah stepped past Levi and peered out what was left of the backdoor. "Bring your horse closer! Now!"

"My horse?" Levi asked.

Hannah nodded, waving him outside. "The circle of protection extends around the cottage, but not past the wood pile. Leaving her tied to that tree out there will draw the Blood Demon here."

Levi looked over his shoulder at Rebecca. "The Blood Demon?"

"Yes, the Blood Demon," Rebecca said. "Do as she says! Quickly!"

"Better yet, tie her up to the cottage itself, as tight and as close as you can," Hannah said.

Levi furrowed his brow, looking back at Rebecca.

"Just go, Levi!"

After Levi secured Chancer to a lantern hook outside the now battered backdoor, with his help, they'd moved the Constable up onto the bed. Rebecca and Hannah sat before the fire and caught Levi up on everything that had happened—the Beast, the Constable, Hannah and the Widow's cottage.

Rebecca relayed everything Hannah had told her about the Widow and the missing *Grimoire*, and how they must have it in order to stop the Blood Demon.

Levi sat up stock straight, staring into the fire, wide-eyed. "So, the only way to stop this thing is to have the Widow read the counter curse?" He stood and walked to the window, wedging open the same plank Rebecca had before, and looked up at the sky. "It's nearly dawn already. If we make it out of the woods without that thing killing us, it would be a literal miracle if we could get into town in time to stop the hanging."

"We have to try, Levi. The Widow wants the legacy of her death to live on in a real way, right here, for eternity!"

Levi lowered the board and walked to the fireplace mantel, his eyes wandering over the little vials of liquids and herbs, then turned back toward Hannah. "And you say you've searched everywhere?"

"Yes," Hannah said.

"Levi, you just got here," Rebecca suggested. "Take a fresh look?"

"I'm on it." Levi picked up one of the lanterns and started in the far back corner opposite them, feeling along the wall with one hand.

Rebecca pulled off her boots and set them near the fire to dry. "Tell us how we can get out of here. If we take Levi's horse, can this circle of protection somehow help get us out of the woods?"

Hannah leaned over some gray ash scattered on the hearth and began to draw with one finger.

"She had me remove the tree bark and make the carving. Her fingers were too bad, too much in pain to do it herself." Hannah drew two circles in the ash, a bigger one with a smaller one inside it, the backwards letter C in between the limbs of an X. "She had me carve this symbol into both cottage doors here, and a path of trees that leads toward the main road."

"I saw some of these on my way here," Rebecca said, massaging feeling back into her feet. The bones in her feet ached with cold. "Levi, did you see them, too?"

"No," he said from the other end of the cabin, where he was upturning a chair. "Chancer and I were too busy trying to outrun the Beast. Um, demon, I mean." He looked back at them. "Why can't we just create some kind of shield for ourselves? Draw the symbol on each one, and ride out of here?"

Hannah sat back on her heels. "It doesn't work like that. I carved the symbols under her instruction, but Widow Goodness read the spell bounding the Demon inside the circle."

Rebecca sighed. "And the spell—"

"Is in the *Grimoire*." Hannah wiped the symbol in the soot away with the palm of her hand. "If you're going to try to make it to town, your best bet is to take the old hunter's path out."

She drew a small X in the soot and pointed at it. "We're here." She drew a wide circle around it. "The trees she cursed form a circle in the woods, trapping the Beast inside. The circle starts at our front door—" She nodded to the cottage door "—and one side of it runs along the path of willows, the old hunter's trail, from here all the way to the main road, and stops just feet before it."

"That's why I could see the Beast through the woods on my walk home weeks ago," Rebecca said. "That's why it didn't chase me, or couldn't. It was trapped in here."

Hannah nodded. "There's a jumble of trees that separate the two and keeps the path to the cottage a secret."

Rebecca yanked off her wet stockings, and not caring who saw her feet, propped her heels up on the edge of the fireplace. Angry crimson blisters had formed on the pad of her big toe, and ones with blossoming puffs of white—ready to pop—had lined the back of both her heels.

"Ugh! That looks painful." Hannah stood, pulled another vial from the mantel, and handed it to Rebecca. "Try this paste."

Rebecca uncorked the vial to find it full of a sticky green substance. She swiped some onto her finger and dabbed in on the wounds on her feet. Rebecca glanced up at the mantel, wondering if there was anything else of value up there that could help them out of the woods.

Levi stepped up to the fire, warming his hands. "So, basically, the Beast can stand in this old hunter's path, and run up and down it destroying everything it likes, but it can't cross the path because of the charmed trees? If that's true, why can't we take my horse and go around the circle?"

"You could try, but you'd be trading one danger for another," Hannah said. "There's a river that runs right behind the frozen willows. It was iced over last I checked." She looked back at Rebecca. "The fastest way to town from here is the old hunter's path along the willows—with a lot of good luck."

"That's what we'll do, then," Rebecca said, nodding to Levi. "We'll stick as close to edge of the charmed circle as possible. We'll run into the woods if the Beast gets close enough."

"Now if we only had that book," Levi said, raising his eyes to search the beams of the ceiling. "If I lived here and had something important to hide..." he thought aloud, walking in a circle.

"I'll help you look," Hannah offered.

"We've already searched the table, both chairs, the bed," Rebecca said, sticking her feet near the fire again. The feeling was finally coming back to them, a warm throbbing sensation overtaking her heels. "I was able to slip my hands under most of the window boards."

"We even searched her chamber pot," Hannah said. "I'm happy to say it was empty."

Levi stepped up on a chair and ran his hands along the ceiling beams.

"Anything up there?" Rebecca asked.

"Cobwebs." Levi made a foul face. "And lots of rat droppings." He dusted his hands off on his cloak and jumped down. He dragged the chair over underneath the next beam and checked it. Then a third.

Rebecca slid her throbbing feet as close to the fire as possible. Her knees ached, and she groaned under the stress of her own movement. Between the running, her tumble down the hill, and the cold, she had no idea how she'd possibly stand up again when the time came.

As she watched the flames dance inches behind her feet, something caught her gaze in the rocks that made up the rear wall of the fireplace. It was made of the same sort of gravely gray river rocks that made up the two fireplaces in Rebecca's home. But from her seat on the floor, Rebecca could see a perfectly straight line of dirt that filled a space between three rocks. She leaned forward for a better look.

"Hannah, you searched the chimney, right?"

Hannah left Levi to finish with the ceiling beams and walked over. "That was the first place I checked. I crawled in there, felt my way up the chimney. Nothing but soot."

Rebecca narrowed her eyes at the odd, rectangular strip of dirt.

"What is it?" Levi called from behind.

"Give me something big, something that can block fire for just a few seconds."

Levi hopped down from the chair. "Would this work?" He held up an extra board from the floor.

"That should do." Rebecca sat up, sweeping her feet back underneath her bottom. She nodded toward the fire. "I need you to block the flames while I feel that slot back there."

"I see it too." Levi ducked down, peering inside.

"Is it the book?" Hannah rushed over.

"I can't tell." Rebecca leaned in, turning her face to the side and blinking as the fire's heat dried out her eyes. "Ready?"

Levi stuck the board inside, momentarily smothering the flames as Rebecca dove forward. She quickly swiped a finger over the even space.

"Ouch!" The rocks around whatever it was burned the tip of her index finger.

Dirt would've crumbled against her finger. Whatever this was, it was much harder. She pulled herself back out.

"Again." She tilted her head toward the fire. "And hold it steady, Levi!"

Rebecca dove back in again, this time, looping a finger around one edge of the packed dirt. She pulled. The corner of something thin and square and filthy slid out at her tug. She took it out. A very thin, very ragged book.

"Is this it?"

Levi pulled the board back out after her arm was clear of the flames.

"Yes!" Hannah gasped. "That's it! She must've rubbed it in dirt to change the color when she hid it."

"No doubt." Rebecca wiped the fireplace filth from the book's spine off on her cloak.

The *Grimoire* wasn't like anything Rebecca had imagined: its cover and pages were grimy to the touch and crudely put together. The cover was some sort of browned or burned animal skin. Thick black string had been stabbed through it to bind the pages together. The pages themselves were ancient parchment, yellowed and rough to the touch, possibly homemade years ago. Their edges felt brittle, weathered and uneven.

Rebecca scooted back from the fire, Levi and Hannah taking seats at her side and peering at the *Grimoire* in her hands.

She opened the cover. Its collection of handwritten scribbles, notations and lists were penned in some sort of Latin-based language. Black and brown ink filled the pages–as well as hideous hand-drawn illustrations of animals, creatures—the pieces of their bodies broken. Rebecca flipped through the pages, her stomach churning as she flipped past crudely scrawled disembodied animals with what appeared to be directions on where to cut.

Rebecca turned page after page, feeling relieved she couldn't read it. "Any idea which spell she used to conjure the Demon?"

Hannah shook her head no and stared at the pages. "I'm not sure. I was rarely allowed to see the inside."

Rebecca's fingers stopped. "Here it is." Her voice failed her as the heading stood out to her on the page, even in another tongue. In the upper righthand corner was a scrawled drawing of a muscular animal, upright horns pointing toward the sky. It held what looked like a deer in one claw, black-inked blood dripping out of it.

The three of them stared at it.

"Well," Rebecca swallowed. "We have the *Grimoire*. Now how in the world are we going to get past the Blood Demon?"

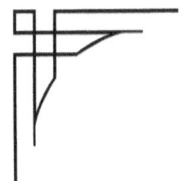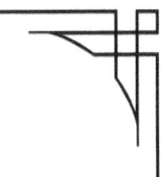

CHAPTER 22
Caleb

The jailhouse door creaked open in front of Caleb to reveal the nervous eyes of a thin, balding man holding the barrel of a gun up parallel to his face.

"Thank the Lord! Come in, Reverend!" the jailhouse guard said through the crack. He swung the door open and stepped aside as Caleb and Marguerite entered. He rushed to secure it behind them. "Lord knows we'll all need you, Reverend!"

Caleb and Marguerite found themselves in the rear of the jail's tiny lobby, which consisted of the Constable's desk, a gun rack that would've held at least a dozen muskets—empty now, a large ship's safe, and a bookshelf of town records. A small row of chairs sat opposite the desk. A fireplace, logs blazing, anchored the wall that stretched in between. The heat in the lobby was sweltering.

"Any sign of Constable Hindstall, my wife, or the hunting party?" Caleb said, loosening the top buttons of his travel cloak.

"No, sir." The guard shook his head, his eyes sunken and nervous in his thin face. "No sign at all. There are only three of us guards left here. The rest have gone to construct the gallows. I'm Isaiah Clark."

"Clark," Caleb nodded, unfamiliar with the man. "Who else?"

"The other two, Asa and Noble, are in the back," Isaiah said, glancing over just then at the front door of the jail-house. Its bolt rattled with the pounding of fists and muf-fled shouts from the mob gathered on the other side. Isaiah took an uneasy step back with a slight shake of his head as if the door were a dam holding back a flood. He gripped the musket barrel in his hands like a flag.

"Two of the Constable's men were stationed outside the door earlier," he whispered, eyes to the door. "But there have been fistfights! Brawls! They had to run off to stop men from smashing in the windows of houses over near the gallows!"

"The Judge is going to have a mob on his hands," Caleb agreed, stashing his cloak—Judge Madden's Bible still wrapped in his black cassock—on top of the Constable's desk. He placed his bag of wine and bread on top of both.

"Where is the accused?" Marguerite asked, her voice oddly professional and calm beyond her years. They needn't wait for Isaiah's reply. Just then, a shriek echoed down the corridor to their left behind a stone wall that di-vided the lobby from the cells.

"Bah! Damn you all!" the Widow howled.

Caleb rushed down the corridor, Marguerite at his heels. Ahead, he saw the last of the jail's four cell doors propped open. A heavyset bear of a man with a gruff black beard stood before the open cell, aiming a gun into it. He peered at Caleb and Marguerite over the side of the gun, one side of his face swollen with a fresh black eye.

"Down here, Reverend!" the guard shouted to them. "We know we aren't to touch her, but there ain't no keeping her still!" The guard glared back at someone inside the cell. "If you're going to do it, get on with it then, man!"

The Widow shrieked in response, the wail echoing through the jail's stone interior.

Caleb's steps picked up. He stepped past the guard to see Widow Goodness seated on a stool inside the cell, dressed in a long brown tunic with torn sleeves. Her bony white arms were tied behind her back, but that wasn't what horrified Caleb most. Behind her stood old Wilbur Hayle, the town's gray-mustached barber. His hands were held high, frozen in the air, a razor blade pinched in between his thumb and middle finger. The top half of the Widow's head was nearly shorn of her white hair. Clumps of it had dropped over her knees and lay scattered across the jail cell floor. A handful of strands still flowed from the back of her head, but all that was left atop her scalp were sharply cut stumps of white hair, cut as close as if she were a sheep shorn while trying to escape. A few light red scratches from the razor traced across her scalp, one ending in a sharp divot plucked into her scalp above her ear. Red blood trickled down in front of her ear. No one had made any effort to wipe it off.

A skinny second guard with red cheeks, whom Caleb recognized from church as Asa Lemmon, knelt at the Widow's feet. He was hugging her white legs against his chest, which she desperately tried to wrestle free. Her toenails were tinged yellow, filthy with dirt around the rims.

Widow Goodness turned her head slightly at Caleb's arrival, glaring at him out of the side of her pale blue eyes, rimmed now with red. Her jaw clenched.

"What in God's name is happening here?" Caleb stepped into the jail cell. Old Wilbur's face looked slack and pale, and his eyes darted between the Widow and the guards as if he'd run off if there weren't so many men in between him and the cell door.

"Judge's orders," the guard who Caleb assumed was Noble answered from the hallway. "Says you have to shave a witch's head to ensure she's not hiding any magical properties on her person. We've already searched the rest of her."

"And what's this?!" Caleb gestured to Asa.

"Her feet can't touch the ground after she's sentenced," Asa replied through gritted teeth, gripping and re-gripping the Widow's right ankle.

"This is preposterous!" Caleb turned back to Noble. "Where is the Judge? I must have a word. Has he not returned from the gallows?"

"We haven't seen him since the trial," Noble said looking past Caleb to Wilbur Hayle. "Get on with it, man! The sooner you're done, the sooner we can all be finished with this!"

"This is lunacy!" Caleb said, as the barber leaned in to take a careful swipe of the razor at long strands that remained on the back of the Widow's head. She howled at the touch.

"They're right, though," Marguerite said from behind. "There are all kinds of rules that must be followed before she can be executed."

Caleb spun toward her. "Rules? What rules?"

"From the book." She shrugged.

He looked down at the thick brown book Marguerite hugged against her chest. *The Malleus Malificarum.* Rules dictated and agreed upon by the two most influential churches in the world. The Judge was deaf to Caleb's pleas for mercy, a doctor's exam, an offer of repentance—but the Judge couldn't ignore his own set of rules by which he practiced.

Caleb pointed at it. "Does your book say anything about carrying out a sentence? About how fast it must happen?"

"Yes."

"Show me." He rushed out of the cell and led her back up the hallway as the sheering of the Widow continued behind him.

"I can see the shadow around her," Marguerite said as she trailed him. "It's dark. Gray and black mixed together."

Caleb darted into another empty cell, grabbed a stool, and dragged it out into the hallway. Marguerite plopped the heavy book on top of it and flipped it open.

"I know it says a hanging must happen as fast as possible, you know, to eliminate bad people, evil people, from the world." She flipped back to the final third of the *Malificarum*. "See. Here."

Caleb ran his eyes over the Latin text and a handwritten translation in the margin, careful to compare them both for accuracy.

"Sentences cannot be carried out on the Sabbath—" Caleb read aloud. That was no help. Today was Thursday.

His eyes continued down the passage and stopped at the phrase "dies santus." He compared the Latin with the handwritten English, double-and triple-checking what he was seeing.

Dies santus.

He had to be sure.

Caleb straightened himself and rushed back down the hallway to Noble.

"I need you to do me a favor, now!" Caleb said, plucking the musket from the guard's hands.

Noble jumped back, squinting down at his hands through his black eye, shocked he'd allowed his gun to be taken away so easily.

"Run around to the front of the building and pull down one of those public notices with the Widow's name on it. Bring it back to me!"

"What? Why?"

"I'll keep watch on the Widow! Go!" Caleb lifted the gun a touch, in the direction of the Widow, just enough to satisfy the guard. Inside, Wilbur Hayle had worked quickly, Widow Goodness having only a few strands of long white hair remaining. "Go! Now! Quickly!"

"Yes, Reverend!"

After Noble disappeared from sight, Caleb propped the gun against the outside of the cell bars, leaving it there. He stepped inside. The old barber continued with his razor, keeping his eyes down.

The Judge had forbidden Caleb to speak to Widow Goodness earlier. Caleb knew he had only moments before Noble—or Judge Madden—returned.

"Widow Goodness, it's Reverend Easton," Caleb said. "I'd like to talk to you."

She glared at him.

"What are you doing, Reverend?" Asa whispered. He flashed a sour face as her filthy toes grazed his cheek.

Caleb held a hand up.

The Widow studied him out of the side of her eye. Her face was now yanked back in a grimace, the skin on her cheeks so thin, it was nearly translucent. Her eyes lined with red. Clumps of her white hair fluttered to the floor like feathers with each stroke of old Wilbur's blade.

"I want to die!" she hissed at him. "When do I die?"

Caleb took another step, holding up both hands as she thrashed her legs again against Asa's grip. Wilbur backed up into the corner.

"We're...we're going to see about that, Widow Goodness." Caleb nodded slowly. "But as your Reverend, I'd like to give you a chance to repent."

"Repent?" The Widow stilled herself and smiled, her cracked lips stretching to reveal her gapped and rotting teeth.

Caleb stepped closer and ducked down to her level. "Evanora, you didn't really mean all those things you said during the trial, did you?"

She laughed. Wilbur stuffed himself even deeper into the corner of the cell.

"Her shadow, Reverend—" Marguerite called to him from out in the hallway. "It's growing, sir."

Caleb continued. "I offer you the chance to repent, Widow Goodness. Why won't you take it? Won't you tell me?"

The Widow cackled. At her feet, Asa ducked his head, looking away.

"I was once like you, Reverend," she said. "Begging God to forgive me. To save me from everything. Influenza, starvation, winter. I prayed he'd protect my husband on his hunting trips, and he died, painfully."

Caleb closed his mouth. All he knew of Elias's death was that parts of his body were found, never the whole thing.

The Widow stared Caleb in the eye. "Wolves tore him to pieces on our very property. They ate parts of him right in front of me. All I could do was scream. They left only the top half of him for me to bury."

Asa mumbled a prayer under his breath.

Widow Goodness leaned toward Caleb on her stool and continued. "I knew then I'd worshipped the wrong being all along. I'd closed my eyes my entire life and mumbled words to a deaf God with no power, while the Devil sent creatures to tear apart my husband. With power, with force, with violence. There is power in violence. In death. There is no power whispering and wishing." She sat back, her legs slack in Asa's grip. "I'll never worship your God again. My mother was right. All the things she'd tried to teach me—"

Caleb squatted down, looking her in the eye. "Evanora, the death of your husband was a tragedy, but you cannot let it mislead you."

"My husband's death showed me the truth."

"Don't you want to follow the Lord? He offers an everlasting life. It's never too late—"

"It is too late." Her pale blue eyes were cold and certain. "I've already made sure of it."

Caleb closed his mouth and rose to his feet. He'd truly hoped the Widow would repent if given the choice, or if she'd shown some obvious sign of sickness or confusion, he could take it to the Judge and convince him to change her sentence. If there could be hope for the Widow, there could be hope for his wife.

Instead, Caleb stared at the ruined old woman tethered to the stool in front of him and felt himself go empty.

The Widow closed her eyes before him and then did something he hadn't expected. She began to hum. The tune was no song he knew, but the notes from her throat issued with certainty, as if it was a familiar melody to her.

"Let me talk to her."

Caleb looked down, surprised to see Marguerite standing at his side.

Caleb waved her back. "I don't think it's a good idea, child."

"It's Judge's orders that I ask for names," she whispered. "I cannot disobey him."

Caleb studied her for a moment, wondering what this child's life as the Judge's ward could possibly be like. If the Judge was such a monster to grown adults, how did he treat this child if she veered out of step?

"All right." He stepped aside, letting her through. His hand went over his mouth as he watched the Widow continue her humming.

"What are you doing?" Asa glanced up at Caleb, mystified. "The witch will infect the child for sure!"

But Caleb held a hand up and let Marguerite continue.

The child took a step forward, tilting her head, her blonde braids shining in the light.

"I can see the dark shadow. It hangs about you," Marguerite said. Her tiny voice got the Widow's attention. Widow Goodness opened her eyes, studying Marguerite. A smile appeared again, as if she was humored by the child's appearance.

"It's stronger than I've ever seen. It never lets you sleep, does it?" Marguerite stopped within arm's reach of her. "I must ask you, are there others in town like you?"

"There are no others."

"In your acts of witchcraft, you acted alone? Entirely alone?" Marguerite pressed.

The Widow's smile spread into a laugh, her hideous brown and yellow teeth revealed again.

"You have no idea what I've done." Widow Goodness's eyes shifted to Caleb, addressing him as if he'd asked the question. "You have no idea what's coming for you. But you will never forget."

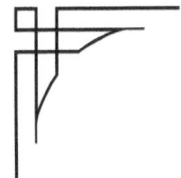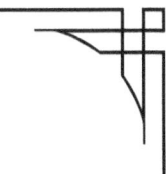

CHAPTER 23
Caleb

The jail's backdoor squeaked open again. Within seconds, Noble appeared, puffing down the hallway toward them. He waved a torn-edged public notice at Caleb.

"Here you are, Reverend!" he said, running a hand over his bushy black beard. "I nearly didn't make it back through the crowd!"

Caleb snatched it up and read the date on the notice.

8 December 1662

The Eighth of December!

"Dies santus," Caleb said. "Dies santus!" He turned and gripped Noble's shoulder. "Good man, run and get the Judge! Tell him he must delay the execution. Go now! Off with you!"

But before Noble could take a step, the front door flung open. Boos and shouts from the mob outside flooded in.

"Tell him yourself, Reverend," Noble said seconds before Judge Madden appeared, flanked by two of Constable Hindstall's men wrapped in wolf fur-trimmed cloaks. The Judge stormed down the corridor toward them.

"The gallows are ready, and the crowd is near riot! Are we finished in here?" his voice boomed.

Caleb stepped in front of Judge Madden in the hallway. "Judge, I must protest!"

"Of course you do," he said, brushing past. "Your nonsense is getting tiresome, Reverend."

The Judge stepped into the cell, examining the Widow, who, at the sound of the Judge's voice, had begun thrashing again to pull her feet free from Asa's grip.

"No! No!" she shouted.

"What's this?" Judge Madden barked at Wilbur Hayle, who still cowered in the corner. "Why haven't you finished?"

Wilbur, offering no words, ducked his head and moved in closer to the Widow, his wrist moving quickly behind the base of her scalp.

Judge Madden turned to Marguerite and pulled his gloves off one by one. "Has she named names? Given a list?"

"I asked, but she didn't name anyone," Marguerite answered from her place in the hallway, seemingly undeterred by his forcefulness. "She was quite adamant that she acted alone. Though I can see the darkness around her."

"That's it, then." Judge Madden pointed a finger at Wilbur. "Finish your job, barber. Now. It's almost sunrise."

He spun around and nearly ran into Caleb, who held his hands up to stop him. "Judge, I insist that the Widow's sentence be delayed until tomorrow at dawn."

Judge Madden blew out as he stormed past. Caleb ran after him, pausing to grab the *Malleus Malificarum* from the stool where they'd left it.

"It says in your own book here that no sentences can be carried out on the Sabbath or—"

"Today is not the Sabbath, Reverend," the Judge said. He stopped at the Constable's desk where Isaiah waited, whose eyes were darting back and forth between Caleb and the Judge.

"Ready her death warrant," Judge Madden barked.

"Already prepared, Judge." Isaiah swallowed and slid a piece of parchment across the desk to him, followed by a quill and bottle of ink. The Judge leaned down. As he did, his elbow bumped against Caleb's bundled cassock on the edge of the desktop. Caleb cringed, balling his fists and praying the cassock wouldn't slip off to reveal that he'd stolen the Judge's Bible. By some miracle, the wrapping stayed in place.

Judge Madden took up the quill and leaned down to sign the death warrant.

"You're correct, Judge. It's not the Sabbath, but hangings are also forbidden on *dies santus*, Holy Days. Today is the Eighth of December, look." Caleb laid the public notice Noble had retrieved on the desktop in front of him, pointing to the date. "It's the Feast of the Immaculate Conception, a Holy Day." He dropped the *Malleus Malificarum* on top of it. "There." Caleb pointed to the phrase *dies santus*. "Her sentence must be postponed until tomorrow, by your own rules."

The Judge paused, quill in hand. His eyes narrowed, a line forming between them.

"The Feast of the Immaculate Conception is celebrated by vulgar Catholics. It's not a Holy Day celebrated in the colonies," the Judge said. "I don't need to tell you that any act of Catholicism in the Colonies is considered an act of treason." He leaned back down, dipping the quill's nib into the ink bottle.

"You're correct, Judge." Caleb grabbed the Judge's wrist, the nub of the quill pausing an inch above the death warrant. "Catholics recognize the Feast—but so does the King of England."

The Judge glared at Caleb from underneath his heavy eyebrows.

Caleb moved behind the desk, looking at him, face to face. He put his hands on the desk and leaned toward the Judge.

"The King is the head of the Church of England, and they continue to mark the Feast every Eighth of December," Caleb said. "With only Governor Winthrop standing in between you and the King himself, surely you wouldn't want any of your decisions to appear disrespectful to the Crown. Not when the Governor has been in England for more than a year, as you said, trying to win Connecticut an independent charter."

The Judge stood silent for a minute, scowling at him and twisting the quill in between his thick fingers. He stared down at the page. Behind him, a log collapsed in the fireplace, sending up a heap of sparks. Down in the corridor, the Widow began humming again in her cell.

Then, without a word, the Judge leaned down, pushed the *Maleficarum* and the public notice aside, and finished his signature in silence.

He penned the date next to his name as the Ninth of December, Sixteen Sixty-Two.

"Oh, thank you, Judge!" Caleb said. "This delay will give me time to counsel her. To determine if she can be led back to the flock. Maybe we could even get a doctor to—"

"You misunderstand, Reverend." The Judge dropped the quill on the parchment and pushed it back to Isaiah. "There will be no delay. The Widow will hang immediately. I do thank you though, Reverend Easton, for preventing me from recording a...clerical error in the date. You're right. It could be upsetting to the King." Judge Madden turned and bellowed down the hallway. "Ready for execution!"

He turned back toward a stunned Caleb.

"Since you're suddenly so well-versed in the rules in the *Maleficarum*, I need a reverend to give the accused the Last Supper one final time. I'll give you that, Reverend Easton." The Judge pointed a finger in his face. "But understand me, you are not to cause any additional delay. You have minutes to do this. Minutes. Do you understand?"

"But Judge—" Caleb said, his voice faltering.

"Do you prefer she die without it?"

Caleb cleared his throat. He felt numb. "I have the wine and bread in my bag."

"Do it. Now."

Caleb snatched up his satchel and cassock-wrapped Bible and rushed back to the Widow's cell. Noble still stood in the hallway, the end of his gun now tipped toward the floor, mouth agape at having overheard the exchange between the two.

"Reverend!" Old Wilbur Hayle shot out of the Widow's cell just then. He met Caleb halfway down the hall and fell to his knees, reaching up toward him.

"Reverend, she touched me!" He moaned, shaking. "The Widow touched me! I was finished! I went to step past her just now and she touched my arm with her hand!" The old man's eyes teared up and his voice shook. "A witch has touched me! Am I destined for Hell now?"

"You're not destined for Hell, good sir. Bless you," Caleb said, squeezing his shoulder and moving past him into the cell.

"Oh, thank you, Reverend! Bless you!" Wilbur called from behind.

The Widow sat on her stool, bald. The skin on her head was whiter than that of her face, a color of pale that Caleb would've thought unimaginable. Even more crude red scratches traced her scalp, evidence of Wilbur's hurriedness. At her feet, Asa still sat holding her legs up off the ground, his boots now planted against the wall as leverage.

Widow Goodness continued to hum. Her eyes had gone vacant, and she stared off into nowhere.

Caleb hurried into the cell, estimating he had a few precious seconds before the Judge followed him inside. Judge Madden, the lying, immoral, unmerciful bastard—and murderer of women—would surely follow him this time. Caleb quickly pulled the bread and wine out of his bag and dropped them onto the floor. He shook the Judge's Bible from his cassock, allowing it to slip inside his satchel. He reached in with one hand and cracked the book's cover. The tiny red bottle of teeth fell out of it and into his hand. He pulled his hand back and dropped the vial into his pocket with one movement, secured the satchel's latch, and dropped the bag to the floor.

"Was anything found on her?" the Judge barked over Caleb's shoulder, just as he'd lowered his cassock into place.

Asa gave him an exhausted look over his shoulder. "No, sir. No items of any kind, nor a witch's mark either."

Caleb stepped forward into the cell, standing inches from the Widow's knees, ignoring them both.

She hummed before him, an odd seven notes, then paused. Then repeated.

Mmm, mmm, mmm,

Mmm, mmm, mmm, mmm.

Caleb held up the wine bottle. "Widow Goodness, I'm here to offer you the Lord's Supper."

"I don't want the Lord's Supper," she hissed, snapping back to life. She tried to pull her legs free from Asa's grip again. She looked at the bottle Caleb held, sickened. "My love wants me pure, without your poison in me when we meet in Hell."

"You will take it, witch!" Judge Madden instructed, stepping inside behind Caleb.

Caleb pursed his lips, ignoring him, and pulled his own Bible out of his cloak pocket. He flipped it open to The Book of Matthew.

"The Lord's Supper seals one's belief in Christ by faith," Caleb said, determined to ignore the Judge and direct his voice to the Widow only, who squeezed her eyes shut and looked away. "It is the closest a human can come with the divine while on earth. It's our opportunity to renew our faith by holy vow. It's not a form of repentance, but rebirth. Won't you do this with me?"

Caleb stared at the side of her face, which remained turned away. He set the wine on the ground, held the bread high in one hand, and continued to read from Matthew 26.

"Now, as they were eating, Jesus took bread, and after blessing it, broke it and gave it to the disciples, and said 'Take, eat, this is my body.'" Caleb broke a bite of bread from the loaf.

The Widow let out a furious wail, as if the ripping of the bread had torn a part of her. Caleb hesitated, studying the painful expression that had formed around her eyes. Asa, at her feet, turned away again toward the corner of the cell.

"Continue, Reverend!" the Judge barked from behind.

Caleb lifted the wine.

"'And he took a cup and when he had given thanks, he gave it to them saying, 'Drink of it, all of you, for this is my blood of the covenant, poured out for many for the forgiveness of sins.'"

"No!" she screamed, as if in pain. She began humming again, loud and furious, trying to drown out Caleb's words.

Caleb searched the Widow's face for any sense of remorse as she tugged at the ropes that tethered her wrists together behind her back.

"Reverend!" the Judge pushed.

"The cup of Christ, poured out for you," Caleb said. Realizing he'd forgotten to bring a cup, he pushed the hunk onto the top of the wine bottle and sloshed a bit onto the bread. He held the bite over to her mouth. She pursed her lips and turned her head away like a defiant child, continuing to hum behind her teeth.

Caleb pulled his arm back, a spot of wine dripping red onto her tunic. "Evanora, your soul deserves a chance."

"Enough coddling!"

"Compassion is not coddling!" Caleb said, dipping the bread again.

"We cannot waste any more time! If she doesn't want the Supper, you must force it upon her!"

"Excuse me?" Caleb turned and glared at the Judge, who leaned over him, his nostrils flaring. Caleb looked back at the Widow, her skin as white as bone itself, her body drowning in the ragged tunic.

"I said, *make her!*" the Judge bellowed.

Caleb lowered the wine bottle. "I cannot and will not force the Supper upon her or on anyone! The Supper is a sacred gift from our Lord. One has to receive it with an open heart, not under duress! To force it upon her would be an abuse of my Christian authority!"

The Widow stilled, watching.

"You want me to follow the rules—" the Judge yelled. He turned and snatched the *Malleus Maleficarum* from Marguerite, who stood behind him in the hallway. He threw the enormous book at Caleb, the volume smacking him in the thighs and tumbling to the ground, pages splayed. "There they are! If a condemned refuses, you must force it upon them." The Judge took a step forward and pointed a finger at Caleb. "Now, you'll do as I say or—"

"I'm curious," Caleb interrupted, taking a step over the spilled book toward the Judge, not caring that the Widow was watching, or Marguerite, or Asa, or Noble—or Isaiah—who now stood with one eye peeking around the corner. Caleb moved forward until the Judge's finger poked him directly in the chest.

"Does the Governor know how you've run your trials?" Caleb's eyes narrowed, staring at the Judge, unwilling to break eye contact. "How you've treated your reverends, your witnesses?" He nodded a chin toward Marguerite, who was watching from between the cell bars. "How you've collected a female child from a family you sentenced to die and continue to transport her with you to dangerous trials? Jailhouses? Executions?"

"Are you threatening me, Reverend?" Every inch of Judge Madden's skin flushed beet red, as his bottom lip curled under and his eyes narrowed. "Thinking about going to the Governor, are you?" He spoke slowly, the tone of his voice deepening into a rolling growl.

The Judge snatched the bottle from Caleb's hands and batted him out of the way with one arm. He rushed over to the Widow and grabbed her delicate face with one wide hand. Then he dug his thumb into one cheek and his pointer finger into the other side, squeezing, forcing her lips open. She tried to close them, but the Judge moved too quickly. He mashed the rim of the bottle into her lips, knocking it against her teeth. A large slosh of wine went into her mouth, the overflow dribbling out of the sides. He then reached down, grabbed a thumb-sized crumb of bread that had fallen onto the floor, and crammed it her mouth with one finger.

"May God have mercy on what's left of your soul!" the Judge yelled into her ear. He clamped one hand down over her mouth and pinched her nose shut with the other, tilting her head back and blocking her breathing, forcing her to swallow.

Caleb stood back, horrified at the sight of the Widow's pale head, tiny in his grip.

The Judge, satisfied, released her and stepped toward the jail cell door, stopping in front of Caleb. He shoved what was left of the bread into Caleb's chest and held it there, leaning in.

"You go to the Governor, and I'll be sure your wife will be next," he hissed between gritted teeth.

He stomped past him, out into the hallway, where Noble and Isaiah stood together, stunned, their backs against the opposite cell.

"Ready the execution! Now!" the Judge yelled back over his shoulder as he passed them.

Noble rushed into the cell, squeezing past Caleb. Asa got to his feet and the two of them slipped their hands under the Widow's armpits, silently lifted her, and hurried her out of the cell. Isaiah trailed behind.

Caleb's gaze followed, dismayed. As he turned and watched them vanish down the hallway, his eyes fell to Marguerite, who rushed into the cell and gathered up her book that lay spilled at his feet, her expression unreadable.

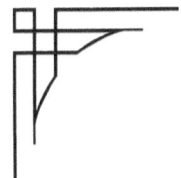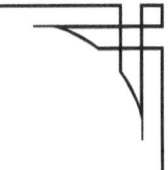

CHAPTER 24
Rebecca

Rebecca pushed open what was left of the cottage's back-door and took a cautious step outside. She looked into the forest behind the cottage. The frozen weeping willows that had led her to the front of the Widow's secret cottage thinned out and blended into the natural forest of evergreens. Everything was still. There was no hint of wind, no sound of cracking branches. No scarce bird left dared to chirp. Rebecca looked around slowly. It felt like the entire forest was holding its breath.

She brushed her hand against her pocket, feeling the Widow's *Grimoire* securely tucked inside.

Rebecca heard a small crack off to her left and looked over at Chancer, still tethered to the cottage where Levi had left her. The horse chomped at her bit and pulled her head back, her eyes on Rebecca as if asking to be untied.

"It's dawn," Levi whispered, as he stepped outside behind her. Rebecca glanced up at the sky, which was now tipping into an eerie violet color.

She nodded. "We're already too late."

"Do we still go then?"

"We must. In the chance that Caleb was able to delay the trial. To get help for the Constable—and Hannah." She pressed against the book in her pocket. "Maybe the Judge will accept the Widow's *Grimoire* as proof that I had nothing to do with this. And if he comes here, sees this place... if he brings men into the woods and they're able to capture the Beast for him..." Her voice drifted off.

Levi stepped over and untied the horse. "If we have to veer from the path, I can use the early morning sky to navigate, find our way out. If it really is an old hunter's path, I should be able to figure it out."

"And the Beast? That doesn't solve our biggest problem." Rebecca reached up, rubbing Chancer's muzzle as Levi walked her over. The horse dipped her head, gazing at Rebecca through her liquid brown eyes. Such a lovely horse. It struck Rebecca each time she looked at Chancer how much she resembled Belle. Rebecca closed her eyes. Hurt waved over her as she dared to think of happier times from her childhood. She glanced down at the shiny pink scars that ran up Chancer's front legs—scars from wolf hunting last year, Levi had said. Such a brave girl. Rebecca leaned her forehead against the horse, just for a second, saying a silent prayer that Chancer would make it safely through what lay ahead. Rebecca thought of Bow. Of Cooke. And Cooke's horse. Then pushed those thoughts away.

Levi led the horse quietly around to the front of the cottage, while Rebecca followed behind. Hannah waited with the front door cracked open. She passed the Constable's gun and hunting bag out to them. Then took one single step out.

"If the Beast tracks us," Levi said as he looped his gun over his arm, "we'll ride as fast as we can."

"No! It will hear you," Hannah warned in a whisper. "Remember, it's a Blood Demon. It hunts by blood. It hears the rush of a heart. Smells it, senses it."

"You mean we have to go as slow as possible?" Rebecca asked.

Hannah looked between them both. "That might be your best chance."

"As slowly and as quietly as possible?" Levi looked at Rebecca. He shook his head. "Then that's what we do. That, and we'll stick as close to the symbols in the trees as we can. If we're quiet as a mouse, maybe we'll have a better chance at hearing it approaching."

Rebecca didn't respond. She only looked back up at Chancer, stroking her muzzle again. She was one of four horses that entered the woods last night, and now she was the only one left.

"You're our best hope. Did you know?" Rebecca said to the horse.

Chancer turned her head and nipped at Rebecca's fingers, hopeful for oats.

"Will she be okay carrying two?" Rebecca asked Levi. "She's smaller than the Constable's horses."

"She's smaller, which means she can get through the brush easier," Levi said defensively. He stepped past Rebecca and undid Chancer's saddle. "That's where the Constable got caught up. With the Beast, I mean. When he was attacked, his horse couldn't turn fast enough to retreat."

"Promise me you'll both be careful." Hannah stepped toward Rebecca and squeezed her forearm, her green eyes serious. "Stick near the symbols of protection if you can. But once you're past them—"

"I know." Rebecca licked frost from her lips, which burned from the cold. Levi stepped up next to her and was refilling the Constable's gun with gunpowder. "Then it's a race for town."

Levi passed the Constable's gun to her.

"Do me a favor and keep the Constable alive," Rebecca said to Hannah as she slipped back into the cottage.

Hannah nodded. "I'll do my best." She shut the door. Rebecca heard wood scratching on wood, followed by a thud as Hannah dragged something heavy behind it, reinforcing the front door. If anything happened to Rebecca and Levi, Hannah would be stranded here with the Constable, and no one would know they were here. Of course, if anything happened to Hannah and the Constable, the best proof Rebecca had of the extent of the Widow's guilt and Rebecca's own innocence would be lost.

Rebecca swung the Constable's musket over her shoulder and looked past Levi and Chancer into the pathway ahead. The line of frozen willow trees on the left and the snow-drenched evergreens on the right were still. In the growing purple light, she could see now the mess the Beast had left on its chase. Branches and dirt from knocked-down trees lay scattered across the path. The spot where Rebecca had found the Constable had been trampled over. The nearest tree snapped in half and tipped to the ground in the direction of the cabin.

"Here, I'll give you a boost," Levi whispered. She turned to see him squat down next to Chancer and lace his fingers together between his knees. "Trust me, I ride with my little brother all the time. Quiet now!"

Rebecca placed a hand on his shoulder and stepped up on his gripped hands with one foot. Levi pushed her up high enough so that she could swing one leg over the horse.

The plan was for Rebecca to drive the horse. Levi would cover over her shoulder with gunfire if needed.

She grabbed Chancer's reins and looked down to see that Levi had brought a chair from the cottage out with him.

"Careful!" she hushed.

He got on it, placed both hands on the horse's back, then stepped a foot up onto the chair back and swung his leg up over the horse. He slid into place behind Rebecca, placing the Constable's pack in between the two of them. She looped the reins around her hands.

"Ready?" Rebecca lifted her eyes back to the pathway ahead. Aside from the broken branches, there were no marks, no tracks from where the Beast had chased her here. Did demons leave tracks? She thought for a second how different the forest had seemed when she and Caleb had first moved here. Then, it had been an endless blanket of color—leaves painted all sorts of oranges, yellows, light and dark browns—populated with animals that chirped, chattered, and scattered at any sound of a human. Now, that same forest lay stretched in front of her, a frozen skeleton of itself. All life had departed.

"Right," Levi whispered in her ear as he looped one arm around her waist for balance. Out of the corner of her eye, she could see his musket, aimed up into the hill to their right.

She closed her eyes and took a deep breath in, willing her pulse to slow. "Steady hearts. And go. Slow."

Rebecca made a soft *click-click* noise in the back of her jaw, simultaneously giving Chancer a gentle nudge in the side with her boot, away from the safety of the cottage and into Blood Demon territory. Chancer took a healthy trot forward, and Rebecca jerked back on the reins, slowing her down and quieting her hooves on the path.

"Shh!" Levi urged the horse over Rebecca's shoulder.

Chancer chomped her bit, not understanding. Her teeth made a clacking noise against the iron, the loudness of which sent prickles up Rebecca's spine. She closed her eyes and exhaled hard, expecting the Beast to crash through the woods at any second. Then Chancer's tail swished, the thickness of it brushing through the air and whisking against her rear end. Rebecca's shoulders hunched as she sent a frantic glance back into the woods next to them, certain they'd been heard.

"She only seems louder than she is," Levi whispered over her shoulder. "We'll go slower. Pull her to a stop."

Rebecca did so, holding her still for a few seconds, then slowly letting up the slack on the reins. The horse took the direction this time and moved at a cautious pace down the path. On both sides of them, glassy willow trees stood frozen in place.

Riding double with a man she barely knew—again—reminded her for a moment of Cooke. His response to Levi offering to join the hunt and what he'd told her about the church burning his family's home played across her mind. Uneasiness filled her stomach whenever she thought about it.

"Levi," Rebecca spoke softly. "Cooke had mentioned something to me back on the road, right after you joined the hunt. Something about the church and your house?"

"Mm."

She dug her thumbnails into Chancer's leather straps as they continued forward. "He said the church burned down your house. He said he was there when it happened and saw it with his own eyes. Is that true?"

"Well, I don't know if he was there, but yes, it's true."

Rebecca twisted to look back at him, nearly losing her balance atop Chancer.

"Why?" She pursed her lips together, as the word had come out far too loud. She went silent for a few seconds, waiting, but the trees stood quiet as they moved past. "Why on earth would they have done such a thing?"

No response.

"Levi?"

Levi's breath exhaled in mist over her shoulder. "They needed the nails."

Her forehead crinkled, certain she'd heard him wrong. She pushed her hood back and tilted an ear toward him. "Sorry?"

"They needed the nails. It's what they do here," Levi said, pointing over her shoulder at a thick branch that blocked their path. Rebecca directed Chancer around it.

"It was two years ago. They were planning on building South Puritan and they needed nails. You can see yourself, we've plenty of wood, but nails...At one point, nails were more valuable than coins here," he said. "When they'd build something new, they'd burn down old houses, vacant buildings, homes of criminals in jail. Gather up the nails from the ash."

"But your house? Why your house?"

The horse's ears perked up in front of Rebecca. It slowed a touch.

"We'd gotten word my grandfather was dying. He lived all the way in Massachusetts Colony. My father rounded up my brothers and I, and we rushed to see him, only the message was a bit premature. He didn't die for another two months."

Before Rebecca, Chancer's ears perked and twitched again. This time, the horse turned its head to the woods on the right. Rebecca looked ahead to see the path littered with debris. She glanced up at the hillside, seeing the shadow of the path of destruction through the trees that led from the top of the hill to the bottom. She swallowed. It was the path the Beast had taken chasing her through the forest to the cottage. Entire evergreen trees were snapped in half, their top halves dangling, leaves green and shaken free of snow. Some had been knocked entirely to the ground, roots pulled from the earth, dirt upturned. Rebecca sat up as a chill brushed over her arms, even underneath both cloaks and her dress sleeves. She turned her eyes back to the path.

"And?"

"And we ended up staying for weeks," Levi continued. "I guess Father should've left word with a neighbor or some-one, because when we returned, everything was gone."

Rebecca sat stunned. "That's horrible! What did the church do when they found out?"

"Nothing," he said. "That's why we ended up living above Father's blacksmith shop in town. It's a bit snug for the five of us but trying to find nails to build a new house...Well, that's also why my father and brothers and I never set foot inside South Puritan."

"Levi, I'm so sorry," Rebecca said. Her face flushed and she suddenly found her throat filled with words no decent woman could say aloud. "I promise you if there's anything I can do, anything my husband can do, we will."

Levi was quiet for a moment.

"It was a long time ago," was all he offered.

Her eyes ran over the path ahead of them, her mind still distracted by the atrocious mistake her own church had made, when her eyes landed on a tree with the hacked branches and symbol carved into it.

Now, in the softer light of early dawn, the details of the symbol were more visible. Whatever blade had been used to etch it was jagged, the lines rough and sharp, as if the markings hadn't been carved into the tree but stabbed.

"Levi," she spoke over her shoulder and nudged her chin down toward it.

"I see it."

She shifted the horse's reins in her hands, the pain of the cold embedded in her knuckles, and kept her eyes on the woods to their left.

They'd continued down the thin trail, riding in silence for a while, the safety of the cottage long gone behind them. Rebecca counted each of the Widow's symbols on the frozen willows as they passed. Hannah had told her there were about fourteen that led into a patch of thick brush concealing the trail from the main road. Just as her eyes caught on Number Eight, Chancer jolted a few steps beneath them.

"What is it?" Rebecca whispered, looking up the hill to her right. She crushed the reins in her fists and pulled Chancer far left, close enough to the frozen willows that Rebecca's sleeve brushed against the trees. Beneath them, Chancer's hooves moved through what sounded like deep, sticky mud.

Rebecca leaned over ever so slightly to look at what the horse had walked into. She stared at a pool of something dark beneath them. The path here had quickly turned to mud, which flecked everywhere.

"It's blood," Levi hushed.

"Are you sure?" Rebecca said, still staring at the dark pool that flooded across and down the path. "From what?"

"The Constable's horse."

She clapped a hand over her mouth, her heart pounding and her stomach rising simultaneously as she gaped at the puddle of blood beneath them. She looked to the ground again. Hannah had been right, the Blood Demon had emptied the creature of every drop of it, violently. Blood—not mud—had splattered chest-height on the trees to their right, sinking into the snow.

But there was just blood, no remains.

"Do you see the horse?" Rebecca whispered, searching the spaces in between the trees beyond the puddle with her eyes, but finding nothing.

Chancer began to buck against her reins. Rebecca pulled back, jerking herself against the horse's movements, trying to get her under control.

"We have to calm her down!" Rebecca said. Levi quickly shouldered his gun and slapped his hands on top of hers, tugging the reins.

"She can smell it," Levi said, as Chancer spun them in a half circle in the middle of the path. Rebecca turned her head in all directions, not knowing which way to look.

"What? The Beast or the other horse?" She struggled to get Chancer to stop, as the horse spun them farther down the pathway.

"Don't look!" Levi commanded, pulling the reins from her hands.

"Don't look?!" Rebecca immediately turned her head in the direction of Levi's voice.

Up ahead on the right side of the path, two thick branches jutted out from the tree line at the edge of the path, at the end of the bloody trail.

"What—?" she started, but instantly, she knew. They weren't branches. They were a horse's hind legs, torn from its body. A puddle of curly entrails pooled out from where the back legs had been ripped off. A wave of dizziness pounded Rebecca in between the eyes. She slapped a hand over her mouth and swallowed a scream, holding it in her chest like a giant pocket of burning air.

The hind legs lay there, hoof to hip, completely detached from the rest of its body, which was nowhere to be seen. Its tail remained, nearly indistinguishable and saturated with blood. Chancer took another step toward the remains, the bloody innards giving off a warm, wet smell. Rebecca craned her neck, searching the woods just steps beyond it. There was no other piece of the horse left to be seen.

"Where's the other half?" she whispered as Levi struggled to hold Chancer still, the horse spinning in the path.

"Whoa!" he shouted. Chancer, spooked, took off in a full-speed gallop down the path.

"Whoa! Whoa!" Levi begged her to slow down, but to no avail. Chancer had seen what they'd seen, smelled it too, and she continued to ignore every pull and kick that Levi tried, dashing down the path, hooves clattering.

"Levi, we have to slow her down!" Rebecca ducked her face against the wind.

"I know, I'm trying!"

"If we can't slow her down—"

"I know!"

"We're making too much noise!" Rebecca touched a hand over her heart as if she could slow it through her cloak.

Just then, a tree cracked behind them.

Rebecca glanced up the hill to see a pine tree, at least thirty feet tall, shaking loose from its place in the tree line and whooshing to the ground.

"Levi!" Rebecca grabbed the reins from his hands, Chancer pounding forward now.

"I heard it!"

"Do you see it? Is it back there?"

Levi shook the gun free from his shoulder. He scanned the forest in the direction of which the tree had fallen. "No, I don't see—"

An enormous *whoosh* issued from the path ahead of them. Rebecca watched a second evergreen smash down the tree line, but this time, it landed on the path in front of them, blocking them from going forward. Rebecca yanked on the reins, and Chancer skidded to a stop. Levi slammed into Rebecca's back. Both teetered for a second atop the horse.

They were trapped.

"Eyes up!" Levi whispered. He unraveled Rebecca's musket from around her shoulder and handed it to her. "Hold her still. Aim forward, I'll cover the rear. It could be anywhere."

Rebecca gripped both reins in one hand as she lifted the Constable's musket into position. Her senses were alive. Her ears were alert to every noise: the dry knock of Chancer's hooves on the earth below, the out-of-breath steamy air piping in and out of her nostrils. Heaps of snow slipped from the evergreen that blocked their path. Its branches shifted, then stilled.

A few moments of silence passed as they held still in the middle of the path and watched for any sign of the Beast.

"We have to get to the main road," Rebecca whispered. "Hannah says it can't leave the edge of the forest because of the symbols. The symbols end just before the road."

Beyond them, Chancer's head turned. Her eyes were wide, her ears flicking a different way every few seconds.

"I don't know if a gun can stop something this size," Levi whispered to her.

"We might be able to startle it."

Levi nudged the tip of his gun toward the felled tree ahead. "It could be waiting there or just beyond."

"Or it could be a diversion."

"True." He glanced at the sky. A pale orange streak now swiped across the dark purple. "But town is that way."

"The way out is the way through." Rebecca's lips parted. She looked back at the tree up ahead. At its thinnest, it must have been ten or twelve feet wide high. "We're going to need to jump it."

She scanned the woods. "Has Chancer ever jumped anything before?"

"Nothing that big. Not on purpose. Can you jump her?"

Rebecca nodded. "We used to jump horses on my dad's farm. We taught them, then sold them to nobles who lived nearby."

"If she stumbles or doesn't make it—"

"I know. But we have no choice, we have to try," Rebecca said. "We're trapped otherwise."

Levi sighed behind her. "How do we do this?"

"I'll handle it," she said, passing her gun back to him.

Rebecca pulled Chancer's reins to the side, turning her on the path. "We have to do this quick, girl," she said, nudging her in the side and leading her back in the direction they'd come from. She drove Chancer back fifteen feet or so, then turned her back again toward the felled tree.

"As soon as we land, I'm going to fire a warning shot into the right side of the forest," Levi said. "If we land okay, it will startle her into racing forward—and hopefully will scare the Beast as well."

Rebecca nodded without a word. She stared at the path ahead. The pine tree they had to jump lay still now, half shed of the snow that covered it. Needles lay everywhere.

"Ready now."

Levi's arms tightened around her waist.

"Chancer, up up!" Rebecca yelled as loud as he could, nudging her with both heels and snapping the reins down hard. Chancer responded, running full force at the tree, hooves pounding on the path. Then, just two horse-lengths before the jump, a hard snap issued from Rebecca's side of the road. At the same time, the cold cloud swarmed her, running up and down her limbs as she looked at the source of the sound.

The Beast, the Blood Demon, had cracked another pine, which was now falling directly down above them.

"Jump!" Rebecca yelled with all the air in her chest.

The terror in her scream made the seconds seem to slow down. Rebecca pulled back on the reins. Chancer's front hooves lifted off the earth just as Levi's gun fired into the air in the direction of the falling tree. Needles showered down on them. Rebecca ducked her head. Chancer's leap cleared the falling tree, her hooves touching down on the pathway.

Levi had been right. The gunshots alone were enough to send Chancer tearing down the path. Rebecca struggled to hold on. Racing hearts and blood be damned. The Beast knew exactly where they were.

"Go! Go!" Rebecca cried, snapping the reins.

Levi leaned forward against Rebecca's back as Chancer tore down the path, trying to balance as he reloaded.

Then, behind Rebecca and to her right, there was a double crack. She turned in time to see two thick elm trees fall. Her eyes caught on something off in the distance. Something the downed trees had revealed. This time, it wasn't the Beast.

"That's my house!" she said, her eyes darting over to the structure she was seeing through the forest. She couldn't believe the words coming out of her own mouth, but there it was, fifteen yards or so away, mostly concealed behind thick elms that backed up to their property. As they dashed forward, she glimpsed the back corner of her house, with its peaked roof and chimney made of black and blue river rocks. A glimpse...and then it was gone.

How could they have never known this path was here? Or the cottage at the end of it?

"It must mean the road is ahead, right?" Levi said, firing a warning shot into the air. Chancer continued to bolt forward. Just feet ahead, the pathway narrowed slowly, the trees creeping back into the path, funneling them in. They'd be trapped, again. It was the brush at the end of the path, the forested area that concealed the path from the main road.

The symbols of protection were about to run out.

"We have to get through that as fast as we can," she said over her shoulder. "Cover us from behind."

Rebecca's stomach lurched as she felt Chancer naturally slow down a touch. The horse weaved right, slipping in between two evergreens, then left, her steps unsteady and searching for even ground. She galloped through the trees ahead.

Behind them, the snapping of branches grew closer.

"On our right!" Levi yelled. A blast issued from his musket before Rebecca could even turn to see what he was firing at. She ducked as trees exploded just feet away from them, bark and branches flying—from the Beast, the gunshot, or both. Upset by the blast, Chancer turned her head while running, smashing her front flank into a tree, then slowing as she rounded past it.

"Where is it? Levi, where is it?"

He didn't answer, only fired off to the right again. Rebecca looked up in the direction of the shot to see a flurry of activity running parallel to them. She could see the Beast's thick horns, the dark of its shoulders, its heaving forearms as they wrecked straight through tree trunks. The image of what it had done to the Constable's horse—what it had left, what damage it could do, flashed through her mind. She gritted her jaw and drove Chancer ahead, steering her around the trees. Branches whipped them all. Snow showered down on them from the trees above. Rebecca and Chancer worked almost as one, the horse following her drive to survive, Rebecca steering her from her higher vantage point.

Boom! Levi's gun blasted again.

Rebecca glanced in the direction of the shot out of the corner of her eye. There it was, not fifteen feet from them. Enormous and black, crouched down on all fours, its spiraling horns pointed forward.

Then, Chancer saw it, too. The horse started to panic, her chest heaving, her eyes wide. A wild instinct had broken open inside her, lit by the sheer will to escape danger. To live.

Rebecca pulled Chancer to the left, directing her away from it, but the Beast launched itself through the trees, pulling itself through the brush with its claws. Rebecca stared straight ahead, searching for any sign of the road. The Beast was going to rush the horse from the side, just like it had done to Cooke's horse.

Rebecca yelled back over her shoulder. "Get ready to stop, hard!"

"What?" Levi yelled, trying to empty what was left of the gunpowder into his musket.

"Just get ready! And don't fall off!" Rebecca said. She turned her eyes to the Beast as it rushed closer, its body shadowed every few feet by a new tree or uprooted trunk. It was running in a diagonal path, preparing to lunge. If it caught either of them, or the horse, they were all done for. Levi wrapped his arms around Rebecca's waist, crushing them together, tradition be damned, and braced himself.

Rebecca watched the Beast's stride as it widened, sidestepping closer toward them every few paces. Suddenly, it was close enough to jump. All at once, the Beast's head turned to the side. Its jaws opened. Its black teeth were visible. The hissing noise began, and—

"Whoa!" Rebecca pulled back on Chancer, twisting her head completely to one side. The horse reared back, stuttering in her steps, just as the Beast launched itself—prematurely—at them. The force of the Beast's jump caused it to tumble though three pines, knocking it off its feet, rolling deeper into the forest.

"Go!" Rebecca yelled to Chancer, snapping the reins. Chancer shot through the forest.

"Do you see it? Is it behind us?" she asked Levi.

"I can't see anything," he said. "Brush is too thick!"

Up ahead, the trees appeared to thin out.

"Levi, I think we're close!" She drove Chancer through two more thick trees and wove around an especially high patch of frozen thorn bushes. There it was! The last few trees that let out onto the main road.

Chancer trotted out, free of the pines. The road was its normal deserted dirt road—the right turn leading to Rebecca and Caleb's house, the left turn heading to South Puritan, then on into Hartforde Town. Rebecca swallowed hard, bringing Chancer to a stop. The sight of the road had brought no comfort. The Beast could be anywhere in the woods behind them. It could be running to a new point to attack them. How far did the boundary extend in the woods? It could be following them. Now, they were out in the open where it could see them. There was no hiding now.

The orange streak in the sky above was spreading. If she wasn't already standing on the gallows, the Widow would surely hang soon. They were almost out of time.

Rebecca glared back at the woods with her lips pursed, thinking of the cabin, their friends trapped there, the Beast who'd tried to kill them, the Widow whose awful plan may just have succeeded.

Her heart raced, now out of anger.

"Give me that?" Rebecca reached a hand back, taking the Constable's gun from Levi.

"What are you doing?"

Rebecca didn't answer. She only gritted her teeth and dropped Chancer's reins long enough to fire one shot back into the woods.

Then, without a word, she looped the gun over her shoulder, picked up the reins, and directed Chancer left toward South Puritan, pushing her into a gallop. They cut through the snow-covered hill, next to the field that bordered church property, and back down the well-beaten hunter's shortcut Levi had taken earlier that night.

Chancer—now unencumbered by obstacles and familiar with the terrain—moved in a steady speed. Her body flattened out and her hooves flew in a clean, clacking rhythm underneath them, setting off as fast as she could for town.

The Widow's *Grimoire*, concealed in Rebecca's cloak pocket, bumped along against her thigh the entire way.

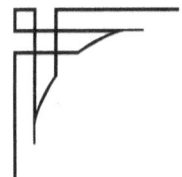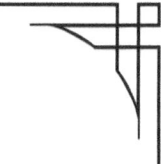

CHAPTER 25
Caleb

"Let's go! It's time!" The Judge tipped his head toward the bolted jailhouse door. "Moral justice must be served."

Caleb waited with Marguerite between the Judge and the door. He watched as Judge Madden plucked a loose thread from the sleeve of his robe, crushed it in between his thumb and middle finger, and let it flutter to the floor.

Next to them, Asa and Noble emerged from the cell, struggling to carry the Widow, their arms wrapped underneath her armpits. They held her aloft, still doing their best to keep her feet off the ground. She cackled and shrieked with delight.

"Do you think I'll wear a lovely gown?" she pleaded to Noble, suddenly turning into an anxious bride. "We'll marry in Hell. Remember that."

She looked over at Asa as they carried her—toes just inches off the ground—up to the lobby of the jailhouse. "My beloved waits for me. I can feel him closer than ever now!"

"Listen to her!" Judge Madden glared at Caleb as he pulled his hood up. "The Widow made a pact with the Devil, and in doing so, knew she was sealing her fate. Now, out of my way!" The Judge brushed him aside with one arm, and within two strides, pulled open the jailhouse door.

The mob outside responded with a deafening roar.

"Sinner!"

"Die, witch!"

"Kill the witch!"

"Hang the Widow!"

"Kill her!"

Two of Hindstall's men immediately appeared in the doorframe, dressed in their wolf-fur lined coats. For a split second, Caleb had hope that the hunting party had returned—until they spoke.

"Ready, Judge?" the taller of the two shouted through the noise.

"Ready," the Judge bellowed.

Caleb hung his head, realizing they were only there to escort them to the gallows.

The shorter of the two men—his upper lip mangled with a bad scar—turned and aimed his gun high, leading the way through the crowd.

"Get back! Everyone, back!" the taller guard shouted as he followed, casting a suspicious eye at everyone around them.

The Judge followed next, stepping outside and holding up both arms in an attempt to calm the screaming mob, which only cried out louder at the sight of him.

Caleb stepped back to make room for Asa and Noble shuffling through, carrying the Widow. Compared to how she'd fought Asa back in the cell, she looked complacent now. Ready to die.

She hummed as she passed by. The same odd tune. They moved through the door.

The crowd roared louder. Small scraps of food and garbage whipped over the heads of others toward the Widow.

"There she is!"

"Hang her! Stone her!"

"Evil woman!"

Caleb took a sharp inhale and followed Widow Goodness out into the gathered mass. Marguerite accompanied him, staying close to his elbow as they moved outside. The little girl blinked rapidly at everything happening around her, for the first time, seemingly taken aback by the anger in the volume and collective voice of the crowd. Or was she looking among the crowd for this shadow she said she could see?

Isaiah stepped out behind Caleb, pulling the jailhouse door closed behind them. He echoed the warning over Caleb's shoulder, holding his gun at the ready, bravery forced into his tone. "Get back! Everyone, back! Justice will be served!"

Caleb's heart thundered against his ribs as they nudged their way through the sea of people, passing faces that were exhausted and terrified and furious. Noble had been right—the crowd had turned into a mob. People yelled from all directions. From the jailhouse front door, it was perhaps a two-minute walk to the dead center of town, where the Judge said the gallows had been set up, but the crowd swirled heavily around them. His eyes landed on the back of the Judge's wigged head. He concealed the red bottle of teeth in his hands.

They passed men and women yelling curses and prayers. Cries echoed down from the windows above.

"Burn in hell, witch!"

"To hell with you and your evil deeds!"

"Don't hang her! Burn her!"

A rotten onion flew over the Widow's head, pelting Caleb in the chest.

"Mind yourself and head to the gallows!" Isaiah yelled louder, as if his voice could push people back. "Justice will be served!"

A red-bearded man jumped in line in between the Judge and the Widow, hoisting a white vessel high in the air. A chamber pot! Caleb identified it a split second too late to warn anyone. The man swung it, dousing the Widow, Asa, and Noble with a foul-smelling liquid. Caleb managed to shove Marguerite out of the way just in time for the splash to find only the tips of her shoes.

"Bastard!" Noble loosened his grip on the Widow, his face burning red. He thrust a hand into the man's chest, pushing him back into the crowd as the Widow splashed down onto the muddy ground.

Asa scrambled to pick her up. "Noble! What are you doing?"

The two hurriedly scooped her up. The back of her brown tunic was now stained with mud. One of Hindstall's men, the shorter of the two, tore off into the crowd after the offender.

"Order here!" Judge Madden bellowed into the crowd.

"Whatever you do, keep moving! Don't stop!" Asa yelled to the group, a slight hint of fear in his tone.

Caleb grabbed Marguerite and gathered her in front of him, hands on both her shoulders, walking close. The girl covered her ears as the crowd's boos picked up, and browned lettuce soared past her.

"Whore!"

"The gallows are too good for her!"

"Hell is too good for her! Witch! Witch!"

"Order, I say!" Judge Madden snapped at the crowd as the pink entrails of rabbit or other small game cartwheeled over his shoulder toward the Widow.

Hindstall's men, now both back in order and leading the way, picked up the pace, walking double-speed toward the platform. The Widow didn't seem to notice or care that she was now doused with human filth and mud. She alternated between humming and mumbling about her "beloved." The closer they came to the gallows, the more her words drowned out the hate shouted by the crowd.

"Let her swing!"

"Go to hell!"

"The Devil will burn you!"

Hindstall's men joined forces at the front of the group, guns aimed in the air in warning, yelling red-faced at those who stood before them to move. It worked. Before them, those few left standing between them and the gallows parted. Caleb's breath caught in his chest when he saw it: a platform had been cobbled together from dark dead wood—likely throwaway pieces from the carpenter's stock blackened by mold from being left outside for the winter. An upside-down L-shaped frame stabbed straight through the middle of the platform. A noose dangled from the center of it. A stool identical to the ones in the jail cell sat positioned beneath the rope.

Hindstall's men paused at the stairs, turning toward the crowd, arms still held high as Asa and Noble hoisted the Widow up the stairs and onto the gallows platform. She kicked her filthy feet with glee, like a little child.

"Reverend," Judge Madden paused, speaking over his shoulder to Caleb. "You will join me on the platform. You are to instruct her to offer last words and nothing more."

"What if she offers to repent, Judge?" Caleb asked, even though he knew it was unlikely. He ran his finger over the cork in the Judge's bottle of teeth in his pocket.

"She won't." With that, Judge Madden turned back and stepped up onto the platform. Caleb said a silent prayer for guidance, for help, and then followed the Judge, his legs weak, his heart pounding. The crude structure measured just about six feet in length and width, and as Caleb stepped up, he saw that it littered with stinking rotten food, wilted cabbage, and worse.

Judge Madden strode to the far end of the platform where a handful of members of the Particular Court waited in their dark robes and expensive white wigs. The Judge turned back and summoned Marguerite over. She left Caleb's side and took a place next to him.

Caleb looked out at the crowd, seeing so many angry faces spread out before him. People flowed from the edge of the platform and filled the entire main square in town. From there, the mob swept down the street in one direction past the butcher's and the tailor's, all the way past the magistrate's office. In the other direction, they filled the vast road that ran before some of the oldest homes along the town wall. The first glimpse of the cursed sun beamed through leaf-bare trees over the east wall toward them. Dawn.

People continued barking wicked words from every direction.

Caleb folded his hands in front of him and watched Asa and Noble drop the Widow's feet on the stool—Asa placing one hand on her back to keep her steady. She closed her eyes, peacefully, continuing to hum. Noble stepped behind her and lowered the noose around her neck.

The crowd roared. More food was flung. More hate.

Caleb's eyes swept over to the Judge, who stood just beyond the Widow. He was looking out into the crowd, that half-smile creeping back onto his face again, his fists on his hips, taking it all in, absorbing the attention, the power.

"Reverend, I think it's time," Asa called him over, keeping one hand on the Widow's back to keep her steady.

Just as Caleb took a step toward her, a jar of something brown landed on the deck a foot in front of him, shattering and showering his boots in something rancid. Laughter followed. Before his feet, he saw a cluster of young boys laugh, their chests pressed against the gallows platform in the exact same place he'd watched his first hanging as a boy, years ago. Their wide eyes raked over the Widow as they whispered to one another. He wondered what effect this would have on them.

Caleb felt every step as he moved. The pounding of his feet was like the ticking of a sick clock he couldn't stop if he wanted to— a heart with only so many beats left. He paused directly in front of the Widow. The stool she stood on bumped up her height so that she was only a smidge shorter than Caleb. The noose fit taught around her jaw, tilting her chin upward. Her crudely shaved head—stained now not just by trickles of blood but also thrown food and splashes of human waste—was held still under the pressure of the noose. One of Hindstall's men had re-bound her wrists tightly in front of her.

The crowd hushed behind him.

Caleb folded his hands, feeling each second evaporate, knowing he didn't have much time before the Judge interfered. "Evanora, this is your chance to share your last words with us. Please. Speak."

Her eyes landed directly on him, but she didn't respond. She smiled, her cheeks straining against the rope.

"You can't hate God for what happened to your husband, nor turn your back on him," he continued. "Please, listen to me." Caleb's eyes flitted toward the Judge, who was directing the guard to come tighten the noose. He swallowed and leaned toward her, pursing his lips and holding his breath, determined not to recoil at the smell of foul breath and dirt and body odor. He quickly continued.

"I must ask you now, and I can only ask this once more... Do you wish to repent for your sins? Do you wish to renounce your connection to the Devil in the hopes that the Kingdom of Heaven will offer mercy on your soul and welcome you back?"

"The Kingdom..." the Widow said, her words coming out choked. She shook her head no the best she could, straining against the rope. "I am going to rule my own kingdom, Reverend. Everyone will see. Everyone will remember. You have no idea what I've done, Reverend."

"Reverend, it's time!" barked the Judge.

Caleb took a step back, looking at the Widow in her stained brown tunic. Asa followed him, taking place next to Marguerite. The Widow pressed her lips together, forming a tiny smile that made Caleb, for the first time, think it was a shiver of excitement.

He exhaled and nodded numbly as he backed up, joining Isaiah opposite the Judge and the men from the Particular Court. He looked to Judge Madden, who nodded just once.

Judge Madden stepped to the front center of the platform and raised his arms. The crowd went silent.

"Men and women of Hartforde Towne," he began. "We've gathered this morning to witness evil being extinguished from the world. For those of you who've not heard, Widow Evanora Goodness has been convicted—and admitted to— the legal and moral crime of witchcraft."

The mob erupted into a roar—a mix of boos and jeers. Caleb glanced at the boys at the edge of the platform, then, seeing their excitement, quickly looked away.

The Judge waved one arm and the crowd was silenced.

"I must remind everyone within hearing distance that there is no greater sin that that of witchcraft, other than perhaps, the sin of not believing that such evil exists." He marched across the stage, looking out over the people. "To knowingly and willfully turn against your Creator, in order to cause malicious harm to others, without an ounce of sorrow or regret in one's heart can only be understood as evil incarnate."

Caleb bowed his head as the Judge continued, and as he did so, noticed a bit of movement at the opposite corner of the stage behind the Particular Court. A line of women— four or five that he could see—stood huddled in a cluster with horrified looks on their faces. Only, they weren't looking at the Widow.

"What's going on over there?" Caleb whispered to Marguerite.

She craned his neck to see, then stiffened as if she was unsure if she should speak while the Judge addressed the people. "They've been gathered for questioning."

Alarmed, Caleb looked back at the line of women. He could see seven of them now, rounded up, their wrists bound to one another in a line. Among them were a few faces he recognized: dark-haired Ellen Cooper, the town's midwife; Edra Bells, an elderly nursemaid with a lisp and nervous hands; and Faithly Stevens, a skinny farmer's wife who tend-ed children at South Puritan. The Judge must've ordered them gathered when he'd inspected the gallows earlier.

"Why are they tied up if they're just being questioned? The Widow gave no names!" Caleb said. "Was it you? Did you say you saw something?"

"Aside from the Widow, I didn't see anything."

In the middle of the platform, the Judge continued pacing in front of Widow Goodness. "As Judge of the Particular Court, I publicly sentence you, Widow Evanora Goodness, to immediate death You will suffer the deprivation of glory for all of eternity."

The crowd exploded into cheers. Two men standing at the base of the stage threw their fists in the air and pounded on the stage.

Judge Madden turned to Caleb. "Your Bible, sir."

"Mine?" Caleb grabbed his Bible from underneath his arm and handed it over.

The Judge flipped it open to a random page, then balanced the book in one hand. He thrust a pointer finger in the air, his voice booming. "In the Good Book itself, it says upon occasions of witchcraft, we are to show no mercy." He paused and moved his finger to the page. "In fact, we are to 'completely destroy them', otherwise, they will trap you with the detestable practices in worshiping their gods, and convince you to sin against the Lord."

Caleb took a step forward, seeing that Judge Madden had the book opened to Psalms.

"That's not what it says!" Caleb reacted before he could realize the words had even come out of his mouth. He snatched the book from the Judge. "Psalms has nothing to do with witchcraft. You're using the Bible to lie!"

Judge Madden spun on his heels to face Caleb. "What did you say?"

Caleb's face flushed red. His hands shook as he stepped in front of the Widow to face the Judge. "I said, you're a liar! You can't misuse God's word to kill people!"

Caleb plunged his hand into his pocket and pulled out the jar of teeth, throwing it at the Judge's chest. Judge Madden's nostrils flared. His body flinched as he made an instantaneous movement toward picking up the vial, then thought better of it.

"I've had enough of your hesitation, Reverend," the Judge hissed.

"And did you bring your dolls with you? The ones you plant inside houses just to make convictions easier?" Caleb yelled loud enough for the crowd to hear. A turning of heads rippled through the men from the Particular Court. "Look at the Widow's hands, look at them!" He paused and turned to her, grabbing her bounded wrists and holding them high in front of her. "Her fingers are twisted with age! Do you think hands in this condition could produce the bounty of dolls that were presented in this case?"

Out of the corner of his eye, he saw little Marguerite Cross tilt her head. Her lips parted as she looked from Caleb to the Judge.

"Judge Madden is a liar! He lies to convict!" Caleb shouted toward the crowd. "This woman is old and sick! She's been devastated over the death of her husband. She needs help! She needs mercy! Aren't those the things Jesus Christ taught us all?"

Judge Madden spun on his heels, grabbing Asa and Noble by their cloak sleeves and thrusting them toward Caleb.

"Reverend Easton, that's enough!" Judge Madden's face was bright red. His eyes bulged as if his entire head would burst.

But Caleb continued. "The Widow believes herself to be guilty, but if we hang this woman based on misquotations from the Bible and questionable evidence, it won't be mercy...It will be murder!"

The Judge stepped up and grabbed Caleb's forearm, twisting it behind his back up toward his shoulder. "Guards, arrest this man on the charges of committing heresy against the church! Reverend Easton has continually refused to comply with the Church's battle against the Devil. To show disbelief in the existence of witchcraft is against the law, per the Protestant Church. Arrest him immediately!"

"No!" Caleb yelled as Asa and Noble grabbed him underneath his arms and dragged him to the edge of the podium.

Judge Madden walked to the center of the stage, picked up his vial and pocketed it, looking Caleb in the eye as he did so. He took two more steps, still staring Caleb down as Isaiah bound Caleb's wrists behind his back. Behind the Judge, the Widow began her sing-song hum again, her voice constrained, the rope tight around her neck.

And then her hum turned into song. Her voice was dry, her throat stretching to push out the words.

"*Tongue and eye and blood be spilled,*" she sang, slowly. "A corpse-sealed vow very soon fulfilled."

Somewhere in the middle of the crowd, a baby shrieked. A few who stood around the squealing baby turned as the mother tried desperately to soothe it.

The Widow continued, repeating the lines.

"*Tongue and eye and blood be spilled.*" Her voice got louder with each word, her tongue slapping against the roof of her mouth.

"*A corpse-sealed vow very soon fulfilled.*"

Then, suddenly, it seemed all the babies scattered in the crowd—any child young enough to cry in their parents' arms—began to.

"What's this?" Judge Madden turned, glaring into the sea of people. "Silence your children! Silence, I say!"

Caleb looked back at the Widow, horrified.

"*'fore the ring of the midnight bell,*
A queen be crowned.
And all who listen,
In my blood be drowned!"

"It's a spell!" one man from the Particular Court yelled from the end of the platform. "Someone, do something!"

With one quick move, Judge Madden launched himself across the platform and kicked the stool out from underneath the Widow's feet.

Caleb flinched as the Widow plummeted down the sharp two-foot drop. Her delicate old neck snapped with the force of the drop alone. The crowd cheered as the old woman's body bucked in midair. Her arms went rigid within seconds—her whole being swinging awkwardly above the overturned stool.

Caleb closed his eyes and dropped his chin to his chest, the Widow's haunting voice still in his head. Her words.

"Come on, Reverend. Back with us." Asa yanked at Caleb's tethered wrists. "Let's get you inside and away from the crowd."

As Caleb was pulled away toward the jail, Judge Madden stepped onto center stage before the body of Widow Goodness. He raised both arms in the air.

"You have nothing to fear! We will eliminate evil, one by one, if we must!"

The town cheered.

The babies screamed.

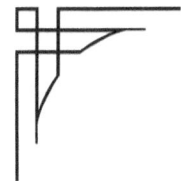 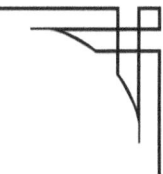

CHAPTER 26
Caleb

"Heresy! Heresy!"

The Judge's ugly accusation echoed in his ears as Caleb stared down at his bound wrists, dumbfounded. Isaiah had used the same type of itchy twine they'd used to tie Widow Goodness, and it was already digging red lines into his wrists. He leaned back against the jail wall, his cell opposite the Widow's now vacant one. The remains of her white hair still lay scattered across the floor, her cell door propped open.

Caleb looked up at the crisscrossed wooden planks that made up the ceiling of the jail. Oh, the irony of Judge Madden of all people charging *him* with heresy. He lifted both hands and yanked the white wig from his head, whipping it across the cell. He ran his hands over his face. The punishment for heresy in the Colonies ranged from a few days in the stockades to public hanging depending on severity. Trying to unmask the Judge for fraud in front of the entire town didn't bode well for his chance at only the stockades.

And what of Rebecca? Dear Jesus. Caleb folded his knees up toward his chest and ran his thumbs running over his eyelids. Would he ever see her again? Had she come upon that creature in the woods? Had Constable Hindstall made good on his promise to keep her safe?

Caleb clung to the thought for a few seconds. What would Judge Madden do if he had the chance to question her?

Would Judge Madden round her up with those other women, who'd been herded like cattle through the crowd? And where were they now?

The thought of the Judge going after Rebecca was enough to jolt Caleb to his feet. He paced about in his narrow cell, restless, when excited whoops issued from the outside of his boarded-up jail cell window. Caleb rushed over and peered out of a slit in the shutters. The crowd was dispersing from the gallows in all directions. A group of only twenty or so men rushed forward toward the platform, torches in their hands despite the gray daylight. They shouted with red faces as Asa and Noble cut the Widow's body free of the noose, catching her body as she fell.

"They're going to burn her now."

Caleb spun around to see little Marguerite standing in the hallway behind him. She stood there, arms at her side, her eyes directed at the floor.

"It's what they do to all the witches after they're dead. They're taking her body out into the woods to do it," she said. "That's what happened to my mother." She poked her toe at a spot on the floor and twisted her ankle back and forth.

"I'm sorry."

The child stared at the floor—a question stuck in her throat. She pulled her foot back.

"Was what you said out there the truth?" Her voice was slow and hesitant. She reached down into the pocket of her well-tailored blue coat and pulled out the Judge's vial of teeth.

"Was this really his?" She rolled it slowly between her fingers. "He threw it into his bag after they arrested you. He gave me his bag to hold while they took her body away."

Caleb looked at her tiny face. Her pure white skin. Her perfect, unblemished blue eyes framed with fair eyelashes. Anger burned inside him for her, for the irreversible damage that had been done to the girl's life because of this murderer.

"Yes, it's true." He took a step toward the cell bars. "I found the vial among his things. But I'd noticed he's been misquoting the Bible."

"Anyone can misquote the Bible," she said, turning the vial over in her palm.

Caleb could see the wheels turning in her mind, wondering who to believe. What to believe. He'd seen that look from many.

"Judge Madden is a dangerous man," Caleb said, quietly. He nodded up toward the front of the jail. "You've seen yourself the power he has in every town he holds court in. People die."

She squeezed the bottle in her palm and looked away. He knew she couldn't deny the power the Judge forced over others, not after what she'd seen on the platform.

She looked back at him suddenly. "You don't believe in witchcraft, do you."

It wasn't a question.

"I believe," Caleb paused, "that there is evil in this world. Good and evil. But that it is man—men and women—who can choose to act on that evil. That they have the choice of how to behave, how to treat others. When they make the wrong choices, intentional decisions to harm or destroy, that is evil. The Devil is not the source. The Devil does not make people do things."

Caleb shifted his feet. The Widow's haunting hum and the accusation that her final words had been a spell ran through his mind again. Did he believe in witchcraft? He'd been so certain the Widow was ill, but now...He pushed the thought away.

Marguerite looked down at the tiny vial in her palm again.

"I also believe that Judge Madden has planted evidence in order to get convictions in the past," Caleb continued, softly. "In the Widow's case, she confessed to witchcraft. But the Judge also presented evidence, poppits, that he said had been found in her home. I believe that to be false."

Her eyes snapped back at him. He could tell she hadn't expected this.

She shook her head. "What do you mean? To accuse a Judge of doing such a thing—"

"I know, I know." He held his hands up. "You weren't present for the trial, but you heard Widow Goodness. She said she started worshiping...the Dark One...so she could marry him. There was never a mention during the trial of wanting to harm any individual resident in our town. There were no witnesses to her dark deeds. That's what I believe he used the dolls for. To seal her fate. And to seal the fate of others in the past."

Marguerite stood quiet. She tucked the vial back into her pocket. Caleb knew his next question would change everything. Marguerite would either trust him entirely or turn on him and go running to the Judge with accusations of treason.

"Marguerite, did your mother and grandmother teach you how to make dolls like that? Dolls made of sticks?"

"Dolls made of sticks?" She locked eyes with him, a little scrunched line appearing between her eyes. "I had dolls made of rags. Why?"

Caleb walked up toward the bars and ducked down, putting one knee on the floor so that they were at eye level. "The Judge told me on our way here all about your mother's trial. He told me your testimony about your mother and grandmother was what sealed their fate after the poppits were presented as evidence. That you told the court they'd taught you how to make them."

"I never made those dolls they found." She backed away, shaking her head. "And I never testified in my mother's trial! The Judge told me that my mother confessed!"

"What?"

"I wasn't at the trial. My mother didn't want me there, so my neighbor kept me at their home," Marguerite recalled, as if speaking to herself.

He watched as her own words sank in, as her young mind piecing everything together. Her ears turned red against her blonde braids, her chest began to heave as her breath picked up, deeper and deeper.

Caleb felt his own heart physically hurt in his chest. He knelt down, the bars between them.

"I'm so sorry, my child," he said, offering his hands to her. "Would you like me to pray with you?"

But she hadn't heard. Her brow scrunched and her eyes twitched as tears made their way in, but didn't fall. He could tell she was replaying everything in her mind.

"The Judge lied to me." Her words fell out in a whisper.

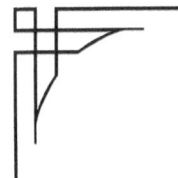
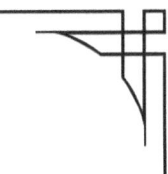

CHAPTER 27
Rebecca

"Stop her up here," Levi said.

Rebecca pulled Chancer to the very edge of the Connecticut forest. The two dropped down off the horse and looked ahead at the small valley that stretched between them and the Hartforde Towne wall. A misty gray fog had sunken into the space like soup in a bowl. Only the brown jagged top of the wall was visible in the distance. Just above the wall to the east, the sun flamed orange, like a miniature canon ball of fire, burning through the dark trees. The sky above them had lightened into a lifeless gray.

"Well. Then. That's it." Rebecca put her hands on her hips and stared in dismay at the burning, undeniable sun. "We're too late."

The deadline had passed for her and Constable Hindstall to bring the body of the Beast back to town to prove her innocence. And instead, the Constable lay dying—if not already dead—back in the cottage in the woods. And the Beast was still on the loose.

"Damn," Levi muttered behind her.

She looked back to see him stooped down, wiping Chancer's fore legs with a handkerchief. Fresh scratches ran up and down both legs, her shins shredded from running through the rough bush. Thin streams of blood trickled down over her right hoof from at least two nicks near her knee, though the horse didn't seem to mind. Levi reached down and scooped up handfuls of snow, wiping away the blood and dabbing at two deeper nicks in the horse's coat.

"Poor girl!" Rebecca said, then looked down at herself. The front and sleeves of her cloak were punctured with pine needles and covered with Constable Hindstall's blood. The bottom of the cloak had been shredded and caked with mud and slush. She shifted her weight, her feet stiff in her boots. She tried to curl her toes, but they were so numb that the movement felt indistinguishable. She took a step, her hips and ankles aching from running for so long on the uneven forest terrain.

Rebecca looked back toward town and the mist in between. She reached up and pushed back her hood, undoing her hair—there was no time to care if Levi saw. She shook it out, pine needles falling everywhere. She wiped off her face. As she did, her finger brushed against a spot on her cheek that felt tender. She dabbed it gingerly with her middle finger, unsure if it was a scratch or a bruise.

"Good Chancer," Levi comforted the horse behind her, rubbing her forehead and muzzle. "Brave Chancer! We'll fix you up, girl. There'll be extra oats for you when this is all over."

Chancer blinked her dark, syrupy eyes and whinnied in response, as if she understood. Rebecca stepped up and gave her muzzle a rub as Levi took her reins and tethered her to the nearest tree. They'd agreed on the route here to leave Chancer on the forest's edge. They'd sneak in through a back way Levi knew of, so they could avoid danger from the mob and head straight for the Widow at the jailhouse. The symbols of protection the Widow had had Hannah set up tethered the Beast to Rebecca's side of the forest on the other side of the road. Chancer should be safe in this part of the forest.

"What now?" Rebecca asked.

Levi stepped past her and Chancer, examining their foggy distance to town. The back of his riding cloak was littered with brambles and pine needles. The wrists of his sleeves were smeared white with gun powder.

"The fog will give us cover. It will conceal her for sure," he said, glancing at the horse. "Not that anyone would be looking out our way right about now, with a hanging going on." Levi crossed his arms over his chest. "You have the *Grimoire?*"

Rebecca nodded as she quickly tied her hair back and yanked up her hood. She pulled the tattered book out of her pocket and held it tightly in her hand. She stared into the fog ahead. "On three?"

He nodded.

"One. Two. Three!"

They took off for the wall, sprinting into the fog-filled valley side by side, Rebecca's frozen feet pounding across the snow-covered field. The Constable's gun, still draped across her back, smacked her in the hip with every other step. She kept her head down as they entered the fog, gray swirling around her, smothering her vision. After, she kept her eyes locked on what she could see up ahead—the murky shadow of the brown barricade of mud and logs that made up the town wall. Levi ran a few steps ahead of her. As they moved, the dark mud lines that separated the log wall grew more visible. Rebecca felt that same awful vulnerability that she'd felt back on the main road washing over her. Being so exposed, out in the open...Anything could jump out of the fog and snatch her.

The closer they puffed to the wall, Rebecca's worries changed to what lay inside town. She could hear the muffled echo of shouts and voices grow louder as they neared. Levi's long legs carried him faster to the wall. He beat her by a few yards and stood there, panting and waiting.

"We're too late! That's too much noise for this time of day," she yelled ahead to Levi. He ducked down and pushed in two loose boards that acted as a patch at the base of the wall.

"My brothers and I sneak out of town through here." He paused, thumping a fist on them. "An old mare my father was shoeing crashed into this spot here. My brother Abe was supposed to fix it, but—" He sunk to his knees and crawled inside first, then held the boards open for Rebecca to follow.

She climbed through and stood up to find herself in the deserted alley that ran between the town wall and the back of the first row of buildings. The interior of town was dim. The surrounding buildings were tall and blocked out a lot of dawn's light.

"This way." Levi nodded to their left. She followed him through the filthy alley, which was crowded with snow-covered crates and stunk of garbage.

"Maybe we aren't too late?" she whispered. Somewhere in the alley behind them, a donkey brayed.

"We'll see," Levi said over his shoulder. "It's just a bit this way."

She followed him, hurrying past the rear of the hay bailer's, which was crowded with bundles of hay covered and wrapped for the winter and piled with snow. They moved on past the rear of the shipbuilder's warehouse, a handful of snow-dusted canoes propped up behind it. Levi paused for an instant at the next building—a dark wood two-story with a double chimney, all lights blazing inside—long enough to look back at her and nod up toward it. She could hear the muffled metal clang of a hammer coming from deep inside the first floor. Levi's father's blacksmithery. They continued moving on past a thatched roof house with a pair of crows perched on its steaming chimney and stopped at the rear of the jailhouse.

Rebecca had only seen the front of the jailhouse a handful of times on her visits to town with Caleb. From the front, it was an aging stone and mud structure with barred up windows. But from the back, it looked as if it could come toppling down at any minute.

Rebecca padded up to the backdoor and put an ear to it, listening for any commotion inside. Levi hung back, keeping watch for any approaching neighbors.

Hearing no noise from inside the jail, Rebecca looked back at Levi and shrugged. She slowly pushed against the backdoor, the metallic sound of the lock clicking. Unbolted. Rebecca paused, expecting some reaction to the door opening, her pulse quickening. But no reaction came. Finally, something in their favor. She gripped the *Grimoire* and the Constable's gun—ready to hand them both over as evidence so she wouldn't be immediately arrested—and nudged the door open farther. She slipped a foot inside.

She turned and exchanged a look with Levi, who stood behind her. He pulled his wolf-skin cap off his head and ran a hand through his brown hair in an attempt to tidy it, suddenly looking his age in such a serious place.

"Hello? Sirs?" Rebecca called to no response. She pushed the door all the way open and found herself in a small stone lobby behind a wooden desk. Levi stepped in behind her. She'd expected the jail to be brimming with people, guards, the Judge—but the lobby was empty and still—save a solitary lantern glimmering on the table and a fire blazing away in the fireplace.

"Hello?" she called, louder. Rebecca pivoted, looking toward the corridor that she assumed led to the cells, and listened for any signs of life. Just then, a loud bang landed on the front door of the jail, followed by a laugh. Had something been thrown, or had someone's fist caused the noise? Something stiffened in Rebecca's gut as she froze, waiting for the front door to push open.

"Rebecca?"

She turned toward the corridor on her left. Her mind couldn't process the voice she'd just heard.

"Caleb?"

"Back here!"

She pivoted and rushed toward the jail's cells.

"Levi!" she called over her shoulder. "We aren't too late! My husband's here! He—" Rebecca's words left her when the last cell came into view. She'd expected to see her husband sitting at counsel at the Widow's side in a cell. Instead, Caleb stood behind bars himself, his arms bound in front of him. His white wig and cassock were discarded in one corner of the floor, leaving him dressed in his normal black pants, white shirt, and plain black-buttoned waistcoat. Deep crevasses were etched underneath Caleb's reddened eyes, making him look as if he'd aged a decade.

"Caleb! Good Lord! What happened?" She rushed over, Levi following behind.

Caleb hurried to the cell bars, holding his bound hands up in front of him. "Rebecca, darling!" His eyes widened at the sight of her. "Is that blood?"

He gripped her fingers through the bars.

"It's the Constable's. He's hurt. You've no idea what's happened to us tonight. The Beast is real. Men are dead. The Constable is in trouble. And the Widow, she—"

Caleb tightened his fingers around hers. "Listen, you must get away from here! The Judge has had me arrested!"

"Arrested for what?"

"Heresy!" Caleb glanced over her shoulder at Levi and the boy nodded. There would be time for introductions later.

She looked at him with disbelief. "But that's absurd!"

Caleb hushed his voice. "I confronted the Judge. We were right, he's been planting evidence in trials, not just in this one—and not just in the Martins' either. There have been more. Many more."

"I can't leave." Rebecca glanced at the empty cells around him. "And I won't leave you! And besides, we've come for the Widow. She's the only one who can stop the Beast. We must get this to her!" She held up the beat-up *Grimoire*. "It's her spell book."

"A spell book?" Caleb looked at her. "Rebecca, didn't you hear what I just said? None of this witchcraft business is real. It's the Judge! He's been using the law and speculation and planted evidence—and the fear of the people— to murder these women!"

Rebecca dropped her hands from his. "Not in this case, Caleb! You haven't seen what I've seen," she said. "Look, I'll explain everything later, but right now we need to get to the Widow. We need her to read a counter curse in order to—"

Caleb waved his bound hands to stop her. "Rebecca, the Widow is already dead!"

"Dead? But we need her! Hannah—the Widow's servant—told me that the Widow's voice and *her voice* alone can destroy the creature!"

"The Widow was hanged thirty minutes ago," Caleb said. "Everyone's gone off to see her body burned."

"What are we going to do?" She pivoted to Levi. "How are we going to stop it now?"

"Where's the Constable?" Caleb said, his eyes roaming over the Constable's gun strung over Rebecca's back. "Have they captured the thing? Found what it really is?"

She turned to face Caleb, her face flushing. "It's a demon, Caleb. A demon! And no, the hunting party hasn't returned with me. Most of them are dead!" Her voice cracked. She turned in a circle, arms raised. "Look at me! I've been chased through a forest. The horse I left the church on was pulled out from underneath me and killed. I saw a man get torn to pieces—" The tone of her voice heightened. "It's a Beast. A Blood Demon. And you don't understand how dangerous that thing is. Bullets don't stop it. We shot at it—I shot at it—again and again, and it did nothing! It chased Levi and me through the woods and halfway here, and we barely escaped. The Constable—" She held his musket up. "I'm not certain he's even alive anymore. And Cooke. And Banks. And the horses! Caleb—"

Caleb opened his mouth to speak again, but Rebecca handed the gun to Levi and held up the Widow's *Grimoire*, flipping through it. "It's here, see." She pointed at the sketch of the Blood Demon. "I have a drawing of it, from the book the Widow used to summon it. Here, look. That's exactly it."

Rebecca watched him as his eyes ran over the words, a wrinkle appearing between his brow. She shoved the book to him through the bars. "Don't tell me the Beast isn't real," she continued, watching Caleb examine the book, holding it precariously between his bound hands.

"Where is the servant?" Caleb asked.

"Where's the servant?" Rebecca repeated, her tone rising. "Stuck in a cottage in the woods. She's there caring for the Constable. They can't leave. The Beast—the Blood Demon—is tethered to the woods around it."

Caleb studied the ugly sketches of monstrous creatures in the tattered *Grimoire*.

"Caleb, what do we do?" Rebecca begged. "If you don't believe in witchcraft, don't believe the Widow or any of this, that's fine." She leaned forward and gripped the bars with both hands. "But as your wife, I need you to believe me."

"She's telling the truth sir. Reverend, I mean," Levi piped in from behind her. "Anything she says I can testify to as well. I've hunted in these woods for years and have never seen anything like it."

Caleb glanced at Levi over Rebecca's shoulder.

Rebecca stared at Caleb. "Can you believe me?"

Caleb closed the *Grimoire* and looked off into the corner, chewing the inside of his cheek.

He sighed. "All right."

"All right?"

Caleb stepped back from the bars, nodding his head, studying his bound hands. "These are things I've never faced. The Widow, before her death, she...I don't know what she did, but it terrified everyone."

"So what do we do now?"

He looked back at her. "I think you need to run."

"I can't leave you! I won't!"

"If you truly believe what this servant said, what this book is...that doesn't change the fact the Widow's dead," Caleb said. "She can't help you, and Judge Madden surely won't. I'm locked in here. The Constable is trapped. There's no one left."

"That's not necessarily true," a small voice said.

Rebecca jumped at the sound. She turned to see a young girl sitting atop a stool just inside the door of another cell, the door propped open. A thick book sat on her lap. Rebecca had been in such a rush to follow Caleb's voice, she must've missed the girl on her way in.

"Marguerite?" Caleb called through the bars. "You're still here?"

The girl rose and walked toward them. Her blonde braids were the neatest Rebecca had seen since she'd arrived in the colony. The girl's eyes were red, and her lips were pinched in a tight straight line.

"Who is this?" Rebecca asked, almost afraid to take her eyes off the girl. She felt wary of trusting anyone other than Caleb and Levi at this point. Even a child.

"Miss Marguerite Cross," Caleb said. Rebecca was surprised at the calmness in his voice. "She's the Judge's ward."

Rebecca glanced at Caleb to see if he was serious. "His ward?"

"She travels with him to help identify witches, and until recently, she believed the Judge to be a just man."

"I know just about everything there is to know about witchcraft," Marguerite said. "You say the Widow summoned a demon? Is that what she called it? A demon?"

Rebecca nodded stiffly, eyeing the little girl and wondering how the word "demon" could come out of such a young thing, so calmly. "That's what her servant called it, yes. A Blood Demon."

"If it is a demon, I may know how you can stop it." Marguerite hoisted up a thick book in front of her. "I have instructions on how to destroy a demon—in here."

"They're the Church's instructions," Caleb said.

"The Church has instructions on this?" Rebecca said.

The girl pushed the book into Rebecca's hands and cracked it open, turning the pages. She stopped at page one hundred, ninety-eight. Unlike the *Grimoire*, the girl's book was finely bound, with the title *Malleus Maleficarum* embossed in gold across its tan hide cover.

"Here," the girl said, peering over the edge of the book. Rebecca lowered it so she could see. Sure enough, a heading in bold black typeface read, "Diminishment of Demonic Beings."

Caleb pressed himself against the cell bars, peering down at it.

"Caleb, what is this book?" Rebecca asked.

He exhaled. "It's a prescription to rid the world of witchcraft. I wasn't familiar with it before tonight. It was written by the Catholic Church, but somehow also approved and used for use by the Protestant Church. It appears to be legitimate, at least in the eyes of the Particular Court."

She met his eyes.

"Apparently they're already using it throughout Europe."

"See." The girl pointed to handwritten notes in the margin of the page. "There are specific prayers you can say, biblical passages that should help you destroy the demon, if she really did summon one."

"It's Latin." Rebecca scanned the text, picking out a few words here and there.

"There's English translation scribbled in the margin," Caleb said, looking over Rebecca's shoulder at the page.

"Can you read it?" the girl asked.

"Rebecca can read Latin better than I can," Caleb said. He leaned against the cell door.

"My family had a very old Latin Bible when I was growing up." Rebecca looked back at Caleb. "But I always preferred the English." She ran her finger down the page, shifting the book in the light. "Luckily, Latin's pretty easy to pronounce. Diabolus, devil? Mortem, death? Christus, Christ?" She put her fingers to her lips, not believing what she was seeing. "So, most of the Christian world not only agrees that witches and demons are real, but that one can follow these steps to stop them?"

She looked down at Marguerite. "So, if my husband sees the Beast—the demon—and recites these specific prayers here." She pointed to a passage set in block text. "You believe he can rid the forest of the demon?"

"How can I? I'm locked in here." Caleb raised his wrists.

"We'll have to have them let you out!" Rebecca said, folding the book closed, her thumb marking the page.

He shook his head. "Judge Madden won't listen. If he sees you, he'll arrest you, too!"

"Then we'll break you out!" She turned to Levi. "Go and look for a key or something to pry the bars open with."

"You have no time," Caleb said. "Listen, the crowd's getting louder."

Levi dashed up to the lobby and peered out a window. "They're on their way back. Two of Hindstall's men and several jail guards."

"She'll have to do it," Marguerite said, pointing at Rebecca.

"Oh, no!" Rebecca stammered. "My husband, he's the Reverend—"

"I'm about to go on trial for heresy, remember?" Caleb said. "The girl is right. The Judge could return at any moment." He stepped up to the cell bars, leaning in toward Rebecca. "Even if I could break out of here, they'll come looking for me. Looking for us both. As far as they know, you're not here. You're still out on the hunt for the Beast."

"You can do this," the girl said, not taking her eyes off Rebecca. "A Reverend isn't needed to follow the directions in the *Maleficarum*. A woman can. Preferably a White Witch."

"A what?" Rebecca recoiled.

"A White Witch." The girl nodded, her expression serious. "They exist as well. They've been given powers by God to help others."

"A White Witch? What do you mean?" Caleb said through the jail cell bars. "My wife is no witch!"

"White Witches are different—they are women who have some kind of special ability, like a knack for healing others, or the ability to foresee certain elements of the future."

"I have no special abilities. Certainly not the gift of healing." Rebecca held up her hands, which were riddled with scratches. "It has to be my husband!"

"Rebecca! Reverend! They're a bit closer now and the Judge is with them—but the Judge has stopped and is shaking hands with people," Levi called from the lobby.

"Your special ability can be your faith," the girl said. "It might work. If you can read the passages and, I assume you know the Bible well enough."

"So, the Church persecutes witches, but this White Witch—it's something that's considered okay?"

Everyone stood quiet for an instant. The sound of men's laughter grew louder outside.

Caleb looked at the little girl. "Excuse us a moment?"

Marguerite nodded, then bent and picked up the Widow's tattered *Grimoire* at Rebecca's feet. She turned and ran back to the Constable's desk at the front of the jailhouse. Rebecca waited until she heard a squeak of the wooden chair, then spoke.

"You seriously want me to try this? Go back into the forest?" She leaned into the cell bars, gripping them with both hands. "What if this book is wrong?"

"It might be."

"What if I can't stop it? What if I fail?"

Caleb studied the ground for a minute. "Rebecca, I'd be fooling you if I said at this point that I knew what danger was. It's dangerous for you to go back into those woods. But it's also dangerous for you to stay here. No one here in the Colony is powerful enough to stop that Judge. He does what he wants." Caleb wrapped the fingers of both his tethered hands around one of hers. "But the last thing I want is to see my wife hanged before I die."

"Stop."

"I also know it's dangerous out there." He nodded his chin toward the jail's backdoor. "I haven't seen the Beast, but I do believe you. Look at you. Look at the boy who brought you here, he's just as shaken as you are. It's all over his face."

Rebecca looked back up the hall at the girl, oddest of them all, who was paging through the Widow's *Grimoire* with great interest. Rebecca looked down at the *Malleus Malificarum* the girl had swapped her for in her hands. She lowered her tone. "But the Bible condemns witchcraft. How can the Church also prescribe becoming a—" She couldn't finish the sentence.

"A White Witch?"

"Well, isn't it sacrilegious?" she whispered to Caleb.

Caleb took a deep breath and looked down at his hands. His thumb dug into the loose end of the rope's knot.

"Do you remember the story of David and Goliath?"

Rebecca pulled her hand away. "You're going to compare that to this!"

"You're right, I'm not. Think about what happened just before that story. Goliath was fighting for King Saul. King Saul was so terrified his army would lose the war that he—"

"Sought out a witch," Rebecca finished.

"Exactly. In First Samuel, Chapter Twenty-Eight." Caleb nodded. "Saul sought a medium to speak to the dead and find out what the outcome of the war would be before it even started. There are dozens of references in the Bible to witchcraft, sorcery, necromancy, spells. The Judge only shared the ones that referred to killing witches, not using them."

She gripped the *Maleficarum* with both her hands, pulling it against her chest and curling her fingers over the top.

He looked deeply at her. "My faith is shaken, Rebecca. With the Widow and the Beast and the Judge—and now what you've gone through." He took a step back in the cell. "I feel as if my mind is a mess." He put a finger to his lips. "What's the difference? What's the difference between a spell and a prayer? Both are utterances of words asking for help to control something we cannot. What's the difference between a medium and a prophet? Both are sought out to seek answers—prophet after prophet was praised in the Bible for foreseeing the future, including Jesus."

"While witches were condemned for doing the same," Rebecca realized. She held the *Malleus Malificarum* in her hand, turning it over and over again. "Simple words for the same things. One word can get you killed. The other earns you praise."

"Luke, Chapter Eleven—" Caleb started.

Rebecca raised her head. "Jesus cast out a demon out of a mute man, enabling him to speak. But I'm not Jesus. How can I be certain that if I try this, God won't be angry with me?"

"Rebecca! Reverend! They're coming this way!" Levi called from the lobby.

"Faith," Caleb hurried. "Faith is the only thing we can rely on now. What does your faith tell you is right, my love?" He raised his tethered hands up. "If God has destined me to be in here and you to be out there, what is right?"

Or what is brave, she wanted to say.

"I love you, Caleb." She pressed her fingers down on his through the bars, then turned back toward Marguerite, who sat up at the Constable's desk, staring into the pages of the Widow's *Grimoire*.

Rebecca walked toward her. "I'm going back for the Beast," she called. "What do I have to do?"

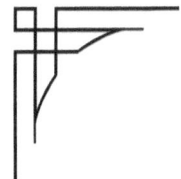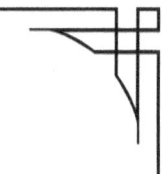

CHAPTER 28
Rebecca

Rebecca crept out the backdoor of the jailhouse—the copy of Marguerite's *Malleus Malificarum* tucked tight under her arm—and headed up toward the loosened boards to meet Levi outside the wall. He'd run ahead to grab more ammunition, rope, and anything else that might be useful to them, while the bizarre Marguerite had shown her exactly where in the book to find instructions on how to destroy a demon.

Rebecca kept her head down and walked with purpose toward Levi's secret exit. She glanced down at her feet, watching as her black boots propelled her steps forward in the white snow that covered the alley. She felt an invisible leash pull her back with each step—sick that she was leaving Caleb behind to such an unknown fate. Would she ever see him again?

Rebecca pulled her hood down over her cheeks, just in case she came upon someone, and continued forward. She passed the old houses, eyed Levi's father's blacksmithery in the chance that Levi hadn't departed yet, but there was no sound or sight of him. The metallic banging she'd heard coming from inside previously had also ceased. She traced Levi's tracks in the snow up past the shipbuilder's and the hay bailer's, to where they seemingly disappeared into the wall. She stood at the wall for a few seconds, listening to the quiet in the alley, making sure she was alone. There was no sign of anyone coming in either direction.

She tugged the two loose boards inward toward her shins and lifted them high enough to duck down and step under.

"That her?" a man's voice said from outside the wall before Rebecca had a chance to get her entire self through.

The remark struck a jolt of shock to her heart, and she froze—crouched half in, half out of the wall.

"Shh!" a second voice, deeper than the first, said. "Levi said to keep quiet, you half-wit! Father will hear!"

Levi?

The boards slipped backwards over her shoulder, and Rebecca stepped outside the wall. Before her stood two brown trotter horses, held by boys about Levi's age, give or take a year. Each looked like an alternative version of Levi with the same brown hair and brown eyes, but the older one stood short and stocky, his arms crossed over his chest in a wall of muscle. Thick whiskers stretched across his jaw. The other boy, maybe younger than Levi, stretched a bit taller with thicker eyebrows and a long face—and like Levi, his cheeks were completely bare of whiskers. They both wore weather-beaten cloaks with guns draped across their backs.

"If we're really going to do this, we're going to need help," Levi said, a pant in his voice.

Rebecca stepped to the side and saw Levi marching Chancer out of the fog behind the boys' horses. "These are my brothers. Abe," he nodded to the older one, then to the younger, "and Josiah."

"Hello!" they said in unison. Levi stopped beside them, now wearing a clean coat and fur hat. He threw Rebecca a dark maroon man's cloak.

"How on earth did you get horses so quick?" she asked, shedding her bloodstained one for the new option. She tossed it at the base of the wall and slipped into the clean one.

"Abe and Josiah rode them out—no one would suspect them," Levi said. "I ran back for Chancer."

Just then, a third and obviously much younger boy with a shock of unruly black curls, scurried out from behind one of the horse's legs.

"I'm going, too!" The boy stood before Rebecca with his lips pinched shut, his arms crossed dramatically over his chest.

"Who's this?" she asked. The little boy's hair stuck up nearly on end. Freckles shaded his nose and forehead.

"Charles," Josiah groaned.

The boy grinned, one of his front teeth missing.

Levi looked down at him and continued. "He's seven years old and he's going back home and has promised to keep quiet."

Charles looked back at Levi, his eyes pinched and full of disagreement. "I am not! If you're all going on a hunt, I want to go, too!"

The older brother, Abe, ducked down to his level. "But we need you to do something really important—we need you to keep a secret! A real one! You must stay at home in case Father comes looking for us. Tell him we've gone off hunting with some friends and don't know when we'll be back."

"Yeah," Josiah said. "And you've got to promise. A brother's vow!"

"A brother's vow?" Charles whined.

"Aye, a brother's vow," Levi said.

"Remember, if you break it, all your hair falls off," Josiah said.

"Fine," Charles scowled. "A brother's vow then!"

"Now back inside with you before Father wonders where we've all gone," Levi said.

Little Charles sighed and stamped his feet a few steps to the town wall, then disappeared as quickly as a rabbit underneath the loose panels.

"Levi, are you certain you want to get your brothers involved in this?" Rebecca said, buttoning the new cloak up to her throat. "You know how dangerous it is."

"He didn't have a choice," Josiah said, climbing up on his horse, his boots squeaking in the leather stirrups. "He told us that the Judge who sentenced that woman to die has been a real king-pisser to you and the Reverend."

"Yeah, and we caught Levi trying to steal our guns off the back porch," Abe added.

"Abe!" Levi scolded.

"Anyway, the whole town's gone off," Josiah said, settling into his saddle and pulling a pair of leather gloves on. "Why'd anyone want to watch a lady get killed?"

"Ahh, don't listen to him. He's gone soft because he's betrothed." Abe rolled his eyes as he mounted his horse. "I want to hunt this thing down. It obviously came after our brother, bad. I mean, look at him!"

Levi frowned and smoothed down his unruly brown hair.

Rebecca looked at the boys. South Puritan had burned their house down, and yet here they were, offering her their help. Seeing these brave and healthy boys in front of her made her feel even worse about what her church had done to them.

"It's going to be dangerous," she said, holding her hands up. "I'm grateful for your help, but please understand that this is...a demon we're chasing. Not a wolf or a bear or another animal you're used to hunting. It can't be killed. It has to be...destroyed."

"And you've got to listen to us both." Levi pointed a finger from himself to Rebecca. "If one of us tells you to stop, duck, run, leave us to save yourselves, whatever, you must do it."

"I think we can manage to take orders from you, brother," Abe said, crossing his wrists over each other and glancing over at Josiah with a crooked smile on his face. "For once in our lives, anyway."

"So, what's the plan?" Josiah said.

"Levi and I will lure it out of the woods and onto the main road," Rebecca said. "We must make sure it doesn't turn and make a run for town. Everyone is within the town walls because of the hanging. We can't let it get there."

Abe scratched his chin. "What'll you use as bait?"

Rebecca released an exhale she didn't know she'd been holding. "Me. We'll use me."

"And me," Levi said.

"Levi—" Rebecca started.

"There's a reason."

Josiah brushed his hair out of his eyes with a gloved hand. "You can't be serious!"

Rebecca looked down at the *Malificarum* in her hands. "We've seen it run. We've seen it kill. I know it, certainly more than either of you."

"Really, it should be one of us to go after it," Josiah said. "Abe is strong as an ox. I'm the best shot in town and you two...well, you look hard terrible."

"She's right," Levi said. "It will chase her. And me." He turned to Rebecca. "The little girl back in the jailhouse showed me some notes in the Widow's *Grimoire*. It seems the most valuable kind of blood to the Beast is the blood of the unbaptized. That's me."

"Aye, whatcha mean?" Abe sat up straight on his horse.

"The creature we're hunting is a Blood Demon. It hunts by blood," Rebecca said. "We're not sure if it can hear it or smell it—or just sense it—but the blood of the unbaptized would be more valuable to it."

"Why's that?" Josiah asked.

"Unbaptized blood is the blood of a living being whose soul hadn't been dedicated to God yet," she said.

"So, it would have the chance to be dedicated to someone else," Abe finished.

Levi squinted up at him. "You're the oldest. I'm pretty sure you were the only one of us who was baptized, Abe."

"He's probably right. Because of the fire," Josiah said, tugging his horse still, "Father never took us back again."

Rebecca looked from boy to boy, the level of danger feeling like it was flaring up even more. She knew she'd be traveling into the woods with the most attractive type of blood to the Blood Demon.

The others sensed it too. They stared at the ground for a few seconds. Only the horses moved.

"So, it's off to the woods then," Levi said, his tone resolute. He took a step forward, pulling Chancer over and ducking down on one knee. He put his hand out for Rebecca to use as leverage to climb up.

"No," Rebecca said, adjusting the *Malleus Malificarum* under her arm and placing a foot up on his palms. "We need to make a stop at South Puritan first."

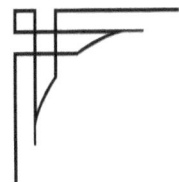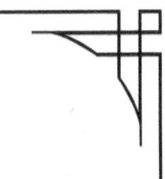

CHAPTER 29
Caleb

Caleb sat alone in his cell, elbows on his knees, hands tethered. He stared at a beam of light that filtered in through the window in what had been the Widow's cell across from him. How had his entire world shifted in less than a day? How many innocent lives had been put at risk in just a matter of hours?

"Marguerite?" he called. No response. She'd walked Rebecca to the backdoor but hadn't returned.

Caleb felt his stomach growl, his midsection hollow with hunger. He ignored the sensation—as well as the ache of his bladder—and stood up, stretching.

This time yesterday, he'd been sitting at home, paging through Deuteronomy in preparation for his next sermon. Rebecca had been cooking stew and the whole house had smelled of it. The memory of the smell made his mouth water. And now, not even a day later, Hartforde Towne would be known for having a witch. And instead of making history as the youngest reverend in Connecticut Colony, he'd be remembered as the town reverend who was hanged for heresy.

He sighed. The Widow was dead, and he'd just sent his precious wife off to fight a battle he had no control over. Their goodbye had been gut wrenching. Would he live to see her again? Would she?

He closed his eyes and pictured her face: her smooth white skin, the cheeks he loved to caress, her dark hair and how she let it fall wavy and long in their bedroom just before she laid down to sleep. He pictured her as she often was, running to and from the fireplace cooking supper, singing. She was always singing. Sometimes hymns, sometimes tunes she just made up. Could he still hear the gentle tone of her voice in his mind? He tried and couldn't.

Caleb stared across the way at the Widow's cell. What would he do if Judge Madden tried to hang him? He pictured himself standing on the rickety boards of the gallows, Judge Madden slipping that noose over his neck to the cheer of the crowd, piss and rotten vegetables being flung through the air. Would he try to run? Fight? He put his head in his hands. His heart rattled in his chest.

Outside the jail cell walls, the people had begun chanting again, words he couldn't make out. A bottle smashed near his jail cell window.

Caleb closed his eyes and automatically recalled—as he always did on the occasion when he felt his temper rising out of control—that Jesus said in the Book of Matthew to turn the other cheek to violence. Love thy neighbor. Do not retaliate. But what if it was a violent act that prevented his death at the hands of an evil man? Or an action that prevented Rebecca's death? That question was too much. It pushed its way into Caleb's mind, filling him with an uneasy mix of despair and worry and anger all at once. He glared at the bars in front of him that separated him from Rebecca, and from freedom and fresh air that the evil Judge right now enjoyed without a thought.

"Ahhh!" Caleb screamed. He ran across the cell, ramming his body against the jail cell door as hard as he could. The bars rattled, but didn't budge. He stepped back, panting.

Just then, his ears perked at the rattle at the jailhouse's front door. A rush of cold air swept down the corridor, followed by the sound of boisterous men's voices and the wooden clatter of guns being re-racked by the desk.

"The old girl really went up in flames, didn't she, if you know what I mean, eh?"

The voice was slurred. They'd been drinking.

"I'd never seen a body burn before. Not intentionally, anyway," said another.

"I'm glad to be done with it," complained a third.

"Still, something to tell the wife and children about, yeah?" the first voice said.

Their glee over the Widow's death made Caleb's stomach felt like it had been placed in a vice. He put his face up to the cell bars, looking down the corridor as far as he could see.

The shorter of Constable Hindstall's men, who had been guarding the outside of the jailhouse before the hanging, took note of him and meandered down to his cell. His nose was flushed red and his breath stunk of ale since the last time Caleb had seen him barking orders at the crowd. "Any sign of the Constable yet, Reverend? Or should I say...inmate?" The guard broke into laughter, slapped his thigh, and pointed back toward the others.

"Leave him alone!" a voice called from the lobby. Asa's voice.

The front door opened again. The men immediately hushed.

"That was a magnificent burning, gentlemen," Judge Madden's voice boomed as he addressed the guards. "You should be proud of yourselves."

"Normally, we'd ask Constable Hindstall this, Judge, but are we to leave the gallows up, or shall we tear them down?" Asa asked. His tone was tired.

The Judge's voice grew louder as he neared the corridor. "Leave them up for now," he called over his shoulder. "I have more people to consider. Witchcraft does travel from one female to another, you know."

"Speaking of, sir," the short drunk said, his tone hushing. "Don't we need to be cleansed or blessed or whatever by the Reverend? We were the ones who touched her, after all."

"In time, in time. Let's make sure the hangings are done for the day first."

Caleb eyed him through the cell bars as he got closer, but as the Judge's pace picked up, it was clear it wasn't Caleb he was looking for.

"Marguerite?" Judge Madden called, heading past Caleb's cell. "Child, where are you? Your talents are needed now. I've rounded up some potential others for you to take a look at. There were some women out there who attempted to protest the hanging and—"

So that's why they were rounded up. Marguerite had told Caleb the truth. She hadn't identified anyone else.

Judge Madden walked clear past Caleb's cell, his boots squeaking to a stop. He pivoted and called back to the guards. "My ward, the little girl who sat here reading before. Where is she?"

"I haven't seen her, sir, since right after the hanging," Asa said.

"Me neither," another replied.

The Judge launched himself back down the hallway. "Well, go and look for her," he shouted. "All of you! I need her! Now! And don't think of returning without her!"

"Yes, Judge," the short, drunk guard said, followed by a shuffling of boots and a creak of the front door.

The Judge paused in the hallway, just past Caleb's cell. At the sound of the front door closing, he made a sound of disgust, wiping a hand over his face. "Idiots."

He turned toward Caleb, narrowing his icy eyes at him.

"You." He reached deep into his pocket. Caleb watched as he pulled out the jailhouse key ring, rammed a key into Caleb's cell door, and turned it, the lock clicking. "Come! Now!"

The Judge swung the door open, but Caleb hesitated, shifting on his feet.

"I said, now! Outside with you!"

Caleb held his bound hands up. "Judge, you can't hang me without a trial. It's unjust. No one will stand for it!"

"You and I are going to have a little discussion," the Judge said, reaching into his pocket again. He pulled out a dagger, the same one Caleb had found hidden inside the Judge's Bible. Someone must've grabbed Caleb's satchel and given it to the Judge after he'd been thrown in the cell, no doubt.

Judge Madden pointed the dagger at him.

"I said...*now*."

Caleb took a tentative step forward. The Judge grabbed him under one arm and thrust him forward, rushing him past the other jail cells and up into the lobby. There on the Constable's desk lay the rest of Caleb's belongings, his Last Supper items, his satchel, and the Judge's Bible, stacked on top of his.

"Outside," the Judge said. Instead of pushing him toward the front door, he shoved him toward the backdoor, his hand thrusting Caleb over the threshold and out into the alley behind the jail. The lane was empty, dusted over with a light coat of snow. Caleb was thankful there were no footprints, no evidence Rebecca had ever been back here.

Judge Madden followed him out, pushing him up the alley, a few buildings away from the jailhouse.

Caleb spun around. "Judge, do you really intend to use that little girl to try and charge more women in this town? Don't you understand what the first hanging has done? You saw them yourself!"

Judge Madden still had his blade pointed at him. "You accused me of being a witch hunter. In front of everyone."

Caleb closed his mouth. The Judge shoved him away, the dagger still pointed at him.

"I found my Bible after they threw you in jail. Mine. It was wrapped in your extra cassock you'd brought from town. You stole it and had it in your hands the whole time."

Caleb glanced past him, willing someone—anyone—to walk in on the Judge's mad conversation.

"And you found my bottle. Trying to be bold, aren't you? I have..." He tilted his head. "I have something to show you." The Judge passed the knife from one hand to the other as he dug into his other pocket. He pulled out something tiny and held it up. Caleb blinked. The Judge stomped forward, shoving the object inches from his nose. It was another tooth; this one with all four roots still attached, the bottom tip of one root nicked.

It smelled of fresh blood.

"Do you see this?" He rolled the tooth back and forth slowly between his fingers in Caleb's face. "This is all that's left of your Widow now. Do you understand? I destroy evil! I'm not sure what you hoped to accomplish by performing theatrics back on the gallows, because I can always start again." He put the tooth back into his pocket and shrugged, speaking slowly. "If I want to use the dead women's hair as stuffing for my pillow, I will do so. I can do whatever I want."

Caleb's stomach turned at the vileness of the Judge's threat, but he stood his ground, determined not to let his fear show. "But why do you do it? Keep souvenirs of the dead?"

"Because that's where evil women belong." The Judge squinted, the point of the knife tapping against the outside of Caleb's black waistcoat. "Forever at the mercy of those who would dare to bring them to task."

A very light *clang, clang, clang!* started up from the back of one of the nearby businesses. Caleb shuffled a slow step back, deeper into the alley, hoping to step out into the sightline of a neighbor or shopkeeper.

"And your knife?" Caleb said, glancing down at the dark blade. He must stall long enough for someone to walk by, hear them in the alley. "What's so special about it that it had a place in your book?"

"I killed my first witch with it," Judge Madden said, not blinking. He pulled the knife back and turned it over in his hand, admiring it. "When the rope snapped at her hanging, I slit her throat with it." He sneaked a look up at Caleb. "What do you think about that?"

"I think you're going to hell," Caleb said.

The Judge's prideful face collapsed, his features narrowing with anger as he lunged at Caleb.

"Ahhh!" Caleb jumped back, but not before Judge Madden's blade stabbed into the side of his belly, right underneath his ribs. Caleb looked down, stunned, at the blade sticking half in and half out of the darkening spot on his waistcoat. He felt lightheaded.

"Help!" Caleb yelled as the Judge yanked Caleb toward him, holding him shoulder to shoulder as he shoved the blade in deeper and held it there. The Judge twisted the dagger in the side of Caleb's belly, once, twice, again. The pain seared through Caleb's entire left side, from the base of his rib all the way down to the top of his hip.

"To hell with you, Reverend," Judge Madden whispered. "And remember who sent you there."

Caleb felt the blood pour out of him—warm and sticky and awful—a living part of his body, drifting away, defying him. He wavered on his feet a few seconds. Then collapsed in the snowy alley. The shadow of Judge Madden hovered over him.

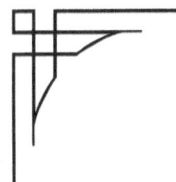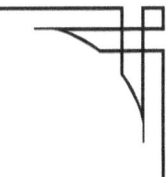

CHAPTER 30
Caleb

Caleb opened his eyes to find himself lying on his side, half of his face mushed in the damp dirt of the alley behind the jail. He put a hand up to his belly and twisted his head around, looking for any sign of the Judge.

Around, the buildings were silent. Snowflakes fluttered down on him, blurring his vision. He was alone.

Caleb made a weak attempt to move, but the pain in his side was searing. The throb that radiated between his ribs was so strong that he wondered if the Judge had left the dagger stuck in there.

Caleb faintly tapped the wounded area with his fingers and winced at the pain. His waistcoat felt heavy with blood, but there was no knife left as far as he could tell. Caleb ran his tongue quickly over his teeth, relieved to feel all of them accounted for. He laid his head back down. The sky above was gray and heavy with snow. How long had he been left to die?

Farther up the alley, the metallic *clang, clang, clang!* started again.

Caleb rolled onto his one good side and used his right elbow and thigh to squirm through the dirty snow up toward the source of the noise. He'd passed two old houses after he'd walked out of the jail with the Judge. He knew the next building was the hay bailer's, which was stacked with squares of hay, but there was no sign of life. He continued his awkward crawl, pausing now and then to set his head back on the ground when the dizziness set in. Caleb struggled to pull himself up to the next structure—a two-story building that looked like a converted business and home—with lights on inside.

"Help! Please!" he yelled. A wave of dizziness hit him between the eyes, and he rolled onto his back. As he did, the clanging stopped. A few seconds later, a husky man with a wide black beard stepped out the backdoor holding a hammer clutched in his fist.

The man froze—an appropriately startled look on his face at the sight of Caleb laying before his feet.

"Good sir, please! I need help!" Caleb said, looking down at his side. Blood flowed out in an even stream, and had, the entire distance of his crawl, painting a bloody trail in the white snow.

The man stepped out into the alley, sliding the grip of the hammer through the side of his belt. His eyes darted quickly in the direction Caleb had dragged himself and nodded.

"Let's be quick, Reverend."

"Thank you!" Caleb looked the stranger over, certain he was not a member of South Puritan. He wore a thick blacksmith's apron. Black smears marked up his fingers. A shiny pink line—a long-healed burn— marked the back of his wrist.

The blacksmith knelt down, pulling a rag from his apron pocket, and pressed it on the wound.

"Hold this here, now."

"Oh, thank you!" Caleb said.

"Can you stand?" the man asked.

"I'm afraid I may need help."

The man stooped down and slid one thick arm underneath Caleb's shoulder. Caleb gritted his back teeth as the man helped him to his feet, holding back a scream. He said a silent prayer that his insides would stay where God had intended them as he pushed himself up onto his feet. When the blacksmith finished helping him up, a young boy with curly black hair broke out of the house's backdoor toward them in a run, the door slamming behind him.

"Charles! What did I say?" the man barked. "Stay in the house! They're hanging people in town! Lord, it's enough that your brothers have run off with Levi! Left me with three times the work."

"Did you say Levi?" Caleb said, leaning all his weight onto the man as they moved toward the house.

"Aye, my son. One of my four," the blacksmith said.

"I met him, just a bit ago. He was helping my wife with—" Caleb glanced at the man's face. "—something critical. Her life may depend on it." He glanced down at his side. "Mine as well."

Levi's father helped him hobble toward the backdoor of the shop where curly-headed Charles waited.

"Well, apparently, he recruited my oldest two for something. Those three, always getting into trouble. The little one here tells me they ran off, along with your missus, in the direction of that blessed house of the Lord a bit ago."

"South Puritan?" Caleb paused, causing Levi's father to look over at him. "They went to South Puritan? Are you sure?"

"Charles, didn't you say that's where they were headed?"

"Yessir. Heard it through the wall, I did!" The boy nodded.

Caleb pushed Levi's father away and sat down on an up-turned barrel outside the shop door, his hand still pressing the rag to his side. "Blacksmith Poole, I hate to trouble you, but can you take me there? As soon as possible? My wife's in real danger. And if my wife's in danger, so are your sons. I can explain on the way."

The blacksmith must've seen the seriousness in Caleb's eyes. Without a reply, he turned back to Charles, who stood waiting at the door.

"Fetch the Reverend a spare coat and shirt, then help me set up whatever horses your brothers haven't taken."

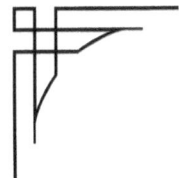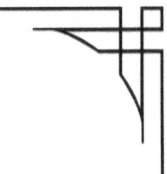

CHAPTER 31
Rebecca

"Wait, repeat that?"

Josiah stood before the altar inside South Puritan. His broad forehead crinkled as he stared down at Rebecca, who was kneeling on the floor with the *Malleus Maleficarum* spread out in front of her, open to the page little Marguerite had marked.

"I said we need to lure the Blood Demon here," Rebecca repeated, looking up at each of the three boys who stood huddled around her. "Into South Puritan. And trap it inside."

"Lure the demon inside?" Abe asked, resting his weight on his gun like a walking stick. "Won't it destroy everything?"

Rebecca sat back on her heels and considered the empty aisles around her. "Probably, but consider the alternative. We need to trap it somewhere. A place large enough for it to fit into. A structure sturdy enough to hold it." She looked up at Levi, who stood with one hand a pew back. "It would be impossible to trap it anywhere out in the woods. We need to set a trap for it, right here."

She slid the book around to face them. "According to this, the first step to set a trap for a demon is to write this phrase here in the shape of a cross. The Demon has to be lured on top of this written cross and held there."

The boys exchanged looks above her.

"That's it?" Josiah said. "That doesn't sound too hard. What is it you have to write in the shape of a cross?"

"This line here." She drew a finger across the line, printed in dark ink, in Latin.

IESUS NAZARENUS REX IUDAEORUM

"Jesus? Nazareth? That much I can pick out, I think." Josiah shrugged.

"Close," Rebecca said. "It says, 'Jesus the Nazarene, King of the Jews.'"

"How do you know?" Abe said.

"I can read Latin. But that phrase is significant. Those were the words that Pontius Pilate carved on Jesus's cross when he was crucified," she said. "The phrase represents the ultimate sacrifice Jesus made for the world, giving his life."

"Makes sense," Levi said, squatting down to getting a better look at the book.

Rebecca read on. "Once the phrase is in place and the demon is held atop it. The—" She skipped reading the phrase "White Witch" in front of the brothers and continued, pointing to a handwritten notation in the margin that said "Read John."

"Apparently, I read the Gospel of John until the demon is destroyed."

"That's a book in the Bible, yeah? What's so important about it?" Abe asked.

Rebecca bit her lip and thought for a second. "I'm not sure. It's one of the four synoptic gospels in the Bible."

All three boys showed blank faces.

"Matthew, Mark, Luke, and John, and the synoptic gospels. They're different books in the Bible that each tell a slightly different account of Jesus's life, his birth and the miracles he performed, like turning water into wine—"

"I've heard of that one!" Josiah said, raising a fist.

"—healing the blind, walking on water," Rebecca continued. "Then his death and resurrection." She paused, glancing down at the *Maleficarum*. "But why they'd choose to read from the Book of John compared to the others, I have no idea."

"Does the Book of John tell you how to beat a demon?" Abe asked, shifting his gun from one hand to the other.

Rebecca looked around for a Bible. They strangely had had no luck finding one of the church's copies since they'd walked in. "No."

"So maybe we buck the whole idea and go out and hunt it down?" Abe said, running a hand over his beard.

"No, we can't. You have no idea how strong and how dangerous this thing is," Rebecca said.

"We've shot at it, many times. So did the Constable. We know that doesn't work," Levi reminded them.

Abe held up his gun. "But with the three of us armed—"

"It moves too fast," Levi stopped him. "It could kill you before you have a chance to reload."

"What does it look like exactly, so we know that we've got it?" Josiah asked.

"You'll know," Levi said.

Rebecca nodded in agreement. "It's massive. Picture a bull that can walk upright—no, run— on its hind legs. Only bigger and with thicker horns."

"Its horns are something," Levi added. "Longer than a steer's, but they twist straight upward."

Rebecca looked up at them. "And it's strong enough to knock down entire trees with one arm."

"Right. We follow Mrs. Easton's plan then." Josiah turned to the others. "If it really is this strong, how can we make sure it stays on the cross?"

Rebecca snapped the book shut and rose to her feet. "The Beast is huge. I think our best chance is to use the church itself." She stepped back, examining the path the aisle led toward the front of the church. "Look. The walkway in front of the pews here and the aisle that runs from the door up to the altar form a natural cross shape on the floor. If we write in massive letters that stretch the distance, the floor itself might trap it."

"What do we write with? Certainly not a quill. That would take hours," Abe said, looking up and down the aisle.

"There are a few inkwells in Caleb's office." Rebecca's voice faded. For letters big enough to stretch down a full church aisle, there surely wouldn't be enough.

"We could water down the ink. Use the snow outside to make more," Abe said.

"We could paint the letters ourselves with our hands," Levi added.

They looked at one another in silence. No one had any argument. It could work. Or it couldn't.

Rebecca stared down at the *Maleficarum* lying open in front of her and chewed on her thumbnail.

"If this works," she continued, staring ahead. "In in the chance it works, I mean, we need proof. We need proof to take back to town to show the Judge, so he clears my name and frees my husband."

Josiah raised his thick eyebrows. "And if it doesn't work?"

Rebecca ducked her head and tucked the book under her arm.

"We need to get snow."

Without a word, the four of them gathered the ink bottles from Caleb's office and three buckets of snow from outside. Rebecca emptied black ink bottles into each one, while Levi stirred them with his hands until the snow turned gray. Abe took the *Malleus Maleficarum* and began pacing out the spaces needed for "IESUS NAZARENUS." Josiah lifted the first bucket of snow and went to work, slowly scooping out handfuls of gray slush to form the word "IESUS" as the horizontal part of the cross, while Rebecca palmed "NAZARENUS" up the aisle. Within minutes, the trap of ancient words was in place.

When they were done, Rebecca stood at the entrance to South Puritan. She peered up at the delicate wooden cross that hung high above the altar at the very front of the church—one of South Puritan's only decorative elements. Caleb had asked her back at the jail to make a judgement on what to do, to follow the *Malleus Maleficarum* and destroy the demon, if that's what her faith told her to do. She glanced around at the boys. Levi walked the aisle slowly, double-checking the spelling of both words. Josiah knelt near the letter Z, wiping up a drip of slush up the floor so there could be no mistake. Abe stood at the head of the church, placing the *Malleus Maleficarum* on Caleb's lectern.

Rebecca began to feel her heart expand. She wanted to weep, because everything felt right. And because everything felt...final.

"Men," she called. "It's time."

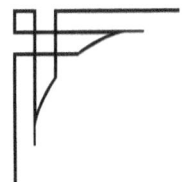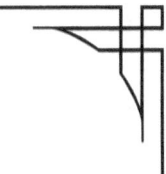

CHAPTER 32
Rebecca

Snow spun down on Rebecca and Levi as they departed South Puritan atop Chancer. The churchyard had turned into a blanket of white. New snowfall blotted out the road that lay down the hill in front of them. Beyond the road, the forest's trees also hung heavy with white. The forest was fully visible now in the daylight, not that that meant much. The daytime sky had revealed itself an appropriate dark gray, with clouds hanging over the earth like a pillow, trapping in the suffocating cold.

"Up, up!" Levi directed Chancer, turning her out of the churchyard and onto the main road. Rebecca rode behind him this time, clinging onto the back of his coat. It was safer, they'd decided, to share Chancer again. Both Levi's musket and the Constable's hung from her shoulder, packed and ready with two shots each.

As they turned left onto the road, Rebecca looked behind them to see the trap set. At the top of the hill, South Puritan loomed tall, with both front doors propped open. Torchlights flickered bright in each window. Abe and Josiah were in position atop their horses, guns in hand, waiting to funnel the Beast into the church. Josiah had followed them down the hill and was now waiting in the road behind them, blocking the Beast from running down the main road, past South Puritan, and into town. Abe was positioned up the hill in the field to the right of the church, where he'd block the Beast from running back into the forest. If it headed to the left of South Puritan, well, they'd have to rely on it getting tripped up in the snow-covered graveyard.

"Thank you, Levi, for going with me," Rebecca whispered, as he eased Chancer down the road along the forest line. "Especially after your family's history with South Puritan. What they did to your home. No religious body should treat anyone that way."

Levi cleared his throat. "Well, these are my woods, too. Not much left to hunt if you've got a demon snatching up everything, right?"

Rebecca paused for a second.

"I want you to know that...after this, if everything is okay, I mean...I'll make sure that South Puritan makes good on your family."

Levi gave no response, only shifted his hands to snap Chancer's reins, speeding up the horse a touch.

Rebecca looked back at the woods and dropped the topic. Around them, the temperature seemed to drop, and the snow seemed to pick up the deeper they got to the forest. With every step Chancer took, Rebecca kept a careful eye on the trees next to them, watching every branch for any sign of movement. She stared into the still and silent woods and wondered how Hannah and the Constable were fairing back at the cottage. Was the Constable even still alive? She thought of the wounds, the salve Hannah had produced... she didn't dare ask the question aloud. Not now.

Levi drove Chancer farther down the road.

"How sure are you that Chancer can outrun it? Out in the open, I mean?" Rebecca whispered. She glanced around Levi at the back of the horse's head, watching her mane swish back and forth. Chancer moved her head back and forth now and then, as if she were studying the woods as well.

"If we can lure it out in the open, our chances are...well—" Levi hesitated while Chancer's hooves continued to clack beneath them. "She managed to outrun it once. That bodes in our favor, right?"

He kept Chancer at a steady trot, also keeping his watch on the forest the entire time.

As they moved, Rebecca ran through the plan in her mind over and over again. She said a silent prayer that she'd be able to do what she needed to do when the time came.

Suddenly, Levi slowed the horse to a stop and nodded ahead to their right.

"Look!" he whispered. "There's where it chased us out!"

Rebecca looked over his shoulder to see a spot on the road where it looked like a whole caravan of horses had smashed through the forest line—damage they couldn't have seen when it was still dark. Several trees stood snapped in half, their top halves dangling toward the ground by sinews of bark, the tips wiped against the road. The smell of evergreen and sap was everywhere. The smoothness of the road itself had been scraped up into a muddy mess only lightly dusted with snow, and a scrambling of hoof marks was littered with pine branches and twigs.

Levi drove Chancer a few more steps, then stopped. Rebecca could see a small willow tree set back from the front of the forest line, visible only now as the thick elm in front of it had been knocked down. The tiny frozen willow had the symbol carved into it—or had had the carving etched into its bark.

Levi must've seen it too, as he turned and spoke over his shoulder to her.

"Um, Rebecca?"

"What?"

"If the Widow trapped the Beast into the forest around her cottage with those symbols—"

"The circle of protection."

"Yeah, about that," he said, still talking over his shoulder. "The Beast can't chase us if it's tethered to that side of the forest. So, how do we get it to chase us?"

"I know." Rebecca sighed. "We have to let it out."

"How?"

Rebecca unraveled the Constable's gun from her shoulder. "Seems the Beast can smash any tree in its path, so why hasn't it smashed one with a symbol on it and freed itself? Run all over town killing everyone?"

Levi looked back at her.

"Because for whatever reason, it can't. The spell and the marks the Widow put on those trees keep the Beast inside the circle of protection," Rebecca continued, gripping the gun with one hand. "Turn me toward the trees. We have to do it now. I want to be done with this."

Levi tugged on Chancer's reins, turning her back to face the direction they'd just come from.

She raised the musket, aiming it at the tiny willow tree, her eyes focusing the barrel on the symbol carved on the tree's trunk. Her heart pounded. The heart the Beast could hear. Rebecca felt the cold sensation creep in the base of her neck. It was already close by.

"Wait!" Levi said. "The blood! Don't you want to get it over with first? It will give us a few seconds of a head start."

He was right.

Rebecca swung the gun back over her shoulder and dug the Constable's hunting knife out of her satchel. "Keep an eye out," she whispered. She felt Levi's body tense in front of her, leaning forward, reins taut, ready to launch Chancer back toward South Puritan at her signal.

Rebecca took the tip of the blade and placed its point directly on her palm. She stared down at her hand as if she could see the blood inside—the life inside—pulsing through it.

"You sure you don't want to use my blood?"

"I'm sure." Rebecca stared at the tip of the blade. "I want it to follow us. You're unbaptized. I don't want to risk strengthening it."

She looked back down at the knife and blew out.

"On three, right?" She counted silently this time. One. Two. *Three.*

Rebecca jabbed the tip of the blade into her palm a quarter of an inch or so. The sharp sensation instinctively made her jump. She wanted to pull her hand away, but she knew she couldn't. The Beast was attracted to blood. They needed to be certain that it would follow.

The tip of the knife burned in her palm. She gritted her teeth and yanked the blade down and across, from her forefinger to the base of her palm.

"Ouch!" She dropped the bloody knife to the ground next to Chancer, instinctively squeezing her fist shut around the pain and feeling the hot stickiness of blood. She held her fist out over the side of Chancer and waited for her blood to drop.

She squeezed. Three drops—dark red—fell onto the white snow below them.

"Get ready." She pulled the gun back up and aimed it at the symbol of protection. Her grip on the butt of the gun slipped a little in her bloody palm. She steadied it against her shoulder, aimed, and fired.

Boom!

The shot blasted the front of the tiny tree nearly in half. Smoke cleared within a second. The symbol had been obliterated.

"The circle's broken. Go!" She looped the gun around her shoulder and wrapped both arms around Levi's waist.

Levi launched Chancer back down the road.

"Any sign yet?" he called back as Chancer veered back and forth, the trees speeding by on their left.

Rebecca glanced behind them.

"Not yet." She pulled her wounded hand back. Her fingers shook as she uncurled them. The cut had been deeper than she'd anticipated, and it pulsed with blood. The cut throbbed to the point where it felt almost numb with pain.

She glanced down. Blood had dripped all over the side of her leg and ran down Chancer's side.

She held her hand out over the side of the horse again and forced her fingers open, blood trickling down on the road as they moved. Within an instant, the cold seemed to rush them from behind, slipping down inside the back of her cloak and sliding over her shoulders—as if two freezing hands had grabbed onto her collarbones, touching her, pushing her down. She shook and pulled herself closer to Levi's wool-cloaked back.

"Is that it? That feeling? Is it some sort of warning?" Levi called, keeping his eyes on the road ahead.

"Yes. It's coming."

Chancer thundered forward, her hooves clattering. Her speed tore up an icy wind that blew Rebecca's hood back, her brown hair flying.

"Can you see it?" Levi yelled.

Just then, a rumble came from the woods behind them. Branches shook and snapped.

It was here.

Rebecca looked over her shoulder in time to see the Blood Demon burst out of the forest where she had destroyed the tree. Her stomach twisted. The Beast could leave the woods now.

"Levi, it's here! Behind us! Speed her up! Go! Go!" Rebecca nudged her shoulder forward so the musket strap would drop down to her elbow, making it easier to grab, if need be, while keeping her arms around Levi's waist. "It's behind us! Go! Go!" she shouted.

She stared over her shoulder at the Beast—this unholy creature summoned from Hell solely for the purpose of causing death and stealing the source of life from anyone and anything. It was the first time she'd seen it unencumbered by the trees and in full daylight. It looked even bigger out in the open. Its twisted horns, which rose up and away from its head, seemed to fill up the entire width of the road.

The Blood Demon crouched down on all fours, and its body, made of black bone and muscle, sprinted down the road toward them like a dog. Its fur was matted against its body now, saturated with blood from all its kills the night before. Its claws ripped at the earth, the icy road no hinderance. The creature stared at Rebecca in its pursuit. Its eyes were pitch black and contained a strangeness that turned Rebecca's stomach. The narrow gleam in them wasn't feral—it was fury.

The Beast closed in on them with each leap forward. It lowered its horns, as if it would gore them from behind if close enough.

Rebecca swallowed. She hadn't accounted for the fact that the Beast would be faster out in the open.

"Hurry, Levi!" Rebecca shimmied the strap to Levi's gun down into her hand. She grabbed the musket with one hand and aimed back at the Beast. Between the two guns, she had three shots left—and at the speed Chancer was moving, the best she could do was a warning shot. Anything else would risk her losing her balance and falling from the horse.

Rebecca turned and fired the last shot from the Constable's gun.

Boom!

"Huah!" Levi shouted, smacking the reins down on Chancer.

Chancer weaved right, then left in the lane, Levi keeping her unpredictable. Prey running from predator. The horse's lungs heaved.

The hissing noise started behind them. It rose in an echo against the frozen earth and trees, surrounding them.

Rebecca gripped Levi and tilted her ear to her shoulder, drowning out half of the volume. She looked back at the Beast.

"Don't let the noise in!" she yelled. "Get her away from the noise! It does that before it attacks."

Levi responded by yanking his cloak up over his ears and snapping Chancer's reins again.

Rebecca turned in time to see the Beast slow its run just a beat to lower itself. Then it plunged forward directly at them, horns forward, claws reaching out.

"Levi!" Rebecca yelled.

Levi responded by jerking Chancer's reins hard to the left. The horse whinnied. The Beast missed, landing next to them. It skidded in the road just a foot off to their right for a split second, until Chancer—seeing the Beast in her peripheral vision—took off running for her life, her hooves gathering and pushing, gathering and pushing.

"Shoot it!" Levi yelled.

"I only have two shots left!"

"Keep him off of Chancer!"

But the Beast was already on its feet, charging toward them again. Rebecca let go of Levi with one arm, lifted his musket, aimed, and fired.

Bang!

The shot missed it entirely. Chancer whinnied and dashed to the right so fast that Rebecca dropped the gun and grabbed onto Levi. The musket's strap, thankfully, caught on her wrist. She pulled it up into her hand again.

"Did you get it?" he called back.

"No! Keep going!"

She hoisted the gun up and turned to see the Beast within one jump away from Chancer's tail. Rebecca fired her last shot.

Bang!

A hit! The bullet landed in the middle of the Beast's hairy forearm. For a second, the creature slowed its pace as it looked down at its wound and shook its arm. Then it took off after them again, in no apparent pain.

"I got it, but it did nothing! Keep going!" Rebecca said

The forest surrounding them whizzed past as Chancer sped toward South Puritan, which came into view ahead.

"Wait, what's he doing?" Levi shouted ahead. Rebecca looked up at the sloping snowy lawn that led up to the church. Abe and his horse—who'd been stationed to block the field between the church and the forest—had seen them approaching and was riding down toward the road where Josiah waited. A horrified look was on Abe's face, gun clutched in one hand.

"He's riding down to help Josiah block the road!" Levi yelled. "We're going to have to change our plans. The field to the forest will be wide open. You'll need to jump off in front of the church."

"Jump off?!"

He nodded, shouting over his shoulder. "I'll get you as close as I can and then turn to block the field."

"Are you sure?"

"We don't have any other option!"

Fifty feet up ahead of them in the road, Rebecca could see Levi's brothers, steady in their saddles, guns drawn, barrel pointed in their direction.

Rebecca ducked her head into Levi's back as they made the sharp turn into the churchyard and shot up toward South Puritan, the building twenty yards ahead uphill. Suddenly, Chancer stumbled as her hooves slipped underneath her. Rebecca glanced at the ground. Her back hooves flicked up ice.

"It's too icy! She's slowing down!" Rebecca cried.

Bang! Bang! Bang!

A trio of shots rang out from behind them as Abe and Josiah fired everything they got at the Beast.

"Come on, girl!" Levi said, driving the horse harder than Rebecca had ever seen him do.

Rebecca looked behind them to see Beast had slowed in the road, annoyed but undeterred by the brothers' gunfire. Then it turned its great head, watching Rebecca and Levi charging up the hill.

Chancer found her footing and drove forward. Levi pounded the reins down and the horse galloped for the church.

Ten more yards.

"Get ready to jump!" Levi said.

Rebecca tossed the Constable's gun to the ground and shifted back from Levi. She gathered up the front of her cloak and dress in a fist, tossing the ends of both over the left side of the horse. She grabbed onto Levi's back to steady herself, then swung her right foot up onto the horse's back, shifting her hips to face the left, getting ready to push herself off.

Twenty feet away.

Bang! Another blast from behind.

Fifteen feet away.

The Beast's hissing noise began again from behind them.

Bang! A blast closer. The boys must be following it up the hill.

Ten feet away.

"Now!" Levi yelled.

Rebecca let go, simultaneously pushing herself off the horse and feeling Chancer bolt out from underneath her. She dropped to the ground, crumpling in the snow at the feet of South Puritan's stairs. Levi quickly turned Chancer, driving her off to guard the field to the right. Rebecca scrambled to her feet and darted up the church stairs in two strides. She ran inside, the torches flaming around her, and headed for the pulpit. She leapt over the letters they had painted in ink on the floor, careful not to ruin any. She could hear the Beast hissing outside now, near the base of the stairs. She dared not turn around now. The hiss grew louder. The freezing sensation swept in.

Rebecca grabbed Caleb's pulpit and pulled it in between her and whatever came through the door. The *Malificarum* lay open before her. She looked up, waiting, but the Beast hadn't yet come inside. Was she to begin to read now? Should she wait until the Beast was in place on the cross?

Seconds passed, and her eyes locked on the meeting house door. Rebecca held her breath. The hissing outside stopped suddenly. Nothing. No sound. No Beast.

Nothing at all.

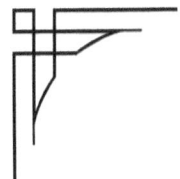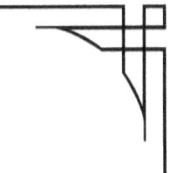

CHAPTER 33
Rebecca

Seconds later, a male voice screamed outside the door.

"No! No!"

The tone was filled with terror, so much so that she couldn't tell which brother was screaming. Rebecca gripped the edge of the pulpit, terrified, her eyes on the open front door. But no one and nothing emerged.

Boom! Boom! Two gunshots cracked the air, making her jump.

"No!"

Another scream—this time, one of anguish.

Rebecca abandoned the pulpit and sprinted down the aisle. Her feet hit the threshold of the meeting house door, and she froze, looking down at the base of the stairs and trying to make sense of what she saw.

The Beast stood poised at the bottom of the church stairs—its back to her. Its spine, dark red and ridged, poked out of its silky back as it stood hunched over something the width of its body blocked. A river of blood gushed down each of its legs, saturating its fur. Nausea waved over her, and for a minute, all sound was lost. Rebecca gripped the doorframe. Whose blood was it? Her eyes flitted to the right. Abe had dismounted from his horse and was now standing on the ground, holding Levi back from charging at the Beast. Levi, red-faced, desperately batted at his brother's arms, trying to free himself. He was screaming. Why couldn't she hear it? Behind them, Josiah was riding on horseback up the hill toward them, his face twisted in horrified confusion as he fired his gun again at the Beast. Why couldn't she hear the gun? She looked down at the Beast, still not understanding.

Just then, it stepped to the side, its back hoof wading through the puddle of blood collecting around it. Rebecca covered her mouth as she felt herself inhale her own scream. Before her, the Beast held something blood-smeared white between its jaws, tearing at it with its claws.

White.

White and gray. Dapple gray.

Dapple gray and covered with blood.

Chancer.

The Beast turned another step. It stood above the horse's body—Chancer's dismembered head hanging from the Beast's jaws as blood drained out of it and onto the ground.

Rebecca legs weakened beneath her.

Not Chancer. No.

She could still feel the roughness of Chancer's speckled hair against her palms. Hear the sound of her heavy exhales, the trot of her hooves in her ears. But no, the beautiful horse's gentle eyes had stilled, her blood draining out over pink tissue that dangled from where its neck should be as the Beast tore at it with its black teeth.

Rebecca tried to process it. Chancer's life...gone.

The Beast took another step, leaning down and dragging the horse's dismembered body back toward it with one claw. Rebecca kept her hand over her mouth. Chancer's body lay just a few feet past where Rebecca had jumped off. Chancer must've blocked the Beast from getting her.

She felt the cavity in her chest where her heart beat rapidly. Beautiful, innocent, brave animal.

She heard a whisper move somewhere deep inside of her.

Be brave.

Rebecca opened her eyes and exhaled, clinging onto the doorframe with one hand. Her senses started returning to her. Levi kept screaming, his voice cracking now.

"Bastard! I'm going to tear you to pieces!"

Rebecca took a deep breath and pushed herself upright. She'd gotten Chancer, Levi, all of them into this situation. She looked at Josiah as he fired again.

Boom!

Bullets didn't stop it. It was up to her now.

"Iesus Nazarenus Rex Iudaeorum!"

The creature twisted back from where it stood and stared at her with its hateful eyes. Chancer's head dropped from its mouth, landing with a sickening thump on the bottom step, rolling off and splashing into the puddle of blood. Rebecca winced at the motion.

She kept her eyes on the Beast and swallowed. She couldn't let herself look anywhere else.

"Iesus Nazarenus Rex Iudaeorum!" she repeated, louder.

It took a step.

Rebecca held her breath, her lungs pushing against her ribs. She stood before the Beast with nothing, her hands empty. No Constable's gun. No ax. Nothing to defend herself with.

"Faith. Faith can be your power."

The words little Marguerite had told her back in the jail rang in her ears.

She stared at the Beast and pursed her lips. She thought of what Caleb used to tell her, about how reading the Bible filled his heart with so much joy that his chest overflowed with words of light, of love, of life. She exhaled the breath she'd been holding, thinking of Caleb.

Rebecca took a step backward into South Puritan, still holding onto the thought of him. If she was going to die, that's how she wanted it to feel. To die with bravery. To die filled with rebellious joy. To die fighting for good. Until the end.

"Abe. Josiah. Levi," Rebecca said, slowly and clearly, keeping her eyes on the Beast, who slowly crouched down on all fours before her. Bits of Chancer's flesh hung from its jaws, the kill already forgotten. "I'm going inside. If it follows, shut the doors behind us."

She heard no dispute.

Rebecca took another step back into the church, reaching up and pulling down a torch that hung just inside the door.

The Beast took another step toward her. Its black eyes narrowed, its heavy brow tilting forward, its horns lowering.

"Ho!" She lunged a step toward it and swiped her torch. It recoiled at the light, then tilted its head to the side and hissed.

"Cover your ears!" she yelled to the brothers.

The Beast moved forward and pounded its front claw down onto the church porch. It smashed straight through, demolishing the wood.

"Iesus Nazarenus Rex Iudaeorum!" Rebecca shouted again, holding the torch out between the two of them.

This time, the Beast opened its jaws wide enough to show four rows of black teeth—two on the bottom, two on the top—and hissed in response.

She shifted her thumb, tightening her grip on the torch. It would follow her now. What next? She pursed her lips. The words. From the Gospel of John. They'd never found a copy of the Bible inside, but she didn't need it. She knew the words by heart.

"In the beginning was the Word...and the Word was God..." Rebecca backed over the threshold into the church. The Beast lowered itself on its haunches. Its spine curved up into an arch. It hissed at her again. Josiah and Abe shouted at the pain of the noise, but Rebecca continued.

If it would hiss, she would scream.

"Through Him all things were made," she shouted, staring at it. She shifted her hips, turning them back toward the aisle, readying to run for the pulpit.

"In Him was life...the light of all mankind."

The two stared at one another, woman and Beast. Then, all at once, the Beast launched its blood-smeared body up the stairs toward her. Rebecca pivoted and sprinted into the church and down the aisle, leading the Beast over the cross of words.

"Rebecca! No!" Levi yelled behind her.

The Beast landed in the doorframe and pushed itself upright onto its back legs, walking like a human, following her inside. Its horns scraped clean through the top of the doorway. As it moved behind her, it reached both clawed hands out, smashing the pews on either side of the aisle. Wood shattered, the tops of pew cracking off with one slam of its clawed fist. Shards of debris flew past Rebecca's head.

She skidded to a stop at Caleb's pulpit just as the church doors banged closed behind them. The boys had listened. Now it was just her and the Beast. She looked up as it paused midway down the aisle, standing atop the "Z" in "Nazarenus." She watched the Beast's muscular body waver in its steps, as if its hooves were stuck in mud. Its head looked back and forth, confused.

The Gospel of John rushed from Rebecca's lips, the words speeding out as fast as she could remember them.

"In him was life and that life was the light of all mankind. The light shines in the darkness, and the darkness has not overcome it!"

The Beast squinted its eyes shut, threw its head down in its hands, turning its head to one side with a grimace. It widened its jaws open all the way. Its black tongue, long and thin like a snake's, slipped out as it hissed.

Her fingers gripped the sides of the lectern. "Iesus Nazarenus Rex Iudaeorum!" she shouted.

The Beast tottered on its hooves and leaned forward, placing its clawed hands on its bony knees. It arched its red spine again— once, twice, a third time—turning in a circle as it did so. She watched its face as it stared back at her out of its shiny black eyes.

But it wasn't a look of pain.

"Iesus Nazarenus Rex Iudaeorum!"

The Beast arched its back yet again, only this time its red spine protruded awkwardly. The Beast shook itself back and forth, spinning to face the church doors. Its feet paused as its muscular back, divided by the red spine, suddenly split in half and lifted up from its body into two parts that stretched farther and farther.

The Beast's back spread out into two enormous wings before her.

At the same time, the church door cracked open behind it, and Levi slipped inside. He glanced at the Beast and then past it at Rebecca, his eyes wide.

The Beast's wingspan was easily double the reach of its arms. One flap of those wings, and it could use its horns to burst through South Puritan's roof. Rebecca exchanged a look with Levi. They both knew if it got out of the church— if it flew away—they'd never stop it.

The Beast turned once more in a circle, then turned back to face Rebecca.

"Burn it down!" she yelled to Levi as she launched herself down the aisle toward the creature. "Burn the church down!"

Levi wavered in his steps, then disappeared, the door slamming behind him.

The Beast raised its wings high, throwing them down, attempting a lift-off. Its hooves lifted up off the cross of words just as Rebecca slid feet-first underneath the Beast. She wrapped both hands around one of its legs. The blood-less flesh felt cold—the black fur sticky and slick with blood. She lay on the ground, pulling down with all of her weight, yanking its leg until its hoof landed in between her knees. It hissed above her and instantly yanked back, trying to free itself. Knowing she couldn't hold it long, Rebecca sat up, scooted forward, and wrapped her whole body around its leg, desperate to keep it grounded down onto the cross.

She recited the Gospel of John again.

"In the beginning was the Word...and the Word was God..." she yelled.

It hissed above her and flapped its wings, trying to break free of her grasp.

Behind the Beast, the church door slammed open. Rebecca saw Levi, Josiah, and Abe slip inside, their eyes wide at the sight of the Beast's wings. They each shed their cloaks into a pile and pulled a torch from the wall, lighting them. Abe ran around the back walls, jumping over the scattered debris. He pulled the remaining torches down and slid them underneath the nearest pew, waiting for them to ignite from below.

Rebecca turned back to the Beast, which hissed and batted its wings again and again. kicking its leg, trying to shake her off.

"Go!" she yelled to the boys. Josiah and Abe headed to the door.

Levi paused a step, unsure. He nodded once, then rushed out behind his brothers.

Rebecca held on tighter. Her sliced palm throbbed.

"Through Him all things were made—"

The Beast spread its jaws and hissed down at her.

Over its shoulder, a church curtain caught ablaze. Fire shot up as if the material was dry kindling. The flames from it licked the rafters seconds later.

"—we have seen his glory, the glory of the one and only Son, who came from the Father, full of grace and truth—"

As the words left her mouth, the Beast folded its wings back and slammed its hooves down hard on the ground. Rebecca lost her grip, falling flat on her back. The Beast lunged down with its claws and slammed her into the ground. Rebecca's head cracked hard against the wood floor. Pain and dizziness washed over her from the back of her skull. For a minute, all sight was blotted out with black sparks. All sound was lost.

Her head throbbed.

Her thoughts ran in a slow drip.

Rebecca blinked, her vision blurred. The Beast's black body appeared in a dark silhouette to the orange fire that was creeping across the rafters high above them both.

Levi and the boys had done it.

She blinked.

The boys.

The throbbing sensation in her head worsened. The Beast's claws felt like icicles stabbing through her shoulders. Tears flooded her eyes. So selfless. The boys had done everything to help her.

Her thoughts floated. The boys. What was the last thing she'd said to them? Abe's question. The Gospel of John. What's special about it.

Jesus. Miracles. *The power of God*, she'd said.

But John didn't work.

Rebecca inhaled a mouthful of smoke and gagged.

Read John, the handwriting in the margin of the *Malificarum* had said.

John.

What's special about John?

She watched the Beast hover above her. Its wings spread out again.

No. Her own voice whispered somewhere deep in her mind, slipping through her fog of pain. *Read John. Not the Gospel of John.*

John the Baptist.

The recognition shot something through Rebecca—a wild spark of light that sprang through her heart and filled her chest to the point where she felt it would burst. That was it. That was the difference. It all made sense.

John the Baptist, Jesus's older cousin.

John, whose words proclaimed the coming of the Savior.

John, the outcast who lived in the woods.

Read John.

Rebecca's vision steadied on the creature as the light she felt in her heart grew, warming her from the inside. She reached up, putting one hand on its forearm. Her lips parted, spilling the words of John the Baptist.

"I am the voice of one calling in the wilderness! Make straight the way for the Lord!"

Before she'd finished the word "Lord," the Beast snapped a claw around her neck and began to squeeze, pinning her throat closed. She tried to gag, but her windpipe was smashed so tight, there wasn't room. Her chest heaved, her lungs burned. She wrapped both hands around the Beast's claws and yanked back as hard as she could. Its claws sliced against her fingers like knives. She opened her mouth to scream, but didn't have enough air. The blood trapped in her head rushed to her face, heating her cheeks.

Rebecca mouthed the words, starting again, choking them out.

"I am the voice...of one calling in the wilderness...make straight the way for the Lord."

Energy from the light she'd felt inside before pulsed through her. She found the Beast's eyes above hers—cold and black and glimmering with death—staring down at her underneath those immense horns. She'd seen the Beast's strength in the woods. She should be dead. It should've cut her head off, torn her to pieces by now. But the way it stared down at her, its eyes wide and waiting. She understood. It was no longer battling just her.

Rebecca pulled harder, yanking back against the claw around her neck. The flesh of her fingers melted against the sharpness of the Beast's claws.

She pulled harder.

The Beast's hoof trembled against the outside of her thigh.

"I am the voice—" She choked the words out between her clenched teeth, struggling to draw breath in through her nose. She felt a tremor flow through the Beast's arm that pinned her shoulder. Its wings collapsed into two folds behind it.

Above them, a ceiling beam snapped. Red hot ash rained down as a portion of it fell and crashed down onto the pews to her left.

The words would be her last or the Beast's. The words of John the Baptist as recorded in the Gospel of John, handed to her by a little girl outside a jail cell where her own husband waited to die. Rebecca pulled as hard as she could against the Beast's claws. She felt the energy's light flow from her filled heart, through her arms and into her hands. She felt no pain. She peeled the Beast's claw up an inch off of her throat.

An inch was enough.

"Iesus Nazarenus Rex Iudaeorum!" She looked it dead in the eye and yelled the clearest and strongest voice she'd ever had. "Make straight the way for the Lord!"

The Beast roared its head back, pressing its eyes shut in response. Rebecca sat up, still holding onto its claw. The Beast yanked itself away. It lurched back a few steps, seemingly unable to move off the cross of letters. Rebecca scrambled back away from it, sliding up the cross's words written on the floor as the Beast fell to its knees. Its fur shed instantly from its body. Its skin beneath aged in an instant, thinning and then sinking into its bones. The Beast's bones began to twist awkwardly inside its hairy body, the jaggedness of them poking out in strange angles underneath its flesh. Then they broke apart, crumbling like a puzzle. All at once, the Beast's black jaws clamped shut and its lips melded together, rending the sharp teeth underneath useless. Its clawed arms became limp, the muscle appearing to deflate, the tissue of its massive arms and legs wasting away before her.

Rebecca coughed, smoke burning her eyes from her place on the floor. The fire was closing in on them both from every angle. Where she couldn't see smoke, she saw flames. Pews on both sides of them were engulfed. South Puritan's cushions, rugs, curtains—everything—had spread the fire quickly.

Another beam cracked above the Beast, sending two huge planks of burning wood down in front of it. The Beast fell down on its knees, howling and hissing in pain as its bones rotated inside its black body. Its horns sank into its head and teetered back and forth. Flames from the planks licked its legs. It hissed faintly, doubling over in pain.

Rebecca stood. The edges of her ruined cloak brushed the flames, but didn't catch. Above her, the ceiling groaned as two more beams cracked. Pieces of them fluttered to the ground around her.

She walked forward, standing eye to eye with the Beast, still sunken to its knees. Her breath was shallow, the smoke thickening too fast. Black spots began clouding her vision again. She shook her head trying to get rid of them. She lifted her cloak up over her mouth, breathing slow deep inhales underneath it. Her eyes watered. Her blood ran down her fingers.

But the light inside her propelled her to continue.

She stared at the creature as she moved toward it. This Beast had haunted the forest, taken life after life, killed her dog, her friends, her protectors. Chancer. She looked into its black eyes—empty and soulless.

Rebecca reached up and placed both of her bloody hands on its shriveling shoulders. The Beast shook.

"I am the voice of one calling in the wilderness," she said. "The light shines in the darkness, and the darkness has not overcome it."

And with that, the Beast's skin tore apart into jagged panels, peeling back and separating into flakes like curls of burnt bark.

Flesh and bone crumbled to ash from underneath her hands. The fire roared through what remained, the flames glowing green and devouring it all.

But as the flames narrowed in on what was left of the Beast, so did the smoke.

Rebecca, her hands still held in midair, backed up, gasping for breath.

Then she dropped to the ground.

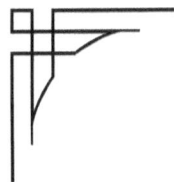
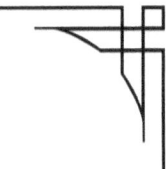

CHAPTER 34
Rebecca

The next thing Rebecca felt was the sensation of being dragged. Two sets of hands were underneath her arms, her boots sliding on the ground. Men were yelling, but she felt tired—so tired that she felt like she could finally sleep. Sleep for hours. Sleep for real, with no nightmares.

Someone lifted her up off the ground and tossed her over their shoulder. They carried her somewhere cold.

Her lungs gasped for air. Fresh air rushed in so fast that it burned her nose and throat. Whoever had a hold of her let go and laid her back against something cold. Her stomach surged violently. Rebecca flopped to the side and vomited into the snow. Someone put a hand on her back.

"It's her!" The voice of the person turned away. "She's alive!"

Rebecca opened her eyes, using all her energy to breathe. She raised her head, her attention drawn toward a burning light. Her eyes stung. She wiped them with a fist. She was laying on the snow in South Puritan's graveyard. Yards in front of her, South Puritan sat engulfed in flames, the white structure of the building turning solid black. Flames choked the first and second stories of the building from the inside. All windows had blown out and dark smoke was piping out of each one. Its porch overhang sloped down toward the ground on an angle, smoke rolling off it. The roof had completely sunken in on one side, ready to cave in at any moment. Only the steeple resembled remained pure white—for now.

Rebecca coughed, her chest heaving to catch up on clean air. Her body pushed out the smoke.

"Darling, are you okay?"

She turned her head to see a stunned-looking Levi standing a few feet away, to her left. She squinted at him. He pointed behind her.

Rebecca rolled onto her back to see Caleb kneeling over her, covered in blood from the chest down.

"Thank God you're alive!" He ducked down, wiping something off her face, then smoothed her hair and pushed his forehead against hers. He wrapped her in a full embrace—in front of everyone—but she held on and tried to breathe in his smell.

"Caleb!" she said, letting him hold her. "Did you escape?"

"Your friend Levi has a helpful family," Caleb said. Past him stood a wide man with a black beard. He was holding Levi's younger brother Charles she'd met outside the wall on his hip, and a musket in the other hand. Charles stared past them, entranced, by the sight.

"The Judge attacked me," Caleb said, his breath heavy. "Levi's father found me just in time."

"He attacked you?" Rebecca panted. "That's your blood?"

"More importantly, the Reverend ran in there and saved you," Levi's father said.

She looked at Caleb.

"Through the side door." Caleb grabbed her hand and helped her sit up.

"Did you do it?" Levi stepped forward and knelt down at her side. "Is it gone?"

"Yes," she replied.

"You're sure?"

She nodded. "It's destroyed. It's over."

Levi quietly glanced back toward the front of the church where the remains of his horse lay.

His father stepped forward, letting Charles drop to the ground. "Shall we see if there's anything at all we can salvage?"

"No!" Rebecca grabbed Caleb's sleeve. "Let it burn to the ground. Let the remains of the Beast burn to ash."

She looked to Levi, suddenly alarmed. "Where are your brothers?"

"In the woods. As soon as the Reverend got you out, I sent them into the woods after Hannah and the Constable."

Rebecca lay back and smiled at Levi—the smartest, most clever, most selfless boy she'd ever met.

"Reverend, you must run. You know that, yes?" Levi's father interrupted. "That Judge tried to end you. He'll hunt you down the minute he realizes you aren't lying in the back alley behind my shop."

"He's right," Caleb said to Rebecca. "We must go. He'll come after me. And there's no Beast left to bring back. If he finds you, he'll declare you guilty of witchcraft. You'll be dead within an hour."

Suddenly, the front porch collapsed into a heap of smoke. The motion tugged South Puritan's roof forward and the steeple tipped over, cracking in half. The church's bell and the speared tip of the steeple plunged directly into flames steaming up through cracks in the roof.

"But the Judge," Rebecca protested. "Someone has to stop him. If we leave, he wins. He'll just continue accusing women like me, women who are simply trying to help."

"You can't think of it that way," Levi said. "You destroyed a demon! You risked your life and saved the town. They may never know, but you did."

"We did," she corrected. "We all did."

"Rebecca, if we run, we keep our lives and the Judge loses," Caleb said. He looked back at the burning church. "It appears the Devil lost today, too."

"If we go—" She thought for a minute. "Where will we go? What will we do?"

Caleb rubbed the back of his neck. "Back."

"Back?"

"Home. It's the safest place now."

Everyone was quiet for a moment.

Caleb stood. "We'll head for the coast. As far as we can make it."

"Take my horses, Reverend," Levi's father said, digging into his cloak pocket. "These are all the coins I have on me. I wish it were more."

He handed a small sack to Caleb.

"Thank you, sir. I'm so grateful for, well, your entire family," Caleb said. "My horse is in the barn out back. Run and get him before the fire spreads. Consider him yours now. Let them think my wife and I perished in the church."

Levi's father nodded, gripping Charles by the wrist. "Thank you, Reverend."

Rebecca staggered to her feet. "Levi, assuming the Constable is okay, can you tell him everything? Him and no one else?"

Levi nodded. "Certainly."

She squeezed his arm. "I'm so sorry about Chancer. She was the best. So much more than a horse."

Levi gritted his jaw. "Yes. She was."

Behind her, Levi's father readied both his and Josiah's horse for her and Caleb.

"And Levi, thank you," Rebecca said.

"Come," Caleb beckoned, holding a hand out to her and glancing up at the black smoke that billowed up into the sky. "We must go."

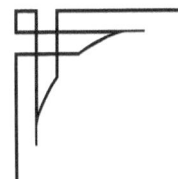
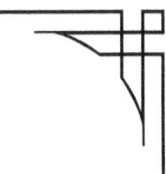

CHAPTER 35
Rebecca
April 1662 (Four Months Later)

"Hello?" Rebecca called as she stepped into the first floor of the Milford Town Grist Mill. A smoke-colored puppy wiggled in her arms as she held the door open with her foot, waiting for the other. The tiny front room was empty, but warm. A healthy fire crackled in the fireplace where the contents of a black pot bubbled against its lid.

Whatever was inside smelled delicious.

She turned back and whistled over her shoulder. "Here, boy!"

Out on the walkway, the pup's brother marched carefully in the snow, curious to examine the white stuff underneath his feet. He put his nose down to it, then backed up, whimpering as it stuck.

Rebecca smiled, then took a cautious glance back down the lane that led to the mill. It was empty as usual.

"Ah, how did the little ones do today, Mrs. Alexander?"

Mr. Middleton, the owner of the mill, walked out from the back room, wiping his hands off on his apron. His white mustache highlighted his wide smile as he leaned down to stroke the head of the pup in Rebecca's arms.

"They're still learning," Rebecca said, as the pup's brother braved his way up the walkway and into the mill. She dropped its brother back on the floor. "They're sure to make great hunting dogs someday, though. Just wait."

"Have you come up with names for me yet?" Mr. Middleton said. Both pups bounded into the backroom, where their mother often slept in a basket of blankets.

"I was thinking Cooke for the tall one, and Banks for the chubby one." Rebecca closed the door behind her, unwrapping the scarf from around her head. She flexed the cold from her fingers, which still ached now and then.

"Both fine names!" Mr. Middleton exclaimed. "Thank you for walking them every day."

"It's a pleasure. How is he?" Rebecca nodded toward the ceiling. She pulled off her cloak and hung it along with the scarf next to the door.

"Eh, so-so." Mr. Middleton flipped his hand back and forth. "It's his side again. Another bad day, you know?"

A liquid noise bubbled and popped from the pot on the fire. Mr. Middleton rushed to tend to it, pulling the lid off and giving it a stir.

"Well, if your husband feels better, the both of you should come down for supper later. I took my bow out this morning and got lucky. I wasn't out but a few minutes when I nabbed a buck. I'll have far more than I can eat alone for days!"

Rebecca suppressed a smile. "Of course. I'll ask." It was the same offer Mr. Middleton made every day. Too much food for him. His own quiet way to ask for company.

Rebecca turned toward the stairs.

"Oh, Missus!" Mr. Middleton called after her. "Here," he said, plucking a bundle of parchment from the table near the door. "A message arrived for you today."

Rebecca's heart jumped. Only one person knew where they were.

"Oh! Thank you, sir," she said, taking the weathered package in her hands. It was addressed to the Alexanders of Milford, still sealed.

She ran up the stairs.

Rebecca and Caleb had occupied a room on the second story of Milford Town Grist Mill for the past four months, ever since they arrived. Milford was a small town on the coast that neither of them had any tie to. Yet, it was south enough of Boston to make it a quick journey once the winter calmed, and the ships started running back to England.

They'd ended up here by accident. After Levi's father had urged them to escape, they had traveled seventy-two hours straight on horseback, stopping only to re-feed and re-water the horses. When they got to Milford, they'd stumbled into the town's only inn and public house, and ordered food for themselves with the last of the coins Levi's father had given them. The inn's owner had served them, unable to look away at how they sat hunched over from sleep deprivation, riddled with wear from the elements. He'd watched as they'd devoured their plates of rabbit, leaving not a trace except for a pile of tiny bones. They looked like people in need, he gently told them without asking the reason why. Then he let them stay the night in one of the inn's unused rooms.

They'd slept for two straight days.

When they finally woke, the inn owner listened to them, fascinated by their peculiar story: Mr. Alexander had been a Reverend, but upon his arrival at his new church in a new town, he'd found the building to be burnt to the ground. Naturally, that must be a bad omen, and they must return home to England. (It was the story they'd stick with for now, also temporarily taking on Rebecca's maiden name of Alexander, for safety).

The kind inn owner had told Caleb of his brother-in-law, a Mr. Middleton, who owned a grist mill five miles south. Mr. Middleton had recently been devastated over the death of his grown son, his only child, and was looking for some sturdy arms who could help ready the mill in time for the spring thaw. In exchange, they'd receive a room and a few pennies a month.

The reality of the partnership was even better for them all. Mr. Middleton gave them a roof, and Caleb, wages. Caleb and Rebecca gave Mr. Middleton a house that felt not-so-empty. Caleb especially had become a great companion to Mr. Middleton, often staying up late, sitting in front of the fire and reading the Bible. With Puritan ministers throughout the Colonies battling one another over how literal to interpret the Bible, Puritanism seemed to be falling to pieces. Ministering one-on-one to Mr. Middleton seemed to give Caleb purpose again, and Rebecca could see how, slowly, each day, Mr. Middleton's grief was soothed just a mite, even if it was to return the next day.

"Darling!" Rebecca called, as her foot hit the top step of the mill's second floor. She pushed open their lodging room door to find her Caleb in bed—lying on one side, his head bent back in sleep, and his mouth slightly open. The room was tiny, offering enough space for just a bed, a fireplace, and a desk with one chair. But that was all they really needed.

Caleb awoke to the sound of Rebecca's voice and pushed himself up onto his elbows, blinking into the afternoon light that filtered through one of the windows. He rubbed a hand delicately over the stab wound on his side.

"We've a letter!" She held it up.

"Really?" The drowsiness immediately lifted from Caleb's eyes as he slid over in bed to make room for her to sit down.

Rebecca and Caleb had written two letters only after arriving in Milford. The first was to Constable Hindstall, both to confirm their safety and inquire about the state of their friends who remained in town.

"It's from the Constable." She unrolled the letter, running her eyes over every precious word. "I'll read it to you..."

"Reverend and Mrs. Alexander—

I hope this letter finds you in good health and pleasant spirits as you reside in the confines of safety and prepare for your upcoming journey abroad.

I am putting ink to parchment, which I almost never do, to update you on the current situation in Hartforde Towne. You may be interested after the unfortunate events that surrounded the burning of our beloved South Puritan."

"Beloved?" Caleb shook his head.

"The town, overall, is in fair spirits now that the worst of winter has most likely passed. We are already working on raising funds to build another meeting house, which we estimate will take a year or so before it's completed. In the meantime, we are holding what we call 'Bible sessions' over in a barn on the old Hatcher farm. Not quite as organized as a sermon, but it's been keeping most of the young boys out of trouble at least.

"The Poole family is doing well, especially young Levi, whom only last week, chose to take the Goodness's servant girl, Hannah, as his bride. The family had taken her in after the day of the church fire, and it wasn't long until the two were seen all over town with one another, inseparable. Sickening for a happy and aged bachelor like myself, but good on them! They plan to marry when the new reverend arrives in summer. As for a source of income, Levi plans to start his own stable business breeding horses next year—"

Rebecca paused, putting her fingers to her lips. "That's perfect for him." She flipped the page and continued.

"—but in the meantime, I've hired him to help train a few new men in the art of hunting and tracking. As for your home in Hartforde Towne, it has been pulled down and the remains burned. It was already quite aged when you moved in, and after the tragedy, the townsfolk thought it best to pull it down and did so without question (yesterday they burned the remains and sifted the ashes for nails)."

Rebecca exchanged a look with Caleb.

"As ordered by Governor Winthrop, there's now a copy of the 'Malleus Malificarum' in every constable's office and jailhouse throughout Connecticut Colony, with instructions to be on the lookout for suspected witchcraft behavior and, if seen, to act immediately according to the legal steps as outlined within it. As

Mrs. Alexander appeared to have left her copy behind, I hope you do not mind my keeping it, considering it's been proven to be a lucky treasure at least once."

"Lucky?" Caleb cringed. "Ah, Hindstall. Always a seer and never a believer."

"He'll get there someday." Rebecca tilted her head at what came next, squinting her eyes at the script and running a thumb midway down. She read silently for a minute—Mr. Middleton clanging pans downstairs—until Caleb reached over and rubbed her thigh out of anticipation.

She shook her head. "Sorry, this part is just a bit odd. Maybe you can understand?"

"The whereabouts of a young girl with blonde braids—Marguerite, I'm told her name was—disappeared the day South Puritan burned. Judge Madden was quite disturbed by her disappearance prior to his own departure after the Widow's hanging and left word with the jailhouse and me that he's offered a personal reward of a healthy sum for the child's safe return. All that I can determine is that the girl must've departed our jailhouse before I returned after the cottage in the woods that day, for I seem to be the only one who never laid eyes on her."

Rebecca tapped her finger on the letter. "You and I were both in the jailhouse that afternoon. That's when the child gave me the *Malificarum*. According to this, you would've been one of the last to have seen her. Did she mention wanting to run away?"

Caleb lay back on his pillow and ran a hand through his hair, thinking. "Last I saw her, she was terribly upset over the truth about her family, and the Judge." He readjusted himself on the bed. "She'd figured out for herself that the Judge planted evidence in the conviction of her family then lied about her being a witness to their supposed acts of witchcraft. I guess it wouldn't surprise me if she'd run away. But where would she go? Especially in that weather? She couldn't have gotten far alone. She had no relatives left to run to."

They locked eyes. From downstairs came the clatter of dishes being laid out.

Rebecca shrugged. "I guess it's a mystery."

"And Judge Madden? Any more mention of him?" Caleb asked, leaning up again.

The second letter they'd composed once arriving in Milford, they'd done so anonymously, penning a plea to Governor Winthrop regarding the treatment of accused persons—male and female—who appear for judgment before Judge Mordecai Madden of the Particular Court.

Rebecca's eyes scanned the letter for anything more on the Judge or the Governor.

"No. It says here the Governor is still abroad in England. Nothing more."

Constable Hindstall had concluded by offering his best wishes on a safe journey and a happy life.

Rebecca refolded the parchment and set it on the table next to the bed. She wished more than anything she could write to Levi, congratulating him on his betrothal.

"Cheer up," Caleb said, reading her thoughts. He grabbed her hand. "We'll write them someday, once we've safely returned to your parents' farm. After all, we too will soon have much to be happy about."

Rebecca ran her hand over her abdomen and the wide bump that was growing—slow and steady every day—across her midsection. She smiled and stood, the thought of a life soon filled with horses and babies and familiar faces and wide-open fields was positively energizing.

"Mr. Middleton invited us to supper again," she said.

"Of course." Caleb buttoned the white sleeves of his shirt. "And what's he planning tonight?"

"Not sure." Rebecca leaned over, handing him his black waist coat from the foot of the bed.

He kissed her forehead. "Sounds ideal, White Witch."

"I'm no White Witch." She batted him away, then took a step toward the bedroom door. "I am a voice in the wilderness."

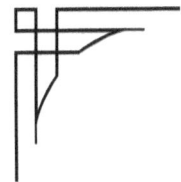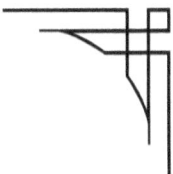

CHAPTER 36
Judge Mordecai Madden
LATER THAT EVENING

"Hurry up, fool!" Judge Mordecai Madden shouted up to Fineas. He pounded his walking stick on the interior ceiling of his warm carriage as the Connecticut forest slid by at a moderate pace outside his window. Snow fell fast and heavy as glimpses of what remained of the sun burned orange set between the trees.

He tossed the walking stick aside and propped his feet up on the empty seat across from him, scowling at the heavy clouds that were certain to bring more heavy snows. He felt restless. There was urgent court business to get to in Wethersford again. A late-season blizzard had already delayed his travel by a full week. Unacceptable.

The Judge pulled his travel case to his side and unlatched the top, pulling out two scrolls a messenger boy had delivered to his inn an hour ago as they'd loaded the carriage to depart. More charges had been filed, no doubt. After the hanging of Widow Goodness—and the terror she incited in her own trial and hanging—the accusations had started rolling in. And not just in Hartforde—neighbors, mothers, wives all over Connecticut and Massachusetts were being called in for questioning. He could barely keep up.

The Judge popped the seal on the first scroll and unrolled it across his lap. The text was brief and informal, confirmation for a Bill of Sale.

Judge M. Madden—

We have received your six-pounds payment for the SB and are writing to inform you that it will be shipped next week. You can expect it to arrive within three months' time.

In thanks,

Galbraith Metalworks

Edinburgh, Scotland

A small smile formed on the Judge's lips. SB. Code for the Scold's Bridle. This model, featuring a spiked gag, would lacerate the tongue if the wearer dared speak and would surely bring about confessions more urgently than their current methods allowed. The Europeans used all manner of devices to draw out a witch's confession. One could almost be jealous.

He rolled up the Bill of Sale and pocketed it. As he did, his fingertips brushed against the tiny tooth in his pocket. He pulled it out, rolling it back and forth in between his fingers, admiring the first addition to his new collection. Another witch—this time, the town's midwife—admitted to baptizing newborn babies in the name of the Devil when their mothers' backs were turned. She'd been an annoyingly strong one, holding out over three days of testimony. In the end, the midwife had survived the dunk test, able to stay afloat, screaming as loud as if she were being stabbed after they threw her into the river. (This time of year, that was quite a feat for the local constable's men in town, needing to break away chunks of ice in the river to make room). Seeing that the midwife floated, he'd had her taken to a tree in the woods nearby and hanged immediately.

He rolled the tooth back and forth, back and forth. That made six so far this year.

Of course, his collection would've been much larger if that damned Constable and the town blacksmith hadn't appeared in Hartforde Towne when they did, shouting about South Puritan's fire, claiming that the Reverend and his wife were trapped inside.

The liars.

The Judge had been certain that Reverend Easton was dead when he'd left him in the alley behind the jailhouse. There was no way he could've made it to South Puritan without help. After the Constable's reappearance and pronouncement that both Reverend and Rebecca Easton had perished in the fire, the Judge had run out back only to find a bloody trail remaining in the alley, ending a few buildings up. He was certain the Reverend had run off, but the Constable wouldn't hear of it, not when the biggest building in their town was ablaze and in danger of spreading to the forest next to it.

The Judge returned his gaze outside the carriage window, snowflakes now sticking to the glass. The sun had set fully, and the forest had grown dark against the purple night sky. One would think they'd move faster as a single coach and no longer a pair of two, yet Fineas seemed to drive slower on nights when there was not a hint of moonlight. The Judge sighed, then remembered the second letter. He drew the scroll onto his lap and ran his finger over the unfamiliar gold seal, bearing three chevrons and a lion. The lion, standing on its back legs, gave him pause.

It couldn't be. Its author had been abroad for more than a year.

The Judge broke the seal and unrolled the parchment. He checked the signature first: Governor John Winthrop, Jr., Connecticut Colony, the loops of the letters J and both H's in the name spread wide and circular, the descender of the letter P curling back to underline itself.

Judge M. Madden—

It has been brought to my attention that a fearfully increasing number of cases of witchcraft have sprouted in the Colonies during my absence. While I thank you for trying these cases as

I have been abroad with the King these many months, I need to inform you of my plans to return to Connecticut as soon as possible to investigate these charges myself.

Having spent the past year in Europe, I've witnessed fearful and ungodly misjustice against innocent souls, with individuals tried more through public opinion and panic than procedure. I've been horrified to see with my own eyes the devices and methods by which judges, magistrates, and even members of the clergy are putting to use here in Europe to solicit confessions and testimony. Because of this, I can no longer endorse the swiftness with which those accused of witchcraft are tried in the Colonies.

Troubling rumors have caught my ear about the way you carry out justice, and your overall treatment of the accused in both the Massachusetts and Connecticut Colonies. So troublesome in fact, that I've decided to return sooner than planned and request your immediate presence at my residence in Hartforde, as fast as a horse's hoof can travel.

You are to return immediately upon reception of this message.
Regards,
Governor John Winthrop, Jr.

The Judge dropped the letter on his lap and slammed his fist against the seat next to his knee.

"Request my presence, indeed!" he said. He crinkled up the letter and thrust it to the bottom of his travel bag, feeling somewhat unnerved. What had been said about him, and by whom? The Governor couldn't prove anything. Let him ask what he would. The Judge had been careful. He'd seen that the documents—all records of the trials he'd overseen—had been burned. He'd collected them from the Particular Court and burned them himself in the fireplace in his room at whatever establishment he'd occupied after Reverend Easton's disappearance. The graves too, of each woman hanged, had been left unmarked at his direction. No churchyard would host the body of a witch, so he'd seen the women's burnt ashes were buried deep in the forest, with only himself and the town's gravedigger present. While the fear of their crimes would remain in the minds of those surviving them, the record of their deaths would have been lost to history.

He had the dolls, of course. The Judge ran his hand on the seat below him. Physical evidence of dark behavior he could offer up as proof of the deceased's guilt. He could easily share them with the Governor. They'd fooled so many thus far. Or he could toss them in the river before meeting with Winthrop. It would be his word against the families of the condemned, and who would dare believe them?

The Judge sat back and looked out the window again, seeing only his reflection in the dark mirror of the window. Of course, it would bode well for him if Marguerite had been found. The sight of such a sweet young girl by his side would surely make him appear more sympathetic and—dare he think it—fatherly?

The disappearance of Marguerite had troubled him since that very afternoon in Hartforde Towne. The last he recalled seeing her, she'd been standing on the gallows platform to witness the Widow's hanging. He'd left the jailhouse guards under strict orders—and an offer of a generous reward of twenty pounds!—to find and return the girl to him, but so far, he'd heard no word. Her powers as an Innocent were irreplaceable, and he'd spent entirely too much time grooming her to start over with another child.

He buttoned his cloak, finding the interior of the carriage suddenly chilly, and tried to roll it over in his mind why or how Marguerite disappeared. She'd always been such a loyal child. Wanting to know. Wanting to learn. Desiring justice. She read voraciously on the topic of witchcraft, every book she could get her hands on. And hadn't he satisfied her curiosity by purchasing her each and every book she'd asked for?

The Judge's thoughts were interrupted by a violent shimmy that rocked the carriage. He reached both hands out instinctively to steady himself, bracing himself against the carriage wall. Then the carriage rocked harder, bumping to the right, this time so hard and fast that the Judge braced himself for the possibility of a tip-over.

"What in God's name is this?" the Judge yelled.

Outside, the carriage righted itself again and stilled. Fineas's lantern slipped from the driver's seat and smashed on the ground. A bump from behind tossed the carriage a few feet forward. The Judge gripped the edge of his seat, propping up one foot against the bench opposite to keep from sliding off.

Then, Fineas screamed from his seat up above.

"Fineas?" The Judge sat up, grabbed his walking stick and knocked it against the ceiling. The carriage immediately shot forward again. Then stopped.

The horses began screeching an awful sound, screams.

"What's this now?" Judge Madden thundered through the ceiling. "Get control up there, man, or I'll have a new driver by morning, and you'll be—"

A hard, wet thump knocked on the window where the Judge sat. He looked over to see Fineas dangling down as if looking into the window from above—except his forehead was bloody and smashed in, his eyes glassy.

Savages? The Judge slid his hand underneath the carriage seat opposite his own and retrieved his dagger. He damned himself for failing to carry a musket, but perhaps he could use the dagger to scare them off. He waited a few seconds and listened. The carriage had stilled. No sounds came from outside. The horses had fallen silent again.

He peered out his window, seeing nothing but dark forest and falling snow in the few strips of moonlight that shone through the trees. He cracked the carriage door open as softly as he could. Nothing.

The Judge stuck his lantern out into the night and waited for any movement. There was nothing but wind in the trees. Moments later, he stuck his head out and looked toward the head of the carriage. Up ahead, there was a puddle of something—no, it was too large—a *pool* of something dark lay dead in their path. He listened, immediately alarmed at the absence of sound. He'd heard the horses scream just moments ago, but now he heard nothing—not the tap of a hoof or a jingle of harnesses.

The Judge slid out of the carriage, immediately annoyed at the frosty air. He reached back into the carriage, yanked a fur from his seat, and wrapped it over his shoulders. He turned the dagger over in his hand and took three strides up toward the horses, or to where the horses should've been. Before him, was a giant pool of blood. He turned in a circle, raising his lantern, aiming his dagger into the dark. His wrist shook as he looked for the pair of white horses that pulled his carriage. He turned to find more blood splattered all over the front of the carriage, over Fineas's legs and boots. He gazed farther out, past the trees that surrounded them on the forested lane.

"Who goes there?" the Judge barked. "Where are my horses?"

But there were no savages, no bandits, no sight of a bear or wolves that could've done this much damage this quickly. There were simply no signs of horse nor man—only blood and Fineas's body, dangling from his driver's bench. Numb with befuddlement, the Judge pocketed the dagger and bent down, picking up the torn reins and examining the ends of them, which appeared to have snapped in half. He lifted the rough ends up to his eyes, baffled. He looked back at the bloody puddle. So much blood. He took a horrified step back and glanced down to see his own boots stuck in a slick puddle.

A few feet off the path into the woods, a twig snapped. He raised his light to it, not believing what he was seeing, not trusting his own eyes at what he saw. The silhouette of a little girl with swinging braids ducked behind a tree just feet in front of him.

"Marguerite?" The name fell from his lips.

But there was no response. Only a miserable hissing noise that arose from the dark behind him.

Historical Notes

The Hartford witch panic hit a fever pitch in 1662 that lasted through 1663.

The character of Widow Goody was loosely inspired by accused colonist R. Greensmith's fearful testimony of colluding with the devil, an admission that led to her hanging of both her and her husband. The characters of Rebecca and Caleb Easton are works of fiction.

The Particular Court and its three-month meeting schedule is historically accurate, and while the character of Judge Mordecai Madden is also fictional, he was designed to represent the opinions and actions of an amalgamation of religious and political figures in the Connecticut area at the time.

The *Bible* verses referenced throughout the story was taken from the Geneva *Bible*, one of the first mass-produced *Bibles* produced in the world and the one adopted by the Puritans. The font developed for the book's front cover was also inspired by the look of the Geneva *Bible*.

The sigil (artwork) that appears as a dedication at the front of this book is a nod to the medieval practice of using pictorial representations to summon spirits as outlined in *The Key of Solomon* and predates witchcraft in the early United States colonies. This sigil, hand-drawn in charcoal, calls on the protection of women from tyrannical men and was created specifically for this text.

This novel also references the *Malleus Maleficarum*—a very real historic text penned in 1486 in response to a 1484 papal bull by Pope Innocent VIII that formally established the Catholic Church's belief in the existence of witches, incubi, succubi, and devils. Combined with the religious fervor of the time, the *Malleus* was later also endorsed by the

Protestant Church and became one of the most widespread witch-hunting manuals in the world.

The *Malleus Maleficarum* remained a worldwide bestseller for nearly 200 years, second only to The Bible.

For related historical reading, I suggest the following texts: *Connecticut Witch Trials* by Cynthia Wolfe Boynton; *The Witchcraft Delusion in Connecticut Colony* by John M. Taylor (1647-1697); *The Malleus Maleficarum* by Heinrich Kramer.

Acknowledgements

I began putting pen to paper on what would become *Widow* during a summer session at Harvard University in 2019, where I sat at a bar in a sweltering July, imagining a cold, dank and dangerous Connecticut forest, while devouring my first-ever lobster roll.

My interest in the Connecticut witch trials had begun earlier that year, after stumbling upon a surprise in my husband's genealogy: his 12x great-grandparents, Nathaniel and Rebecca Greensmith, were an elderly couple accused of witchcraft—but in Connecticut, years before the Salem Witch Trials in Massachusetts. If recorded accurately, Rebecca, being aged and married, had offered a vivid and detailed confession. As a result, the Greensmiths were both hanged—but *unlike* most witch trials, her grown daughter Sarah survived. (Otherwise, my husband's line would've ended there).

Rebecca's grisly confession inspired the following curiosities – was her confession a reclamation of her power against her accusers? How had others reacted to such a graphic admission? And with no division between church and state, what were the real motivations of those who sought to persecute women (and men) during the Connecticut witch trials?

This book would not be complete without the support of author Seth Harwood (and his writer's group), the endless encouragement of author Andrew C. Peterson, the editorial excellence of author Maithy Vu, and the assistance of the staff at Harvard's Widener Library who helped me track down a scan of an original *Geneva Bible*, among other miracle requests.

Thanks are also due to my husband, Chad Baker, for inheriting rather adventurous DNA. He is also a descendant of Vlad III, Prince of Wallachia, otherwise known as the inspiration for Bram Stoker's Dracula.

www.ingramcontent.com/pod-product-compliance
Lightning Source LLC
Chambersburg PA
CBHW030242120726
47903CB00005B/1585